Hugh Dempsey is the author of many books on western Canadian history, but is perhaps best known for his biographies and histories of the First Nations of the Plains, including *Crowfoot: Chief of the Blackfeet*, *Charcoal's World*, *Red Crow: Warrior Chief*, and *Big Bear: The End of Freedom*. He is an honorary chief of the Blood tribe, has honorary names from the Blackfoot and Peigan, and has served as honorary secretary of the Indian Association of Alberta.

Hugh Dempsey is Chief Curator Emeritus of the Glenbow Museum, an active member of the Historical Society of Alberta, and has been editor of the quarterly magazine *Alberta History* since 1958. He was awarded an honorary doctorate from the University of Calgary in 1974, and the Order of Canada a year later. He lives in Calgary with his wife, Pauline.

To all the Elders
who so generously shared with me
their knowledge of the past

———————————————

The Amazing Death of Calf Shirt and Other Blackfoot Stories

Three Hundred Years of Blackfoot History

Hugh A. Dempsey

University of Oklahoma Press
Norman

Library of Congress Cataloging-in-Publication Data

Dempsey, Hugh Aylmer, 1929–
    The amazing death of Calf Shirt and other Blackfoot stories :
three hundred years of Blackfoot history / [collected by] Hugh A.
Dempsey. — Oklahoma paperbacks ed.
        p.   cm.
    Originally published: Saskatoon : Fifth House Publishers, c1994.
    Includes bibliographical references and index.
    ISBN 0-8061-2821-6 (pbk. : alk. paper)
    1. Siksika Indians—History.   2. Piegan Indians—History.
    I. Title.
    E99.S54D37   1996
    970.004'973—dc20   96-38302
                                                                  CIP

Oklahoma Paperbacks edition published 1996 by the University of
Oklahoma Press, Norman, Publishing Division of the University, by
special arrangement with Fifth House Publishers, 620 Duchess
Streeet, Saskatoon SK Canada S7K 0R1. Manufactured in the U.S.A.

            1   2   3   4   5   6   7   8   9   10

Contents

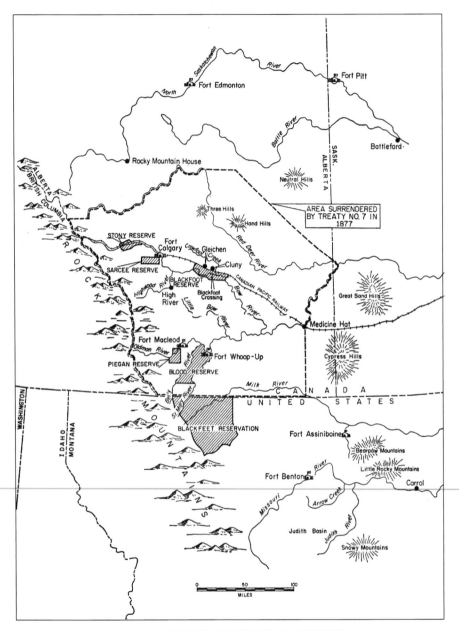

PLACES SIGNIFICANT IN THE LIFE OF CROWFOOT

The map is from *Crowfoot: Chief of the Blackfeet* by Hugh A. Dempsey, copyright © 1972 by the University of Oklahoma Press. Reproduced with permission of the University of Oklahoma Press.

Introduction

The members of the Blackfoot Nation of southern Alberta and northern Montana—the Bloods, Blackfoot, and Peigans—have seen massive changes in their way of life in the last century and a half. Once free and independent buffalo hunters, they were forced onto reserves in the 1880s and were expected to adapt easily to the new way of life.

But some refused to give up their old traditions and customs, and though government officials viewed them as "troublemakers," they were openly admired by their own people. Others did accept reservation life, but under their own terms.

This book draws together many stories that at one time were well known to Blackfoot elders but that have been slipping away with each succeeding generation. Retention of tribal history has become a daunting challenge in the face of integrated education, loss of language, and that great leveller of all cultures: television. This book tells the stories of some of the Blackfoot in the days before and after reservations; one tale even goes back to the 1690s, virtually the beginning of time for the tribe. Other accounts deal with the men who would never have survived reserve life, such warriors as Calf Shirt and Low Horn. But most of the stories are about people who tried to cope with the changing world. Some, such as Flying Chief and Dave Mills, compromised by keeping their old beliefs while accepting a new economy. Others, such as Big Rib and The Dog, simply rebelled against the government's authoritarian control over their lives.

The stories are all factual and are based on extensive interviews with elders, as well as research into government documents, accounts of early travelers, and missionary records. Many contain a strong element of mysticism. This is not a coincidence, for such beliefs were a significant part of Blackfoot life. People accepted the supernatural as part of their everyday lives and did not try to analyze or rationalize it. They believed that their entire universe was inhabited by good and evil spirits who could wield their powers at will. As an elder sat and told me his stories, the supernatural was just as real to him as buffalo hunts or war parties. Nothing in Blackfoot life happened by accident; their whole existence was governed by a litany of spirit protectors and supernatural forces.

Even today, the spirit world is important to the people. Young people seek spiritual help in an increasingly complex society, while the elders find solace in the rituals of their tribes. Many have found a delicate balance between their belief in Christianity and their faith in the Native beliefs. There are Blackfoot people who are ordained clergy and others who are respected medicine men. The Blackfoot have found room for both in their lives.

As a result, the approach in this book has been to accept the Indians' supernatural as reality. It was truth in the minds of the speakers and is delivered here as their truths. And just as the elders accepted that Calf Shirt spoke to rattlesnakes, so did they believe that Small Eyes had a vision in which he met Jesus Christ. Rather than be judgmental, I have accepted the stories as they were told, supernatural elements included.

Many of these tales are based largely upon oral history. When the elders tell a story, it is recounted just as if they had been there, complete with conversations. I recorded them that way and I now present them in that fashion. These conversations are a part of their narrative style.

I wish to thank the many Indians who shared their stories with me, including Jack Low Horn, Shot Both Sides, John Cotton, Suzette Eagle Ribs, Rides at the Door, Jim White Bull, Bobtail Chief, Jenny Duck Chief, One Gun, Harry Mills, Laurie Plume, Big Sorrel Horse, Vickie McHugh, Iron, Ed Yellow Old Woman, Cecil Tallow, Yellow Squirrel (Mrs. Bruised Head), Ambrose Gravelle, and a host of others. I will always be grateful that they were so generous with their time and that they were willing to provide me with a rare glimpse into their culture and beliefs. My interviews started in 1951 when I began to travel to the Blood, Blackfoot, and Peigan reserves with my late father-in-law, Senator James Gladstone.

Since that time, many changes have taken place. The Blackfoot tribe is now called the Siksika Nation, the Peigan tribe is the Peigan Nation, and the Sarcee tribe is the Tsuu T'Ina Nation. I respect these political moves to free themselves from government-imposed titles, but I have retained the use of Blackfoot, Peigan, and Sarcee as terms that are more familiar to readers, and to many of the Native people themselves. I want to extend my gratitude to Jane Richardson Hanks, who made available the field notes compiled by her and her husband, Lucien Hanks, between 1938 and 1941. Their work among the Blackfoot was monumental. Thanks also to Dr. John C. Ewers, formerly of the Smithsonian Institution, Washington, D.C., and especially to my wife, Pauline, for her support and for her assistance in translating many of the Blackfoot names.

Other acknowledgements go to the Glenbow Library and Archives, Calgary; National Archives of Canada, Ottawa; Hudson's Bay Company collection in the Provincial Archives of Manitoba, Winnipeg; and Historical Society of Montana, Helena. Finally, I wish to acknowledge the cooperation of the chiefs of the Blood and Blackfoot reserves, to whom this manuscript was submitted for comment long before it was ever sent out for publication. I am proud of the fact that over the years, the tribal councils have never objected to my writing about their people, and in fact, the Bloods have made me an honorary chief of their tribe, while the Blackfoot and Peigan have given me honorary names.

The Wise Old Ones

$\mathcal{T}$hese were the wise old ones. They sat around the Sun Dance camp or in their tiny one-roomed cabins, remembering how it used to be when they were young. In 1880 they had been wandering freely over the plains; the next year they were camped in the river bottoms near Standoff, in southern Alberta, accepting handouts of beef and flour from a reluctant government. Their old way of life had vanished with the disappearing buffalo herds; a vacant prairie and a government ration house were all that remained. Almost overnight, Indian agents expected them to forget all about buffalo hunting, warfare, and their Native religion and become good Christian farmers who were content to stay at home. In two or three years, they said, the Indians would be self-sufficient agriculturists.

In the early 1950s, as I wandered freely through the Blood Reserve, listening to their stories, it was obvious that many things had not changed. The elders still spoke their own language and followed their own religion, but they preferred to live in the happy past rather than in a questionable present. They wore white man's clothing because buckskin was no longer available (although some still wore moccasins), and they could no longer travel the plains. Instead, they moved about within their reserve, knowing they were surrounded by an alien world.

When I began asking questions, they were amazed that a young white man wanted to hear their tales; no one else was interested. The only white people who ever visited him, commented one man, were Indian Agency employees, missionaries, bootleggers, and Mormons seeking conversions. I didn't fit any of those categories, but perhaps the fact that I was married to a Blood Indian woman whose father was a respected member of the tribe made my presence understandable.

First there was Bobtail Chief. He sat crosslegged in his tent at the Sun Dance camp while he spoke about life in the old days. He made

Bobtail Chief was a blind patriarch of the Blood tribe when the author interviewed him in the 1950s. He is shown here holding a pipe. *Courtesy Glenbow-Alberta Institute/NA-1757-14*

graceful motions as he described portions of a story, then clapped his hands at a new development. He was tall, with a large aquiline nose and thin gray braids wrapped with gray cloth that once had been white. As he spoke in the Blackfoot tongue he was listened to attentively by two Native visitors—his brother from Montana, Charlie Revais, and the chief from the Blackfoot Reserve, Joe Crowfoot.

He told us in a matter-of-fact way about his decision not to kill an enemy. "There was Crazy Crow, Bruised Head, and me," he began. "We were on a horse-stealing raid down in the Bears Paw Mountains in Montana; we were on a hill looking down on a shed and corral, likely a sheep corral. We saw a man, a Cree or a half-breed, come up to the shed. He got off his horse and went inside.

"We crept up and he must have heard us, for he came outside. I immediately grabbed his ax and someone else got his knife. The man was so frightened he just stood there and trembled and I could hear his teeth chattering. Crazy Crow was going to strike him with his war hatchet, but I said, 'No, don't do that.' If he had had braids we would have killed him and scalped him, but he had short hair, even though he was an Indian."[1] So they let him go; there was no point in killing him if they couldn't take his scalp.

A little later, I visited Charlie Pantherbone in his one-roomed log home at the southeast corner of the reserve. Nobody called him Pantherbone except the people at the agency; to everyone else he was Sinew Feet. He was a mild-mannered man, thin as a rail, with one of the most gentle faces in the whole Blood tribe. My interpreter/father-in-law, James Gladstone, sat with me on an iron bed while Sinew Feet sat on the bed opposite the door. His wife and two grandchildren were asleep on the south side of the room. I noticed immediately that the layout in the house was the same as in a traditional tepee: doorway facing east, the man of the household at the west, the fireplace (stove) in the center, the women on the south side, and the male guests on the north. There was no way to make an altar on a wooden floor, so he had filled a shallow box with soil and placed it between him and the stove. Here he kept his sweetgrass, buffalo stones, and other ceremonial objects. Behind him, hanging on the wall, were his medicine bundles.

Sinew Feet liked to tell stories about his famous grandfather, *Sotai'na*, or Rainy Chief, the head chief who had signed Treaty Seven with the Canadian government in 1877. Sinew Feet also had a few ghost stories, such as this one:

"One time when the Bloods were in camp, the chief sent out a crier at dusk to invite everyone to his lodge. As the people were going in, one man held back. 'Why are you so slow to enter the lodge?' he was asked. The man did not answer but stood all alone, so the man asked him again.

"When he refused to reply, the Blood picked up a stick and hurled it at him, but it just passed through the man and hit the side of a lodge with a slap. It was then the Blood knew the stranger was not a real person. As the man turned and walked away, the ghost followed him to the lodge and stood outside. 'I came here to smoke,' the ghost said at last, 'and instead you try to hit me.'

"Everyone inside heard the voice, so a pipe was filled but no one would take it out. Finally, the chief asked a woman if she would pass it. She accepted the pipe and handed it out the door, but the ghost grabbed her and began to drag her away. The others tried to stop them but the ghost just pulled them all. At last a young man picked up a burning stick and struck where the ghost's hand should be. When that happened, the ghost released the woman and disappeared.

"However, the shock was so great that the woman went crazy. She was taken to the lodge of a medicine-pipe owner, and after the ceremonies were held and prayers were given for her, she returned to normal. From that time onward, she was known as *Sta'awpitaki,* or Ghost Old Woman."[2]

John Cotton, another elder, was living in the newly established village of Moses Lake, just north of Cardston. He lived in one of the tiny frame houses, ten-by-twelve feet in size, which were intended for senior citizens. But, as usual, the government didn't understand Indian ways. As soon as the old people had a roof over their heads, they were joined by sons, daughters, in-laws, and grandchildren. The extended family would never permit the old people to be shunted off by themselves and forgotten.

Cotton, round-faced, dynamic, humorous, and a member of the tribal council, took his responsibilities seriously. He could speak good English, but he preferred to tell his stories in Blackfoot, a language that was common to the Blood, Peigan, and Blackfoot tribes. He was much more at home with his own language, and besides, there were many old words for which he knew no English equivalents.

On one of my first visits, he told me how he had received the name of John Cotton; his own people called him *Minit'siko,* or Favorite Ill Walker. "About 1884," he said, "when I was in Fort Macleod, I got a job working for Superintendent John Cotton of the North-West Mounted Police. I used to look after his three big dogs, feeding them and keeping them combed. Then one day Superintendent Cotton said he was going to war against Louis Riel and the Crees, and he left. I didn't see him again until some time later and as I approached him, somebody said, 'Well, here's young John Cotton.' And that's how I got my name."[3]

There were many others who shared their stories with me—Jim White Bull, who had been crippled when he was shot in the back by a Montana lawman; Rides at the Door, whose wife was the holy woman at the Sun Dance; Shot Both Sides, the old and venerated chief; Iron, who at ninety-eight was the oldest man on the reserve; and Jack Low Horn, who could tell stories by the hour.

Their tales of the last days of freedom and the destruction of their old ways of life were not filled with bitterness or anger. They were told plainly and simply as facts that could not be changed through the passage of time. A few of these men had been warriors before they settled on the reserve and some had continued to go to war even after they were supposed to have settled down.

Shot Both Sides, who was head chief of the Blood tribe from 1913 until his death in 1956, had been on five raids against his enemies, capturing two horses on each venture.

Shot Both Sides, head chief of the Blood tribe from 1913 until his death in 1956. He took part in five raids against enemy tribes. This photograph was taken in 1927. *Courtesy Glenbow-Alberta Institute/NA-21-13*

"There were three of us—Big Plume, Plain Woman, and me," he recalled. "We went across the line to raid the Gros Ventres. It took us four days on horseback to reach their camps. During the night we went through the brush in the valley and stole the horses from their camp. There was one tepee near us. I took two horses. One was tied near the tepee and the other was hobbled. One was a white and the other a bay.

"After each of us had taken two horses, we rode northeast, and it took two days and nights of steady traveling before we arrived home. I never used my captured horses but just kept them around the camp."

"I never killed an enemy," he concluded.[4]

At the time of Treaty Seven with the Blackfoot, Blood, Peigan, Sarcee, and Stoney Indians in 1877, the buffalo were still plentiful on the southern Alberta plains, but within two years they seemed to have disappeared like magic. Some Indians thought the Blackfoot were being punished for signing the treaty. As proof, they pointed out that three of the Blood chiefs who signed the treaty did not live to see the next payment. Others thought that the Sun spirit was angry with the Indians for letting the white men slaughter his herds. So he had taken the last of his creatures and driven them into a huge cave. In a matter of months, the Canadian prairies became a barren desert, with only the bleached bones and a few prairie wolves reminding the Indians that the land had once been black with buffalo.

By 1879, the last herds had been drawn into a tight circle in the

Judith Basin in central Montana. Tribes from all parts of the northern plains were present, sometimes forgetting old animosities in the face of a common disaster. It was there that most of the Bloods congregated for their last taste of freedom. John Cotton remembered his first trip, probably in 1879.

"It was spring," he began. "That year we held our Sun Dance across the line, at the confluence of the Missouri and Yellowstone rivers. Both the Bloods and the Blackfoot were there. After the Sun Dance we traveled south. Our chiefs were White Calf, Bad Head, and Medicine Calf. There were still plenty of buffalo, and from some of the hills as we traveled towards the Yellowstone, there were buffalo as far as the eye could see.

"I saw them killed and butchered but I was too young to kill any myself. I was asked to kill a buffalo calf but I took one look at him and I was too scared.

"When we arrived near the spot where Billings now stands, we met the Crows. Because we had promised in our treaty to live at peace with the other tribes and the Americans had stopped their Indians from going to war, we made a peace treaty. Bad Head got together with two Crow chiefs, Was Kicked and Pregnant Woman, and said: 'To make this peace lasting, we must smoke the pipe.' After this was done, we were at peace with the Crows.

"Our camp was about a half-mile from them and there were at least a thousand lodges in each camp. After a while, we were joined by the Gros Ventres and Assiniboines and we made peace with them as well. At first we all watched each other, but after a while we started to trust our neighbors. During the two seasons we stayed in camp, we didn't have any trouble with the Crows.

"My father had a Crow friend named Heavily Whipped and he had two children, a boy and a girl. The boy, Pierced Ears, was about my age and we used to play together. We talked in sign language at first but I soon got so that I could understand Crow.

"From our big camp, the Bloods and Crows would go out hunting together whenever the scouts located buffalo. Whichever tribe killed the first buffalo was in charge of that hunt. Because the Bloods had the fastest horses, they were usually in charge. I must tell you that the Bloods had some excellent race horses. There was a famous sorrel owned by Eagle Shoe and another sorrel of Little Ears. He sold it to the Crows for three good runners and a blue roan that had come third in a race to kill the first buffalo in a hunt."[5]

By the autumn of 1880, the last slaughter had been so great that the buffalo were virtually gone. A few scattered herds remained, but they were so harried by hunters that they stampeded at the first sign of danger. Sadly, the Cheyennes, Shoshonis, Gros Ventres, Assiniboines, and other American tribes went back to their reservations. Meanwhile, military authorities harassed the Canadian Indians, telling them that they were trespassers and ordering them back across the line. But as long as there were buffalo to be hunted, bands of Bloods, Blackfoot, Sarcees, and Crees stayed near the Judith Basin.

John Cotton's family lived in the united camps of White Calf and Medicine Calf all winter, but in the spring of 1881 they had to say farewell to the Crows. The Bloods were going home.

"Our people were starving," said Cotton. "We traveled on the American side in search of buffalo until at last we came to a place where the soldiers were issuing food to the Indians.

"'We can't give you any rations,' they told us. 'You're Canadian Indians. We're feeding only American Indians.'

"Then one of the soldiers noticed the big silver medal that Medicine Calf was wearing around his neck.

"'What's that medal?' he asked.

Hunting camp in the Judith Basin of Montana in the early 1880s. By this time the buffalo were scarce; only a few scattered herds remained on the Great Plains. *Courtesy Glenbow-Alberta Institute/NA-5084-2*

"'This is the medal given to me by the Americans on the Yellow River in 1855,' he told the man.

"When the soldiers learned that our chief had signed the American treaty, they welcomed us and gave us all the rations we needed.[6] There was flour, bacon, beans, coffee, and all kinds of food, which we packed on our horses. After we were well supplied, White Calf said we shouldn't continue our search for buffalo. He said it would be foolish to travel towards the Bears Paw Mountains, as we would probably run into war parties of Crees, Assiniboines, and Sioux, and we would all be killed. But we wanted buffalo meat so we decided to go.

"After we had traveled for a few days and were camped for the night, our scout heard someone singing the Buffalo Song. When he investigated, he found a lone Blackfoot Indian who told of killing eight buffalo from a large herd. He had picked out the strays and had not disturbed the main herd. He told the scout they were about two days' travel ahead. As soon as we heard the news in the camps, everyone lit their campfires and began singing. Soon there were lights shining in every tepee and everybody was happy.

"The next day we broke camp and traveled towards the Wolf Mountains; on the second day we came to the place at the foot of the mountains where there are two hills covered with timber. We called them the Hairy Caps. Winding out from there is a wide coulee which we call Beaver Creek. It was in this bottom where we found the buffalo.

"White Calf told us to ready our buffalo horses. When everyone was prepared, he shouted the signal and we all rushed over the edge of a hill overlooking Beaver Creek. On the other side of the creek the valley was black with buffalo. Our hunters' horses rushed into the main herd and we were successful in killing many buffalo before the herd dashed away.

"When the women saw that the men were successful in their hunt, they took their knives and cut open the bottoms of the sacks which held our rations. They left the flour, bacon, beans, and coffee strewn over the prairie as they came down to skin the dead animals."[7]

John Cotton paused in his story. It was Boxing Day and he had just finished a huge turkey dinner at my in-laws' house. But at that moment he was far away from the comfortable surroundings of Christmas and was back on the open plains, watching the women expertly butchering the carcasses that lay strewn along the coulee floor. Later, the fires were lit, the iron pots put on the fire, and songs of happiness echoed along the valley.

"That was the last time I ever saw a wild buffalo," he concluded.

"We rested for a while at Beaver Creek, and by the time we passed Fort Benton our people were starving again. We had not seen another buffalo. When we realized there was no more food on the prairies we returned to Canada, where we were fed by the Mounted Police."[8]

As they straggled across the border, the Bloods were in pitiful shape. At Fort Benton, the townspeople had refused to allow them to come into the village to trade for food. But during the night their camps had been visited by whiskey traders, who "in return for the remnants of their buffalo robes, revived their falling spirits with some more Yankee Doodle rot gut."[9] Then they were harassed by white horse thieves who ran off almost a hundred animals in three separate raids.

To add to their misery, children were dying with measles and scarlatina, the horses were suffering from scabby mange, and the elderly were succumbing to starvation and the rigors of the journey. As the Bloods came to the reserve located south of Fort Macleod, they formed a slow, ragged line. A few were on horseback but many others were afoot, their worldly belongings pitched over their shoulders as they trudged along. Only the jingling of a few bells on a staff or the yapping of a dog betrayed the presence of the new arrivals. They were hungry, tired, and sick.

Within a few weeks, more than two thousand Bloods wandered into the valley of the Belly River, joining the eight hundred who had stayed in Canada under their chief, Red Crow. Tattered tepees were pitched beside the cottonwood cabins that had been built over the winter. Tiny garden patches of turnips and potatoes were overrun by grazing horses, the fences knocked down and used for firewood.

"Just after we settled on the reserve I remember that we were starving," recalled Bobtail Chief. "We were camped near Whoop-Up and in the late winter and early spring we were so hungry that we ate our dogs. At the beginning of winter we had fresh meat but that ran out. Then we had dried meat, then bacon, and then pemmican. We were so hungry that we begged for flour to keep alive.

"The first flour that was issued to us was black, made from frozen wheat. It was quite a few years before we got white flour. The black flour was edible and was better than starving. When we got it, we would make a batter and put it on the red coals of the campfire and cover it over with hot ashes. When it was cooked we would take it out, brush off the ashes, and eat it.

"The pemmican that was issued to us was made by the half-breeds. A lot of it was rotten and had maggots in it, but it all went into the black iron pots and was cooked and eaten. The dried meat was better; it was never rotten.

"Our first houses were made of cottonwood logs. There were half-breeds to help us build them. The chimneys were made of rocks and were either at the back of the room or in the middle. We used sacks for windows before there was glass, and had canvas for doors."[10]

The Bloods suffered through those early years on the reserves. Deaths greatly outnumbered births, blindness became prevalent because of the small, smoke-filled cabins, and tuberculosis was added to the list of diseases that were causing a high mortality rate within the tribe.

Now that the buffalo were gone, the Bloods had three choices for their future. They could exist on rations of flour and beef; they could learn to fend for themselves; or they could simply die off. Disappear. Become the "vanishing American" of popular literature. To leaders like Red Crow, and many young men, the choice was obvious. If the white man lived by farming and raising cattle, the Bloods would do the same. By the 1890s, after a decade of despair, they finally overcame government inefficiency, red tape, and adverse conditions to farm their little plots of land and to send growing herds of cattle out onto the rich grasslands of their reserve.

Big Sorrel Horse, one of the respected elders who lived near Bullhorn Coulee, remembered those days.

"When I was a boy," he said, "my father, Left Hand, was one of the few farmers among the Bloods. He grew corn, onions, potatoes, and other vegetables. He also had a patch of oats that was all sown by hand. First, the oxen from the agency were used for breaking and plowing. Then my father harrowed it with pieces of brush from the valley. When the oats had matured, he cut them with a scythe. He built a log corral inside of which he spread the coverings of his tepee. On this he piled his oats. Then he opened the corral gate and drove his horses inside. He drove them around and around so that their hooves threshed the grain.

"When there was a good wind blowing, he threw the grain into the air so that the chaff separated from the oats. The oats were put in grain sacks and loaded on a travois to be taken to my father's house.

"When he went to sell his oats in Fort Macleod, he and my mother dressed up in their best blankets and blanket coats. Five or six sacks of oats were piled on the travois until it was bowed under the weight. There were no fences between our home and Fort Macleod. With the load, it took us two days to reach the town; we took our time on the trail and stopped for dinner at the Standoff springs. It took us one day to come back. On the way home we were all very happy."[11]

The dynamic leader of the Bloods at that time was Red Crow, head chief of the tribe. His pride and independence were an inspiration to his people. He was a successful rancher, sent his favorite child to boarding school to get the white man's education, and treated the government officials as though they were his equals, not the superiors they perceived themselves to be. Yellow Squirrel, the wife of Bruised Head, who was staying in Red Crow's tepee in 1900, remembered the tragedy of his death.

"Red Crow went across the river to round up his horses," she said. "When he didn't return, his wife, Longtime Singer, went to look for him. She found him lying on the gravel at the edge of the river. I saw her crying and we knew what had happened. We all went across with Red Crow's wagon and brought his body over.

"Red Crow had used some stones between the pegs of his tepee, and before we moved camp, we made the circle of stones complete. Then we placed four radiating lines of stones. We did this because it was the custom as far back as the days when we used dogs. They were the marks of a warrior chief.

"That night, Bull Horn (who was unaware of the death) moved his tepee to the next river bottom, and during the night he heard someone calling loudly from our deserted camp. He told his wife about it and next morning he went to the campground. When he saw the stone markers around Red Crow's tepee site he began crying. He went back to his lodge and said, 'We have lost our chief.'"[12]

This circle of stones with the radiating lines—or medicine wheel, as white people call it—marked the site of the chief's last camping place until it disappeared under the backwaters of the irrigation dam on St. Mary's River in the 1950s. Perhaps it is still there today, but like many features of Blood culture, it has been inundated by the relentless onslaught of the white man.

The early years on the reserve were difficult, but the Bloods adapted to the new conditions as best they could. They continued to practice their religious beliefs, followed as much of the traditional lifestyle as possible, and maintained a healthy sense of humor. For example, when the Shooting Up Band settled on a backwater of the Belly River and it dried up, everyone laughed. They said the family was so lazy that all they did was sit around all day and drink tea. In that way, they had drunk the backwater dry. So they renamed them the Interfering Band, because they had interfered with the flow of the river.

My father-in-law, James Gladstone, had his own recollections of humor during that period. "Somewhere between 1908 and 1912," he recalled, "the Bloods used to have a laughing contest dance. It was held during the evening, maybe at a rest period during the regular round dance." People listening to the story nodded when they remembered the event.

"Two societies would choose a representative, usually a man from one side and a woman from the other. They would face each other and try to get the other one to laugh first. They might sing, use sign language, talk, or sometimes a man would even pull at the woman's face to make her laugh. Or he might point to a homely person and say, 'That's your boyfriend over there.'

"Both of them would try to stay serious, but the contest usually lasted for less than a minute. The first person to smile was the loser and their [age-grade] society had to sponsor the next dance. It would probably cost them fifty dollars for meat, bannock, and other food, so it was an expensive contest."[13]

In the 1950s, the wise old ones enjoyed telling these stories. There was no electricity on the reserve then, no television, and few radios. Storytelling was a favorite way of passing the time, so whenever a few people got together the stories flew thick and fast. If they were recollections of the past, the teller made sure he adhered strictly to the truth. His reputation depended on the accuracy of the telling. After telling a story, Iron, at that time the oldest man on the Blood Reserve, said to me, "Many men told lies about their experiences and they died early. I tell only the truth and that's why I'm still alive."[14]

If the stories were humorous, the sessions were quite animated. Often the teller arose and acted out portions of the story or, if he was too feeble, he waved his arms in the air to make a point. After a huge guffaw or laugh, he cleared his throat and spit into the indispensable tobacco can that most old men had by their bedsides. Then he was off on another story.

They were home to stay on their reserve, but their minds and hearts were far away. The past was filled with reminiscences of buffalo hunts, exciting raids on enemy camps, and freedom to wander the prairies. There was much happiness in these memories of the days when their people had been the masters of the plains.

The stories that follow are the results of those many happy hours of listening, asking questions, and taking notes. Often, it was possible to find additional data in the records of the Mounted Police and the Indian Department. Sometimes there were variations, particularly when officials had no real understanding of Native culture, but it was surprising how often the accounts dovetailed. Essentially, however, these are Indian stories, told to me from an Indian perspective and offered in the same way. They are the stories of a proud and self-reliant people who prized their freedom and independence.

A Friend of the Beavers

The autumn sun caressed the little valley and bathed the gnarled cottonwoods with its warm rays. Nearby, the Red Deer River gurgled and splashed contentedly as it wound its way through the high hills as though hurrying to reach the prairies far to the south. Overhead, a peregrine falcon hovered silently, waiting for an unsuspecting ground squirrel to venture from its burrow. Closer to the riverbank, a few swallows dipped and curved, twittering constantly as they searched for flying insects.

Along the valley, close to the trees, a Blackfoot camp blended with its surroundings. The leather lodges were a golden brown, becoming darker towards their tops until they were almost black at their smoke holes. A few churlish dogs slept in the shadows of the lodges, always with an eye half-open to snap a piece of stray meat or to slink away in case of trouble. In the woods, some young girls collected firewood, laughing and giggling as they used their long, curved poles to break the upper limbs off old dead trees. High on one of the nearby hills, a lone scout watched the wood gatherers for a few moments, then resumed his vigil.

This was the decade of the 1690s, and for the first time in several years, the Blackfoot Nation was at war. The Crees to the east were peaceful, while the Kootenays still crossed back and forth through the mountain passes and the Beaver Indians lived quietly in the woodlands north of the big river.

The trouble had come from the south and it had all started so innocently. The two tribes had been friends for a long time, right from the days when the first Shoshoni warriors had drifted northeast, leaving their fellow tribesmen in the mountain valleys. The Bow River, an unpredictable little stream that could rage like a buffalo bull in the spring and become a turgid trickle in the fall, was the acknowledged dividing line between the two nations. The Blackfoot hunted as far north as the Saskatchewan River and east to the Eagle Hills, but ventured south of the Bow only when joined by their Shoshoni friends.

Yet there was plenty of land and lots of buffalo for everyone. The horse had not yet been introduced to the Plains tribes, so travel was measured by a day's walk and baggage was limited to the goods that a dog could pull on a travois. No white man intruded upon the land and no European goods, guns, or metal tools interfered with the way the Indians had lived for generations.

The trouble all started at a children's game. The Blackfoot and Shoshoni had been camped together when the boys organized a football match. This was a uniquely Shoshonian game called *tanasiikwito'koin*.[1] A ball made of deer hair and covered with leather was dropped into the middle of a playing field and the teams kicked, passed, and ran, until one side crossed the goal line. It was a rough and tumble sport, as vigorous as the boys themselves.

During one fateful game, a Shoshoni boy was hurt and in retaliation the father angrily clubbed a Blackfoot boy to death. While threats and insults degenerated into pushing and shoving, an old Blackfoot sat down on the ground and threw up his hands. This was a sign that the man did not want to fight, and in the past his wishes would have been respected. This time, however, feelings were running so high that he was killed by Shoshoni warriors. When the two tribes parted, each to go to their own side of the Bow River, the days of peace were at an end.

"Thereafter," recalled an aged patriarch, "the Blackfeet had no mercy for their enemies."[2]

The Blackfoot camp in the valley of the Red Deer River was always on the alert after the incident, but daily life continued in the same way as it had for generations. The men went out in the morning to stalk the fat buffalo cows while the women tanned, cooked, and tended the camp. Some went farther upstream to pick berries while others looked for wild turnips on the open prairies.

One of the members of this camp was a poor young man named *Eksikoka*, or White Clay.[3] He lived with his grandmother and provided enough food for their lodge, but he could not afford to acquire religious objects or to have fine clothing made for him. And because the Blackfoot had been at peace, there had been no chance for him to earn battle honors.

White Clay was in love with a young married woman, and she was in love with him. But he had never tried to win her because he was ashamed of being poor. He realized that her recent marriage was no problem; she had become the fourth wife of an older man specifically so that she might later marry White Clay. The old man had only one real wife and she was as old as he. The other two women, like White Clay's beloved, were under the holy man's protection.

This was not an unusual situation; explorer David Thompson noticed the same practice when he lived among the Peigans during the winter of 1787-88. He observed that an old Indian had three teenaged girls in his lodge whom he called his wives but whom he treated as daughters. "The whole three were betrothed to three young men," explained the husband, "and would have been given to them, had not three Men of two powerful families who have each already four or five wives, demanded that these young women should be given to them; as their parents are not powerful to prevent this, these three young women have been given to me, and in my tent they will remain until this camp separates . . . when they will be given to the young men for whom they are intended."[4]

The practice was so common that periodically the Blackfoot had the young women perform a special dance. It was customary for them to wear the clothing of their lovers during the evening to reveal to everyone their true sweethearts.

White Clay's beloved was married to one of the most powerful men in the Blackfoot nation. Not only was he rich, but he possessed the sacred beaver bundle, which was the most important religious object in the camp. He was a kindly man who was devoted to his people and to his faith in the spiritual world.

One evening when the camp criers announced that the women's dance would be held, the man noticed that his young ward had made no move to join the other women.

"What's this?" he chided her, "you haven't gone to the dance? Don't you have a lover then?"[5]

The woman knew that White Clay was ashamed of being poor, but she wanted everyone in the camp to know that she loved him. She also understood that she had to do something to make him break out of his despondency and challenge him to win the right to demand her as his wife.

When she went to his lodge, she discovered that he was out hunting, so she asked the grandmother for his clothes.

"Oh my poor girl," said the old woman, "those clothes are not beautiful at all and such a young woman as you shouldn't wear them. They wouldn't suit you."

"It doesn't matter. Give them to me anyhow. Those are the clothes that I want."

She put on his badly worn shirt and leggings, tied a strip of wolf skin in her hair, and wrapped his old robe around her. The skin was scabby—it was never properly tanned—and was so worn that it was round in shape. People always laughed at this garment and had given the poor man the nickname of *A'pikoh-kominima*, or Scabby Round Robe.

As she approached the dance, the woman cut a small stick which she smeared with white clay and decorated with bird feathers, just like her lover carried. Then, dressed in this shabby costume, she joined the other women in the dancing circle. She was newly married and people had tried to guess the name of her lover. Now they saw her and laughed that she had chosen White Clay, the poorest man in the camp.

While she was dancing, her lover returned from the hunt and watched in surprise and humiliation as the beautiful woman paraded proudly in his clothes. As she moved in rhythm to the drums, she constantly pointed her feathered stick along the downstream course of the river. White Clay could not stand the jokes from the people around him, but before he fled, he asked his comrade, Double Runner, to report anything his sweetheart said or did.[6]

The old man who was in charge of the dance was puzzled by the young woman's performance, so he halted the drum. "This girl has come to dance tonight for the first time in her life," he said. "We want her to let us know what she intends to do." The woman stood defiantly in front of the whole camp and then, speaking as though she was the man whose clothes she wore, she again pointed her stick downstream and exclaimed, "When the river gets warm next summer, I will show you what I will do. I will go to war."

The drums rolled and the people applauded, for they understood that she had challenged her lover and if he failed to go to war he would lose her forever. Not only that, but he would be branded a coward. Yet White Clay was a man without spiritual protectors and without power. Even in daily life the world was filled with dangerous forces that could cause a man to be trampled by a stampeding herd of buffalo or attacked by a grizzly bear. Nothing happened by accident; all the good and evil that occurred in the world was controlled by spiritual forces. If a man went to war, the dangers were even greater, and only if someone possessed his own spiritual powers could he expect to overcome all the dark forces that awaited him on the war trail.

It was autumn and already a few leaves were turning yellow and the grass was a crispy brown. In a few weeks, the first flakes of snow would swirl down from the north, and soon everyone would be huddled in their lodges, venturing out only when the air was cold and clear. Then, wearing sturdy snowshoes, the men would set out with spears in hand to trap unwary buffalo in snow-filled coulees. In weather like that, no man could search for spiritual help.

As soon as he learned of his sweetheart's challenge, White Clay gathered his few belongings and headed upstream from the camp, vowing not to return until he could meet her challenge. After traveling for several days, he came to a small stream where beavers had built a dam. Out in the pond he could see the rough pile of sticks and mud that marked their lodge.

White Clay knew that the beavers possessed great magical powers, so he dug a pit near the shore of the pond and made a shelter for himself. He watched the beavers as they busily cut saplings and hauled the branches to their lodge for their winter supply of food. Guided by their actions, he gathered bullberries and hunted buffalo and stored the food in his own shelter.

And there he stayed for the winter, praying and seeking spiritual guidance. At last he had a vision in which a young beaver came to his shelter and told him to close his eyes. When he opened them, he found he was inside the beaver lodge in the middle of the pond. Only now, the lodge had become a tepee and the beavers had taken on human form.

"My son," said the beaver man, "sit down and tell me why you are here."

When White Clay explained his problem, the beaver man offered to help him and to teach him songs and rituals that would protect him from his enemies. As the lessons drew to a close, one of the young beavers took the man aside. "When our father offers you a gift," he said, "and tells you to choose whatever you wish, take the thing that is closest to the door, for that is the best our father has, and has strong power."

As predicted, the beaver man offered White Clay a gift. The Blackfoot looked at all the fine costumes and wonderful articles hanging on the walls and for a few moments he was tempted. But remembering the words of the young beaver, he said, "I'll take the object that is closest to the door."

"But that's just a stick that's used to close the door. It's no good for anything."

"That's what I want."

Four times the beaver man urged him to take something else, but each time White Clay chose the stick. "Very well," said the beaver man, "you have been good and remained true to your choice. This is my strongest instrument of power."

When White Clay awoke, he was back in his crude shelter, the strange little stick by his side.

He seemed a different man when he returned to the Blackfoot camps in the spring. Though still poor, he was now calm and self-assured. He spoke to no one about his experiences, but the stick—with a rawhide cord attached to each end—was worn proudly like a bandoleer. Shortly after his return, when a huge war party was organized to go against the Shoshonis, White Clay was the first to volunteer. But the others laughed at him, still remembering the frightened man who had fled when his sweetheart had danced.

The others set out, but White Clay and his friend Double Runner followed resolutely in the rear. They stayed just out of sight of the main party so that no one would try to force them back to camp. From the valley of the Red Deer River the war party marched out to the plains, the scouts constantly on the move, running ahead of the others and watching for signs of danger. A restless milling of a buffalo herd or a few antelope bouncing across the distant prairies could signal the presence of enemy hunters. A scent of smoke in the air or the noisy scolding of a magpie might reveal a party of Shoshoni warriors hidden in a nearby coulee.

But the prairies were devoid of enemies as the Blackfoot ventured south. Not until they were almost in sight of the Bow River did their scouts report that the main Shoshoni camp had been found. It was located in the valley along the south bank of the Bow near a major crossing known as *Soyo-powah'ko*, or Ridge Under Water.[7]

As the Blackfoot warriors approached the river, they boldly marched down a narrow coulee that led to the broad valley below. The Shoshoni, seeing them approach, pointed and milled restlessly. A few minutes later, the two enemy camps stared at each other from across the wide expanse of the Bow River, then began shouting and making defiant gestures. Because it was spring and the river was high, the only safe crossing was a narrow ridge a foot under the water where men had to walk in single file. The only other crossings nearby were several miles upstream.

The leader of the Shoshonis realized that the Blackfoot were in no position to attack, so using a form of sign language universal to the Plains Indians, he challenged any of his enemy to meet him in single combat.

Meanwhile, White Clay and Double Runner had circled west of the main party and watched from a hill upstream as the challenge was delivered. Without hesitation, White Clay said, "I'm going to kill the great chief. Stay here. Don't go farther down the river. I'm going to bring you the body of the Snake [Shoshoni] chief."

Stripping down to his breechcloth, White Clay remembered the prayers and songs given to him by the beaver man. As he slipped into the water, he sang, "When we try hard, we escape danger. When we dive we are safe."[8] He took the beaver stick in his teeth and, without weapons, he floated downstream towards the river crossing.

The Blackfoot were surprised and excited when they saw someone floating and swimming towards the Shoshoni camp. None of the warriors or chiefs could recognize him in the water and they knew that no one had left their war party, so his identity was a mystery. The Shoshoni saw him, too, and hooted and jeered when they noticed he was unarmed. All he had was a strange stick in his mouth.

At last White Clay reached the ridge that marked the river crossing. As his feet touched the gravelly bottom, he arose and waded towards the enemy. "Here I am," he shouted defiantly to the Shoshonis. "Tell your chief to come into the water and here we will meet in combat."

Giving a loud war cry, the Shoshoni leader grabbed his spear and jumped into the water. As he waded along the ridge, White Clay steadily backed away, as though afraid of the oncoming enemy. As he did so, he moved into deeper and deeper water, the unsuspecting chief following him. At last, when he thought he was close enough, the Shoshoni hurled his spear at the retreating Blackfoot, but the water was so deep that it spoiled his aim and White Clay easily deflected it with his beaver stick.

Now the fight had taken an ominous turn and suddenly the cheering Shoshoni were silent. As they watched in horror, White Clay grabbed the spear, waded back to the shallow ridge, and hurled the weapon with deadly accuracy at his foe. The Shoshoni, trapped in the deep water, was killed instantly. As his body bobbed to the surface, White Clay grabbed it by the hair and dived into deeper water.

A great cheer arose from ranks of the Blackfoot, and the warriors excitedly rushed downstream to meet the warrior as he floated ashore with his victim. Not only did they want to greet the unknown warrior, but they knew that great battle honors would go to the man who

This illustration of Blackfoot Crossing in 1881 shows that it was still a narrow ford across the Bow River, just as it had been when Scabby Round Robe killed the Shoshoni chief in the 1690s. The crossing was washed out in a 1901 flood. *Courtesy Glenbow-Alberta Institute/NA-1190-9*

scalped the Shoshoni and to the first four men who struck the dead body with their coup sticks. It did not matter if they had taken part in the fight; to be the first on the scene was an honor in itself.

But White Clay had no intention of giving these prizes to the men who had rejected him. So instead of floating downstream, he swam upstream like a beaver until he reached the place where Double Runner was waiting for him. Together, they pulled the body onto the shore where White Clay scalped it and cut the grisly trophy in two. One for himself and one for his comrade.

When the other Blackfoot warriors discovered they had been tricked, they dashed upstream; the first four men to find the body were not the great chiefs and warriors of the tribe, but young men who had been left behind when the leaders had gone downstream. By the time the chiefs got to the scene, the body had been scalped and the war honors taken.

Across the river, the Shoshoni had accepted defeat and were sadly taking down their tepees and preparing to move. It was the beginning of an exodus that ultimately took the entire group back across the mountains to rejoin its main tribe. With this one brave act, White Clay had opened the land south of the Bow to occupation by the victorious Blackfoot.

Now that he was a great hero, everyone wanted to be White Clay's friend. They listened with awe to his account of the fight and of the protection he had received from the beaver people. He was no longer an outcast or the butt of their jokes. He was a great warrior.

Because of this deed, White Clay announced that he was taking a new name. That was his right. There were many important names which had once existed within the tribe that he might use, or, if he wished, the event itself might cause him to create an entirely new name, such as Beaver Young Man, or Water Chief, or Swims Under. But no, as he stood before the respectful throng of warriors, he chose none of these. Instead, he announced that henceforward he would be called *A'pikoh-kominima*, or Scabby Round Robe, a name that was once a source of derision and now would be a symbol of honor.

Days later, a breathless scout entered the main Blackfoot camp and announced that the war party was returning. It had been successful, there were no Blackfoot casualties, and the Shoshonis had been defeated. The great hero was White Clay, now called Scabby Round Robe.

As soon as he heard the news, the husband of Scabby Round Robe's beloved called for the woman. Everyone searched for her and at last she was found gathering rose hips; she was wearing her oldest dress and was grimy from her work. As soon as she heard the news, the woman squealed with delight, cast aside her berries, and hurried back to the camp. Her husband's second wife immediately dressed her in the finest clothes and when the victorious war party reached the camp, she was ready to greet them.

The warriors marched in solemn order while the people of the camp gathered in a huge semicircle and sang a song to honor the returning warrior. Scabby Round Robe was in the lead, followed by Double Runner, then the four young men who had counted coups, and finally the rest of the expedition. The woman came forward to greet her sweetheart, shook his hand, and they kissed. Then Scabby Round Robe presented her with the scalp and the spear he had taken from the enemy warrior.

"Give these to your husband," he said.

That evening, as a great victory dance and scalp dance were being organized, the husband called Scabby Round Robe into his lodge where he sat with the young woman.

"Here is our wife," he said. "I give her to you in place of the presents you gave to me. And here is my lodge; I also pay that to you. And also one of my dogs, the yellow one."[9]

In this way, Scabby Round Robe became rich and won the woman he loved.

Now that he was a hero, people looked to Scabby Round Robe for leadership. They were at war and he had proven himself as a fighter, so he could lead them. Some time later, when they were at war with the Kootenays, Scabby Round Robe headed an expedition where he killed another enemy and took the man's arrows and scalp. He led the party home, and when they neared the camp he climbed a hill and signaled to the people. We had a good raid, he told them in sign language, and we were victorious.

When they entered the camp, his wife was waiting for him. Again he kissed her, and this time he presented her with a quiver full of arrows and the Kootenay scalp. She in turn gave them to her former husband. The older man was pleased, for he realized that the future of the Blackfoot depended upon leaders such as Scabby Round Robe. Not only was he fearless in battle but he had spiritual protection from the beaver people, just as the man himself had.

That evening, he invited Scabby Round Robe into his lodge and there he gave him his second wife and the most important of all his possessions, his beaver bundle. The beaver people had given the bundle to the old man many years earlier, and everyone believed that it guided and protected the Blackfoot people. Now he was passing it along to a younger man. Included in the bundle were the spear and Shoshoni scalp from Scabby Round Robe's first victory.

Later, Scabby Round Robe went on a third raid. This was a long expedition, and it took them many days before they finally found their enemy. Again he led the charge and took the scalp and spear of an enemy he killed in battle. As he was the only man to take a life, he cut the scalp into small pieces and gave a lock to each warrior who had accompanied him. When they returned, he gave the spear to the former husband and in turn the man presented Scabby Round Robe with the third and last of the women he had under his protection.

Because of these three successful raids, which took place after so many years of peace, Scabby Round Robe's war honors enabled him to became the chief of the Blackfoot nation. He replaced Scar Face, the great leader who first taught the tribe to venerate the Sun spirit. Scar Face was said to have visited the sky people and was given the rituals of the Sun Dance by the Sun spirit himself.

Years later, when Scabby Round Robe became old and tired, his place was taken by Shaved Head, the man who discovered horses. He found them among the mountain Indians about 1725 and brought the first animals to the Blackfoot people.

But the people always remembered Scabby Round Robe and venerated him. Over the years, the tales of his exploits became so enmeshed with the religious beliefs of the tribe that he was remembered as much for his ownership of the beaver bundle and his winter vision in the beaver lodge as he was for being a great warrior chief. He was said to have brought the first calendar sticks to the Blackfoot, given to him by the beavers so that the Indians might know and record the changing seasons. He is also credited with giving them the tobacco rituals that were followed when they cultivated their only agricultural crop.

The site of Scabby Round Robe's first victory is on the Blackfoot Indian Reserve, east of Calgary. The Ridge Under Water, better known by its name of Blackfoot Crossing, was destroyed in a flood at the turn of the twentieth century, but the site is still known and recognized today by the Blackfoot people.

The Reincarnation of Low Horn

$\mathcal{O}$ n 1835, when *A'tsitsi,* or Screech Owl, was thirteen, he decided to go to a lonely place to seek a vision. He had not yet been to war, but he knew that he would need spiritual protection when his time came to join a raid on an enemy horse herd. When the entire Blackfoot tribe assembled in camp for their annual Sun Dance, Screech Owl climbed to the top of a high hill, carrying with him only his robe and his pipe. There he remained, stretched out in a crude shelter of stones, without food or water, gazing eastward towards the rising sun and praying each day that a spirit helper would visit him.

On the third night, a violent storm swept over the prairies, the rain pelting down on the Blackfoot camp, the thunder roaring overhead and the lightning flashing with such brilliance that it turned night into day. As the people watched, they saw that the lightning concentrated on the hill where Screech Owl lay fasting. Again and again the lightning bolts struck the crest of the hill, until everyone was convinced that the boy was dead.

Next morning, to their amazement and delight, Screech Owl returned safely from his vigil. He never revealed what had happened on that stormy night, but from that time onward, he possessed the song of the thunder spirit and could sing it when he needed help.

Later, perhaps in a dream, Screech Owl was out hunting when a large jack rabbit, obviously very frightened, bounded between his legs and huddled there. Overhead, the Blackfoot boy heard the piercing cry of a sparrow hawk, and then, to his surprise, the bird spoke to him.

"Son," it said, "stand aside so I can get that jack rabbit. I've been chasing him for a long time. If you move, I'll give you my body.[1] I'm the fiercest of birds and you'll have my powers."

"No!" the rabbit argued. "Don't listen to that bird. You see he can fly quickly but he can't capture me. Save me and I'll make you a great leader of your people. I'll give you wonderful powers."

"Wait!" responded the bird. "I'll let you have the song that goes with my powers." He then sang his sparrow hawk song and gave it to the boy.

But Screech Owl had taken pity on the rabbit, so he gathered it in his arms and offered the sparrow hawk some gophers and small birds that he had killed. Carefully he made a mound of buffalo chips and sagebrush, skinned the gophers and birds, and placed them on the pile. As the sparrow hawk came to eat, Screech Owl sent the rabbit scurrying into the safety of some bushes.

That night, with the warmth of the frightened rabbit still clinging to his skin and the sparrow hawk's cry racing through his head, he had another vision in which the rabbit came to him and gave him a song. "Because you saved my life," it said, "you'll be a leader of your people. You'll escape from many dangers." The next night, the sparrow hawk appeared in the boy's dream, forgiving him for setting the rabbit free. "I give you my power," said the bird. "In battle you must wear two feathers from my wings and you'll never be beaten."

Because he now owned the sparrow hawk song, Screech Owl often looked for the birds, watching them as they swooped down on some tiny animal scampering across the prairie. One day, a sparrow hawk passed close to him, diving at its prey. As it rose in the air, Screech Owl fired an arrow, causing the bird to drop a tiny mouse, which fell into the boy's hands.

The mouse, known to the Blackfoot as *kaina-ski'na*, or "old rotten face," was considered to be the source of supernatural power. Red Old Man, one of the famous warriors of the tribe, had received his power from that little creature. Now Screech Owl held one in the palm of his hand. It had been slightly hurt by the sparrow hawk's claws but the boy was able to make it well. In gratitude, the mouse gave him a song.

A Blackfoot was lucky if he had one vision in his lifetime and was promised the aid of a spirit helper. But Screech Owl, while still a teenager, had acquired the holy songs of the sparrow hawk, rabbit, thunder, and mouse. That is how he took his first steps to become a great warrior of the Blackfoot tribe.

By the 1830s, the Blackfoot were at war with most of the tribes around them. They had always traded with the Hudson's Bay Company at Fort Edmonton or Rocky Mountain House, but in 1831, the first American forts in Blackfoot country were opened on the upper

Missouri River. As American trade goods found their way into their camps, the Blackfoot began traveling farther and farther south with their Blood and Peigan allies. Finally, they spent the entire winter of 1834-35 in the Missouri River country, over two hundred miles from their usual wintering grounds. Here they were exposed to a new enemy, the Crows, who usually hunted south of the Missouri into the Yellowstone country.

It proved to be a disastrous winter for the Blackfoot. In one surprise raid alone, fifty-two Blackfoot and eight Bloods were slaughtered by the Crows. In the summer of 1835, the rest of the Blackfoot tribe went back home, near the banks of the Bow River. It was while they were camped there that Screech Owl had experienced his adventure with the thunder and lightning storm.

During the rest of the year and well into the winter months, more fights took place between the Blackfoot Nation and their enemies. In one encounter, a combined party of Crees and Assiniboines killed eight Peigans near Rocky Mountain House, while in another incident Cree and Blood war parties fought over stolen horses and several Bloods were killed. In a confrontation near Fort Pitt, one Blackfoot was killed while the Crees had one killed and four wounded. During the late winter, three Blackfoot died at the hands of the Assiniboines.

These killings were the last straw. When the news of the tragedy reached the hunting camp of the Blackfoot, Bloods, and Peigans, a large war party set out for the north to wreak revenge upon the Crees and Assiniboines. When Screech Owl heard the news, he went to his father's lodge.

"Father," he said, "many of my cousins are going with this war party. I think that now I'm old enough to go to war, and I'd like to join them."

"My son, I'm willing; you can go."

So the fourteen-year-old boy who had never been on the warpath before, joined his cousins for the attack. Because this was his first expedition, he was expected to go as a servant, collecting firewood, making temporary shelters, and preparing the food. He would not take part in the raid itself.

In times of war, the Blackfoot organized two different kinds of raiding parties. If the Indians were merely seeking horses, a few warriors would set out, often on foot. Their goal was to creep into an enemy camp and escape undetected with as many ponies as possible. However, if the tribe had suffered some indignity at the hands of their enemy, then a revenge war party was organized. It could have a dozen or even a hundred warriors whose sole objective was to kill as many of their enemy as possible. Screech Owl had joined a revenge party.

Before he left, his father gave him a very fast horse; it was black with a white spot on its side. He also offered the boy a number of weapons but he refused them all. Instead, he went to war armed only with a small tomahawk. "This will be all I'll need," he said.

The war party traveled northeast until it reached the North Saskatchewan River near Fort Pitt. From there, it traveled a few miles downstream where scouts sighted three Crees who had been out hunting. Noting their direction, the Blackfoot made a wide sweep around them to ambush them farther along the trail. When in position, the older warriors began to ready themselves for the attack, painting their faces, donning their war clothes, and singing their songs.

Then they noticed to their surprise that Screech Owl had stripped down to his breechcloth, placed two sparrow hawk feathers in his hair, and had begun to ride around, singing his sparrow hawk song. The older men thought the fourteen-year-old boy was making fun of them.

"Here, look at this boy!" one of the warriors cried. "Has he no shame? He'd better stay behind."

But Screech Owl would not be denied. When the attack began, his black horse dashed ahead of the others and soon he was leading the war party, still singing his sparrow hawk song. The three Crees, seeing the horsemen burst from cover, urged their horses to a gallop, staying close together for their own protection. As Screech Owl drew near, one of them turned in the saddle and fired a shot but missed him. Quickly, the Blackfoot teenager drew alongside his enemy and struck him with his ax, knocking him to the ground. The body was left behind for the others to count their coups as the boy raced along to the second Cree. As he approached him, the enemy fired his musket directly at Screech Owl, but at the last moment the youth slid to the side of his horse and the ball whistled harmlessly over his head. Then, in a demonstration of superb horsemanship, Screech Owl swung back into place and in one sweeping motion knocked the second Cree from his horse.

By now, the other Blackfoot were far behind but were cheering his victories and shouting, "*A-wah-heh*, take courage!" The third Cree, riding the fastest horse, was farther ahead; he too was armed with a flintlock. Screech Owl did not want to overtake him until the gun was fired, but his big black horse thundered on, caught up in the excitement of the chase. The young Blackfoot shifted his body from side to side to make himself more difficult to hit and when the shot finally came, he easily avoided it.

Screech Owl now urged his horse to greater speed, and as they overtook the hapless Cree, the young warrior swung his ax and brought it down in a crushing blow to the man's side. Then, another slice to the head sent the body of the third Cree crashing to the ground.

Wheeling his horse around, Screech Owl got back to the scene just as the other warriors were counting coup and scalping the third body. They were amazed at the daring exploits of their young companion, and when they returned to the south, they proclaimed his bravery to the entire camp. In the victory celebrations Screech Owl was praised by the warrior societies, and even though he was only fourteen, he was recognized as a man. Because Screech Owl was a boy's name, it was no longer suitable. Instead, he was given the respected and honored name of *E'kaskini*, or Low Horn.

And so began the career of one of the Blackfoot's greatest warriors.

The skirmishes between the warring tribes had become so bitter that in the summer of 1836 a peace treaty was made between the Bloods and Assiniboines. Soon, peace spread to the other tribes and the chiefs tried to keep their young men at home to hunt and look after the horse herds. But the treaty proved to be short-lived, for in the spring of 1837 a war party of fifty-five Assiniboines raided a Blackfoot camp, killing a woman and two children, and suffering seven wounded themselves.

With the tribes again at loggerheads, Low Horn resumed his role of warrior. Whenever the opportunity arose, he left his father's lodge and joined the older men in attacking enemy camps. On these occasions he was not bent on revenge but on capturing horses. But unlike some young men who accumulated sizable horse herds and became wealthy, Low Horn gave away all the horses he had taken. His father, his cousins, and others in the camp benefited from his exploits on the war trail.

His powers seemed to make him immune from danger. Time and time again he entered a Cree or Assiniboine camp to take a prized buffalo runner or race horse. Wearing his sparrow hawk feathers and quietly chanting his holy songs, he seemed to move through the camps like a shadow, leaving his enemies angry and afoot.

As his reputation grew, Low Horn became a leader. While he was still a teenager, older men came to him and asked him to take charge. They knew he was brave and lucky, as well as having powerful spiritual protectors. Even the enemy, during brief periods of peace, learned the name of the warrior who had been raiding their camps with impunity.

When he was about twenty-three, Low Horn married *A 'watoyi-kipita 'ki,* or Deer Old Woman, and together they moved to their own lodge. Even though he now had a wife to think about, he still went to war whenever possible, but kept a few animals to start his own herd.

One day, early in the summer of 1846, Low Horn organized a war party of seven men to raid the Crees. One of the group was a close friend, another was Low Horn's age, while the rest were teenaged boys. They left their camps at Blackfoot Crossing and traveled on foot to the Red Deer River, where they found the water so high that they had to build a raft to cross. When they reached the other side, they discovered that some of their gunpowder had gotten

"*Ínkas-Kínne, Siksika Blackfeet Chief.*" Low Horn, Blackfoot chief and warrior, in his heavily decorated war shirt of otter skins. When this leader died, his name was taken by young Screech Owl. *Painting by Karl Bodmer, 1833; reproduced courtesy Joslyn Art Museum, Omaha, Nebraska/Gift of the Enron Art Foundation*

wet. They made a camp in the shelter of some trees to see if they could salvage the powder by setting it out to dry. Next morning, just at sunrise, they were surprised to hear Low Horn singing his sparrow hawk song. Usually he did this only when they were meeting an enemy. As the others stirred, he called them to his side.

"The reason I sang my song," he told them, "is that I had a very bad dream last night. I saw all of you being killed while a buffalo with an iron horn was goring me. In my dream I was looking down at my own dead body."

"Let's go back home," said Low Horn's friend. "We can get the holy men to make sweat baths; then we can pray and start over again."

But some of the young men protested, saying Low Horn's interpretation of the dream may have been wrong. They were intent on capturing horses and didn't want to go home just because of a bad dream. "We've started," they said. "We'd better go on."

Low Horn reluctantly agreed with the boys, but secretly he wanted to turn back, not through fear for himself, but for the young members of his war party.

All that day they traveled on foot across the prairie, their scout constantly running ahead and keeping a sharp eye open for an enemy camp. They were still far south of the place where they expected to find the Crees at that time of the year, but Low Horn was taking no chances. That night they camped; next morning he again sang his sparrow hawk song and called his war party together.

"Now I'm sure," he said. "I've seen it for certain."

But still there was no consensus in the party. Although Low Horn was their leader, the opinions of all members of the party were respected. A warrior could lead only as long as his people wished to follow. They camped for two more days, still trying to dry out their gunpowder, but they found that most of it had caked and was spoiled. Already exasperated, Low Horn now had further reason for concern.

"Here, let's use some sense about this," he said. "We have very little ammunition. We can't defend ourselves. Let's turn back from here." Finally, they all agreed.

Traveling south, they recrossed the Red Deer River and reached Serviceberry Creek, on the edge of the Wintering Hills. Here, the monotony of the short prairie grass was relieved by high rolling hills and a few groves of aspen and saskatoon bushes. While the war party stopped for a rest in a broad coulee, their scout saw a large group of people coming from the north. Low Horn was relieved, for they were now deep in Blackfoot territory, only twenty miles (32 km) or so from their main camp. The travelers must be friendly Sarcees on their way to Blackfoot Crossing. Low Horn sent two of his party to greet them and to invite them to smoke.

But they weren't Sarcees.

The Crees and Assiniboines had been angry over the losses they had suffered at the hands of the Blackfoot during the previous year. All winter they had planned their revenge, and in the spring a Cree chief named Bunch of Lodges had sent a messenger to camps all the way from Fort Edmonton to Fort Pitt.

The emissary carried Bunch of Lodges's medicine pipe, and when he entered each camp, he presented it to the leader and called for warriors to join in a retaliation raid against the Blackfoot. If the camp was willing, their own chief's pipe was offered to the messenger.

In the spring, all of those who had heeded the call gathered at the Battle River, south of Edmonton. Among them were two famous warriors of the tribes—Horned Thunder, an Assiniboine who had made several successful raids against the Blackfoot, and *Kominakoos*,[2] a leading warrior of the Crees and a member of Lapotac's band near Edmonton. When *Kominakoos* was still a small boy, his father had been killed and his mother kidnapped by the Blackfoot. His hatred of that tribe was such that when he was only eleven, he tried to join a Cree war party; they rejected him but he followed behind and saw them become trapped by the Blackfoot. Slipping away, he found another Cree war party and led them to the rescue of their beleaguered friends, making *Kominakoos* the hero of the day.

He began going on raids as soon as he was in his teens, but when he was fifteen he disappeared for two seasons. No one ever knew what had become of him, but when he returned he could speak Blackfoot as fluently as his native Cree. Soon, he was just as feared among the Blackfoot as Low Horn was among the Cree.

Horned Thunder and Kominakoos were rivals, one always trying to better the other in war. At the Battle River gathering, Horned Thunder ridiculed his fellow chief's war record and claimed that in any battle, the Assiniboine warrior would always be in front. *Kominakoos* listened to these boasts and vowed not to be overshadowed by his rival when they went to war.

The huge party set out from Battle River, threatening to kill the first Blackfoot they met. In their party were women and even a few children, for their numbers were such that they had little fear of attack. This was the party observed by Low Horn's scouts.

When the two Blackfoot reached the strangers, they had already pitched camp and a woman was standing beside a creek, preparing to fetch water. The warriors greeted her in a friendly fashion, first in Sarcee then in Blackfoot, but instead of returning their salutations, she screamed and ran for the camp, yelling that the Blackfoot were upon them.

Realizing that they had stumbled into an enemy camp, the two warriors plunged into the creek and made their escape. Meanwhile, Low Horn and the others were walking along leisurely, still unaware of their danger. When the leader saw a number of Indians coming towards them, he believed they were a welcoming party of Sarcees, but their war cries and brandished rifles soon disabused him of this idea. In a few moments, the Blackfoot were surrounded by Cree and Assiniboine warriors but Low Horn shouted defiantly, "People, you can't kill me here, but I will take my body to your camp, and there you shall kill me."

Saying this, he rushed towards the Crees, killing two of them as the rest of the warriors fell back. Then, as he and his companions fought their way forward, the Crees and Assiniboines gathered on each side of them, but were afraid to shoot lest they kill one of their own men. Another two Crees died in the next few minutes of battle; then one of Low Horn's companions dropped.

"Take courage," he told the three survivors. "These people can't kill us here. Where that patch of chokecherry brush is, in the very center of their camp, we'll go and take our stand."

As lead balls and arrows whistled through the air, the men reached the bushes and another Blackfoot died as they frantically dug shelter pits. There, outnumbered and with scant protection, they kept up a steady fusillade against their enemy.

Kominakoos had been one of the leaders of the attack, but once the Blackfoot were entrenched, he warned everyone to be cautious. He told the Crees that he had had a bad dream several days earlier. "A bear attacked us," he told them, "and my body was chewed up by it." He saw in Low Horn the ferociousness of the bear in his dream.

The battle lasted all that night, and even though his enemies died around him, Low Horn kept fighting without being wounded. Sometimes he would rise defiantly from his pit and sing one of his four holy songs. At other times he stayed in hiding, shooting at any shadowy figure that might appear in the light of the fires the Crees had lit to make sure he didn't escape. During this time, the Blackfoot leader announced that he was the great Low Horn and dared them to attack, but the Crees preferred to wait until morning.

Kominakoos admired the bravery of the Blackfoot warrior and noticed with concern how his own men were being killed in the fight. At one stage, he crawled close to the trenches and called out in Blackfoot:

"Low Horn, there's a little ravine running out of that brush patch, which puts into the hills. Crawl out through that, and try to get away. It's not guarded." He said that the Blackfoot had already caused enough grief; he should escape and leave the bodies of his comrades behind.

"No, I will not go. You must remember that it's Low Horn that you're fighting with—a man who has done much harm to your people. I'm glad that I'm here. I'm only sorry that my ammunition is going to run out. Tomorrow you may kill me."

By morning, all the other Blackfoot were dead; only Low Horn was left. He had used up most of his precious powder and soon would have only his large, double-bladed knife.

As the first streaks of daylight filtered across the prairies, *Kominakoos* again approached the trench.

"Low Horn," he shouted, "try to get away."

"No! You've killed all my men. I'm here alone but you can't kill me."

"If you're here after daylight, I'll go into the brush myself and catch you with my hands. I'll be the man who puts an end to you."

"*Kominakoos*, don't try to do that. If you do, you'll surely die."

By mid-morning, after twelve hours of battle, it was evident that it soon would be over. Cree and Assiniboine bodies had been dragged away from the site, although a few men who had ventured too close to the trenches still lay where they had fallen. With the great Blackfoot chief now within his grasp, *Kominakoos* was ready to fulfill his threat and prepared to attack. As he moved forward, taking cover behind bushes and rocks, he was joined by Horned Thunder, the jealous Assiniboine.

At first, *Kominakoos* led the other man, but Horned Thunder was not to be outdone and, heedless of the danger, he crept past the Cree chief until he was far out in front. There, with nothing to protect him, Horned Thunder was an easy target for the Blackfoot marksman. A moment later, a groan escaped from his lips as he rolled over lifeless on the grass.

Triumphantly, *Kominakoos* slithered behind the Assiniboine's body and whispered, "My friend, you shall continue to be in front," and pushed his body along as a shield between him and the Blackfoot warrior. In this way, the bullets passed harmlessly over his head or struck the dead Assiniboine as *Kominakoos* moved forward behind his grisly barrier.

At last, nearing the rifle pit, *Kominakoos* jumped to his feet and attacked, grabbing Low Horn around the waist. But before he could hurl the Blackfoot to the ground, Low Horn swung his vicious twin-bladed knife in a deadly arc and slashed off one of the Cree's fingers. As the attacker stepped back, Low Horn fired his gun wildly, the ball glancing off the Cree's face, putting out an eye, and tearing into his scalp. A cry went up from the Cree spectators as the wounded warrior fell to the ground.

The battle continued into the morning until Low Horn was left with only one charge of powder for his gun. Knowing the end was near, he stepped from his trench, past the bushes that had been shot away during the fighting, and shouted to the Crees.

"I'm thirsty," he said. "Give me a drink before I die."

A warrior named Acts Like a Woman hid a knife under his shirt, then took a vessel of water to the Blackfoot. As Low Horn drank, the Cree pulled out the knife and tried to kill his enemy but Low Horn dropped the pail and stabbed the man to death.

When this happened, the Crees and Assiniboines resumed shooting but the bullets seemed to graze the Blackfoot warrior without hurting him. Then they attacked him; the first into the fray was the Cree chief, Bunch of Lodges. He jumped over the trench but before he could shoot, Low Horn slashed out with his dagger and killed him. Others now swarmed into the entrenchment but to their amazement their knives could not pierce his chest; not until a man plunged an elk horn spear into his ear did they kill the magical Low Horn. He was twenty-four years old.

According to a fur trader, Low Horn's invincibility was more than just superstition. When the Crees stripped his body, they found he was wearing Spanish mail. Although rare, such armor was used by the Blackfoot, one owner receiving the name of Iron Shirt because of it.[3]

The price the Crees and Assiniboines had paid was a high one, as the bodies of thirty of their dead were scattered about near the earthworks.[4] *Kominakoos* was still alive, but would spend the rest of his life as a one-eyed warrior.[5]

From this point on, the tale of Low Horn becomes one of pure mysticism, as if the warrior's exploits could only be explained in supernatural terms. Some accounts treat the affair as a simple battle between two opposing parties.[6] In the Native versions, however, the Crees chopped Low Horn's body into small pieces, then lit a huge fire and tossed his remains into it. As they did so, a mentally handicapped boy from their camp began to dance around and sing the sparrow hawk song that he had heard from the lips of the Blackfoot warrior a few hours earlier. At that moment, a burning ember popped from the fire, and when it struck the ground, a huge bear arose from the spot and slashed out at the terrified Indians, killing five of them.

The others fled from the scene and began to travel northward, but they had gone only a short distance when the handicapped boy began to sing Low Horn's rabbit song. At that moment, a pack of seven huge prairie wolves, their mouths frothing, darted among them, attacking and killing anyone they found in their way.

Thoroughly frightened, the Crees and Assiniboines continued their northern odyssey and their terror increased when the handicapped boy began to sing Low Horn's thunder song. The sky turned black, the winds arose, and the Indians found themselves in a vicious summer storm. As the rain started pelting down, the thunder suddenly crashed overhead and bolts of lightning came down, striking the Crees and Assiniboines. As they fled from the scene, more bodies were left strewn behind.

The mentally handicapped boy, who was believed to be possessed by the spirit of Low Horn, stayed with survivors until they reached the Red Deer River. Then he burst forth again in song, this time repeating the mouse song of the Blackfoot warrior. It had great supernatural powers and as the music drifted across the valley, seven large buffalo bulls roared out from a nearby coulee and dashed among the Indians, goring and trampling several hapless victims.

By this time the war party was completely demoralized. Their chiefs were dead, their greatest warrior seriously wounded, and now the spirit of Low Horn was destroying them. In desperation, the war party separated, some traveling north to the Beaver Hills and others going towards Fort Pitt and the Eagle Hills. The Blackfoot believed that many of the Indians never found their way home but traveled about the county in small bands, always fearing the vengeance of Low Horn.

Meanwhile, the two Blackfoot who had escaped at the outset of the battle remained hidden among some willows along the banks of Serviceberry Creek. They heard the sound of battle, and when quiet reigned over the valley, they knew Low Horn was dead.

When they thought it was safe, the two slipped from their hiding place and hurried to Blackfoot Crossing, where they found the main camps of their people. When the news was spread that Low Horn had been surrounded and attacked only twenty miles (32 km) away, the

Blackfoot were horrified. Scouts were sent to nearby hills to guard the camp, while Low Horn's father led a band of warriors to relieve his beleaguered son. But when they arrived at the scene, the camp was deserted. All they found were the scalped and mutilated bodies of the other Blackfoot warriors, but of Low Horn, nothing remained. The charred embers of a huge fire told the grim story.

Meanwhile, as Low Horn was fighting and dying near the banks of Serviceberry Creek, another adventure was taking place a hundred and fifty miles (241 km) away. In the camp of Red Crow, head chief of the Blood tribe, a woman had withdrawn to a tiny shelter to give birth. It proved to be a healthy boy with a lusty cry that pleased and amused the midwives who were helping with the delivery. Then, as a woman tied the umbilical cord and washed the infant, she noticed something strange.

"Look at his ears," she exclaimed. "They're already pierced for earrings!"

"And see his back!" said the other. "He has two black marks that look like bullet wounds."

They puzzled about these strange sights, but the mother, Riding Together Woman, wasn't worried. She already had a daughter and now she was thrilled that she had a healthy boy to add to the family. Later in the day, she proudly introduced the new arrival to his father, Slow Talker, a half-brother of the head chief. After due consideration and proper ceremonies, the boy was given the child's name of Only Person Who Had a Different Gun.[7] The name was based upon a war experience of the giver. He had taken a gun in battle that was different from all the others; this was a sign that spiritual helpers were on his side, so he wanted to pass his good luck along to the child. The name would remain with him until he was old enough to earn an adult name.

About 1852, when the boy was six, a large band of Bloods decided that they would go to Fort Edmonton. Usually they traded with the Americans, but a leading chief named Bad Head had become displeased with his treatment and chose to go north. A number of families joined him, including Slow Talker.

They traveled first to Blackfoot Crossing to join up with the main camps of the Blackfoot. In this way, they could go to the fort in large numbers and have no fear of marauding Crees.

While the Bloods waited at the crossing, Different Gun demonstrated that he was not an ordinary child. One day while he and his sister were playing outside their tepee, a Blackfoot woman walked by.

"Ah," said the boy, with a twinkle in his eye, "there goes my wife."

His sister was shocked by this breech of etiquette, for young children were taught to be respectful to adults.

"You're a *mini'poka*, a spoiled brat," she raged. "I'm going to tell her what you said."

"Go ahead," he challenged.

Indignantly, the girl ran to the woman and repeated her brother's words. As the woman came back towards Different Gun, he repeated the comment he had made before.

"Here's Deer Old Woman," he said solemnly. "She was my sweetheart when I was young."

The woman laughed, then kissed him and told him not to be foolish. "Yes," she said, "I'm Deer Old Woman. I'm the widow of Low Horn."

Next day, the Bloods and Blackfoot set out for the north, crossing the Bow River and striking off over the prairie. Different Gun, who was riding with his mother, remained strangely silent and then unexpectedly began to cry. His father, coming up beside them, said to his wife:

"Why is my boy crying? Did you hit him?"

When she shook her head, Slow Talker took his boy onto his own horse and asked him if he was in pain.

"No, father," Different Gun replied. "I'm crying because this is the place where I was attacked and killed by the Crees. I am Low Horn."

Shortly afterwards, when the party camped for the night, Slow Talker told his wives to pitch their tepee and to prepare a feast. When this was done he called the elders to his lodge, and after they had eaten he addressed them.

"There's something strange I want to tell to you," he began. "Today when my boy was crying I thought my wife was beating him so I took him with me on my horse. When I asked him if there was any pain in his body or head, he told me there was none. He said he cried because he was Low Horn and this was the place where he had been killed by the Crees."

A murmur of surprise and disbelief spread through the gathering. Low Horn's tragic death was well known, but the Bloods lived far to the south and were unfamiliar with the actual site of the battle. However, the Blackfoot knew they had passed the spot just when the boy started to cry. But it was hard to credit the story of a six-year-old.

"We don't believe the boy," one of the elders said at last. "This is all in his mind."

"No!" responded Different Gun. "Back at the place of the fight, I hid my whip under a rock and a little farther down the slope I buried my skinning knife near the trench where I was killed."

"It's not far back to that place," said a holy man. "In the morning let's go back to see if we can find the whip and dagger."

Next day, the men caught their horses, and while the women struck camp, they went back to the spot the boy had indicated. As they approached the creek, the boy held back.

"Let me stop here. I don't want to go any farther. I'm afraid. Go to that rock you can see, move it and you'll find my whip. Farther down the hill in that hollow, if you look around you'll find my knife."

The men went to the places that the boy had indicated. When they moved the rock, the whip was lying there just as Low Horn had left it, but when they tried to pick it up, it was so rotten that it fell to pieces in their hands. Then they went to the hollow and dug away the earth and leaves in the shallow trench. There they found Low Horn's old skinning knife. It was so rusty that it had holes in it. Low Horn had returned.

Although he was only six, Different Gun was given the name of Low Horn and in succeeding years he added to its prestige and fame.

When he was a teenager, he went on a vision quest and the white-headed eagle became his spiritual helper. Slow Talker was so proud that he announced to the camp that he would honor his son. On the appointed day, Low Horn was sent to a high knoll within sight of the camp. When all was in readiness, his father took his finest buffalo runner, saddled it, and decorated it with neck ornaments and feathers. On the saddle he tied a beautifully decorated suit of buckskin clothing.

Amid singing and drumming, Slow Talker took the horse to the knoll, dressed the boy in the clothing, and led him back through the camps. When they reached their lodge, the father announced that the horse and clothing now belonged to his son. It was a great honor.

Low Horn went on to become a warrior, joining successful raids against several enemy tribes, but particularly the Crow Indians. His comrade during those years was a Peigan Indian named Mountain Chief, who in later years became a prominent chief of his tribe.

Even when Low Horn was young, everyone knew of his strange reincarnation and believed that he would become a holy man. Therefore, no one was surprised in the 1870s when he began visiting with the medicine men of the tribe, listening to them, and gradually learning their ways. He became an apprentice to one of the men, assisting him as a servant during prayers and incantations.

The typical medicine man of the period used a combination of talents to cure the sick. The most important was through prayers to his spiritual protector, calling forth the forces of nature to drive away the evil that was causing the sickness. To do this, the medicine man had his own way of painting his face and he possessed his own bundle of religious objects used in the rituals. Basic among these were sweetgrass for incense, paint to conse-

Blood storyteller Jack Low Horn is shown here making a headdress, 1958. His father was the reincarnation of a Blackfoot warrior. *Courtesy Glenbow-Alberta Institute/NA-1757-1*

crate the sick person, and a whistle to drive away evil spirits. Other objects might include a drum, rattle, pipe, tobacco, sagebrush, and an object that symbolized his spiritual protector. Low Horn, for example, would likely have worn an eagle claw necklace or the head of a white-headed eagle in his hair.

Besides offering prayers, some medicine men had a thorough knowledge of roots and herbs that could be used for certain ailments, particularly to treat wounds and broken bones. To reduce a swelling the holy man might chew a piece of alum root and place the poultice on the affected area. Juniper berries were boiled to make a tea to stop vomiting, while the dry, powdery center of a toadstool could stem a bleeding wound.

A third form of treatment was through ritualism and incantation. A good medicine man learned to impress his patient by performing acts that seemed to substantiate his mysticism. Through drumming, dancing, and using a sucking tube to draw evil spirits from the body, he created a feeling of authority and power that went a long way in effecting a cure.

After he had become a healer, Low Horn would disappear for days and people suspected that he was seeking spiritual help. In addition to the white-headed eagle's power, he had the songs of the previous Low Horn to help cure people of their sicknesses and to perform magic deeds.

Low Horn took four wives during his lifetime: Black Face Woman, High Woman, Another Woman, and Last Killer. From them he had a number of children, although only two, Jack and James, reached maturity.

With the disappearance of the buffalo in 1881, the Bloods were obliged to settle on their reserve. Low Horn, like other members of the Fish Eaters clan, lived in a buffalo skin tepee until it wore out. Then he built a cabin in the valley of the Belly River, about six miles (10 km) upstream from the trading post at Standoff. There, for the next several years, he was called upon to treat the sick and the dying. With poor food, a new and strange life, and disease rampant in the camps, he was constantly in demand.

His most famous cure occurred in 1891 when a Blood warrior named Steel was shot through the chest by a North-West Mounted Police officer. Left for dead and abandoned by white doctors, he was turned over to Low Horn for what the officials thought were his last hours. Using four of his most sacred paints and the power of the mouse inherited from the Blackfoot Low Horn, he performed his rituals. Twelve days later, after constant attention from Low Horn, the wounded man was strong enough to ride a horse to the medicine man's camp so that he might continue to be treated. Steel did not die as predicted; in fact, he lived for another fifty years.[8]

But sometimes even Low Horn could not help. In 1894, a woman named Only a Flower became despondent and wandered away from the camps. When a young boy found her hanging from a cottonwood tree, he rushed to the medicine man's house for help. Low Horn went to the site and cut her down, but there was nothing he could do for the unfortunate woman.

In spite of failures, many of them due to white man's diseases, medicine men like Low Horn had considerable success in treating members of the tribe. However, their actions were ridiculed and vilified by Indian agents, who saw them as detriments to progress. Even more vitriolic in their attacks were the Indian Department doctors, who carried on running battles to have the medicine men suppressed. One such advocate was F.X. Girard, medical doctor for the Blood Reserve during the 1890s.

"When a Medicine Man is in a lodge or house," he wrote, "he is the ruler—the patient and the family abide by him. Besides the tom tom used by the Medicine Men and their incantations against the evil spirit, they use the red embers, flint stone, etc., to cut the poor patient who would no doubt prefer a quick blow to put an end to his sufferings than a slow death by knife and fire.

"Many times I have called for sick people. At my arrival at the lodge, the tom tom was in full swing—impossible to get admittance—the door was locked and guarded. I was plainly told to go back, that my presence was of no avail. This by order of the Medicine Man."[9]

Yet in his 1899 report, Dr. Girard admitted that a quarter of the deaths for the previous four months had occurred in his own hospital and "if there is no stop to this state of things, it will not be long before the band is completely extinguished."[10]

After Low Horn settled on the reserve, he continued to seek visions. In one instance, a spirit appeared before him and warned him never to sleep in a white man's bed. Later, Last Killer furnished their log house with chairs, table, and a four-poster bed, but Low Horn slept on the floor.

Then, one warm day in the spring of 1899, Low Horn came into the house for a rest after working outside. Without thinking, he sat on the bed, dozed off, then rolled over into a deep sleep. He awoke with a start and, with a feeling of foreboding, he called Last Killer, his favorite wife, to his side.

"I've done something my guardian spirit warned me not to do," he said, "and I know that in the month when the saskatoon berries are ripe, I shall die."

His wife muffled a gasp of fear, but before she could cry, Low Horn held up his hand for silence.

"Yes," he continued, "I'll die, but you can bring me back to life. Just as the spirit of Low Horn the Blackfoot came to life in my body, so can I come back into my own body. Here's what you must do. The moment I die, pitch our old tepee inside out with the entrance facing east. Set my body up inside at the back, facing the doorway, cover me to the waist, and paint a strip of yellow across my forehead."

He paused as his wife nodded in assent.

"You must then go outside the tepee and sit some distance away, facing the entrance, holding in your hands my pipe filled with tobacco. When all is in readiness, four leading men of the tribe with four of the fastest horses must race towards our tepee, and one who is armed with a rifle must come inside and shoot me in the chest, at the same time shouting: 'Here is your smoke, Low Horn!' When they remount their horses they must ride close to you and pass near you. I'll come out of the tepee, you'll give me the pipe to smoke, then I will mount a horse and chase after the riders."

Last Killer believed every word he had spoken. Low Horn was a great medicine man who had not only inherited the powers of the Blackfoot warrior but had gained his own spiritual protectors.

In late June, the Bloods started to gather near the base of the Belly Buttes for their annual Sun Dance. Low Horn and his two wives began their preparations but discovered that their tepee poles were too rotten to last for another year. So Last Killer joined a number of other Bloods who were going to the foothills to cut lodgepole pine. Meanwhile, Low Horn and his second wife, Another Woman, loaded their belongings in their wagon and began the ten-mile (16-km) trek to the Sun Dance camps.

The Blood Reserve had experienced a wet month and the potholes and ditches along the way were filled with water. As they came down a small hill, Low Horn's wagon hit a soft spot on the trail and overturned into the ditch. His wife was thrown clear, but the great medicine man of the Bloods was caught under the wagon box and was drowned. He was fifty-three years old.

Low Horn's second wife, Another Woman, knew nothing of his power to come back to life. With other grief-stricken Indians, she helped pull the body from the muddy water and prepare it for scaffold burial in the forks of a cottonwood tree. When Low Horn's favorite wife returned from the mountains several days later, it was too late.

Sadly, Last Killer mourned the loss of her husband, and wondered. This man, whose spark of life had been reincarnated from a Blackfoot warrior and who had committed great feats of magic—could he have returned to life? As she cried, she believed in her heart that the answer was yes.

The Amazing Death of Calf Shirt

S ixteen bullets from the guns of Fort Kipp traders late in 1873 ended the life of Calf Shirt, one of the greatest war chiefs of the Bloods. He was gunned down by Joe Kipp and his fellow whiskey peddlers after the chief had demanded the return of his war shield and threatened to kill the white men if they failed to comply.

Besides being a war chief, Calf Shirt was leader of the Lone Fighters Band, which consisted of some twenty-four lodges or almost two hundred followers. Born about 1815, the son of Cracked Ear, the chief was described as being "a man of commanding presence, over six feet [1.83 m] in height, weighing over two hundred pounds [91 kg], and with regular and comely features."[1]

A relative named Iron Collar had been the original leader of the group, but by 1855 Calf Shirt had taken over and was recognized as one of the six leading chiefs of the Blood tribe. In that year, he was present on the Judith River when the United States government negotiated a treaty with the Blackfoot nation and other tribes in the area. The purpose of the treaty was to establish peace among the warring Indians and to set aside huge hunting grounds for the nomadic tribes.

Though Calf Shirt may have signed the treaty, he was not a proponent of peace. In his youth, he earned a deserved reputation of being a brave, reckless, and ruthless warrior. This aura of strength and power was a contributing factor in his rise to prominence in the tribe.

His greatest mystic power was given to him while he was still a young man. The Bloods were camped near the east butte of the Sweetgrass Hills when Calf Shirt decided to go on a vision quest. This meant that he would seek a lonely place and fast for four days, hoping that a spiritual protector would come to him and bestow upon him some supernatural gift. Calf Shirt went to the top of the east butte, and there, while fasting, a grizzly bear spirit visited him but refused to give him the supernatural power he sought.

"To receive power you must give me a woman," the bear spirit said.[2]

Calf Shirt returned to his camp, where he told the youngest of his four wives to dress in her finest buckskins. Then he escorted her to the summit of the butte where he stabbed her to death and piled a cairn of stones over her body before returning to camp to mourn and bewail his loss.[3]

That night Calf Shirt had a dream in which the bear spirit returned to him and told him that henceforth no bullet, arrow, or knife could penetrate his body.

Calf Shirt, as sketched by Gustavus Sohon, 1855. The Blackfoot believed that no mortal man could kill this Indian warrior. *Courtesy Glenbow-Alberta Institute/NA-360-13*

This incident gave Calf Shirt a reputation of invincibility and resulted in him receiving a second name—Impervious to Bullets. As one trader noted: "The 'Calf Shirt' had gained a name for himself ... as he was known among all the nation as being the greatest Indian desperado of the day, having run through a bloody career of many years, escaping from every engagement without a scratch. The Indians regarded him with genuine superstition, firmly believing that no mortal man could take his life."[4]

In the spring of 1871, for example, he was heedless of danger when he helped to repulse a Cree war party. Iron Collar and a number of Bloods were camped on the Belly River, awaiting the arrival of some other bands that were going to travel northward to hunt in the Hand Hills, near the Red Deer River. However, their small village was discovered by a Cree war party, even though the tepees were well concealed among the cottonwoods along the river bottom. During the interval while the Cree scouts were reporting back to their main attacking force, Calf Shirt and his family arrived from the hunt.

That night, if the Crees noted the addition of a single tepee, they attached no importance to it. Instead, they followed their usual practice when raiding a small enemy encampment. First, a warrior slipped quietly into the village, cutting loose any horses that had been picketed near the lodges. The Crees knew that the finest race horses and buffalo runners were always tied up at night, while the common travois ponies were herded on the open prairie under the watchful eyes of two or three young boys.

The Crees expected their scout to cut the horses loose and then let them wander out of the camp. When this had been done, the Crees planned to open fire on the tepees, then attack and despatch any survivors.

On this occasion, the Cree who crept into the camp undetected had already turned loose about thirty-five horses when he came to Calf Shirt's tepee. There, as he cut the ropes, he made a slight noise that was instantly heard by one of Calf Shirt's wives. Without panicking, she quietly nudged her husband, and when he looked out the door, he saw the Cree leading a horse towards the edge of the camp.

Calf Shirt did not hesitate; he grabbed his rifle, dashed from the tepee, and shouted to the Cree to stop. The raider fired a wild shot at the chief but Calf Shirt responded with deadly accuracy, seriously wounding the Cree invader.

The other Crees were unnerved by the sudden discovery of their raid, but resolutely started to shoot back at the Bloods while some of their number went to round up the stray horses. Discovering that their scout had been cut down, the Crees gradually withdrew, taking the horses with them. The Bloods, not knowing the strength of the raiders or whether another assault might be made at dawn, remained in the camp, guarding against a possible attack.

In the morning, Calf Shirt discovered that the Cree raider he had shot was not dead. His leg had been broken by the bullet, and he had dragged himself into the bushes where he tried to hide by covering himself with branches. Calf Shirt found him there and killed him without a moment's hesitation. Then every Indian who had suffered a loss of horses came forward and pumped another bullet into the body. Afterwards, the remains were turned over to the women to wreak their final vengeance on this person who had violated their camp.

On another occasion, Calf Shirt was with a large body of Bloods who were traveling south to hunt near the Sweetgrass Hills. At the same time, a party of nine Crees who had raided a Peigan camp were hurrying north. In the early mists of dawn, some Blood hunters saw the fleeing enemy and alerted the camp.

Calf Shirt took immediate command. When his followers found the tracks of the Cree raiders, he split his party into two groups, Seen From Afar taking one and Calf Shirt the other. While the former followed the clear trail in the frosty grass, Calf Shirt went towards the Cypress Hills, hoping to cut off the marauders before they reached the timbered slopes.

The pincer movement trapped the Crees near a prairie lake, and although they fought bravely and wounded several Bloods, by nightfall the nine attackers had been killed and scalped. "Upon our return to camp," recalled Red Crow, "all the people painted their faces black, and we had a gala time because it was a complete victory."[5]

Yet this type of warfare had its tragic consequences for Calf Shirt. One day in the spring of 1866, a war party of Blackfoot returned to an enormous camp of Bloods and Blackfoot who were hunting near the Red Deer River. The warriors had taken some Cree horses on the South Saskatchewan River and reported the presence of enemy villages that could easily be raided. Accordingly, a Blood warrior named Weasel Horse organized an expedition that went out in search of horses, scalps, and trophies. However, they were ambushed in a snow-filled coulee by watchful Crees, and fifty warriors were killed.

The Bloods and Blackfoot called a great council meeting during the following spring to consider retaliation. As a war chief, Calf Shirt took a prominent role in the discussions and in the decision to move the whole camp of several thousand Bloods, Blackfoot, Peigans, and Sarcees to the southeast to destroy any Cree camps they encountered. Traveling with such an enormous body of warriors meant little likelihood of ambush.

After several days of travel, two leading warriors named White Calf and Eagle Head returned with an enemy scalp. They had found a Cree village on the open prairie at a place called Still Pointing Butte, near the mouth of the Red Deer River, and had killed a woman nearby. With the news that they were close to their enemy, the Indians held a war dance, and as Red Crow noted, "Then off they started, hundreds and hundreds in number—a fine sight."[6]

With Calf Shirt in the forefront, the gigantic war party approached the camp after sunset, remaining undetected in a nearby coulee while a driving rain covered any sounds that may have drifted to the watchful Crees. At daybreak, a few warriors crept into the village and began herding the horses away. However, they were discovered and soon the Crees were in an uproar. Their women and children fled to nearby timber while the men opened fire on the attackers.

At this point, Calf Shirt and the other leaders exhibited their abilities as tacticians. Instead of a bold attack on the village, which would have cost many lives, the Blackfoot raiders retreated, as though frightened by the ferocity of the Cree fusillade. Heartened, the Crees pursued them until they were well out on the open prairie and far from the protection of their camp. Then, on a signal, the Blackfoot turned around and dashed forward in a counterattack, taking the Crees by surprise.

"They did not attempt to make a stand," said Red Crow, "but fled in the wildest disorder, and were slaughtered like buffalo."[7]

As the battle neared the Cree village, the Blackfoot withdrew again, and for a second time the enemy thought they were retreating. They soon discovered their error, and several more Crees died.

When the Bloods and Blackfoot finally withdrew, more than a hundred Crees were dead, and Calf Shirt believed they had scored a total victory. Then someone brought him the tragic news. They had suffered only one fatality in the battle—Calf Shirt's own son, Wild Insect Ear. A feeling of sadness pervaded the expedition, but the war chief rode through the camp, crying: "Be joyful! You do not mourn for my son. You have killed many enemies and captured much."[8] So on a sorrowful father's instructions, the Bloods and Blackfoot held a huge victory dance before returning to their own territory.

While Calf Shirt was a good leader and a great warrior, he had a terrible temper that was intensified whenever he was drinking. This made him so violent that he was given the nickname of *Mini'ksee*, or Wild Person. This descriptive term normally was used only when referring to a wild dog or a wild buffalo bull. In his own camp, whenever Calf Shirt was in this mood, everyone avoided him.

He was known to have killed at least three of his own band during violent arguments. Also, according to reports, he murdered several of his wives over the years after accusing them of unfaithfulness. "When bad whiskey could be bought," noted a trader who was personally acquainted with Calf Shirt, "this chief never failed to keep himself well soaked with it, and he usually ended his sprees by killing one or more of his friends or relatives, if no enemy was near enough to become the victim."[9]

The winter-count for 1859, for example, stated that the Bloods fought among themselves while camped at Yellow Mountain in Montana Territory and that "Calf Shirt killed some of his own people."[10] Similarly, in 1870 the chief was obliged to remain north of the Belly River after he killed two Peigans in a quarrel on the Marias River and grieving relatives had vowed revenge.

James Willard Schultz, who lived with the Peigan Indians and wrote numerous books about them, described the Calf Shirt as "a man of powerful physique, very brave and very brutal. He was greatly feared by all of the tribes with whom he was at war, as well as by his own people."[11] The Indians had the same view of him. Frank Red Crow, a son of the Blood head chief, said he was "a very powerful man. He was strong of muscle and could wrestle down any other Indian. When he was sober he was a very good man, but when he was drinking he became very mean."[12]

Frank Red Crow claimed that Calf Shirt's mother, Tight Eyes, was the only person who could control the chief when he was in a rage. She would grab him by the hair, tap him on the back, and tell him to be quiet. This would cause him to settle down. Such an occurrence was unusual in itself, for when a boy reached the age of six or seven, he was given over to an uncle or grandfather to train, and by the time he was a teenager, he was pretty well beyond the control of his mother. For Calf Shirt to retain this relationship into adulthood meant either that his mother was particularly strong willed or that she commanded his complete respect.

There was one occasion when Calf Shirt's bullying and threats did not work. The Lone Fighters Band was camped near a trading post when a band of Blackfoot came to trade. Among them was a blind old man who bought liquor and then pitched his lodge apart from the others.

Some Bloods warned him that Calf Shirt might try to take the whiskey from him, but the old man said that the war chief was nothing but a bluff. Calf Shirt heard this remark and called out in a loud voice:

"Blind man, bring me what whiskey you have or I'll kill you!"

The old man laughed and ignored the surly chief. Angrily Calf Shirt approached the lodge.

"Blind man," he repeated, "I'm coming closer to your lodge. Give me your whiskey or I'll kill you."

When the demand again was greeted with laughter, the war chief barged into the lodge and grasped the old Blackfoot by the arm. Suddenly he felt an odd sensation and raised the frail man's hand to his lips. As the old Indian's fingers rubbed across his teeth, Calf Shirt could feel a great power exuding from them. It was then he realized the blind warrior was a great holy man. Fearfully, he released him and humbly asked for a drink.

"No," he was told. "Get out of my lodge and return to your people the way you came." Calf Shirt fled without his coveted drink.

Calf Shirt's own supernatural powers, given to him by the bear, were powerful. In one story told by the Bloods, Calf Shirt was at a trading post but would not leave when he had nothing more to trade. In desperation, the white men tried to drag him away but his bear power was so strong that he could not be budged until he was given another drink.

In a similar incident, traders offered to give him a gallon (4 l) of whiskey if he could defeat their best man in a wrestling match. Calf Shirt's opponent proved to be a husky black man who was almost seven feet (2.15 m) tall and as powerful as a bull. In the first encounter, the man tried to throw the Indian warrior but found him to be immovable. Then Calf Shirt picked up his opponent and dashed him to the ground, breaking his leg.

In 1865, Calf Shirt became a key figure in a drama that ultimately had far-reaching effects on the history of Montana. It had its beginnings with the discovery of gold in western Montana in 1862; the result was an influx of Civil War veterans who had little regard for the hunting grounds or legal rights of Indians. At the same time, many young warriors found a new source of instant wealth through raids on the miners' horse herds.

A year later, relations between the Blackfoot tribes and the Montanans further deteriorated when the Indians failed to get the annuities promised in the 1855 treaty and the Indian Agency was virtually abandoned by government officials.

During the winter of 1864-65, the situation turned ugly when three Bloods stole some horses from Charlie Carson (a nephew of Kit Carson) and two other trappers. They pursued the Blood trio, caught them, and killed them.

Then, in the early spring of 1865, a daring group of Blood raiders swept into the village of Fort Benton and successfully took forty horses. Some of the angry residents announced that they would kill the next Blackfoot who came to their town.

About a month later, a party of Bloods arrived to trade, unaware of the animosity that existed in the town. They assembled near the Indian Agency, where they put on a dance and made a demonstration of extolling their war victories. The only problem was that some of their most outstanding feats had been against American trappers or traders.

Two old mountain men named Joe Spearson and Henry Bostwick, who could speak Blackfoot, became so angry at the exhibition that they opened fire on the group, killing a chief and three others. Their bodies were dumped unceremoniously into the Missouri River. Two Bloods escaped to carry the news back to their camps.

No one will know if it was the killing of the three horse raiders during the winter or the slaying of the Bloods at Fort Benton that spurred Calf Shirt to action. It was likely the former, as it was only a matter of a couple of days after the Fort Benton incident when the war chief assembled a revenge party of some two hundred warriors from the Lone Fighters, Fish Eaters, Many Fat Horses, and Black Elk bands to travel south to the Missouri River to retaliate against the whites for killing members of their tribe.

Meanwhile, the captain of a Montana steamboat, Frank Moore, decided that the confluence of the Marias and Missouri rivers would be an excellent place to establish a village to compete with Fort Benton. Four hundred lots were surveyed, several cabins erected, and the budding community was given the name of Ophir. In order to meet the expected demand for houses, Moore hired a manager named N.W. Burris and sent him to the site with a crew of men to cut enough timber for three hundred cabins.

On their way to Benton in late May, Calf Shirt and his war party stumbled upon the Ophir wood choppers.

According to whiskey trader John Healy, "The party of wood choppers were twelve in number, all good men, but inexperienced in Indian warfare. Just above the mouth of the Teton, they were alarmed by the discovery of this formidable band of Indians riding down upon them, and unfortunately for themselves, instead of retreating to a more favorable point of defence or attempting to fortify themselves in any way, they opened fire at once without waiting to find out the Indians' intentions."[13]

As it turned out, the Indians had no thought of harming the wood choppers and when the men opened fire on them, Calf Shirt restrained his warriors and tried to communicate in sign language that they meant no harm. However, the wood choppers continued to shoot, so the Bloods charged their camp and killed them all.[14]

Montana was in an uproar over the slayings. In response to cries for action, Governor Sidney Edgerton announced plans to form a volunteer army to punish Calf Shirt. James Stuart, a Montana rancher, was appointed to organize a militia, but when officials learned that the chief had fled to the British side of the line, a planned military campaign was called off.

The situation between the Indians and whites was now so strained that people began referring to it as a "Blackfoot war." Calf Shirt's destruction of Ophir gave the government the excuse it needed to resolve the problem. Their answer was to respond to Governor Edgerton's call to "take steps for the extinguishment of Indian title in this territory, in order that our lands may be brought into market."[15]

Accordingly, the Indian agent was given instructions from Washington to negotiate a new treaty and to reduce the size of the Blackfoot reservation. When the chiefs of the Blackfoot, Blood, and Peigan tribes gathered for a council meeting with government officials in November 1865, Calf Shirt was conspicuous by his absence. In fact, a report of the treaty session commented specifically: "With regard to the Bloods, it must be noticed that the hostile band by whom the murder of the eleven whites was perpetrated last spring on the Marias River, was not represented, these savages ever since the murder, having outlawed themselves beyond the British line."[16] When the treaty was concluded, the Indians had lost all their hunting grounds south of the Teton River.

After the Ophir incident, Calf Shirt stayed away from the Americans and did not venture south again until the winter of 1868-69, when he visited the I.G. Baker post on the upper Marias River. However, he had not changed his ways, nor his dislike for white people. Even though the traders honored him by presenting him with a fancy uniform, he still demonstrated his hostility towards anyone who crossed him. On this occasion he focused his attention on a Jesuit priest, Camillus Imoda, and tried to shoot him, but just before he fired, trader William Conrad knocked his gun barrel in the air.

Although Calf Shirt's life was filled with many such incidents of warfare, bravery, and conflict, it was his death that really made him an immortal figure among his people. The incident has minor variations as told by the Indians and white traders, but generally follows the same pattern.

One day in December 1873, Joe Kipp was at his post at the confluence of the Belly and Oldman rivers when Calf Shirt came to buy whiskey. A few months earlier, the chief had left a shield with the trader as security for some goods he had obtained on credit. Now he was joining a war party and he wanted his property back. When Kipp demanded that he pay for it, Calf Shirt admitted he had nothing; he was broke.

"I want to fight and must have my shield," he threatened. "You must give it to me."[17]

Kipp realized that the chief was dangerous so he reached for his gun, which was hidden in a pile of blankets. However, Calf Shirt saw the movement and before the trader could grasp his weapon, the Blood drew his own gun from beneath his robe and pointed at Kipp. It was fully cocked.

Calf Shirt could have killed Kipp on the spot, but instead he turned around, walked out of the fort, and returned to his own camp. There he fumed about the insult he

Joseph Kipp built Fort Standoff in 1870 and Fort Kipp in 1871. It was an argument with this trader that set into motion the events leading to the death of Calf Shirt. *Courtesy Montana Historical Society*

believed he had received at the hands of the trader and considered ways of getting revenge. Finally, his anger reached such a point that he became heedless of his own safety—or perhaps he was secure in his own invincibility given to him when he had sacrificed his young wife many years earlier. Stripping to a breechcloth and moccasins, he painted his face and body with his personal war symbols and began to sing his war song. As he did so, he donned his headdress, picked up his revolver, and headed for the fort.

Fort Kipp was built in the same fashion as most whiskey posts of that period. Buildings formed three sides of a square, their outer walls serving as palisades, while all doors and windows opened into a courtyard. The fourth side was enclosed by a palisade with a gate at the center. The chief stalked resolutely towards the main gate.

"Calf Shirt is coming! Calf Shirt is coming!" cried the Indian wife of a trader. "He says he will kill you all."[18]

As the chief approached the trading room, he continued to sing his war song, then paused to perform a few steps of the war dance. Attracted by the clamor, a number of traders who were in the men's quarters playing poker with some visiting wolf hunters grabbed their guns and rushed to the door.[19] Joe Kipp, who was in the trading room with another trader, also came to his door and was confronted by the sight of the chief, painted for battle, approaching him with a loaded revolver.

"Now, what must Calf Shirt have thought," asked an early Montanan, "when he saw all those men come out, with pistols in their hands? He knew that his time had come, that he would never leave that place alive, but he did not hesitate; he kept on singing and dancing."[20]

Kipp shouted to his men to kill the offending Indian. They promptly opened fire, and although Calf Shirt was peppered with lead balls, he just stopped, then slowly turned around and strode out the main gates of the fort. He made no attempt to return their fire.

The men looked at each other in wonderment and surprise. All were good gunfighters who prided themselves on being excellent shots. How could they possibly have missed such an easy target? Was he really invincible?

The fort was still fairly new and about one hundred yards (91 m) away was a deep excavation where the earth had been taken for sodding the roof of the structure. Calf Shirt walked straight towards it, reached the edge, and kept going as though he were in a daze. He tumbled down into the hole, and when the traders cautiously peered over the brink, they saw him lying at the bottom.

"There were sixteen bullet holes in his body," commented James Willard Schultz, "every one of them a fatal shot; he had evidently possessed the vitality of a grizzly bear."[21]

The whiskey traders had little regard for human life, particularly if that life had belonged to an Indian. Dozens of Natives died each year from the effects of the whiskey, freezing to death while drunk, or being shot either by a fellow Indian or a trader during a quarrel. Even though Calf Shirt was a prominent chief and the incident had been spectacular, the traders went to no particular pains to dispose of the body that lay inert in the excavation. A couple of men simply picked him up, carried him to the frozen Oldman River, and pushed him through a hole in the ice that had been made for watering their horses.

Calf Shirt's wives stood nearby, watching the desecration of their man's body but afraid to interfere. Calf Shirt had told them that he had the power to come back to life four days after his demise. He would return through the sacred power of the grizzly bear that he possessed.

After the body was thrown in the hole, it became snagged on a piece of driftwood, so Kipp went to the fort and got a long pole, using it to ram the body free, but without success. However, the next day, someone discovered that the chief's body had broken free on its own and had floated for a short distance under the ice. There it became entangled in more driftwood where there was an open place in the river caused by a large spring.

Several Indians helped to drag the body onto the shore and the two widows began to chant as their husband had taught them to do. Soon word spread through the camps near the fort and curious Indians gathered to see if the women would be successful in bringing him back to life. Among the onlookers was Crowfoot and a band of Blackfoot who had come south to trade at the fort. Hour after hour passed as the women performed their rituals, but the body of Calf Shirt remained unmoved, curled up in the fetal position, the knees bent and the legs drawn up against the body. He had been frozen stiff.

Among the curious was a great medicine man from Crowfoot's camp who watched the ceremony with interest. Finally, he burst forth with his own holy song, then claimed he could bring Calf Shirt back to life by giving him four drinks of whiskey. As he spoke, he produced a keg of liquor and poured some of the liquid into the mouth of the dead chief. Then a horrified murmur passed through the crowd. Slowly but steadily, one of Calf Shirt's legs unfolded like a man awakening from a long sleep.

The medicine man looked pleased but the others were frightened. Crowfoot announced a sudden desire to leave immediately for Blackfoot Crossing, while others found urgent business in the Porcupine Hills, or some other distant location. As the medicine man resumed his singing, the Bloods started to mill restlessly. They remembered the trouble Calf Shirt had caused in life and recalled his promise to come back as a grizzly bear.

"Stop!" exclaimed one of the Bloods. "Don't continue your ceremonies!"

"But I can give him more whiskey and bring him back to life."

"We don't want him back with us. We'll be happier if he stays dead."

A little later, only his sorrowing wives remained to prepare the body for its final resting place in the trees. Calf Shirt was truly dead.

Many tales by the Blackfoot tribes have supernatural interpretations of factual occurrences. Medical science might explain that the thawing of the body or the whiskey being poured into it caused a muscular reaction that made the leg relax. But the Bloods prefer their mystic tales and enjoy having their joke on Crowfoot. They like to remember the time when the Blackfoot chief was frightened.

Peace with the Kootenays

nce again there was peace between the Kootenays and the
Bloods.

Usually they were enemies, but every once in a while a messenger
would come across the mountains bearing a pipe and sweetgrass. It
was the Kootenays who wanted peace, for they were the ones who
needed access to the great buffalo plains. Once or twice a year they
had to leave their protected mountain valleys and travel to the open
prairies, where they killed buffalo, dried the meat, and stored provisions to supplement their meager diets of fish and camas roots.

Sometimes, in early summer, a Kootenay scout slipped through one
of the mountain passes and prowled the region of the Waterton and
Belly rivers. If the weather was warm and the spring had brought plenty
of rain, the Bloods probably would be far to the east, within sight of the
Cypress Hills. That's where the main buffalo herds congregated in
summer, so that's where the Blackfoot tribes were camped.

If the Kootenay scout found the campfires cold and Belly River
country deserted, he darted back through the craggy peaks to relay
the good news. A few days later, the first guards rode out cautiously,
looking carefully for signs of danger. Positioned near the summits of
prominent foothills, they finally signaled to the main camp that it was
safe to come out.

Soon a trickle of riders filtered down the mountain pass, single
file, moving carefully and slowly into the forbidden land. Women
and children and whole families traveled together, their empty pack
horses trailing behind. Ever watchful, the scouts stayed on the
surrounding hills until the small band of riders made camp for the
night.

Over the next several days the hunters searched for buffalo, the
scouts watched for enemies, and the women followed along with their

butcher knives ready. If the Kootenays were lucky, a few stray herds were found on the upper waters of the Waterton River.[1]

But sometimes the valleys were as barren of buffalo as they were of Bloods, in which case the Kootenays ventured farther and farther east, sometimes as far as the St. Mary River. The scouts were out day and night, watching for the tiniest hint of trouble. A herd of antelope bounding away in the distance; noisy magpies in the river bottom; a wisp of smoke in the air. These were danger signals that were heeded and carefully studied.

Usually the scare was a false one, but even if riders were sighted, the Kootenays didn't necessarily flee to the shelter of the Rockies. First the scouts had to determine the number of enemy. Was it just a small family going to the foothills for tepee poles? Was it an all-male war party on its way to raid across the mountains? Or was the main camp of the tribe returning to its fall hunting grounds?

The Kootenay warriors were brave fighters who were willing to die to protect their families. And there were always the younger boys who saw wealth and glory in raiding an enemy camp. So if the visitors consisted of a small band of Bloods, their horses would probably disappear in the night; if they proved to be a war party, they were destroyed.

But usually the area stayed free of enemies and the Kootenays were able to finish their hunt, load the meat on the hardy little cayuses, and head back into the mountains. As they departed, they left a memento of their visit, an offering of thanks to a land that had been good to them. Sometimes it was a deer antler placed on a growing pile of horns left from previous visits; more often it was simply a stone added to a cairn that had grown steadily over the decades with each succeeding hunting party.

But what if the Bloods had not moved eastward? What happened if they were still hunting within the shadows of the Rockies? The Kootenays had two choices; either they could try to make peace, or they could return to their lands empty-handed.

That is when they needed two brave men. Often one of them was a chief, while the other was a pipe bearer. It all depended on who was prepared to make the dangerous journey to the plains, hoping to reach a friendly band before they were set upon by an enthusiastic bunch of young warriors.

Sometimes they entered Blackfoot country and simply sat down on a prominent hill, pipe in hand. When they were seen, scouts would report the strange sight to their chiefs. A guardian of the camp would approach the strangers and, in sign language, ask them who they were and why they were sitting there. They would explain they were Kootenays who had come to make peace.

At other times, a particularly daring Kootenay might slip past the warrior guards, ride into a camp circle, and enter the lodge of the chief before anyone realized he was there. Once within the safety of the tepee, he could offer his pipe as a token of peace. And usually such an offer was accepted, for it was common knowledge that while the young men longed for war, the chiefs and elders wanted peace. They had lived through the horrors of scalping knives and shattered families; they had won their respectability and wealth and now they wanted to be left alone.

If a peace pact was made, everyone knew it probably wouldn't last more than a season. The young Bloods and Blackfoot were well aware that the Kootenays had the finest appaloosas and race horses in the land, so it was only a matter of time before a daring party would slip away from a camp to raid their peaceful friends. Or sometimes it was the other way around; a Kootenay might see the chance to gain war honors that he needed to win the respect of his comrades.

But whatever the reason, the mere loss of horses was not sufficient reason to break the treaty. Rather, it was when the young raiders killed their enemies or were caught in the act and slaughtered on the spot that the troubles began. For death meant retaliation, and revenge meant a return to hostilities. So the peace treaties seldom lasted.

An important exception occurred in 1855 when a peace treaty was arranged by the American government. At that time, consideration was being given to constructing a railway line through Blackfoot country and across the mountains. To avoid the problems of inter-tribal warfare, the government negotiated a treaty and assigned hunting grounds to each of the tribes. Those who signed the document agreed not to make war on their enemies. These were the Bloods, Blackfoot, Peigans, Gros Ventres, Kootenays, Nez Perces, Flatheads, and Pend d'Oreilles.

In the years immediately following the treaty, a number of Blood chiefs made a sincere effort to maintain the peace. It was broken on a few occasions but reestablished almost immediately. Even when a huge war party of Blackfoot wiped out a number of Kootenays in 1858, the Bloods refused to take part. By 1862, relations were so good that a leading Kootenay chief, Bear Necklace, expressed a wish to spend the winter in the foothills or farther east on the open plains.

A meeting was arranged between the Bloods and Kootenays at

the confluence of the Waterton and Belly rivers, and a pipe of peace was passed between them. When the ceremony was over, the Bloods had agreed to share their winter hunting grounds with their former enemies. The occasion was so important to the Kootenays that the pipe they used was treasured, passed down from chief to chief into the twentieth century.

The Kootenays settled into a winter camp on the St. Mary River, not far from where it joined with the Oldman. As weeks passed, they were visited by families of Bloods and people became friends; the only curse on the camp was gambling. At almost any time of the day or night, the high-pitched gambling songs and the beat of drums could be heard in the Kootenay village. Or the ground would tremble with the thundering hooves of horses in a betting race. By spring, the young Kootenay men had lost almost all their possessions and their chief was angry and upset.

"I thought you'd do better than that," he told them. "I thought we would like it here where you can hunt and trap and get rich. But now we're going to get out of here."[2]

At this time the main Blood camp was just west of the Belly Buttes, while the North Peigans led by Bull Head were farther northwest on Crowlodge Creek. As spring came, the young men from all the tribes started to get restless, wanting to leave on war expeditions as soon as the grass was green enough to graze their stolen stock. Bear Necklace noticed these signs and wanted to get back across the mountains before any trouble started.

During the winter, a young gambler from the Blood tribe had admired a Kootenay race horse that was faster than any other animal in the Blood, Peigan, or Kootenay camps. The boy was from a rich Blood family; his older brother, *Aka'kitsipimi'otas*, or Many Spotted Horses, was a chief; his followers were so wealthy that they were known as the *Awaposo'otas*, or Many Fat Horses Band.

Many Spotted Horses was one of the leading chiefs of the Blood tribe. He had signed the 1855 treaty on behalf of his followers and had amassed a large horse herd through his prowess on the warpath. By the time peace was made with the Kootenays, he had killed nine enemies in his battles with the Crows, Crees, and other tribes. Even when he was still a young man he had led a war party against the Crees and scored a major victory in a battle near a place called Man Pointing Hill.

In another battle he discovered two enemy warriors riding on one horse. In spite of the danger, he killed them both with a club, knocking them off opposite sides of the horse. Because of this audacious feat, he was permitted to own a thirty-buffalo-skin tepee. This was a war honor limited to a half-dozen or so warriors who had committed a brave deed with a dual signifi-cance. Reflecting the double nature of the honor, the tepee had two doorways, two fire-places, and was split into two sections when moving camp. Not only did a man need

Many Spotted Horses (Heavy Shield), as sketched by Gustavus Sohon at the American Treaty of 1855, was one of the leading chiefs of the Blood tribe, and was known for his prowess as a warrior. *Courtesy Glenbow-Alberta Institute/NA-360-14*

to be brave to own such a lodge, he also had to be rich. Two of his horses had no other duty than to move the lodge from place to place.

An American trader who knew Many Spotted Horses in the 1860s described him as a political chief whose wealth was measured in pinto horses, while in 1877 a Mounted Police officer observed that the man owned three hundred head, mostly pintos. When the chief signed Treaty Number Seven with the Canadian government in that year, his personal family consisted of ten women and thirty-one children. This, too, was a measure of his wealth.

And his younger brother was spoiled; he usually got what he wanted. This time, he wanted the Kootenay race horse but the owner would not part with it for any price. So when the young brother couldn't buy it, he decided to steal it. One night, he and some companions crept into the unsuspecting Kootenay camp on St. Mary River, cut the racer loose, and were on their way to the Peigan camp on Crowlodge Creek when the loss was discovered. The angry Kootenays caught the young horse raiders and in the melee that followed, the brother of Many Spotted Horses was killed.

The chief was grief-stricken when he heard the news. Three years earlier, he had lost his two older brothers in a drunken fight at Rocky Mountain House. Now his younger brother was dead. As he mourned, he became bitter about the peace treaty that had brought the Kootenays to the east side of the mountains. In his despondency he announced, much to the surprise of his followers, that he was going to visit the Kootenay camps.

"I'm on my way to make a peace," he told them. "The first Kootenay Indian I meet, I'll make peace with him."[3]

Traveling with two companions, he sang his war song as he rode east towards the St. Mary River. As he left, his people looked at each other in puzzlement and wonder.

Meanwhile, during the previous day in the Kootenay camp a young man named White Horse had wanted to go hunting, so he had saddled his uncle's horse. He was just about to ride away when his aunt yelled at him and told him to leave the horse alone; his uncle didn't want it to be ridden that day.

Angrily the young man had stomped out of the camp, determined to get his own horse. His solution was to visit the Peigans on foot that night and to leave with one of theirs. He had hidden his prize in the trees on the Belly River for the rest of the night and was now going home to show it to everyone.

Many Spotted Horses and his companions were about halfway to the Kootenay camps when they saw White Horse in the distance. At Rocky Lake the chief turned north to Wild Turnip Hill, and there the three Bloods dismounted and sat in a row, waiting for the young man to approach. The chief filled his pipe and held it as a sign of peace. As the Kootenay hesitantly drew nearer, the Bloods recognized his horse and knew it was stolen from the Peigans. Many Spotted Horses smiled grimly.

"My enemies made me cry a few days ago," he said, "and now it's my turn to make them cry. I'm not going to show any compassion to this enemy."[4]

White Horse was worried when he saw the three men, but when he recognized them as Bloods, he relaxed. He had taken a Peigan horse, not a Blood one. Many Spotted Horses made signs to him to dismount and to sit and smoke with them.

"Don't be afraid," he signaled. "We have made a peace between you and us. We are all friends."

Warily the Kootenay sat facing the three Bloods as the pipe was being prepared. He explained that his horse had wandered away in the night and he had gone looking for it. Now that he had found it he was on his way home. The Blood chief was not fooled; speaking rapidly in Blackfoot, he told the others that he intended to distract the Kootenay. "I have killed nine enemy," he said to one of the Bloods, "you can kill this one."[5] Many Spotted Horses then told the Kootenay in sign language that there was a short cut he could take to his camp and pointed in that direction. When White Horse turned and looked, the Blood chief expected the man to be shot but nothing happened.

"I guess I'll have to make it ten," he sighed, and shot the Kootenay dead.[6]

They left the body where it fell and when they returned to the Belly River, Many Spotted Horses rode through his camp, telling everyone what he had done. "I made peace," he proclaimed. "I killed a young Kootenay on this side of Turnip Hill."[7] The peace had been made with himself, not with his enemies.

When two old Blood warriors named Chief Standing in the Middle and Wearing Old Clothes heard the news they immediately grabbed their horses and raced to the scene to be first to scalp the dead Indian. However, in their rush to dismount they neglected to tether their animals; in the excitement, both horses ran away and left the men afoot.

When the animals returned riderless to the Blood camps, everyone was sure the Kootenays had killed them, so a few young warriors

This stone effigy was constructed by Blood Indians to mark the spot on Wild Turnip Hill where Many Spotted Horses killed the Kootenay Indian *(centre, rear)*. *Collection of the author*

painted their faces, sang their medicine songs, and set out to find their comrades. When they came over the last hill before Rocky Lake, they saw the two old warriors running as fast as they could, frequently looking back over their shoulders.

The war party could see why. In the distance, a crowd of Kootenays stood around the scalped body of White Horse. Then they were in their saddles, shouting their war cries and waving their guns in the air as they raced towards the hapless old men. Quickly the Blood warriors rescued their fellows, then retreated to their camp, shouting a warning that the Kootenays were attacking.

To prepare for the assault, some Bloods dug entrenchments at the edge of the village and were able to repulse the first Kootenay onslaught. But then the mountain Indians, reinforced by new arrivals, repeated their attack and kept the Bloods pinned down for the rest of the day. Meanwhile, Kootenay chief Bear Necklace ordered his village on St. Mary River to be pulled down and the people to make haste into the mountain passes. By nightfall, when the Kootenay warriors finally withdrew from their positions at the enemy camp, their women and children were already safely within the protective crags of the Rocky Mountains.

A few days after the event, some Bloods went to the site of the killing on Wild Turnip Hill and commemorated it with stones. Three cairns marked the places where Many Spotted Horses and his companions sat; a line of stones marked White Horse's hesitant journey; and an outline effigy of a human body marked where he fell. There it remained for generations as a monument to the revenge of the Blood chief. He said he was going to smoke with the Kootenays, but instead he wanted to make them cry.

A Messenger for Peace

$\mathcal{T}$he Blackfoot and Cree had been continuously, viciously, unremittingly at war for more than a decade. Usually their battles were interspersed with extended periods of peace, but during the 1860s the fighting raged unabated. Young men raided for horses; older men led revenge parties to slay their enemies.

Blackfoot raiders penetrated deep into Cree country, while the Crees waylaid their enemies on their way to trade at Edmonton, Rocky Mountain House, and Fort Pitt. Sometimes peace overtures were made, but one fur trader noted in 1864 that "these great advocates of peace are almost invariably the peace breakers."[1] Later that year, a Cree peace expedition came to Edmonton from the Fort Carlton area, but its members promptly stole thirteen horses. Another group of Crees led by Little Pine arrived at Fort Edmonton just as a Blackfoot trading party was leaving. With a shout of triumph they attacked the scattered flock, killed one man, and captured a dozen horses within sight of the fort.

There were many uncertainties placed upon the tribes during this decade—stresses that made everyone insecure and fearful of the future. In the south, American prospectors and ranchers had invaded Blackfoot country, killing anyone who resisted them. Backing them up was the United States army, looking for the day when the Indians would be confined to reservations. Farther north, the Crees had heard rumors that their lands were being sold. As a trader commented in 1863, "Sweetgrass and a few followers arrived from Fort Pitt quarter, come to enquire if the report of the Company having sold their Lands & that their Fort, &c. were to be given up, were true."[2] Also, the Crees were beginning to experience a shortage of buffalo as the thinning herds concentrated on the open plains. Bands that had lived comfortably in the woodlands during the winter and killed buffalo just south of the North Saskatchewan River now had to go farther and farther onto the plains to find the shaggy beasts. In 1866, for example, the factor at Fort Edmonton remarked that "starving Indians from the Plains are flocking in daily and we have great trouble with them begging food, which is as precious as Furs at present. Fortunately, Rabbits are numerous or many would starve to death."[3]

The problems between the two tribes had started in 1860 when the Crees killed a Blackfoot chief on his way to trade at Fort Edmonton. The southern tribes had retaliated and peace-making efforts by the fur traders had failed. Many Crees had intermarried with Hudson's Bay Company employees and were so friendly with them that the Blackfoot began to see the traders as their enemies as well. On one occasion the Blackfoot even raided Fort Pitt, one of the principal establishments on the North Saskatchewan, which was deep in Cree territory.

During this period, the Crees on the upper Saskatchewan were led by four great warriors—Sweetgrass, Broken Arm, Lapotac, and Little Pine. Among the Blackfoot tribe were three head chiefs—Old Sun, Crowfoot, and Many Swans. It was Many Swans's favorite wife, *Akai'niskimyaki*, or Many Buffalo Stones Woman, who ultimately tried to bring peace to the warring tribes.

Akoi'mukai, or Many Swans,[4] had assumed power in 1858 when he performed a particular act of bravery and took over from his older brother. He was leader of the influential Bad Guns Band, and when the whole tribe gathered together, he took the position of supreme chief. Many Swans disliked the white traders and the feeling was mutual. In 1870 a traveler at Fort Edmonton described him as "a man of colossal size and savage disposition, crafty and treacherous."[5] In 1866, he urged the Blackfoot to attack a peaceful expedition of Cree half-breeds sent out to the plains from Fort Edmonton to trade with them. When the Indians feared reprisals for killing Hudson's Bay men, Many Swans settled for pillaging the cartloads of trading goods. The traders saw him as a warlike, intractable chief.

On the other hand, the Blackfoot considered Many Swans to be one of their greatest leaders. He was a generous man who kept ten valuable buffalo-running horses just so he could lend them to others during a hunt. A Blackfoot patriarch, Crooked Meat Strings, stated:

> Everyone liked him because he was very kind to them, especially to his children. He would feed a bird. No one helped him to keep in touch with the people's needs; he did it himself. He gave out things to old people, especially those

who couldn't go out and hunt. Nearest the chief's tipi were the tipis of old men who liked to be near him.[6]

Yet Many Swans's followers were a wild, unruly bunch, even by Blackfoot standards. Although the proper name of their band was the Bad Guns, they were nicknamed the "studhorses" because so many of them were always chasing women.

On balance, Many Swans was a dynamic leader whom his people could follow with confidence. Yet, unlike chiefs such as Crowfoot and Rainy Chief, he showed no diplomacy, sympathy, or mercy when dealing with an enemy or to anyone who opposed him. On one occasion, his youngest wife deserted him and ran off with a Blood Indian. When Many Swans's brother complained that the action brought shame on the whole family and asked permission to kill the woman, the affronted husband agreed. So his brother went south to the Blood camps and murdered the woman. No one tried to stop him because everyone both feared and respected the Blackfoot head chief.

The sequence of events that led to the peacemaking efforts of Many Buffalo Stones Woman started in the spring of 1869, when some of the Crees decided that the war needed to be stopped. The movement was led by *Maskipitoon*, or Broken Arm, who had come under the influence of Methodist missionaries and had devoted much of his attention towards peace. He was known to the Blackfoot as *Manikapi'na*, or Young Man Chief.

Maskipitoon organized a peace expedition of ten men, including his son and grandson, hoping that a direct confrontation with Blackfoot leaders could bring about a much-needed peace. Previously, their offers of pipes, sweetgrass, and tobacco had been transmitted through the fur traders. The Crees set out from the Battle River country, and when their scout discovered the Blackfoot camps on the Bow River, they all dressed in their finest clothes, cached their horses in a coulee, and made for a hill overlooking their foes. There they placed a Union Jack on a staff and sat beneath it with a Bible, pipe, and tobacco, waiting for the enemy to arrive. Surprised, Blackfoot horsemen galloped to the place where the Crees sat in a semicircle, bravely offering a pipe of peace.

As soon as Many Swans saw them, his only thought was to kill these hated Crees. "I'm going to take away all their guns," he bragged to his followers.[7]

The chief approached the party on horseback, holding his two hands in front of him, clasped together with the right hand on top.

This was the universal sign for peace. Then the Blackfoot chief said that if there was to be a truce, no one should be armed; he himself carried no weapons. *Maskipitoon* agreed, and in a few moments Many Swans had collected all their weapons. He then turned and rode away, shouting to his warriors, "Go ahead! Shoot and kill them!" The Blackfoot dashed among the defenceless peacemakers and in a few minutes all of them were dead.

"Many Swans performed his greatest deed of all," said Crooked Meat Strings, a Blackfoot patriarch. "He was the only one who ever got a whole batch, more than ten guns at one time. It was a 'good' fight [i.e., the Blackfoot had no casualties]; there was none of our blood in it."[8] The victors scalped the Crees, took their fine clothes, gathered up their horses, and rode back to camp, singing their war songs and holding their grisly trophies aloft. According to Methodist missionary John McDougall, the Indians "had cut the old man to pieces, and had dragged his remains at the tails of their horses into their camp."[9] Many Swans gave all the guns to his relatives and kept none for himself.

Later that month, two young Blackfoot Indians went to Fort Edmonton and broke the news that "Old *Maskipeetoon* [had been] killed by the Blackfeet . . . The old man was off to make peace and was killed by the Swan in sight of the camp."[10]

No one told the Crees, however, the details of the killings. They only knew that the Blackfoot had wiped out *Maskipitoon*'s group on a mission of peace, but they had no idea that the Crees had been tricked and slaughtered like sheep.

Over the next few months, a number of retaliatory raids took place, and during the summer, the Reverend George McDougall reported that "since the murder of our lamented chief, the Crees have killed nearly one hundred Blackfeet."[11] But major revenge expeditions often took a year to organize. Messengers bearing pipes had to be sent to each warrior chief and his approval gained as to the time and place of a retaliatory attack.

However, before winter, the scourge of smallpox swept the plains, killing more Blackfoot Indians than could be accomplished in any Cree raid. By the spring of 1870, almost twenty-five hundred members of the nation had perished, with at least six hundred of these being from Many Swans's own Blackfoot tribe. The Crees had been less severely affected and saw the holocaust as an excellent chance to wreak vengeance upon a weakened enemy.

The idea for the raid originated in the Qu'Appelle Valley, where

Crees and Assiniboines had been warring for years on the east flank of Blackfoot territory. Messengers carried pipes to the Touchwood Hills, Battle River, and Fort Edmonton areas, and by early autumn of 1870 some eight hundred Cree and Assiniboine warriors had assembled near the forks of the Red Deer and South Saskatchewan rivers. Among them were Little Pine, Big Bear, and others who sought revenge for the killing of *Maskipitoon.*

The scouts, traveling ahead of the main expedition, found a Blood Indian camp at the confluence of the Oldman and St. Mary rivers, about three miles upstream from the American whiskey post of Fort Whoop-Up. They picked up a few horses and reported that their enemy would be easy prey.

However, the Crees were not aware that a few miles upstream were the main camps of the South Peigans, a part of the Blackfoot nation. Normally, they would have been far to the south, along the banks of the Marias or Teton rivers in Montana. But the American army had descended upon a defenceless camp of Peigans earlier that year and had slaughtered 173 people, mostly women and children. Fearful of annihilation, the Peigans had decided to winter in British territory.

The Cree revenge party attacked the small Blood camp, killing a chief and several women. But before the raiders could celebrate their victory, the Peigans were upon them. The Crees fought gamely, but their flintlocks and bows and arrows were no match for the modern repeating rifles of their southern enemies. Within a few hours the attack became a rout, and as the raiders fled across the Oldman River, according to participant Jerry Potts, "You could fire with your eyes shut and would be sure to kill a Cree."[12] Exact casualties are unknown, but between two hundred and three hundred Crees and forty members of the Blackfoot nation died that day.

Interestingly, neither Many Swans nor any of his followers took part in the fight. They were camped farther north, along the Bow and Highwood rivers. So the Blackfoot chief, whose actions had contributed to the attack, neither lost men in the battle nor gained personal war honors.

The Blackfoot spent the winter of 1870-71 recovering from the smallpox epidemic. Like other chiefs, Many Swans seemed to have been chastened by the destruction wreaked by the virulent disease. While he may not have changed his mind about his hatred for his enemies, he seemed less inclined to go to war. With the havoc created by disease and whiskey traders, a chief needed to work to keep his followers together, to feed them and to protect them; intertribal fighting seemed less important.

Many Swans camped on the plains below Nose Hill, within the present limits of Calgary. Across the Bow River was his fellow chief, *Omux-kukinai*, or Big Necklace. From these camps, some of the men trapped foxes and coyotes in the foothills, while everyone gathered dried meat and buffalo robes to trade.

In May 1871, a French-Canadian named Jean L'Heureux arrived at the camp to encourage the Blackfoot to take their furs and provisions to the Hudson's Bay Company at Edmonton, rather than to the Americans at Fort Whoop-Up. He also brought a proposal for peace from Cree Indians.

L'Heureux was a fascinating character. He had studied for the priesthood in Quebec but had been expelled when he was caught stealing. He came west in 1860 and tried to join the Oblate mission near Fort Edmonton, but was caught in a homosexual act and was compelled to leave. He joined a roving band of Blackfoot and went to Montana, where he passed himself off to the Jesuits as a secular priest, but was proved to be a fraud. He then returned to the Blackfoot and spent the next thirty years wandering with them. He took the Blackfoot name of *Nao'kskatapi*, or Three Persons, after the Holy Trinity of the Father, Son, and Holy Spirit.

L'Heureux was thoroughly hated and distrusted by the fur traders and Methodist clergy, and even the Catholic priests were embarrassed by his presence. In the Blackfoot camps, he often wore a cassock and performed marriages and baptisms. Each time a real priest arrived, the process was repeated to formalize L'Heureux's ministrations. So while L'Heureux was an asset in gaining conversions and acting as messenger and interpreter, his erratic behavior and sexual proclivities were hard to accept.

The Blackfoot had no such problem. Homosexuality was considered to be the result of some supernatural influence and was accepted as a fact of life. Besides, L'Heureux proved to be a trusted friend of the Blackfoot through war, pestilence, treaties, and, later, life on their reserve.

One of his reasons for coming to Many Swans's camp was to pick up his adopted son, a young Peigan boy who had lost his entire family in the smallpox epidemic. L'Heureux's intention was to take him to St. Albert, just north of Edmonton, where the Grey Nuns could care for him.

On arrival, L'Heureux went to the lodge of White Foretop, and after a few days, he told his host, "Friend, I'm going over the river to see Many Swans to ask him if he is going to Edmonton to trade hides, for I want to take my little son there."[13]

The chief considered L'Heureux's offer and agreed to trade with the British. Many Swans and Big Necklace formed a small party that left Nose Hill late in July and arrived at Fort Edmonton on August 3. In light of the competition from the American whiskey traders, the Hudson's Bay factor treated the chiefs royally. They were outfitted with complete uniforms—red coats with brass buttons and gold braid, pants, shirts, and silk top hats decorated with red and blue plumes. He also gave each of them a fathom of twist tobacco and other gifts.

The factor repeated L'Heureux's message about peace with the Crees. He said that a delegation had approached Father Lacombe and the priest had promised to contact the Blackfoot. Two days later, the priest arrived and presented Many Swans with a twist of tobacco, which the Crees had sent as a peace offering.

Many Swans still had no love for his enemies and would have preferred to fight rather than make peace. But he knew that times had changed. In addition, his wife Many Buffalo Stones Woman had her own ideas. She was his senior wife, the oldest of the four in his lodge. And because of her position, she had the privilege of freely expressing her opinion.

Neither she nor Many Swans was young any more. They had plenty of children and grandchildren, and an adopted son, Chief Calf, who was the old man's favorite child. The smallpox, the Americans, and the whiskey traders were causing too much trouble for the Blackfoot. Why not remove one of the obstacles in their lives by making peace with the Crees? She would be willing to carry the message herself to the enemy camps.

So it was settled. Many Swans gave the tobacco back to the priest and told him to offer it to the Crees as a symbol of his acceptance. In a few days, his wife would come to their camps on the Battle River with the chief's tobacco and lead the Crees to the treaty site near the Bow River. When his followers asked Many Swans why he agreed to send a woman, he replied, "If we went it would be taken as a sign of war, but they will let her go into their camp and deliver the message."[14]

Many Buffalo Stones Woman bravely set out alone from Edmonton while the rest of the band went south to prepare for the treaty. When she arrived at the Cree camp, the people saw a lone woman coming towards them, carrying a peace sign—a frame of crossed sticks with tobacco, eagle plumes, and sweetgrass tied to its center. Unlike her husband's treatment of *Maskipitoon*, she was not attacked and killed, even though she was unarmed. Rather, the Crees were tired of war and their leader, Sweetgrass, had taken up the cause of peace.[15]

The woman was led formally to the chief's lodge where all the sub-chiefs and head men waited for her. When she presented the tobacco to Sweetgrass, he accepted it, lit his pipe, and passed it to everyone in the lodge. As the men smoked, they were symbolically signifying their desire for peace.

Tepees on the Blackfoot Reserve, near Gleichen, Alberta, 1885. *Courtesy Glenbow-Alberta Institute/NA-4967-58*

Many Buffalo Stones Woman explained that her people had accepted the offer of tobacco, and she was there to lead them to a treaty site near the Bow River. Everyone in her tribe knew of her mission and the Cree trucemakers would be perfectly safe. Sweetgrass accepted her words and in a few days the delegation set out from the Battle River, crossed the Red Deer, and traveled the open plains to the south. Scattered herds of buffalo could be seen along their path, and to the west the Rocky Mountains formed the "backbone of the world."

Meanwhile, Many Swans and his trading party returned to their camp near Nose Hill, where the chief announced the forthcoming peace treaty and instructed everyone to get prepared. He knew that the hotheads in his band would never attack the Cree party with his wife as one of its members. Soon the scattered lodges were reassembled in a huge circle with four tepees pitched in the center. Each was occupied by one of the main warrior societies, the protectors of the camp. The chief also sent the men out hunting so there would be plenty of fresh meat for their guests.

A few days later, a scout announced that Many Buffalo Stones Woman and the Cree delegation were coming, most of them on foot. "Get ready," Many Swans told his companions. "Don't crowd around and don't make any excitement to alarm the Cree visitors, lest they hurt my wife."[16] The members of the four warrior societies mounted their horses and rode forward to meet the procession. Many Buffalo Stones Woman, Sweetgrass, and three other Cree chiefs stood in a line, one holding the Union Jack and another a frame of crossed sticks with sweetgrass, plumes, and tobacco. A few yards behind the leaders stood the rest of the Crees in an orderly line.

Many Swans approached them on foot, his warriors standing respectfully in the distance. When he came to the first row, he solemnly kissed his wife, then kissed the four Cree leaders. He next went to the second line and shook hands with all the Cree delegation. The Blackfoot chief then signaled to his followers. The members of the warrior societies fell in behind the Crees, and the rest of the Blackfoot formed a fourth group at the rear of the procession.

When all was in readiness, the Crees marched forward, singing their honoring song. The other Indians followed behind in groups, until they all stood before the four society tepees within the huge camp circle. From there Many Swans took the four Cree chiefs and the senior leaders of the warrior societies into the main lodge. There, a holy man sat at the back of the tepee, with the Crees on his left and the Blackfoot on his right.

The old man took his sacred pipe and passed it to the Blackfoot leader. As he touched his lips to the unlit stem, Many Swans passed his hands over the holy man's body, thus indicating his willingness to make peace. The ceremony was repeated with each of the other Blackfoot leaders, and then with the four Crees. After these vows, the pipe was lit and each man smoked in turn until the bowl was empty. Both the Blackfoot and Cree believed that this was a "holy smoking ceremony" and anyone who broke the peace would die.

When the ritual was over, the group emerged from the tepee and Many Swans called out to his people, "Come and choose one Cree as your *takai* [friend] to take home to sleep."[17] Some of the Crees had women and children with them; these families and others were taken to individual tepees where they were fed and given gifts. Although not everyone could speak the other's tongue, all were acquainted with the sign language that was common to all Plains tribes.

Many Buffalo Stones Woman took Sweetgrass and his family to her lodge. Her work in bringing the two tribes together had succeeded. Now the men had the responsibility of concluding a peace pact that would end the senseless killings.

After two days of feasting and visiting, a camp crier went through the village, telling everyone to get ready, for on the following morning they were moving to the Rosebud River, thirty miles (48 km) to the northeast. When they traveled, everyone rode, for all the Crees had been presented with horses as gifts. At last the Indians arrived at a big cutbank on the Rosebud, where again they camped in a circle. After another two days of feasting, Many Swans announced, "Tomorrow I'm going to put up a big dance for the visitors."

He pitched his huge tepee in the center of the circle and tied four horses in front of it. One of them, a white buffalo runner, was his prize horse; it was painted with red designs depicting all of Many Swans's war exploits. Included were symbols of guns, horses, human figures, and representations of objects captured in battle.

When the crowds had gathered in front of his tepee, Crees mixed with Blackfoot, Many Swans began bringing out gifts for a huge giveaway. One at a time, his wives emerged from the tepee, each laden with presents, which were piled on a horse. The first three wives were young and beautiful; they carried the piles of blankets and robes. The fourth was Many Buffalo Stones Woman, much older and greatly respected by the tribe. Because of her role in making peace, she had the signal honor of displaying guns, shields, knives, pipe axes, and other objects that her husband had taken from the Crow, Sioux, Snake, and other tribes. These objects were placed on the painted white horse.

Many Swans mounted the horse and led the procession to a dancing area where four old men began beating their drums and singing. The chief rode to the center of the circle and laid all the gifts in piles. Then he danced, each time picking up a pile and holding it in his arms. Usually, when a man sponsored a giveaway, all his gifts could easily be carried at one time. But Many Swans was so generous that he had to dance four times with his arms loaded before he was finished. Then he gave the gifts to the northern visitors.

The Crees, who had gathered at the southwest side of the circle, were very pleased and impressed. One of their leaders cried out, "Now we know the Blackfoot are the greatest of all the four tribes—the Blackfoot, Blood, Peigan, and Sarcee—and Many Swans is the greatest chief of all of you."

"Yes," agreed one of the Blackfoot. "It is true. We make our chiefs by taking guns, bows, knives, and axes—the things that can kill us. The Crow, Sioux, and the Snakes have been deprived, especially of their tepee flags."[18]

The peace treaty was going well. Firm friendships were made, the Crees had enjoyed the feasts, and now they were going home loaded down with gifts and horses.

But then the Blackfoot spokesman, through his incessant bragging, destroyed the feeling of comradeship that had been developed over the past week. Perhaps he was related to Many Swans and could not resist talking about his leader, or perhaps he was someone who loved to gossip or taunt his enemy. Whatever the reason, he was not satisfied to simply tell the Crees that the Blackfoot chief was a great leader.

"Many Swans is our head chief," he cried aloud, "because he is the one who fooled *Manikapi'na.*"

The Crees looked intently at the orator. They knew that he had spoken the Blackfoot name of their great chief, *Maskipitoon*, the Broken Arm. In detail, the Blackfoot went on to describe how Many Swans had tricked the peace party into giving up their guns under the Union Jack, how he told his men to slaughter the unarmed Crees, and how they had a great victory dance to celebrate the event. Sweetgrass and the others were appalled; this was the first time they had heard about the way their leader had died.

The visitors were angry but quiet for the rest of the day and left the following morning. Along the way north, they talked about revenge, but none was willing to break the pact of peace. Then one of the chiefs commented that during the ceremonies, Many Swans had fallen from his horse and had been badly bruised; perhaps his weakness left him vulnerable. When they reached their camps on the Battle River, the chiefs had decided what they should do. Even Sweetgrass, the peacemaker and convert to Christianity, agreed when the others sent for the most powerful shaman in the tribe. He was known to have great supernatural powers and was both feared and respected by his own followers.

Using songs, incantations, and secrets known only to himself, the shaman placed a curse on Many Swans; he sent spirit messengers to fill the man's body with pain and told the others that after the man had suffered for his treachery, he would die.

The shaman's attack struck Many Swans in his joints. First it was his arms, then his legs, and finally the pain coursed throughout his whole body. The Blackfoot recognized the signs of "Cree medicine," a power that was often greater than anything their own medicine men could combat.

"Save him! Save him!" cried Many Swans's followers. "The Crees have done this."[19]

Many Buffalo Stones Woman sought out the three best medicine men in the tribe, and by the time they gathered in the tepee, the chief was unconscious. His body was stripped, laid on a buffalo robe, and the medicine men tried to see if they could counteract the effects of the Cree medicine. The first man to try was Yellow Coming Over the Hill. As he sang amid the smoke and incense of the lodge, he drew two metal arrowheads from the chief's hip, shot there by the Cree spirit messengers. Then he made his sacred weasel skin come to life; it ran around the fire, stopping at Many Swans's left hip, where it pulled out a metal pin, and then to the right, where it pulled out another. As the medicine man rested, he looked at the crowd in the tepee and said, sadly, "There are more in him."[20]

The second medicine man, Holy Mountain, took up the task. He painted Many Swans's body white, adding a red circle in the arch of each foot. Then, after dancing and reciting his incantations, he used an obsidian blade to cut tiny holes at the center of the circle. Placing a bone whistle in his mouth, he blew it vigorously as he danced, then bent over the prostrate chief and, using it as a sucking tube, drew three needles from the man's foot. Repeating the ritual on the other leg, he drew out three long hairs that had been taken from Many Swans's own head and blown into his body by the powers of the Cree shaman.

The third medicine man, Red Morning, repeated the ceremonies of his fellow doctors and removed metal arrows from the chief's wrist, elbow, and shoulder.

But Many Swans was not cured. His body was still filled with the missiles of the spirit messengers. Reluctantly, Yellow Coming Over the Hill tried again. The weasel skin ran around the body and pulled tiny medicine bundles from three places in the chief's shoulder. But that was all. There was just too much Cree medicine inside the chief to be removed.

Finally, the holy man silenced the drum, took away the incense, and began to pack his things. "His body is full of these things," he said sadly. "We can't save him for his skin is already turning black from the Cree medicine."[21]

That autumn, Many Swans died. Some people said the fall from the horse had killed him. The fur traders claimed he had tuberculosis.

But his followers knew better; the Crees had gotten their revenge for the killing of *Maskipitoon.*

Yet the 1871 peace treaty survived the death of Many Swans. A few small skirmishes took place over the next few years, but the days of pitched battles and the destruction of entire villages were virtually over. Yet Many Buffalo Stones Woman must have wondered about the strange turn of events as she watched her grandchildren playing in the peaceful camp. She had stopped the war between the two tribes, but she had lost her husband in the process. The price of peace had been high indeed.

The Orphan

$\mathcal{T}$he foothills of Montana Territory were bare and the muddy waters of the mountain streams were choked with ice and the flotsam of winter. In the coulees, the winter snow was still packed in among the gnarled cottonwoods and willows. From the brow of the valley, the long procession of Indians wound down a trail towards the tiny village of Sun River Crossing. On the hillsides, cautious scouts watched for anything that might signal danger to the cavalcade of men, women, children, horses, and dogs. Pausing briefly to look at the log houses built since their last visit, the Indians halted near the low, sod-roofed trading post on the north side of the river.

It was early March 1869, and the mixed trading party of Bloods and Peigans were loaded down with the results of their winter hunt. Bundles of buffalo robes and coyote skins made the overburdened travois sag as their dragging poles dug deeply into the prairie soil. The Indians pitched their tepees near the store, just across the road at the bend in the river, and prepared to trade. For the next few days, the two proprietors of the fort, John J. Healy and Alfred B. Hamilton, conducted a lively business, providing blankets, knives, and a variety of other trade goods—and even a little whiskey—in exchange for the hides.

Healy and Hamilton had opened the post two years earlier, located about four miles (6.4 km) from the military post at Fort Shaw in northwest Montana. Trading was forbidden on the huge Blackfeet Reservation[1] that had been set aside through the treaty of 1855, so the pair had built their post on the very edge of the reservation.

As soon as the Peigans finished their trade, they left for the plains, but the small party of Bloods decided to stay on. There were only six or seven tepees—about fifty men, women, and children—under their leader, *Akai-nuspi*, or Many Braids. He was a member of the Many Tumors Band and his followers had spent the winter with the Peigans.

His was the first Blood trading party of the season, and he preferred to wait until other Bloods came down from the north so that his small band would have protection on the trail. Many Braids had met Johnny Healy on earlier visits and had become quite friendly with the trader. Healy suggested that while they were waiting, the Bloods could earn some extra money by hunting antelope for the post and the settlers at the crossing.

A short time later, the silence of the peaceful valley was broken by the sounds of another trading party, whooping and singing as they came in from the eastern plains. They proved to be a band of Pend d'Oreilles who lived on the west side of the Rockies but often crossed the mountains to hunt buffalo. The Blackfoot considered them to be trespassers, so there was no love lost between the tribes.

As soon as Many Braids and his followers saw the enemy approaching, they gathered up their horses, which had been grazing on the prairie, and close herded them while the mountain Indians strutted and mingled around the post. The Pend d'Oreilles were camped, Many Braids discovered, several miles downstream at Flat Creek. They had spent much of the winter in the Judith Basin, making a temporary truce with the Peigans while they gathered a plentiful supply of dried meat and robes.

Many Braids realized that the Pend d'Oreille treaty with the Peigans did not apply to the Bloods, so he watched the enemy Indians carefully. They were boisterous and happy after a good winter's hunt, but they did not bother the camp.

Still, the Blood leader didn't trust the mountain Indians. He saw how some of the young men had looked covetously at the little herd of cayuses and buffalo runners that milled about near the Blood village. After the Indians had gone, Many Braids asked Healy if he might put the horses into the corral that adjoined the trading post. He would not rest easily until the Pend d'Oreilles had left for the mountains.

Healy agreed, and that night the trader decided to visit the Blood leader to see how he was faring. The store was short of meat and he hoped that Many Braids would soon head out to look for antelope. He was even prepared to lend him his old Swiss breech-loader, which would be far better than the Indian's trade musket.

Accompanied by his interpreter, François Vielle, Healy had a pleasant visit in the Many Braids tepee. The whole family was there. Many Braids's wife, *Pi'aki*, or The Dancer, was quietly nursing her baby girl while two girls and a boy sat nearby. The boy, about eight

John J. Healy, in later life. Healy and his partner, Alfred B. Hamilton, established the notorious Whoop-Up trading post in 1869. *Courtesy Montana Historical Society*

years old, was called *Potai'na*, or Flying Chief,[2] while one sister was named *Natoi'si*, Holy Woman. She was blind.

About ten o'clock, when night had settled on the prairies, Many Braids suddenly stopped talking, listened for a moment, and then threw ashes on the fire to cast the tepee into darkness.

"Look out!" the Indian cautioned.

"What's the trouble?" Healy asked his interpreter.

"Something's wrong. Let's get back to the house."[3]

Healy thought a few drunken soldiers might have come from Fort Shaw to stir up some excitement, but Vielle was afraid of an Indian attack. A Frenchman who had lived most of his life with the Blackfoot, Vielle knew how to read the signs. Barking dogs, strange sounds in the distance, the milling horses—all could be indications that an enemy was near.

Many Braids accompanied the two men back to the trading post, then checked his horses to make sure they were safe. He was pleased to see that the gate to the corral had been securely tied with rope. He also accepted the loan of the Swiss rifle and a small quantity of ammunition. He wanted the gun for Pend d'Oreilles, not antelope, for he was sure he had heard their signaling calls. When he returned to his camp, he sat near the doorway, gun in hand, peering out into the darkness and watching for signs of danger.

Meanwhile, the occupants of the trading post settled down for the night. In addition to Healy, Hamilton, and their families, there were the interpreter, three visitors sleeping on the floor of the store, and Healy's older brother, Joseph. About an hour after they had turned out the lights, their dog, Pronto, began barking furiously.

"He was a very fine watch dog," recalled Healy's daughter. "He never slept at night, was always on the prowl, and hated Indians."[4]

About fifteen minutes later, heavy gunfire shattered the stillness of the night. The Pend d'Oreille raiders had swept down on the Blood camp in pitch darkness, hoping to stampede the horses they believed were being herded nearby. Many Braids opened fire on the enemy but the fight was pathetically one-sided. Other than the Swiss rifle, the Bloods were poorly armed with bows and arrows and old muzzle-loading flintlocks and had no defence against the night raiders. Volley after volley was fired into the tepees, and screams of agony and terror were mixed with the barking of the camp dogs and the shouts of the attacking warriors.

Many Braids was one of the first to fall, a bullet lodged in his thigh. Then his wife, The Dancer, and their baby were cut down, while the chief's oldest daughter caught a bullet between her eyes and was killed instantly. In the other tepees, some screamed, others died, while a few lucky ones fled into the darkness.

When the Pend d'Oreilles realized that the Blood horses were gone, they turned their attention to the trading post. Some of the Indians went to the bridge and fired at any settlers from the village who had ideas about coming to the aid of the besieged traders and Indians.

At the first sound of gunfire, Healy shouted to his family to lie on the floor. When the bullets started to strike the logs of the store, he called for his brother to guard the back while he protected the front entrance. Stuffing his trousers full of cartridges, he loaded his Springfield rifle and crept to the door. When he opened it, a bullet whizzed past his face but the trader jumped onto the porch and hid behind a pile of firewood. From where he lay, Healy could see three of the Blood tepees all surrounded by Pend d'Oreilles. When he fired a shot in their direction, the Indians scattered.

Many Braids saw that the enemy had retreated so he hobbled across the road to the store, shouting in Blackfoot, "Open the door, my friend. I am shot. Let me in!"[5] Healy recognized his blood-soaked companion and helped him inside, laying the wounded man on the floor.

The trader then became aware that the attackers had gone to the corral and were trying to chop open the gate. Ignoring the danger, Healy dashed behind the woodpile, then jumped around the corner, intending to chase the one or two Indians away. To his surprise, he was confronted by almost sixty Pend d'Oreilles on horseback, while another handful were working on the gate. Healy opened fire on the closest man, who was less than eight feet away, then fled back to the safety of the store amid a hail of gunfire. Meanwhile, his brother Joseph and the three visitors had been shooting from windows every time they saw something move.

A whoop of victory signaled the opening of the corral, and a few seconds later the entire Blood horse herd went galloping into the night. Not only did the Pend d'Oreilles get the Blood animals, but also seventy-five horses belonging to the traders and the visitors.

In the aftermath of the raid, stunned Indians began to wander into the store. Some were wounded, while others searched for their families. In the Many Braids tepee, Flying Chief and his blind sister, Holy Woman, had remained huddled in their buffalo robes and were unhurt. But the others were dead. As Flying Chief recalled years later, "It all happened so suddenly it was difficult to realize its reality. There lay my mother and my sister, shot dead."[6] And with his mother was the tiny baby, also a victim of the attack.

As the two children went to the trading post, the full horror of the raid became clear. The bodies of seven Pend d'Oreille raiders lay scattered about, one having fallen into the well. Nearby was a Blood woman who had been shot in the back when she tried desperately to reach the store. A little girl with both bullet and arrow wounds lay bleeding and in shock. In all, more than fifty people crowded the store, both Indians and whites.

Many Braids lay on the floor of the trading post. "My father's condition was severe," recalled Flying Chief, "and knowing his minutes were numbered, he called to his side Mr. J. J. Healy and begged him to take me and look after me. Shortly after this, father died."[7]

A few days earlier, Flying Chief had been a carefree eight-year-old, just beginning to learn the lessons of manhood. He loved to ride his own horse, proudly following his father as they moved from place to place in search of the buffalo. A year earlier, he had seen one of the last buffalo hunts where the Bloods had driven the animals over a cliff for a winter supply of food. He remembered how one hind quarter and one front quarter went to each family, while the holy men and women received the tongues. Those were happy family days.

Now he was an orphan, left in the care of a strange white man. When the surviving Bloods moved eastward to seek refuge in a Peigan camp, they took the boy's blind sister with them. She stayed with the Peigans for the rest of her life.

But fate had other plans for the little orphan boy. Johnny Healy took his promise seriously and adopted Flying Chief as his own. He gave him the name of Joe Healy and kept him at the trading post for the rest of the spring. Then, when summer came, the boy began to attend school in nearby Fort Shaw with some of the army children. There he picked up a working knowledge of English and learned the alphabet. He thus became the first Blood Indian to receive a formal education.

Meanwhile, his foster father was away on his own adventure. Healy had built a profitable business in Indian trading, particularly when he could sell illegal whiskey and repeating rifles. The profits to be made in these goods were immense. One of the men who did not agree with Healy's way of doing business was William F.

Flying Chief, or Joe Healy, patriarch of the Blood tribe. After the death of his parents, Flying Chief was raised by John J. Healy, a white man. Later in life, he returned to live among his own people and became an important link between the two cultures. Ca. 1915. *Courtesy Glenbow-Alberta Institute/NA-1228-1*

Wheeler, the local United States marshal. He managed to have a number of dealers convicted and made life difficult for the whiskey merchants.

Johnny Healy, because of his associations with Many Braids and other Blood leaders, realized that he could find a good market for his wares if he moved across the yet-unsurveyed forty-ninth parallel, which separated the United States from the "British possessions," as the Americans liked to call them. Not only would business be good, but the traders would be beyond the jurisdiction of Marshal Wheeler. Accordingly, in the autumn of 1869, while little Flying Chief was attending school, Healy and Hamilton slipped across the northern border and opened a trading post at the confluence of the Oldman and St. Mary rivers. The winter was so successful that they netted fifty thousand dollars for the season and made plans for a bigger and better fort.

As a result of Healy and Hamilton's foray, southern Alberta was launched into a four-year period of uncontrolled exploitation and death. Other traders, seeing the success of the Sun River merchants, followed them north in 1870 to open their own nefarious whiskey trade. Healy and Hamilton's new fort—huge and heavily armed by western standards—was soon dubbed Fort Whoop-Up. Other smaller posts gloried in such names as Standoff, Slideout, and Robber's Roost.

When trading whiskey, Healy started off with kegs of alcohol that he diluted with water on a four-to-one basis, that is, four parts of water to one of alcohol. Then he added a few other ingredients such as molasses, burnt sugar, bitters, etc., to give the mixture both color and kick. Later, when his Indian customers were feeling the effects of the liquor, he further diluted it on a ten-to-one basis. This was nicknamed "Blackfoot whiskey." This flow of liquor into Blackfoot hunting grounds soon had tragic results. The authority of the chiefs was destroyed, laws within the camps were ignored, and hundreds of Indians fell victim to the whiskey. Some killed each other in drunken arguments, others froze to death while intoxicated, and still others were shot by the traders when they became too troublesome. Hundreds of Indians died during those lawless days. Yet Johnny Healy's friendship with leading Blood chiefs enabled him to operate with impunity.

Each spring, the traders returned to Sun River with their bull wagons piled high with buffalo robes. Young Flying Chief, now fully conversant in English, was there to greet his foster father. While Healy was away during the winter, the boy went to school and worked at the Sun River store, sometimes helping with the supplies and at other times interpreting for the visiting bands of Peigans.

Later, when Fort Whoop-Up was firmly established, Flying Chief made his first visit to the northern post. "I was only a boy then," he recalled, "but I remember well the long wagon-trains loaded high with goods and supplies. It was a two-week trip for us, and we passed through many dangers before we reached our destination. I was at the useful stage and knew well how to handle the four-horse team."[8]

Flying Chief moved back and forth between Sun River and Whoop-Up until the summer of 1874. The young Indian's reminiscences of that tragic period were a mixture of sadness and colorful incidents.

Fort Whoop-Up, seen here in the background, ca. 1870s, proved very profitable for its American owners, but signaled the beginning of four years of uncontrollable exploitation and death for the Blackfoot. *Courtesy Glenbow-Alberta Institute/NA-550-18*

"I recall," he said, "going back to Sun River for additional supplies, and on my return, when I reached a high hill about ten miles [16 km] from camp, the Fort Whoop-Up traders would fire a cannon. The volley was a signal to the effect that new supplies were at hand. The first come were the first served."[9]

On one trip, he saw the bodies of three white men who had been killed at Rocky Springs by Assiniboine Indians. But the traders weren't the only victims. "The liquor supply steadily grew," he observed, "until one could even find the dead lying around uncovered. There was no law, justice or a demand for peace."[10]

With the arrival of the North-West Mounted Police in 1874, Johnny Healy turned his attention to his Sun River business. With the help of his adopted son, he added a grist mill to the store and began to produce flour. In 1876, he made his first trip back into Canada when he found that the Bloods were taking their robes to the stores in the Mounted Police village of Fort Macleod. To garner his share of the profits, Healy, probably with Flying Chief in tow, traveled to the Blackfoot camps, buying buffalo robes before the Indians had a chance to take them to the Canadian traders.

But the glorious days of the fur trade were rapidly coming to an end. In 1877, Healy reluctantly decided to give up his Sun River store and move to Fort Benton, where he had an offer to become business manager for the local newspaper. Flying Chief felt there was no place for him in these new surroundings. He was now sixteen years old, almost a man, so he decided to return to his people. He had never completely lost touch with them, and even though he had no close relatives, he had become friendly with Bull Shield and other people from his father's band, the Many Tumors.

"I had lived there just like a white man," Flying Chief recalled of his Montana years, "a son of the family of Mr. Healy. I attended the white schools of Montana, and not till years after did the longing come to me to return to Canada to see my remaining relatives and friends."[11]

Flying Chief—or Joe Healy as he was now being called—slipped easily into the routine of Indian life. Traveling with Bull Shield, he followed the last buffalo herds into Montana. He also joined in the religious and warfare activities of the tribe. In 1881 when a Blood war party met the steamboat *Red Cloud* on the Missouri, Joe Healy was one of its members.

A little later, John Devine, a hotel operator at Sun River Crossing, saw three Indians, a man and two women, riding up to his place. Stepping outside, he held up his hand in greeting and said, "How."

"How do you do, Mr. Devine," replied the buck. "Don't you remember me? I am *Battana* [Flying Chief]." It was the Indian boy that Healy had raised as a white man, returned to the tepees of his forefathers.[12]

The young man had gone full circle from Flying Chief, the orphan boy; to Joe Healy; to Flying Chief, the Blood warrior.

When the Bloods settled on their reserve in 1880-81, Joe Healy was the only member of the tribe who was fluent in Blackfoot and English. Most of the interpreters were mixed-bloods or traders who had lived with the Indians. Healy, on the other hand, had the full confidence of his people. He was outspoken in 1881 when a posse of Americans came to seize a number of horses they said were stolen from them. When they had appropriated fourteen animals, Healy recognized them as thieves who had raided Bull Back Fat's camp a year earlier while he was hunting in Montana. Healy protested to the Mounted Police and in the face of mounting anger, the Americans were forced to withdraw.

Because of his knowledge of English, Healy was in great demand, especially by the missionaries. The Reverend Samuel Trivett, in particular, tried to recruit the young Blood. He even located his mission near Bull Shield's camp, hoping that Healy might use his influence to gain converts. However, Trivett could not even convert Healy, who was quite comfortable with his Native religion. Trivett then turned to prayer.

> Earnestly would I ask the Committee to Pray for him, asking Our Merciful and Gracious God to lead him to the feet of Jesus. He sometimes speaks well and wishes to have prayer but again he returns to the Heathen Dances. Earnestly do I pray for him and I would ask the Committee to make this a Special Case for Prayer, more if requests could be sent to Christian friends. What a Blessing if this poor man could be converted as he might be able to do so much for our Blessed Lord in leading others to the Mighty.[13]

Yet Joe Healy was unmoved by the appeal. Thirty-five years were to pass before he embraced the Anglican faith. In the meantime, he was an outspoken supporter of Native religion. During the 1890s, when the government tried to suppress Indian dances, he defied their decrees. Instead, he put on a beaver bundle dance, and later in the decade was arrested for performing a medicine pipe dance. His defiant actions contributed significantly to the overthrow of the government regulations. By 1900, the Sun Dance and other religious festivals were being held without restrictions.

Joe Healy married First in the Water, the daughter of Little Ears, chief of the All Short People Band, shortly after his return to the tribe. They had one son who died of tuberculosis at the age of three. Healy then married Wide Nostrils, the daughter of Iron Pipe, and they had a large family of six daughters and four sons.[14] Most of them attended the Anglican mission and went on to be successful members of the tribe.

As for Joe Healy, he became a bridge between the Indian and white communities. He was an official interpreter for the government when a new treaty was made in 1883. He accompanied the Blood chiefs when they were taken on a tour of eastern Canada in 1905. He served for a short time as a scout for the Mounted Police, and he helped organize Indian participation in the nearby Lethbridge Fair.

In addition, the Healy home became a focal point for many community activities. At one time, the Northwest Fur Company rented a part of the house to use as a trading post. Actually, the home consisted of two log houses placed end to end with a porchway connecting the two. One was their home and the other a store or gathering place. Mike Mountain Horse described the place:

> It was a common sight for anyone entering the store to make a purchase to see several women squatted on the floor, some with bawling babies on their backs. These women would be drinking tea quite contentedly from large mugs, the beverage slowly simmering in a huge pot sitting on a cast iron stove in the room, while their husbands did their purchasing. There were colored blankets of all grades and sizes, beads and mirrors, and paints for the face. Groceries were also sold.
>
> The company did a land office trade at the house of Healy's, who did their interpreting for them because Joe was the only Indian who spoke English fluently enough.[15]

At other times, Indian dances and feasts were held, while at Christmas, Joe Healy celebrated the way he learned as a child in Montana. On Christmas Eve, he told his children about Santa Claus, equating him with *Napi*, the trickster of Blackfoot mythology. One time, when he told them that *Napi* would be leaving gifts for them, his oldest boy, Johnny, became frightened, for he knew that the Blackfoot trickster could play mean pranks on people. So the boy decided to stay awake to protect the other children. As Mike Mountain Horse tells it:

> Along towards morning, Santa Claus came in cautiously with a bag on his back. Johnny, who was ever on the alert, espied him right away from under his bedding and, thinking him to do them harm, jumped out of the bed and seized the broom that was handy and started to inflict a very telling barrage of blows on Santa Claus.
>
> This unexpected reception caused Santa Claus to retire in quick order, yelling at Johnny at the same time, "Son, you're hurting me!"[16]

Another part of Christmas was a huge feast that Joe Healy gave every year. Dozens of people from all parts of the reserve came by wagon, horseback, or on foot to share the food. This happened during the years when hunger was common among the Bloods, so the feast was a great event. And through the influence of the nearby Anglicans, Healy sometimes had his wife make a plum pudding and brought it into the room, blazing with brandy that he had obtained from a bootlegger.

After several years on the reserve, Joe Healy took a new name, which was the custom of his people. His choice was *Mako'yi-itsikin*, or Wolf Moccasin, a name once used by his father. Then, in 1888, an incident occurred that gave him a third name. He had gone to the Blood timber limit at the edge of the mountains to cut poles for corrals. He was accompanied by an Indian Department employee, Mitchell Hughes, whom the Indians called *Sta'ah*, The Ghost. They had just reached Standoff with their loads and were passing an Indian horseman when a violent thunderstorm crashed about them. Both of the men jumped from their wagons to seek shelter when a bolt of lightning flashed to earth accompanied by an ear-splitting thunderclap.

The Indian, Riding Slight of Hand, was killed instantly, along with his horse, as was one of the horses in the Indian Department team. Both Healy and Hughes were dashed to the ground and lay unconscious. Some Indians saw what happened and took the two victims to a nearby house. Healy recovered consciousness after about two hours but Hughes remained in serious condition. He was taken to a hospital in Fort Macleod where he remained unconscious for several days. "Hughes, I fear, is in a very dangerous condition," reported the Indian agent, "& even though he should recover, it will be a long time before he is fit for work."[17]

The Blackfoot Indians did not believe that anything happened by accident. The fact that Joe Healy had been unhurt by the lightning, while others had been injured or killed, was taken as a sign that the Thunder was his protector. As a result, when he was an old man he chose the name *Maistoi'siksinum*, or Black Crow, for himself, as the crow was considered to be a messenger of the Thunder spirit.

Joe Healy also had the power, because of this experience, to name any children after lightning, thunder, or water animals. Among the names he chose for his grandchildren were White Mink Woman, Three Flashes of Lightning Woman, Quiet Thunder, and Distant Thunder.

When Crop Eared Wolf, head chief of the Blood tribe, died in 1913, the townspeople of Lethbridge tried to persuade the Indians to choose Joe Healy as his successor. Instead, when Shot Both Sides became the new chief, the *Lethbridge Herald* explained why. "Joe Healy, although popular with the entire tribe, was in favor of leasing [land] to farmers, in small tracts, and on this account, and because of his friendly relations with the whites, and of his position in the RNWMP, it is thought the tribe turned him down."[18]

So, in the end, the very strength that the onetime orphan boy brought to the tribe turned out to be his greatest weakness. He understood the white people but he was too close to them.

In 1935, a mission school teacher, Noel Stewart, described a visit with the old man:

> His kind face was full of genuine friendship that night. Seating himself at the table in the center of that spotless room, warmed by a modern heater, he looked the fine-cut Indian. His face was alight by the flame of the coal-oil lamp, and he kept a steady gaze upon me as if revealing my inner character. Yet how stolid his expression was, tinted by the shade of a flickering lamp.
>
> No pen could have portrayed the scene he presented, for his countenance showed up every characteristic so true to his race. Around us sat his many grandchildren, who were as eager as I was, to hear the words of a great grandfather, and never once during my two hour visit did they utter one sound.[19]

Joe Healy saw his foster father only once after leaving Sun River. The trader had gone to the Yukon in the 1890s and had returned to the United States an impoverished and broken man. In 1906, he was on his way to Chicago to see about financing for a new venture when he stopped to renew acquaintances with old friends in Fort Benton and Great Falls. Joe Healy learned about the visit and made a special trip to Montana to see his foster father. Johnny Healy was pleased to welcome Flying Chief, now a man of thirty-five with a growing family. He was happy that the years at Sun River had benefited the orphan, and in spite of his own financial condition, he gave Joe Healy a gift of two hundred dollars.

Joe Healy never forgot how the tragedy of his parents' death had given him a new kind of life, one that most Bloods would not experience for one or two generations. When he died in 1936, the little orphan boy had become one of the most respected patriarchs of his tribe.

Black White Man

S ome time in the late 1830s, a man named Henry Mills arrived at Fort Union on the Missouri River with Chief Trader Kenneth McKenzie and began working as a laborer for the American Fur Company. At once the Blackfoot Indians were impressed and fascinated with the man. They treated him with more than customary friendliness and invited him to their camps. He in turn accepted their offers and soon became great friends with many of the leading warriors.

This comradeship was no surprise to the men at the post, for Mills was Black. They knew that from the time of first contact, the Black race had been a source of curiosity and wonderment to the Plains Indians. The few Blacks who were drawn to the western frontier found they were in a class by themselves and were considered by the Indians in a much more favorable light than by their white employers.

The first record of a Black on the northern plains occurred in 1805 when "Negro York" accompanied the Lewis and Clark expedition on its historic journey to the Pacific. This man was constantly made a center of attention by the Indians. "They had never seen a being of that color and therefore flocked round him to examine the extraordinary monster."[1]

After the establishment of the American fur trade, a number of other Blacks came to the Upper Missouri. Tom Reese, a Black employee at Fort McKenzie, was killed by Blackfoot Indians in 1843; another man named Mose was drowned in the Yellowstone in 1858; and in 1872 a Black named David Green was living with the Peigan tribe. Perhaps one of the most famous Blacks was James Beckwourth, who became a great warrior and chief of the Crow tribe.

Blacks also were employed by the Hudson's Bay Company during the nineteenth century. Sir George Simpson, during his voyage around the world in 1841, was reminded of one particular Black employee who had served in western country several years earlier.

He commented that the Indians "had their curiosity most strongly excited by a negro of the name of Pierre Bungo. This man they inspected in every possible way, twisting him about and pulling his hair, which was so different from their own flowing locks; and at length they came to the conclusion that Pierre Bungo was the oddest specimen of a white man that they had ever seen."[2]

This idea that a black man was an unusual variety of white man rather than a separate race is revealed most clearly in the Blackfoot language. To them, a Black was *Sixapekwan*—literally "black white man"—likely because the first Blacks appeared singly and in the company of white traders. This caused the Indians to conclude that just as an albino is sometimes found in a buffalo herd, a Black would be found among a group of whites. However, even after they learned the truth, *Sixapekwan* remained the Blackfoot name to describe all Blacks.

The situation of Henry Mills, however, was different from most Blacks who came to the frontier in that he apparently was still in slavery. Records of the Upper Missouri Outfit for 1839-40 show that half the wages of "negro Henry," a total of $621.84, went to his master, Kenneth McKenzie.

After serving at Fort Union for some time, Mills was moved to Fort Benton, downstream from the present city of Great Falls. Upon arriving at the post, he formed a relationship with the Bloods and particularly with a band called the Hairy Shirts. There he met a warrior named High Sun and his sister, whom the whites called Phillisy. Deaf and mute, she had been married to a white man known to the Bloods as *Okotok*, or The Stone; he had left the Upper Missouri country a short time before and had abandoned her. By the time the first winter set in at Fort Benton, Mills had married the young Blood woman and was given the Indian name of *Inowow*, or Observed.

Although there are no records to substantiate the exact date, the union likely took place early in 1854 when Mills was forty-six and his bride was twenty-one. During the first winter, the American Fur Company sent Mills to live with the Bloods, gathering furs for the trading post, trapping muskrats, and taking coyote pups from their dens in the spring. Then, like most other employees with Indian wives, he returned to the fort with his furs and went back to his laboring duties.

In the spring of 1855, on April 13, the first child was born to the couple. He was baptized at the fort seven months later and given the name of David. At this time, Phillisy already was the mother of one girl named Mary, who had been born during her previous marriage to the white trader.

Over the next several years, the life of Henry Mills, his Indian wife, and two children was not unlike that of many mixed marriages on the frontier. Their time was divided between the traders and the Indians; sometimes they lived at the fort and on other occasions they wandered after the buffalo herds with the Bloods, trapping and collecting furs. Because of his knowledge of the language, Mills often acted as interpreter while at other times he was a cook, handyman, and laborer. As a Black, he was considered to be on the lowest level of the fur trade hierarchy and was never permitted to rise above menial labor.

In the Indian camps, Mills was strictly a fur trade employee who was interested only in trapping. His wife's band, the Hairy Shirts, were friendly to whites, and its leader, Rainy Chief, was one of the first of his tribe to welcome missionaries into his camp. Henry Mills profited by these good relations, but he was never too far from the trading posts and found employment with them whenever possible. He made no attempt to adopt an Indian way of life but was simply doing his job. Even at that early period, he was a hard worker who took seriously his duties as a husband and father.

By 1870, the American Fur Company had been dissolved, so Mills settled in the growing town of Fort Benton, where he built a house and found local work as a laborer. In a town census taken that year, Mills had real estate valued at one hundred dollars. The family consisted of Henry, who listed his birthplace as Kentucky, his wife Phillisy, and seventeen-year-old Mary. Neither of the parents could read or write but Mary was attending the local school. Young David was away that summer working on the bull trains.

A short time later, Henry Mills was hired as an interpreter and laborer for the whiskey traders who were invading Alberta. He was employed at the I.G. Baker post on the Highwood River and probably was the unnamed Black working as an interpreter for the same firm in 1873 at the later site of Calgary. A traveler at that time commented that "the interpreter was a Negro. I was told that the Negroes master the Indian language more quickly and easily than the white man."[3]

One day during this period, Mills and his wife and daughter were traveling with a small trading party of Bloods when suddenly they were attacked by Pend d'Oreille Indians. In the heat of battle, one of the enemy swept Mary onto his saddle and triumphantly carried her away. The young, educated school girl was taken across the mountains by the victorious attackers and for several years the family didn't know if she was alive or dead. Not until some years later did Mary return safely to the Blood camps. After the raid, she had become the unwilling bride of her captor and had born him a son. When the opportunity finally arose, she ran away and returned across the mountains to the Blood camps. Her son was given the name of Lone Man and remained with the Bloods for the rest of his life.

After the arrival of the North-West Mounted Police in 1874, Mills returned with other Americans to Montana, where his health rapidly declined. He left Phillisy with her Blood relatives and stayed quietly in Fort Benton until his death in 1878; he was seventy years old. During his forty years in the West he had performed no brave deeds nor shown any great leadership. He simply demonstrated that the frontier was not limited to Indians and whites. As a Black whose opportunities were limited, he had found regular employment, looked after his family, and stayed out of trouble. His association with Indians was incidental; he was with them, but was never a part of them.

But he left a legacy in his son, David, a child of a mixed marriage who proved that race or color was no detriment to an ambitious and intelligent frontiersman. Whereas the father was an ex-slave in a world dominated by discriminatory whites, the son lived comfortably in both the Indian and white societies. Perhaps he was never fully accepted by either, but he got along equally well in both. He learned English from his father, Blackfoot from his mother's family, was baptized by a priest, and was given the Indian name of *A'pikanisstumi'k*, or Scabby Bull. Throughout his life, he shared the inoffensive nature and work ethic of his father but revealed an inner strength that made him admired and respected by those who knew him.

A husky lad, as soon as he was old enough to work he joined I.G. Baker & Company as a bull whacker, driving the slow, plodding teams between Fort Benton and Whoop-Up. In later years, his son told about one of his father's adventures with the bull teams.

"They were on their way to Whoop-Up," he recalled, "when the train was attacked by the Assiniboines. The white men wanted to avoid a fight as they were greatly outnumbered, but the Assiniboines were ready to wipe out the whole wagon train. It was then that my father yelled out to them in Blackfoot not to attack.

"'Who are you?' called out one of the Assiniboines who could speak Blackfoot.

"My father thought quickly. He knew that the Bloods were fierce enemies of the Assiniboines while the Peigans, who also are part of the Blackfoot nation, were friendly with them. So he cried out, "'I'm Scabby Bull of the Peigans.'

"The Assiniboine answered, 'The Peigans are our friends so you white men must be our friends too,' and they let the wagon train go unharmed."[4]

On another occasion Mills was en route to Whoop-Up when the bull whackers stopped for the night in a deserted shack. Inside, they found blood stains on the floor and suspected that someone had been killed there. But, having the luxury of a roof over their heads, they decided to settle down there for a sleep.

During the night, the men were awakened by a great clamor as though someone were throwing stones through the windows and pushing cupboards over. Dave and the other men were frightened, but when morning came, they saw that nothing had been disturbed and no stones could be found inside the shack. Dave always believed that the ghost of the man killed in the cabin had been angry with them for sleeping there.

After the Mounted Police drove out the whiskey traders in 1874, Dave Mills divided his time between his mother's camp and his father's little shack in Fort Benton. He took odd jobs that were available, usually working as an interpreter and scout. During this time he received a severe knife wound in his arm, which left a deep scar that he carried to his grave. He would never tell how he got it.

Indian interpreter Dave Mills with Blood Indian woman and child, early 1900s. *Courtesy Glenbow-Alberta Institute/NA-4035-160*

In 1880, when the first Indian agent was appointed for southern Alberta, Dave was hired as his interpreter. But Mills, then a young man of twenty-five, was criticized for showing too much favoritism to Red Crow, the head chief, and was dismissed. Two years later, when Cecil Denny took over the agent's post, he immediately rehired Mills at a salary of thirty-five dollars a month plus rations. The young man had apparently learned his lesson, for he began a service with the Indian Department that was interrupted only once during the rest of his active life. He no longer displayed any favoritism but proved to be of tremendous value, both to the Indians and to the budget-conscious government.

One of his first services was in helping to detect South Peigan Indians who were under treaty in Montana but tried to pass themselves off as Bloods so they could collect the annual treaty money in both places. Mills was so highly regarded that when treaty money was being paid on the nearby Peigan Reserve in 1885, he was taken along. The Indian agent reported, "Morning Plume tried by every means in his power to get a number of South Piegans paid. As I had Mills with me, who knows nearly all the South Peigans, he did not succeed."[5] Also, Mills's ability to remember and classify the names of individuals and sizes of families played an important part in stopping the Bloods from trying to falsify their numbers to receive greater rations.

Mills's work was so appreciated by the government that the Indian agent recommended a salary increase, saying, "His conduct . . . has been highly satisfactory and through his knowledge of the Bloods he has been mainly the means of saving the Govt. several thousands of dollars. Last year it was almost entirely through his actions that a reduction of one thousand souls was made."[6]

Although he undoubtedly caused anger and embarrassment when he proved that a woman claiming to have six children really had only one, or that an old warrior who swore he was a Blood was really an American Peigan, he usually made no bitter enemies. At the same time that he was helping to pare down the lists, he was also correcting inaccuracies, getting Indians on the rolls who had never registered, and sorting out complex family relationships.

As an interpreter, he experienced some trouble in translating Blackfoot names into English, but he was far better than most men of that period. His work was often complicated by the fact that a warrior might have two or three names or might have received a new name since the last treaty payment. For example, two chiefs who signed Treaty Number Seven in 1877 were White Calf and Father of Many

Children. When the latter died in the 1880s, White Calf took his name. So Mills always had to remember that when the white people talked about Father of Many Children, they were referring to the dead chief, but when Indians used the name, they were referring to the man the whites called White Calf.

There were other instances where the Indian Department employees decided to alter a name. For example, his son recalled: "One day an Indian came in and gave his name. It was *Pooksisi*. Without thinking, my father gave it the correct translation of Small Asshole.

"'What?' said the clerk, jumping up from his desk. So my father repeated it. 'I can't write that down. We would spoil the books with a name like that.'"[7]

After some thought, the clerk entered the name in the books as "Small Backside." A year later, the problem was resolved when the Indian came into the office and announced he had received the new name of Not Good. Without hesitation, the clerk scratched out the old name and entered the new one.

During the 1880s and 1890s, Mills was often the eyes and ears of the reserve. He passed disturbing rumors of unrest to the agent, argued about poor rations, and complained about ranchers' cattle trespassing on the reserve. He explained government regulations to the Indians, allayed fears when trouble occurred, and interpreted for countless delegations coming with complaints. The agent also sent him to check on the accuracy of reports, to

Dave Mills, seen here *(second from right)* with Bloods and Indian agency staff, 1886. *(Left to right)* One Spot, minor chief; Red Crow, head chief; William Pocklington, Indian agent; Interpreter Mills; and clerk, E.R. Cowan. *Courtesy Glenbow-Alberta Institute/NA-769-6*

guide Mounted Police patrols investigating crimes, to interpret in court, or testify as an expert witness.

Sometimes he passed along information whether the agent wanted to hear it or not. For example, in 1891, the agent reported angrily: "Interpreter Mills stated to me that the Indians complained of the cattle being on the Reserve, whites cutting hay and timber under my permit, that they were not properly treated, some were starving, that they wanted me & the rest of us moved, discharged, etc., etc. It is the usual spring bellyache only more so."[8]

Yet as a government employee, Mills was never completely free of the suspicion by the Bloods that he could not be trusted. Certainly, when he was placed in the difficult position of choosing sides, he demonstrated that although he was part Indian, he had no option but to support those who were paying his salary. Also, when he was the bearer of bad news, he found that a few leaders sometimes directed the blame against him personally. As the Indian agent commented, "I have heard them tell him openly, 'You are one of us and ought to know better than to talk like that,' and they seem to forget he is merely interpreter."[9]

In 1895, these hidden hostilities and suspicions burst to the surface when an Indian took exception to Mills's single-mindedness. It all started when the brother of police scout Big Mouth moved to the Blackfoot Reserve. When Mills heard about it, he followed the normal procedure of ordering the reduction of the family's ration ticket by one person. Big Mouth, an aggressive man who had no hesitation in wielding his authority, went to Mills, demanding reinstatement of the ration. When the interpreter refused, the scout threatened him and stomped out of the agency. From there he went directly across the river to the shack of a half-breed ex-scout named Jack Wagner, who had recently been released from jail after serving a term for bootlegging. Wagner, a son-in-law of Red Crow, also had no love for Dave Mills, blaming him for the fact that he was barred from the reserve.

One of Big Mouth's duties was to be on hand when rations were being issued, so he was familiar with all the criticisms and gossip that had been circulating in the previous few weeks. Between the two of them, the scout and Wagner drew up a list of complaints against Mills, charging him with "trafficking in tickets belonging to dead Indians, that he had accepted treaty money or part of it from certain parties, and that he had traded in ration tickets."[10] These were submitted to the Mounted Police and an investigation ensued.

There were six serious charges, any one of which could result in arrest or dismissal. However, four proved to be completely groundless, while two represented irregularities that were no fault of the interpreter. For example, one charge stated that Cross Child had been given a second ticket by Mills and was drawing extra rations for three people. In fact, the ticket belonged to Mills's brother-in-law and Cross Child was simply picking up his rations because they were working at the same hay camp. Another accusation was that Mills had conspired with Bobtail Chief to collect rations for dead Indians. When questioned, Bobtail Chief thought at first it was a bad joke. "He most emphatically denied ever having had anything to do with tickets other than his own," said the agent. "He never drew for anyone either dead or alive. Says he never had anything to do with Mills."[11]

When this ploy failed, Wagner enlisted the help of another scout, Ben Deroche, to testify that Mills had given an extra ration ticket to Medicine Calf. However, when the matter was investigated, no evidence could be found to support the claim. Then, in his final last-ditch effort for revenge, Wagner got his mother-in-law to state that Mills demanded a bribe of two dollars to keep her sister's name on the rolls after she had left for Montana. However, it turned out that the woman was listed at the direction of the Indian agent, and that Mills had nothing to do with it. At that point, the entire investigation against the interpreter collapsed.

In appearance Dave Mills was more Black than Indian (a Blood who knew him well described him as "not very black . . . a very nice man and generous to everyone,")[12] and he sported a heavy moustache that added to his handsome appearance. On formal occasions when he was outfitted in a suit, tie, and wide-brimmed hat, he looked more like a Mississippi gambler than an interpreter. But his everyday dress of woollen coat, kerchief, and cowboy hat fitted in better with the western scene.

During these years, Mills lived like a westerner, with his house just off the reserve near the Lower Agency. A visitor in 1884 described his place as "a low, mud-roofed shack perched upon a convenient knoll" beside the river crossing.[13] Reflecting the attitudes of the day, he said it was occupied by "Nigger Dave, the Indian agency interpreter."[14]

"My father was a powerful man," recalled Harry Mills, "and one of the best runners in the country. He was about five feet ten inches tall and very strong. Although he lived all his life with the Indians he was also quite popular with the whites as well.

"He was very good with horses. I remember the time the Indian

Department bought a team from Captain Winder's ranch and my father was the only one who could handle them. They were the fastest team in the country. Whenever my father left the agency for Fort Macleod, some Indians would try to race him with their ponies but they could never keep up with him."[15]

During the Riel Rebellion of 1885, Mills constantly monitored the activities of the tribe and reassured them that the soldiers who were flooding into the West would not attack them. A reporter spoke to Mills about those weeks of tension.

"When the police at Macleod were reinforced," Mills told him, "they thought that there was to be an outbreak against themselves and that the police intended to make war on them. The Indians didn't want war."[16]

"I asked Mills what effect the rebellion had on these people," said the reporter, "and he replied that . . . when they heard of the execution of the eight Crees at Battleford they were glad, because the victims were Crees and they were glad too that Riel was hanged, for they do not like the Red River half-breeds. They wanted to go and fight the Crees during the rebellion and asked the agent to allow them to help the police."[17]

When it was over, the agent praised Mills for devotion to duty during a time when others were taking refuge in Fort Macleod.

Shortly after settling near the reserve, Mills took as his wife a Blood woman named *Poosa*, The Cat, daughter of Chief Standing in the Middle. They were married in Indian fashion but in 1886, at the insistence of the agent, Father Albert Lacombe came to perform a legal ceremony. The couple had three children, Harry (actually, Henry, after his grandfather), David Junior, and Lily (later Mrs. Mortimer Eagle Tail). A fourth child, George, was born in 1899 but died before the year was out. His father had given him the Blackfoot name of *Na'pikwan*, or White Man, as his own form of humor. Picking up a joke that was common among Blacks in the West, he said he had the right to give the name because he was the first white man in the country.

In 1901, Mills's wife gave birth to twin girls—a rare occurrence among Indians—which became the subject of considerable gossip. Some regarded it as good luck, but others weren't so sure. In the end, the predictors of gloom were right; four months later both girls died and their mother passed away a year later.

In 1906, Mills married Holy Rabbit Woman, daughter of the great chief Medicine Calf. They had only one child who lived; his name was Willie.

As he grew older, Dave Mills suffered increasingly from rheumatism. He resigned from the Indian Department in 1900 due to ill health and was replaced by a young boarding school graduate. However, the more experienced Mills proved to be so valuable that he was persuaded to return a few months later. By 1905, the Indian agent commented: "Our interpreter has grown old in the service and is too much crippled to do, in addition to his own work, the labor heretofore performed. I will do the best I can though I would rather pay out of my salary to have water hauled to my house than force poor old Mills to do it."[18]

In spite of his condition, Mills carried on as interpreter for the next thirteen years. When he became too crippled to work, the government put him on a small pension until his death on April 9, 1918. Interestingly, his son, also Dave Mills, died a month later of complications received while he was a private in the 191st battalion of the Canadian army on his way overseas.

With each succeeding generation, the family had moved from Black to Indian, both racially and in daily life. While the original Henry Mills had been a Black who associated with Indians for trading purposes, his son lived between the two worlds of Indian and white. His children, on the other hand, were legally and culturally Indians; young Dave, before joining the army, had belonged to the Doves and the Brave Dogs societies and had participated actively in reserve life. By his generation, their Black heritage was simply a curiosity and a distant memory.

The Wild Ones

This was no life for a real Indian. Seven years earlier when there had been buffalo, the tribes had been free of the white man's yoke. Now only the ration house stood between them and starvation; only the crumbs from the white man's table kept them alive.

The year was 1887, six years after the Bloods had drifted onto their reserve from the buffaloless plains to the south. Now their leather tepees were tattered and log cabins dotted the camps in the bottomlands of the Belly River. The old days were over, gone with the buffalo whose disappearance had so suddenly taken away their freedom and independence.

O'mukopi'kis, or Big Rib, and *Imitah'*, The Dog, had missed the days of glory, for in 1887 Big Rib had just turned twenty-one, while his companion was twenty-three. But they knew about those thrilling times and were not to be denied their chance for adventure and fame. The boys were cousins from the Many Children Band, one of the most warlike families in the tribe. Big Rib was a son of the chief, Running Wolf, and was married to a daughter of White Bull of the Peigans. In the eyes of the Indians he was a good man but to the Indian agent he was "one of the worst characters on the reserve."[1] This meant that he scorned farming, clung to his Native religion, and displayed the arrogant independence for which his family had become famous.

The Dog, on the other hand, was something of a dandy. A son of Bad Horses, he had gained considerable fame in the camps a year earlier when he courted and won an attractive woman who had been married to a white trader. To accomplish such a deed was almost as good as counting a victory on the warpath, so The Dog was hailed and praised by his comrades. Like his cousin, he was no favorite of the Indian agent, who described him as "the ringleader of all the stealing parties,"[2] and as keeper of the war drums, he helped to encourage the warlike traditions of his tribe.

These budding warriors wanted no part of scratching the earth to grow turnips and potatoes. They scorned those who humbled themselves before the Indian agent, but found it hard to keep their independence in the face of hunger and privation. In 1884 Big Rib had been caught stealing a white man's trousers when he was short of clothing, and the following year his name was linked with a horse theft. But not until the spring of 1887 did he and his cousin decide to really strike out on their own. They would prove that the Bloods were "the cream of creation."[3]

Big Rib *(third from left)* was a leader of the 1887 Blood war party that set out to raid the Gros Ventres in Montana. After his release from jail, he became a Mounted Police scout. This photo, taken in 1894, shows part of the Standoff, Alberta, NWMP detachment. *Courtesy Glenbow-Alberta Institute/NA-288-6*

Many young men were ready for war that spring, all because six Bloods had been killed a few months earlier by Assiniboine Indians from the United States. They had been ambushed while trying to recover stolen horses in Montana in October of 1886, but before the Bloods could get revenge, winter was upon them. By the time spring arrived, the older and wiser chiefs were preparing to make a peace treaty with the offending tribe, so the young men now had to find another enemy. Big Rib and The Dog decided to raid the Gros Ventres; they were age-old foes who shared a Montana reservation with the hated Assiniboines.

Late in April, the pair organized a small war party to make the raid. Led by Big Rib and The Dog, it consisted of Rainy Chief, Real Man's Shirt, Coming Singer, and Small Eyes.[4] Most of them were teenagers on their first expedition. Slipping away from the Many Children camp, the party eluded Mounted Police patrols and were free at last from the confines of their reserve. Traveling cautiously on foot, they carried their trusty Winchester rifles and a few other essentials for the trail. As they crossed the barren plains towards the Cypress Hills, they kept a wary eye peeled for police patrols but all they saw were a few scattered herds of cattle.

When far out on the prairie, they killed a cow that was wandering on the range and spent the next few days feasting and drying the meat. They took only what they could carry and traveled until they came to the upper reaches of Seven Persons Creek. By this time it was raining, but the temperature turned cold and soon the heavy snowfall forced them to stop. The war party found a small grove of trees and built a war lodge—a tepeelike structure made of logs and branches. The blizzard lasted for ten days, and when it was over, the war party had run out of food, except for some tea. They killed another cow, dried more meat, then circled past Badwater Lake, heading southeast towards the Gros Ventre camps in Montana.

They had just crossed the Milk River when one of their keen-eyed scouts noticed the tracks of unshod ponies cutting across their trail in a north-easterly direction. The only Indians heading in that way would be another war party, either Cypress Hills Crees returning from a raid or Gros Ventres heading to steal horses from the Cree camps. Either way, the horsemen were enemies.

At the direction of Big Rib and The Dog, the party swung north and followed the trail, their scout riding ahead and watching for signs of campfires or other evidence that their enemies were close. That evening they found the Indians encamped for the night and succeeded in running off their entire herd of twelve horses. They never did find out if they were Crees or Gros Ventres, but it didn't really matter.

From there the victorious Bloods went to the Bull's Head, a grassy promontory that marked the western edge of the Cypress Hills. This had been a favorite summer camping ground of the Bloods for generations. Two decades earlier, a thousand Indians would have been camped within its shadows and the buffalo so thick that they carpeted the prairie with their mass of bodies. Now there was only a lonesome prairie wolf, a hawk circling the blue skies, and bleached bones that marked the demise of the mighty monarch.

The war party hid all the following day in case the raiders tried to pursue them but when no one came near them, they relaxed. They killed another cow, loaded the meat on their horses, and were on their way to a distant coulee when someone pointed out to Small Eyes that he had lost his meat. He went back and was just repacking it on his horse when he was suddenly attacked by a Cree war party. These men were well armed and were not the same ones the Bloods had unseated. Small Eyes dropped his meat and opened fire on the closest attacker. When the others pulled back, he jumped on his horse and dashed away to warn his friends. They took shelter in a grove of trees where they were quickly surrounded by their enemies. Desperately, they dug shallow foxholes to protect themselves from the rapid gunfire. One of the Bloods was grazed by a bullet but their protective position kept the Crees at bay.

The war party lay surrounded all day, and during the night the Crees lit fires to prevent them from escaping. The Dog, leader of the war party, sent a scout to search for an escape route. Meanwhile, each of the men prayed to his spirit protector and made vows. One promised to join a secret society; another said he would dance with the Horn Society staff; and Small Eyes vowed to go through the self-torture ritual at the Sun Dance if they successfully escaped.

A short time later, the scout reported that he had discovered a narrow coulee leading down to a nearby creek. Quietly, the Bloods slithered down the path and when they reached the valley, they walked all night; as soon as the first streaks of light began to color the eastern sky, they went into hiding. They had made their escape, but they were again without horses.

Traveling east, the Bloods entered the Cypress Hills; Big Rib and The Dog had decided they should raid one of the Cree camps rather than make the long trip south to the Gros Ventres. However, after prowling through the eastern slopes of the hills, the Bloods learned that they had come too late. Other war parties had been there before them. Now the Crees were so cautious that their herds were driven into makeshift corrals for the night and were heavily guarded during the day. A raid under such conditions would not be brave; it would be stupid.

Not wishing to suffer the indignity of returning home empty-handed, Big Rib and The Dog announced that they would check out the local ranchers. This immediately led to an argument with Real Man's Shirt, who insisted that they stay away from white settlements. He knew that Indians could show up with a herd of stolen Indian ponies and hardly a word was said, yet if even one branded horse of a white man was brought to the reserve, the whole country would be in an uproar. But Big Rib and The Dog were adamant; they would raid a ranch. Reluctantly, the other Indians followed as the two leaders traveled northward out of the hills until they reached the main line of the Canadian Pacific Railway. There they turned west, following the railway line until they came to the siding of Irvine. A short distance away, they scouted a small ranch owned by Abram Adsit and noted with satisfaction some good saddle horses in the corral. Unlike the Crees, the rancher seemed to have taken no precautions against a Blackfoot attack. Why should he? Everyone knew that Indians raided only Indians.

That night, April 27, 1887, Big Rib, The Dog, and the others quietly crept to the edge of the corral. The Indians were ready to swing the gate open and ride off with their booty but to their surprise the horses were gone; the corral was empty. Puzzled, they checked the outbuildings and finally discovered that the stock had been put in the barn. The door had no lock so it had been tied shut. Muttering under his breath at the delay, Big Rib pulled out his double-bladed knife and began to saw at the cords, hoping that the slight creaking noise would not be enough to wake the dogs.

It wasn't, but the owner's son was a light sleeper and the strange noise outside disturbed him. Clad only in his nightshirt, he picked up his rifle and opened the cabin door just as the Indian had finished cutting the rope. The rancher yelled aloud and fired wildly into the night as the raiders dashed for cover. One of the bullets went through Small Eyes's coat, but he was not wounded. A short time later, The Dog returned, angrily firing two shots at the ranchhouse and threatening to kill the occupants.

Real Man's Shirt had had enough. He refused to pursue the madness of the leaders so the war party split, Man's Shirt taking one of the young Bloods back home while the others continued their raid. The two leaders were determined to prove to everyone, including themselves, that they were fit to be warriors just like their fathers and uncles before them.

When it was reported to the North-West Mounted Police that unknown Indians had fired on a rancher, the telegraph lines were soon humming between headquarters in Regina and the political offices in Ottawa. At dawn, a patrol under Corporal Birtle set out from Maple Creek to search for the miscreants, fanning out from the ranch and following the trail into the hills. From a bushy knoll, the

Bloods saw the patrol approaching. Had they stayed hidden, the police would have passed them by. But these men were warriors so they boldly showed themselves and defiantly fired several shots in the direction of the patrol. The corporal, not knowing the size of the war party, wisely retreated to his detachment. From there he sent out a general alarm: Indians were on the warpath!

The following day, a heavily armed patrol of fifteen men under Inspector Mills left Maple Creek to search for the Bloods. Another force under Inspector Moodie set out from Medicine Hat, and Sergeant Major Lake with twenty-five men formed a flying patrol from Lethbridge to head off the Indians in case they were withdrawing back to their reserve.

But retreat was not part of the warriors' plans. Neither knowing nor caring about the sensation they were creating, the warriors realized only that they still were empty-handed. After Birtle's patrol had fled, the Indians hid in the neighborhood until nightfall, then followed a dry coulee westward. From there, they traveled towards the railway town of Medicine Hat, and when they reached Seven Persons Coulee, they saw three Cree tents with five horses grazing nearby.

Because it was a cloudless night, the moon cast an eerie light over the prairie and there was no place to hide once the Bloods began moving in on the enemy camp. They waited until they were sure that the Crees had settled down, then the warriors crept forward and picked their horses. During the raid, one of the men became frightened and was almost left behind, but a friend went back for him and soon the war party was riding south, into a protective coulee between two ridges. There they stayed for the next two days.

But Big Rib and The Dog still weren't satisfied. They set out again, coming closer to Medicine Hat and were almost on the outskirts of the town before they found what they were looking for: two horses in the unguarded corral of rancher Robert Watson. Silently and efficiently they led the animals away from the buildings and then, satisfied and jubilant, they set out for home. However, they had traveled only a short distance along the trail when they unexpectedly met a man on foot. Recognizing him as a Cree Indian, they fired several shots at him before galloping away with their captured horses. The Cree, frightened but unhurt, carried the electrifying news to the townspeople of Medicine Hat that a raid had taken place almost in their back yards.

Elated, the Bloods rode back to their reserve. Wise to the old war trails, they easily eluded the police patrols and entered the Many Children camp with their faces painted black as a sign of victory and singing their war songs. The stolen horses, decorated with feathers, were paraded through the camp to prove that the old days were not dead.

Some of the older Bloods did not appreciate the efforts of the raiders in attacking white man's ranches. They still remembered how their relatives, the Peigans, had been massacred in Montana when a white rancher was killed several years earlier. Maybe it was different in Canada with the Mounted Police, but maybe it wasn't. Quietly, word of the triumphant return was passed along to the redcoats and a patrol was sent out from Fort Macleod to arrest the raiders. They were interested only in Big Rib and The Dog, the two ringleaders. However, as soon as the police appeared, the wanted men were nowhere to be found.

Realizing that they had little hope of catching the warriors when they were being watched by almost every young man in the camp, Inspector Gilbert Sanders withdrew his patrol to the nearby Standoff detachment for the night. Then, long after sunset, he was guided through the darkness by a half-breed scout until he and his men came to the camp of the Many Children Band. There, at three o'clock on the morning of May 13, they swooped down on the sleeping raiders and had Big Rib and The Dog in handcuffs before anyone was fully awake.

Excitement and anger swept through the camp, with one old warrior even going so far as to urge the younger men to attack the redcoats. But the police held their ground and by sunrise the two raiders were in the Fort Macleod guardhouse.

Four days later, when they were brought before Magistrate James F. Macleod, the two Indians were charged only with horse stealing; no mention was made of their potshots at the police and citizens. The news of the single charge was greeted with some relief by the prisoners, for in the past judges had recognized that horse stealing was an integral part of Indian life and usually imposed a nominal sentence of two months in the guardhouse. Confidently, the two Bloods pleaded guilty but were shocked when each was sentenced to five years in Stony Mountain Penitentiary. Although the shooting charges had not been laid because of a lack of evidence, the Bloods immediately realized that these were the crimes for which they were being punished. To steal Indian cayuses was one thing but to shoot at the police and take the white man's horses was an entirely different matter.

The news grieved and distressed the Indians who had gathered for the trial. A long term in penitentiary in the far-off province of Manitoba was like a death sentence, for many Indians could not survive the cold dank cells and died there of tuberculosis. As the prisoners were led from the courtroom, women wailed and tried to grasp the men's arms, hoping to restrain them. One old woman even tried to stab them so they would not suffer in prison. Amid all the cries of anguish and mourning, Big Rib and The Dog remained stoic to the end, singing their war songs as they were led away.

Next morning, Sheriff Duncan Campbell and two police officers collected the prisoners and escorted them to the nearest railway point at Lethbridge, thirty-five miles away. Upon arrival, they learned that the local train wasn't running so they continued their journey another 110 miles (177 km) to Dunmore, just a few miles from where the original raid had taken place. There, at Dunmore station, the sheriff's bad luck continued, for regular service on the main line of the Canadian Pacific had been canceled and the next train was not due until the following day.

By this time, all fight seemed to have gone out of the prisoners. As they were escorted to the nearby Ford Hotel and chained together in the second floor corridor, they told Campbell they accepted their fate and knew they would die in jail. This should have warned the sheriff that he was dealing with two desperate men who felt they had nothing to lose; instead, he was relieved to find them docile and subdued. When he went to bed, he left them chained in the corridor with police downstairs guarding the only exit.

That night, about one o'clock, a terrific crash shattered the stillness of the warm spring night. Rushing to the corridor, Campbell discovered that the Bloods had jumped through the glass window from the second story and he could hear the clinking of their shackles as they dashed to freedom through the darkness. Running as a team, and holding the chains loosely between them, Big Rib and The Dog did not waste any time to rest or congratulate themselves for a successful escape. By the time red streaks of sunlight began to paint the eastern sky, they had reached the rolling hills far from the law's searching eyes.

Shortly after sunrise, they found a small ranch and, muffling their chains, they crawled through the prairie grass until they reached some outbuildings. There they slipped into the first shack and, as luck would have it, they found a rusty old file. Gleefully, they grasped this key to freedom and disappeared back into the hills. A few hours later, after some hard labor, the shackles were removed and the last vestige of captivity was cast aside.

Within two or three days, the men were back in their home camps where they were greeted as heroes. To the younger Bloods they were great warriors who had made fools of the white man and his laws. Maybe the buffalo were gone, maybe the Bloods were forced to eat white man's food, but they still were men and not cattle to be put into iron corrals. Even the old men were glad to see the boys back home; they may not have agreed with their wild ways, but they did not want to see them die in jail.

For the next few weeks Big Rib and The Dog wandered freely through the Many Children village, for the Mounted Police usually stayed away from the troublesome band unless they were on routine patrols. Not until July 20—over two months later—did Inspector Sanders learn that the wanted men were in the camp. He thought they had fled to the safety of Montana. A patrol was sent to search The Dog's lodge but the warrior was gone. Three weeks later another patrol was told where to find the fugitive, but again he was tipped off by his friends and slipped out of sight. It seemed as though the men were taunting the police, as probably they were.

Not until September 11, almost four months after the escape, did the police sight one of the men. The officers were told that Big Rib was in the bushes near his house drinking beer with some of his buddies. Sergeant Williams and two constables were sent to the spot, and this time they succeeded in grabbing the wanted Indian before he could dash away. Just as the sergeant started to fasten the handcuffs, a number of Bloods, led by minor chief Eagle Ribs, were upon him. In the melee, Constable Gilmore fired a shot that killed an Indian horse, and in the wild confusion, Big Rib disappeared. A few days later, Eagle Ribs was given three months for obstructing the police, while Calf Tail and Lizard Hips were let off with a warning. Constable Gilmore, who appeared before a police enquiry, was fined forty dollars for shooting the horse, the money going to its owner, Yellow Horn.

With those exciting events, 1887 passed into history. The two Bloods continued to enjoy their freedom, and although the police received reports from time to time, there was never enough information to warrant a search. By now, Big Rib and The Dog were considered to be the leaders of the young men, and although some of the elders may have preferred more docile heroes, they were powerless to interfere. As the months passed, the possibility of recapture seemed more and more remote. Then, one day in September of 1888, in sheer bravado, The Dog decided to visit the Mounted Police in their own town of Fort Macleod.

The wanted man and four other Bloods rode into the village unnoticed, made a few purchases in a local store, and almost succeeded in their audacious enterprise. Then, just as they were riding away, The Dog was recognized by an alert police officer who tried to make an arrest. The other Bloods quickly came to their comrade's assistance, and as the officer drew his revolver, he was pulled to the ground. Just then, another officer arrived and shot twice at the fugitive as he prepared to flee. The first bullet, fired at close quarters, would have hit the warrior but his horse plunged at that instant and took the shot instead. The second veered off wildly as The Dog and his wounded steed raced for the safety of the Blood Reserve.

This was the final insult. Within a few days the Mounted Police had placed a fifty-dollar reward on each man's head. It was a lot of money for the destitute Bloods but there were no takers. Instead, Big Rib and The Dog continued to move openly within their camps, joining the religious gatherings and attending rituals of their warrior and age-grade societies. As the months passed, the freedom of the two men seemed to symbolize the independent spirit of the tribe.

Two years later, at the beginning of 1890, the men were still at large. During the intervening months, the Indian agent had received several unconfirmed rumors about them. One was that they had gone to Montana where, with some admiring comrades, they had built a cabin by St. Mary's Lakes, not far from the Canadian border. There, according to the agent, "they had lots of cartridges and if the police wanted them, to go and take them, as they were ready for them."[5] These were brave words from a pair of fugitives who, according to another rumor, had stood off a patrol of United States Indian police who had tried to arrest them.

But the days of glory and freedom for Big Rib and The Dog were almost at an end. No police officer had been able to catch them and no scout had been able to trap them. Yet their presence was becoming a painful reminder of the past. Their chiefs had grown weary of the police patrols and the accusations that the Bloods couldn't be trusted. So in the end, the pride of the tribe was at stake.

Red Crow, the head chief, considered Big Rib to be like a grandson, so he wanted to resolve the problem in the fairest way possible. Since the original conviction, both men had been guilty of a number of crimes, including escape from custody and resisting arrest. If the judge threw the book at them, they would either die in jail or be old men when they got out. However, Red Crow spoke to the authorities in Fort Macleod and received their assurances that if the two men surrendered no further charges would be laid. Besides, conditions had improved at Stony Mountain and more and more Indians were surviving their confinement.

Red Crow met with Running Wolf, leader of the Many Children, who agreed that his son and his cousin must give themselves up to the police. Red Crow himself escorted The Dog into the barracks and two days later Big Rib was sent in by his father. True to their promise, the police reimposed the original sentences without further charges, and the two men were admitted to the penitentiary late in March of 1890.

The sentences proved to be much shorter than anyone expected. Both men were model prisoners and had served only fourteen months when they were released with time off for good behavior. When they returned, a reporter noted that they wore "fashionable clothes and white shirts with high collars and cuffs, talk English fluently and possess other equally useful attributes of civilization acquired at Stony Mountain."[6] They said they had enjoyed themselves, had plenty to eat, and were well treated.

After they parted and went to their separate homes, the two cousins never again worked as a team. They had fought for and won the right to be warriors. They had flaunted the white man's laws, taken his horses, and successfully eluded capture for many months. As a pair they had been the wild ones on the reserve, and although others tried to imitate them, none ever succeeded.

They were no longer reckless youngsters when they returned from prison; Big Rib was twenty-four and The Dog twenty-seven. As the elder of the two, The Dog was interested only in settling down. Using his newly gained knowledge of English, he applied for a job as scout for the North-West Mounted Police. When he was accepted, he was posted to the St. Mary's detachment at the east side of the reserve. From there he went on patrols, interpreted, and did general duties. His tepee was pitched nearby and his wife helped by doing washing for the men.

But it didn't last. In September of 1893, a drunken constable tried to molest The Dog's wife and all the Indian's warlike fury returned with a vengeance. Angrily he drew his knife and when the fracas was over, the officer lay wounded and bleeding on the floor.

When he appeared in court, The Dog testified that he had acted to defend his wife. He claimed he was on his way to the detachment with her when he saw the police officer looking out the window. "I told my woman to go home, they were drunk," he said. "I saw Currie running after us and [he] caught the two of us. He caught my woman on the chest by the blanket and brought us back to the Detachment."[7] Then followed an argument in which the officer struck both the scout and his wife. At that point, The Dog pulled his knife and stabbed the drunken man, first in the arm and then in the head.

The Dog protested his innocence, but the police said the attack had been unprovoked. In the end, the word of an ex-con did not carry much weight with the courts. He was found guilty of assault causing grievous bodily harm, sentenced to two years in Stony Mountain, and this time he stayed there for the full term. When he was released, he was suffering the ravages of tuberculosis and died the following spring.

Meanwhile, Big Rib continued his wild ways on the wrong side of the law. He hung around with a hard-drinking bunch that always seemed to be getting into fights and trouble. In May of 1893 he was accused of raping a girl named Takes a Gun Woman during a drinking party, but was found not guilty for lack of evidence. He was also involved in a number of "women scrapes," and of the trouble-makers on the reserve, Indian agent Wilson considered him to be "the worst among the whole lot."[8]

During this time, inadequate rations continued to be a vexing problem for the Bloods. Among the old people, actual starvation was a reality, while few people ever had a decent meal. The chiefs complained, the missionaries wrote letters, Mounted Police officers prepared reports, and local citizens expressed their concern, but nothing was done to improve the situation.

Some of the young men turned to Big Rib for leadership. Flattered by the attention and always ready to flout the law, he joined with Black Rabbit—a man who had once stood off the police with a gun—to systematically kill and butcher the cattle of nearby ranchers. No one knows whether they did it for excitement, glory, or the benefit of the tribe, but they were eminently successful.

Young boys were shown how to go out late in the day to scout the neighborhood southwest of the reserve and to find stray cattle. These usually belonged to one of the larger ranches, such as the Cochrane, and roamed at will. At night, a team of Bloods, sometimes under the leadership of Big Rib or Black Rabbit, would kill the chosen animal, butcher it, and carry the meat back to the reserve. They were so audacious that some of the killings took place within a mile of the Big Bend police detachment. By 1894, Superintendent

Sam Steele estimated the Bloods were killing 350 cattle a year in this fashion.

The Mounted Police and their scouts could never apprehend the cattle killers, but then the young men started fighting among themselves and growing jealous of each other's success. It was only a matter of time until someone in their anger went to the police and informed on the whole lot. Based on the information, the Mounted Police descended on the Blood camps in August of 1894 and arrested eighteen Indians, with Big Rib among them.

It seemed as though the Indian's checkered life was at last tumbling down in ruins. The evidence was strong and it looked as if the ex-convict would soon be following the lonely trail back to Stony Mountain. But Big Rib had learned about law and justice the hard way, so he and Black Rabbit turned Queen's evidence, told the full story to the police, and were released.

Indian agent Wilson was incensed. "It is a strange thing," he fumed, "that two of the worst men among the whole lot who had anything to do with this cattle killing are allowed free. I am told they are Queen's evidence men but from their past records and from what appears on the face of the committal papers, there is little doubt in my mind that the two principal ring leaders are to be allowed to go free, while a number of young men and lads are likely to be punished for offences into which they have been in a great measure drawn by these two men."[9]

At the trial, Big Rib and Black Rabbit gave evidence that sent six of their fellow Bloods to jail for two years, two for six months, and two for a month, the rest receiving suspended sentences.[10] Not surprisingly, Big Rib was roundly condemned for his actions, but those who knew him weren't surprised. He didn't care what anyone thought, Indian or white. He simply did what he wanted.

Two years later, Big Rib joined the Mounted Police as a scout, demanding and receiving their highest possible salary, twenty dollars a month. From then until the end of the century, his wildness was channeled into arresting law breakers, practicing Native religion, and providing a spirited opposition to the dictates of the Indian agent.

Like many other Bloods, he detested Agent James Wilson. Most other agents were bureaucratic, but at least they seemed to have had the interests of the people at heart. Within the limits of budgets and legal restraints, they tried to make life bearable for the tribe. Wilson, on the other hand, was single-minded about his desire to suppress the Sun Dance and other religious practices. He defended and helped maintain the status quo in the inadequate rationing system, and he seldom questioned the dictates from headquarters, even when he knew they were foolish.

Big Rib soon discovered that the Mounted Police had no more love for the officious Indian agent than had the Bloods. So the wily scout learned to pit one against the other, with the hope that the Indians might be the winners for a change.

During the 1890s, Big Rib's father, Running Wolf, was one of the leading figures in the religious life of the reserve. He was active in the Sun Dance, owned and transferred medicine bundles, and belonged to several secret societies. To him, religion was essential to the tribe and it was a feeling shared by his son.

In 1898, a number of Bloods decided to rebel against the agent's efforts to suppress Native rituals. Wilson had already squelched the Sun Dance for three years, offering the Indians a sports day as a substitute. When Running Wolf announced that he intended to put on a medicine pipe dance, his son joined with him in defiance of the Indian Department. For four days the Many Children camp was alive and excited as the rituals took place and feasts were held, despite the meager rations. Horses, blankets, and other gifts were presented during the religious event.

When Agent Wilson heard about it, he laid charges against Running Wolf, Big Rib, and the wife of White Man, another Mounted Police scout, citing the Indian Act provision that prohibited giveaway dances. The Mounted Police, however, saw the dance as a religious event, so Inspector Davidson simply told the accused not to break the law, and released them.

Heartened by their success, Big Rib and his father decided to tackle the Sun Dance. Together with Red Crow, they visited Superintendent R.B. Deane in Fort Macleod and asked the Mounted Police for permission to resume holding the summer religious festival. The officer told them there was nothing illegal about gathering for religious purposes as long as they refrained from giving away gifts at the time.

Excitedly, the chiefs spread the word that they should assemble in a large camp so that some of the societies could perform their rituals. It was too late for a Sun Dance, as no tongues had been prepared for the sacrament, but at least they would have a gathering. Agent Wilson was furious about police interference and particularly complained about Big Rib. "I hear he is telling that he has been promised a Sun Dance," he chided Deane, "and have no doubt he will try to get one up. He is a Police Scout and ought to be the last to break the law."[11]

A year later, another gathering was held but there was still no formal Sun Dance. Finally, in 1900, Red Crow, Running Wolf, and the other leaders decided they had had enough of Agent Wilson. Red Crow announced plans for a full Sun Dance, with the wife of Eagle Child taking the role of holy woman. With Big Rib's help, tongues were taken as rations by the Mounted Police scouts and turned over to her for the ritual. Agent Wilson had always prevented this sacrament from being performed by cutting any tongues in half before they were issued as rations; he knew that only whole tongues could be used in the ceremony.

When summer came, Big Rib and the other scouts scoured the reserve, rousting people out of bed and bringing them in from the fields to go to the ceremony. By the time the Sun Dance started, the Bloods had their biggest camp in years and the power of the agent was broken.

Big Rib resigned from the Mounted Police the same year. By this time he had become so involved with the Sun Dance that he decided to devote his entire attention to religious life. When he died in 1907, he was recognized as a religious leader who had won the admiration and grudging respect of everyone around him.

During their first years on the reserve, the Bloods had been starved, suppressed, humiliated, and repressed, but their pride could not be destroyed. People like Big Rib and The Dog wouldn't let it happen.

The Last War Party

A chinook breeze, carrying promises of warmer weather to come, drifted over the Blood camps; most of the snow was gone from the prairie, with only a few patches still clinging to the south side of the low hills. In the coulees, dirty mud-sprinkled snow was inches deep under the twisted limbs of the gnarled cottonwoods and in among the thick willow bushes. The streams, which had shrugged loose their winter ice coats weeks before, were choked with muddy water from countless rivulets.

The Blood camps were near chaos in the spring, for it was 1889, just eight years since the last buffalo had been killed en masse by this Blackfoot-speaking tribe. A few tepees fashioned from the hides of the shaggy beasts were still in evidence, but these were becoming worse for wear and now were pitched indiscriminately with the rude log dwellings and canvas lodges. The discards of the winter were strewn carelessly among the camps by a people not yet used to staying in one place for many months. A stench from the semi-decayed wastes clung pungently in the prairie air, mixing with the smoke from fireplaces and campfires. Small patches of farm land along the bottoms of the Belly River revealed the new occupation of many Bloods who, less than two decades earlier, had been feared and respected from the Saskatchewan River to the Yellowstone.

The tribe was officially at peace with its enemies, for the elder chiefs had met and smoked the pipe under the watchful eyes of their Indian agents. But while the old people had set aside their weapons and picked up the tools of peace, the young men still dreamed of glory. The thrilling tales of raids and of heroic expeditions into enemy country inflamed the minds of those who were not ready to cast aside the rifle for a hoe. It had always been so. When the Long Knives[1] had arrived south of the Medicine Line,[2] the young ones resented it, but the old ones wanted peace. When the whiskey traders had built forts in their hunting grounds, the young ones got drunk and then wanted to wipe them out. And now, when the days of the buffalo were past, the young ones wanted war and the old ones wanted peace.

"No more war," said an elderly chief. But the young men scoffed and replied, "Our old ones talk like women. Their wits have grown dull from the handouts of beef; their spirits have been broken by the missionaries and their black books." The bad talk always started in the spring, as though it had been lying dormant while the snow swirled around the camps, and came to life with the green buds. Red Crow, head chief of the tribe, had made his wishes plain: "No more war." The Black Catchers, a police force that had existed among the Bloods long before the whites had come, patrolled the camps at night to enforce their leader's ruling.

April 18 was just another day in the Month of New Leaves. The wind carried the lonesome wail of a coyote through the evening stillness where it mingled with the night prayer song from one of the lodges. In the darkness, six shadowy figures slipped out of the camp one by one, eluding the four Black Catchers who, with their faces painted black and decorated with yellow zigzagging streaks of paint below their eyes and mouths, kept up their constant but unsuccessful vigil. Later, the figures met near a lone pine tree beside the St. Mary's River where each new arrival was greeted quietly by his comrades.

The leader of the war party was Prairie Chicken Old Man, a veteran of the warpath. The spring raid had been his idea; it had taken weeks of planning and days of discussions before he had selected his partners from the eager fledglings and older veterans in the tribe. Most important among his recruits was Calf Robe, a seasoned warrior who could speak four languages; he was from the leader's own band, the Fish Eaters. The others were younger, but showed the ability to be good warriors. Two from the Fish Eaters Band were Young Pine and Crazy Crow; from the Buffalo Followers Band was Wolf Sitting, and completing the complement was a South Peigan Indian from Montana named Hind Gun.[3]

The men tingled with excitement at the thought of what lay before them. The Crows! In their fathers' time and their fathers' fathers' time, the Crows had been their bitterest enemy. Every summer at the Sun Dance, old warriors told of their thrilling raids, and always the Crows were the most dangerous foe. The mountain tribes were poor, the Crees were off in the bush, but the Crow were rich in horses. Their hunting grounds lay about four hundred miles

(644 km) south of the Blood Reserve, across a land that was dotted with the white man's towns, forts, and ranches.

Before leaving their rendezvous, each warrior checked his simple equipment: a rifle, cartridges, rawhide lariat, extra moccasins, knife, firebag, and a small quantity of dried meat. Then, with only two horses among them, they headed boldly across the prairie, using a keen instinct to guide them on their southerly course. Within an hour they had reached a faint, almost indiscernible trail, and by the time the sun had climbed beyond the horizon, the Bloods were well away from their reserve and within sight of the Sweetgrass Hills.

The mind of each warrior was clear, his step was firm, and his eyes were cautious. Although an isolated war party, this one was destined to write the last chapter of a turbulent and bloody era that had kept bitterness and hatred alive for generations. Theirs was to be the last major war party to raid across the Canadian-American boundary on the windswept prairies.

In spite of careful planning, the war party had not been a well-kept secret. Meetings had been held in Young Pine's tepee, and there were times when the place was overflowing with youngsters anxious to go to war. When plans were nearing their final stage, it appeared as though the leaders were willing to take anyone who was inter-

Young Pine was a member of the last major war party to raid across the Canadian–American boundary. This photo, taken in later life, shows him wearing the uniform of a minor chief. *Courtesy Glenbow-Alberta Institute/Atterton Collection*

ested. This was unusual, as a good leader liked to choose a war party with a good mixture of youthful enthusiasm, bravery, scouting ability, and experience. But in this instance, no one seemed to be excluded when Young Pine gathered the recruits together.

"All of you fellows who want to go on this war party had better get ready," he said. "Tomorrow at noon we will have another meeting to complete our plans, and we will start on our war party tomorrow night."[4]

As the young Bloods excitedly slipped away from the lodge, one of the leaders touched Hind Gun and a select few and asked them to stay. When the others had left, Prairie Chicken Old Man told them that they were leaving immediately. He had not informed the others in case a disappointed candidate rushed off to tell the Mounted Police or Red Crow.

Their ruse was successful; no one knew until the following day that they had left. At first, no one was worried about the missing Bloods. Even the Indian agent, William Pocklington, felt it was necessary only to curtail the rations of beef and flour usually given to the absent ones. "I had heard this particular party was gone," Agent Pocklington wrote in his report, "that it was their intention to hunt down by the St. Mary's Lakes where there was plenty of whiskey to be bought. Another report was that they had gone to the Crow Reserve, but I did not credit it, as our Indians have not been that far for a long time."[5]

Agent Pocklington was one of the many interesting types of men found on the Canadian frontier. He was of the British "old school," having been a close friend of the Prince of Wales during Pocklington's days as a military officer and cricketer. Coming west with the North-West Mounted Police in 1874, he had joined the Indian Department in 1881 and since that time had fought an uphill battle to keep his wild wards off the warpath.

Pocklington had been given a handful of trouble when he took over the Blood Reserve in 1884. During the Riel Rebellion in the following year, he had camped among his non-too-civilized wards and intercepted couriers bringing tobacco and peace offerings from the warring Crees and half-breeds on the Saskatchewan. After the rebellion was successfully quelled, Pocklington had hoped the Bloods would see the futility of intertribal warfare and would settle down to a peaceful life as farmers. His hopes were being realized and the people cooperating quietly until September of 1886, when a bombshell was tossed into the laps of his agrarian-minded Indians.

It all started when ten horses were stolen from a Blood named White Elk. Suspecting the Gros Ventres, the Indian stalked over to the agent's house and demanded that he be allowed to lead a retaliation party against them. Pocklington, after a long and tiring argument, agreed to let six young men travel to Fort Assiniboine, in Montana Territory, to recover the horses through the military authorities. Later that week, five Bloods—Dog Running Back, Hog Shirt, Spy Glasses, Small Gut, and a son of Tall Eagle—were joined by Bull Elk's son from the Blackfoot, and rode south towards Montana. A few weeks later their scalped and mutilated bodies were found in a hastily dug trench near the Sweetgrass Hills. Indications were that the Bloods had put up a terrific battle before they had been wiped out.

At first, the Bloods were incredulous. Ru-

William B. Pocklington, shown here in the 1880s, came west in 1874 and joined the Indian Department in 1881. He became the Indian agent on the Blood Reserve in 1884, one year before the Riel Rebellion. *Courtesy Glenbow-Alberta Institute/NA-659-67*

mors were spread that white ranchers were responsible; others said that the American cavalry had caught them killing cattle. But when word came in that Gros Ventres had done the killing and had put on a scalp dance within sight of American soldiers at Fort Assiniboine, the Bloods had no doubts as to who had been the mysterious attackers. At that point, an early snowstorm stopped plans by war chiefs Calf Shirt and White Calf for a full-scale retaliation, but as the winter set in, everyone knew the fight had been delayed, not canceled.

Red Crow, the head chief, tried to reason with his people, but could provide no good reason for holding back the angry warriors. "The younger Indians have decided among themselves to start for the Gros Ventre reserve as soon as the snow goes off the ground, and revenge the deaths of their comrades," observed the agent. "I am informed the party will muster about four hundred strong."[6]

Officials of the Indian Department in Ottawa began to squirm uncomfortably as spring approached, even though Red Crow's impassioned speeches for peace were having a slow but positive effect. Then, in the early spring of 1887, just when Red Crow's influence was beginning to show, four young Assiniboines swooped down on the Bloods and ran off with eighty horses, most of them belonging to the head chief. The Bloods pursued the raiders towards the American reservation that the Assiniboines shared with the Gros Ventres, but when they returned empty-handed, the agent feared that any hope of settlement would be hopeless. At this point, Red Crow showed he was a true diplomat whose interest in his tribe overshadowed his personal losses.

"The only way to settle this trouble between the Bloods and Gros Ventres," he told the agent, "is to go over and make peace with them. This is the only thing that will stop the young men from going to war."[7]

Officials eagerly grasped at the chance for a peaceful settlement of an international situation and arranged for a treaty party to meet with the American Indians to finalize a pact. Although only about half the Bloods were in favor of the treaty ("The other half," said Red Crow, "say they do not care about a treaty until they have killed some Gros Ventres"),[8] all agreed to recognize any truce arranged by their chief.

The treaty negotiation held June 9, 1887, at Fort Belknap, Montana, was a turbulent affair, with the Bloods and Gros Ventres in favor of signing and the Assiniboines against.

"I want to know what the Bloods mean by peace," snarled the Assiniboine leader, Little Chief. "I thought they had it long ago, but the Bloods have been bothering us all along. Now they have no more horses to lose."[9]

Another Assiniboine, The Male, complained that a treaty had been made twelve years earlier. "Where were the Blood chiefs in the sky and on earth that they did not make that treaty lasting?" he asked angrily.[10]

Lame Bull, head chief of the Gros Ventres, cooled the hot spirits of his Assiniboine allies and asked them to let bygones be bygones. "Now I can sleep well," he told the crowd of Indians. "My horses are safe. Should I travel on the prairie, I need not take a rifle. What I say is true."[11]

Red Crow, who led the peace party of Bloods, made a simple speech to the gathering of enemies and former enemies. "I have come over to see you and make a treaty," he began. "I feel good now. I have made a treaty and smoked the pipe at last. Now the Indians must stop fighting with one another. I will not say we do not steal horses; all Indians steal horses and the whites are just as bad. I mean what I say."[12]

As each leader rose and spoke, the strained feelings between the three nations relaxed. Red Crow asked for, and received, the horses stolen from him. In return, he secured the release from jail of the four Indians responsible for the raid. When the Bloods returned north, the prairies again were at peace.

During the next two years, the quiet routine of daily life was interrupted only once when Star Child, a wild young Blood who had been living with the Crows, picked up four Gros Ventre horses on a return trip to his home reserve. As soon as Red Crow learned of the incident, he seized the horses and turned them over to the authorities. Later, when it was shown that Star Child had known nothing about the treaty, he was released.

Through 1887 and 1888, a few small horse raids were made on Cree camps in the Cypress Hills and on a few white ranchers, but generally all was quiet. Perhaps that is why nobody was too worried when Prairie Chicken Old Man and his party disappeared. The leader was an ambitious soul who often talked of organizing war parties, but he was also fond of the rotgut whiskey available from the unscrupulous bootleggers across the line. Officials preferred to believe the latter reason for his absence. A Mounted Police scout reported that the bunch had gone on a horse raid but his statement was filed and ignored.

As the days passed, Prairie Chicken Old Man and his war party slowly made their way southward. They killed a rancher's steer whenever they needed food and carefully avoided white settlements. Stopping at Writing-on-Stone, they marveled at the cryptic symbols carved into the rocks by unknown hands and looked for signs that might foretell the success of their venture. This was a place where a warrior could receive supernatural power from the same spirits who guarded the magic writings. Here, too, was a Mounted Police detachment that had to be avoided as the party crossed the invisible line into Montana Territory.

A couple of days later, after an unsuccessful attempt to pick up some horses from a rancher's corral, the Bloods crossed the Missouri River and continued towards their original prey, the Crows. Each day they went out in small separate forays into the area, their senses alert and their eyes peeled for horses, wild game, and enemies. By a tiny creek they found a cabin, and after making sure that the owner was away, they broke in and replenished their supplies of ammunition, clothing, tobacco, and food. Rolling their booty in part of a canvas tent, they triumphantly carried it to the seclusion of a woody ridge, where they recited prayers and sang their victory songs, marking the success of their first raid.

While perhaps it was not as heroic as the deeds of earlier warriors, they had nevertheless risked their lives in ransacking a white man's cabin, for had the owner returned he would have shot the "lice-picking, gut eating Indians."[13]

Heartened by their success, the party spent several days in the area, searching for horses, but could find no large herds. At last, Hind Gun picked up a rancher's horse to make it easier for the party to continue its trip to the Crows. From then on, traveling was easy, for with three horses among six raiders, they could ride double and cover many miles in a short time. Previously, at least two of the warriors were constantly on foot.

A careful reconnoiter was made before they crossed the Mussellshell River, and by the time they arrived at the wide valley of the Yellowstone, each warrior was alert to every suspicious sound or movement. A restless herd of antelope on a distant hill warned them of a passing party of cowboys; a cloud of dust revealed the presence of a wagon trail. But there were no other Indians, no enemies. The raiders had covered four hundred miles of prairie country, through hostile ranch lands and across two nations without mishap or discovery.

Following the valley of the Yellowstone River, the party reached its confluence with Pryor Creek just before sunset and took refuge in the protective confines of Beaverhead Butte. Next morning, from their windswept vantage point they could see two Crow Indian camps, one small and the other quite large. The younger members could hardly suppress their excitement, but Prairie Chicken Old Man told them they must wait patiently for the setting sun. The day was long and by the time evening shadows were stretching across the valley floor, dark clouds were gathering in the west. Soon a chilling spring

Calf Robe was a member of the 1889 war party that raided the Crows. He later became an active participant in Native ceremonies. *Courtesy Glenbow-Alberta Institute/NA-4812-1*

rain was upon them, and in utter darkness, the Indians made their way down the hill towards the larger of the two camps.

At first, the weather was to their advantage, hiding their movements and covering any noise as they crept into the enemy camp. But no sooner had they rounded up a few scrawny horses than the storm worsened and they lost the whole herd in the swirling rain while crossing the river. Thwarted in their first efforts, the party traveled east to the mouth of the Bighorn River, where they found a hiding place for the following day. There they camped, rested, and dried out from the vicious storm.

The next night, they divided into three groups to search for horses near the Crow camps. Young Pine and Wolf Sitting were the first to pick up a couple of loose horses. Shortly afterwards Hind Gun and Crazy Crow found a larger herd that was completely unguarded. Rounding up the animals, they met Prairie Chicken Old Man and Calf Robe, and together the Bloods began their long trek back home. They had no idea what had become of Young Pine and Wolf Sitting, but on any war expedition, it was a case of every man for himself.

The four men had gone only a few miles when, in the early morning sunlight, they saw another Crow camp in their path. While the main herd was guided around it, Calf Robe and Hind Gun decided to ride boldly through the camp and in doing so they picked up seven fine horses. The Crows were not suspicious, for no one had raided them for a long time, and who would expect an enemy to ride through the middle of a camp? Not even the restless dogs voiced an enquiring howl.

Some distance north of the Yellowstone, the raiders came to a railway line, and before they could hide, a passenger train came rumbling by. Men and women gazed out of the windows, and thinking they were seeing some local Indians on a roundup, they waved and smiled. Puzzled about the strange customs of white people, the war party waved back.

That night, someone was supposed to have kept guard in case the Bloods were pursued by Crows, but the warriors were so tired that everyone fell into a deep sleep. Fortunately, no vengeful enemy descended upon them.

It was here that Hind Gun showed a fine sense of gratitude. As they neared the place where he had stolen a rancher's horse on the inward journey, he now turned it loose to find its way home. "I didn't steal you," he told the animal. "I only borrowed you, and now I am returning you."[14]

The next day, the quartet unexpectedly encountered a white man along the trail. Some favored killing him but others argued that they had set out to capture horses, not to take scalps. The white man, not knowing that his life was at stake, was finally told in sign language to move on. The war party was concerned that he might be a scout from a nearby military base, so they veered due east to throw any pursuers off their track. This took them within sight of the Little Rocky Mountains where they observed a couple of Indians on the trail. Fearful of ambush, they crept up on the pair and discovered to their relief that they were Young Pine and Wolf Sitting. They had failed to take any more Crow horses but had stolen three from local ranchers along the way.

Once the war party was united, they decided to abandon the three branded horses, fearing that the American military would have little mercy on them if they were found with white men's livestock.

For the next two days, the weather turned cold and snowy and the Indians found themselves without food or shelter. Finally, they reached the Bears Paw Mountains, where they built a shelter and remained in hiding for four days. During the miserable weather, several of the horses died, adding to the ones they had lost along the trail. Although they searched the hills for food, the blizzards and cold weather drove the raiders back to their shelter. There they were forced to eat a calfskin saddlepad, which they boiled and then roasted in the coals of the fire.

When the weather cleared next morning, the raiders set out again, driving their horses before them. They had gone for only a few miles when one of the animals dropped out from fatigue and was left behind. A short distance farther along the trail, the Bloods found two cows, which they butchered, and prepared to eat their first real meal in several days.

As they were skinning one of the carcasses, Hind Gun glanced back at the horse they had abandoned. Instead of seeing one, there were two. Puzzled, he said to Young Pine,

"How many horses did we leave over there?"

"Only one."

"Well, there are two there now."[15]

Then everything seemed to explode. First they saw an Indian in a Hudson's Bay capote examining their played-out horse. And beyond him came a group of riders galloping in their direction. Then the shooting began.

Quickly, Young Pine sent the others along the trail with the horses while he stayed behind with Wolf Sitting to cover their retreat. Once the horses were safe in a dense stand of timber, the Bloods waited for their attackers to come. They had no idea who they were, but they suspected they were Crows who had been following them from the scene of the raid.

As the Indians approached, Calf Robe estimated there were eight of them, and so he arose and called out to them in the Crow language, "Who are you? What are you up to?" The response was a volley of shots that sent Calf Robe falling over backwards and diving for cover. After a spirited gun battle, the Bloods withdrew and were driving the horses down a snow-choked gully when they were cut off by enemy Indians who had guessed their strategy. However, Hind Gun opened fire and killed a horse, throwing its rider to the ground, and the enemy backed away.

At this point, the Bloods scattered, Crazy Crow and Calf Robe guarding the horses, Hind Gun taking the point, while Wolf Sitting, Young Pine, and Prairie Chicken Old Man flanked their enemies and drove them into a grove of willows. The attacking Indians thought there were only three Bloods to contend with, but when Hind Gun opened fire, he threw them into confusion and caused them to retreat into a clump of heavy brush.

As the Indians withdrew, Hind Gun fired a shot at a man wearing a soldier's uniform—blue tunic, pants, and hat. The Indian stopped, then staggered back into the willows, obviously wounded. His friends continued their retreat but the wounded man stayed in the scant protection of the willows until Young Pine shot and killed him.

As soon as the others were out of rifle range, the Bloods swooped down on the fallen victim. Hind Gun was the first to count a coup on the body, and as he took the man's belt and hat, Prairie Chicken Old Man grabbed the rifle. The dead Indian had two braids, so Young Pine scalped one side and Hind Gun the other. Only then did the warriors realize that their attackers were Assiniboines, not Crows.

The enemy Indians were still firing from a distance so the Bloods decided to withdraw. Wolf Sitting had discovered the horses their enemies had been riding, so these were added to the Crow horses that still remained after the battle. One of the enemy horses was particularly attractive and had a fancy bridle and saddle; this was claimed by Wolf Sitting. The Bloods then traveled through heavy snows to a large hill south of the battle scene and hid in the trees. There, Young Pine and Hind Gun cleaned the scalps while Calf Robe served as lookout. On one occasion he saw the Indians searching for them, but if they knew where the Bloods were hiding, they made no attempt to attack.

Later, just as evening was drawing a cover of darkness over the land, the Bloods saw a cavalry patrol out looking for them. A troop from Fort Maginnis under Captain Adams had been sent to intercept the raiders. Their problem, however, was that the army did not know the identity of the thieves. The Crows thought they were Sioux; the cavalry said they were Peigans; and the stock inspector said they were Bloods. The Bloods didn't know about this confusion, so they immediately abandoned their refuge and plowed through the heavy snowdrifts until they were far out on the plains. Riding in darkness, they passed Grassy Lake and camped at Big Rocky Coulee. There, Hind Gun killed an antelope and again they had fresh meat.

"By this time we were so hungry that we had to be careful how we went about eating," recalled Hind Gun. "We ate the raw liver as we dressed out the antelope, but before even beginning to cook the muscle meat we all drank some blood soup."[16] By the time the meat was cooked, the Indians were able to eat heartily without getting sick.

Traveling in a northwesterly direction, the war party passed close to the present towns of Shelby and Sunburst, stopping only long enough to make new soles for their worn out moccasins and to have a victory dance now that they were back in Blackfoot territory.

Meanwhile, the western frontier was in an uproar. The Crows had screamed to their Indian agent about the horse raid; the agent had complained to the military about the lack of protection for his wards;

and the army had sent out patrols to intercept the marauding Indians. The first news of the raid was telegraphed to Canada by R.B. Harrison, secretary of the Board of Stock Commissioners at Helena, who complained to the North-West Mounted Police that forty horses had been stolen from the Crows. This was followed by the more electrifying news from Col. E.S. Otis, officer commanding the 10th Infantry at Fort Assiniboine, that "Bloods with stolen stock passed through Bear Paw Mountains and there killed an Indian."[17]

Impatiently, Agent Pocklington waited for further news. Rumors spread through the reserve that the Bloods had all been wiped out. Some said that white ranchers had lynched them. Constant patrols of the Mounted Police watched the trails leading towards the reserve while newspapers spoke of a war between Blood Indians and cowboys in Montana.

Meanwhile, the exuberant raiders reached their original meeting place at the lone pine on May 13 and had a final victory dance. They had been away almost four weeks. Then, painting their faces black as a sign of triumph, they entered their village, driving their few remaining horses and displaying their scalps and trophies as they proclaimed their success.

The next day, Agent Pocklington sent an anxious wire to Indian Department headquarters: "War party Bloods returned Monday with horses. Scalp Dance last night. Am investigating. Indians gave me four horses."[18]

Within the next couple of days, Young Pine, Wolf Sitting, and Hind Gun were persuaded by the head chief to surrender to the Mounted Police. Once they were in custody, Young Pine made a statement, giving his version of the expedition.

"I thought you would be glad that we killed the Assiniboines," he told the Indian agent. "They started the trouble. They stole Red Crow's horses and gave you lots of trouble to get them back."

When Agent Pocklington tried to explain that the Great Mother did not like her children to murder each other, the Indian replied hotly, "We killed them across the line! The Americans paid no attention to our Indians who were killed. Red Crow made no trouble nor talked bad. That was three winters ago. We killed only one; they killed six Bloods."[19]

While the defiant trio cooled their heels in the Fort Macleod guardhouse, the Mounted Police learned that the rest of the war party were living as heroes in the Blood camps. Prairie Chicken Old Man had displayed the rifle taken from the dead man while Calf Robe had paraded about with the trappings from a captured horse. As soon as the news was received, a small patrol of police rode to the camps on the reserve and singled out Calf Robe for their first arrest.

When he was approached by the redcoats, Calf Robe snatched a rifle from its nearby resting place and leveled it at the officer in charge. Aroused by the noise of the confrontation, a few other Bloods began to gather as word spread that the police were trying to make an arrest. With the gun still pointing menacingly in their direction, the redcoated patrol hastily withdrew and reported the incident to their commanding officer, Superintendent Samuel Benfield Steele.

One thing has to be said about Steele; wherever he went he waved the British flag. He was a typical pompous officer of the Victorian era, the kind of man who helped conquer a tenth of the world's land mass for Queen and country. He was the type of officer who believed that his finest contribution to mankind was to introduce the British way of life to primitive lands, whether the inhabitants wanted it or not. He was so assiduous in this quest that niceties of law and justice often eluded him.

But in this case, when he learned of Calf Robe's foiled arrest, he took no immediate action; he realized that a fugitive on the Blood Reserve was harder to find than a flea in a buffalo robe. Instead, he sent several telegrams to authorities in Montana, urging them to send a representative to claim their six stolen horses.

Strangely enough, the killing and scalping of the enemy Indian was never pursued by the American authorities. Even though Young Pine had confessed to his part in the death, no attempt was made to have him extradited to the United States for trial. In all likelihood, both American and Canadian authorities considered intertribal warfare to be in a special category and outside the usual realm of the judicial procedures. After all, they were only Indians.

During the month of June, most of the Bloods left their tiny gardens and fields to gather for their annual Sun Dance. Held near the Belly Buttes, the ceremony was the most important religious event of the year, giving the prairie people an opportunity to reaffirm their faith in the Sun spirit. It also was an occasion for recounting past war deeds, inflaming the desire for glory and adventure in the minds of the younger Indians. Prairie Chicken Old Man and Calf Robe took prominent places in the circle of warriors and graphically reenacted each action and each movement of the war party during their thrilling raid.

By June 20, there was still no word from American authorities, so

Young Pine, Wolf Sitting, and Hind Gun were released and the charge of bringing stolen property into Canada was dropped. Immediately following this action, Agent Pocklington rode into the fort to find out from Steele what could be done about Crazy Crow, Calf Robe, and Prairie Chicken Old Man, who were still at large.

Steele said there were no charges against the men, but they should give themselves up so they could be lectured about the evils of horse stealing. The three Indians were elated at the news, but only Calf Robe visited the fort and received his verbal reprimand.

"That night," recalled Hind Gun, "we had the biggest victory dance of all. Everybody was there, and those of us who had been on the war party were honored. We told all about stealing the Crow horses, and about the battle. When we told about taking the scalps, everybody fired off their guns and made so much noise that several of the horses picketed nearby broke loose and stampeded."[20]

A white man who visited the camps during the victory dance was impressed with the sight of some two thousand Indians painted and dressed in their finest regalia, dancing to the beat of the drums. The finale came when the Bloods formed a long line, danced through the camps, then sat down to a feast.

"High upon a pole in the center of the crowd," observed the visitor, "were suspended two newly taken scalps, red and gory. The long black hair indicated that they were from the heads of

Hind Gun accompanied Young Pine and the other warriors in 1889 on a raid against the Crows. He is shown here, ca. 1900, after he had become a police officer in Montana. *Courtesy Glenbow-Alberta Institute/NA-1229-1*

Indians. They were the trophies, visible proofs of the powers of their braves of which they were very proud."[21]

When the last drum had been packed away, the last piece of boiled beef devoured, and the scalps lovingly stored away, the incident was over. The horses were in the Mounted Police corrals, all charges had been dropped, and no one seemed inclined to pursue the matter of a killing. To the people of the Blood Reserve, the excitement was finished and they could return to the solemnity of their holy Sun Dance.

A few miles away, bordering the reserve, stood the Mounted Police detachment at Standoff, which was under the command of Staff Sergeant Chris Hilliard. His task was to maintain law and order on the reserve, which, realistically, meant leaving the Indians alone unless they committed a crime that fell under the Criminal Code of Canada. Minor problems were looked after by the Bloods' own police society, the Black Catchers.

Hilliard had heard faint rumblings of the troubles between Prairie Chicken Old Man's war party and the Mounted Police, but the matter had been handled personally by the top man, Superintendent Sam Steele. The only official communication Hilliard had received in his outpost was that Prairie Chicken Old Man, Calf Robe, and Crazy Crow were to be arrested on sight. No one had bothered to tell him that the charges had been dismissed.

On the morning of July 4, Hilliard took two constables and his interpreter, Henry Choquette, on a patrol to the Sun Dance camp. The officer wanted to make sure there was no liquor in the camps to aggravate the excitement caused by such a large gathering. He knew from personal experience that there was whiskey around, as he had taken a few belts to fortify himself before he left the detachment.

The men followed the Belly River downstream for about five miles until they came in sight of the great circle of tepees. In the center of the half-mile-wide camp stood a brush-covered lodge, which was the focal point for all the ceremonies.

Although the Sun Dance itself was a sacred event, the warlike Bloods took the opportunity of the assembly to perform other rites. These included opening their medicine bundles, extolling their war deeds, and permitting teenaged boys to go through a ritual to fulfill vows they had made to the Sun spirit. In the ceremony, skewers were placed in the young men's chests and fastened by a rope to the center pole of the lodge. The candidates then danced until the skewers were ripped free.

As the patrol reached the center lodge, they noticed that a ceremony was underway, so Hilliard motioned to the others to follow him. As they pushed their way through the crowd at the opening of the structure, Choquette tugged at the police officer's sleeve and pointed to two warriors sitting among their comrades. They were Prairie Chicken Old Man and Calf Robe.

Ignoring the religious ceremony underway in the lodge and the excited jostling of young Indians, Hilliard drew his revolver, stalked across the sacred circle and ordered the arrest of the two "fugitives." Immediately, a howl of protest arose from the throng as the sergeant wrenched a rifle from the hands of Calf Robe and jerked him to his feet. The constables grabbed Prairie Chicken Old Man by either arm and pushed him towards the entranceway.

The resentment against the redcoated intruders rose like a tidal wave and swept away any respect that the Indians held for the law. Infuriated warriors and head men crowded around the small group, brandishing knives, rifles, and lances, and they cried for revenge against the white soldiers who had desecrated their sacred lodge and mishandled their heroes. Rough and violent hands quickly freed Prairie Chicken Old Man and Calf Robe from their captors; guns were torn from Mounted Police hands, and scarlet tunics became disheveled and almost ripped from the officers' backs.

The anger of the Bloods was near the breaking point, and Hilliard could see death in the eyes of the usually peaceful Indians when suddenly three prominent chiefs forced their way into the small circle. Red Crow, Ermine Horse, and One Spot, aided by the Black Catchers, rescued the thoroughly frightened patrol and led the men safely to the edge of the camp. Their uniforms torn, their rifles and revolvers gone, Hilliard and his men were given a stern warning by Red Crow and told to keep away from their holy rituals.

When Sam Steele heard that four of his men had been manhandled, he was fit to be tied. Agent Pocklington was equally furious when he learned that the Mounted Police had tried to arrest, without a warrant, two of his wards who had already been cleared of any criminal charges. "The Police had no right to attempt their arrest," he fumed, "and it was a mad act to attempt it at the Medicine Lodge."[22]

Steele, on the other hand, was not about to let a minor detail like a warrant get in the way of his own idea of justice. "In making this arrest," he asserted, "the non-commissioned officer was not in possession of a warrant, but I consider he acted perfectly right. There are so many bad Indians wanted at times that unless a man takes every chance offered he will likely lose his man altogether."[23]

To demonstrate his anger, Steele sent a large contingent of police to the Sun Dance, where the officers arrested five men—Young Pine, Big Wolf, Sleeps on Top, Thunder Chief, and Crop Eared Wolf—and charged them with obstructing the police. These were not a bunch of teenaged hell-raisers. Thunder Chief and Crop Eared Wolf were destined to become head chiefs of the tribe; Sleeps on Top was a son-in-law of Red Crow; and all were respected leaders.

Then, in a neat twist of the law, Steele had Calf Robe arrested and laid a charge of using a deadly weapon to resist arrest; this was based on the incident that had occurred more than a month earlier.

"Calf Robe had already given himself up and was liberated," noted the Indian agent dryly, "yet the Police arrest this man for an offense committed on the seventeenth of May last. But strange to say, the information is not laid until the sixth of July, two days after the fuss at the Medicine Lodge. The day after the trouble I visited the camp and talked with Red Crow and others. They were much excited. The best of their talk was that they could not understand how it was that after Calf Robe had given himself up, the Police should wish to arrest him."[24]

Although the whole trouble had resulted from Prairie Chicken Old Man's war party in the spring, only Calf Robe and Young Pine of the six original were now involved. Hind Gun had dashed home to his reservation in Montana at the first sign of trouble, while the others kept a low profile during the excitement.

A month later, the Indians appeared in court in Fort Macleod. From the outset, it was obviously a battle between two branches of the federal government—the Department of Indian Affairs and the North-West Mounted Police—with the Indians being little more than interested spectators. Both sides had the best legal counsels, the Indian Department engaging Frederick Haultain, who later was knighted and became the premier of the North-West Territories. Hearing the case was Magistrate James F. Macleod, the former commissioner of the Mounted Police. The courtroom was crowded with spectators who came to watch the fun.

The first case was The Queen versus Crop Eared Wolf, Thunder Chief, Young Pine, Big Wolf, and Sleeps on Top, all charged with obstructing the police in the execution of their duty. After a stormy session, the magistrate dismissed the charges and ruled that the arrests had been illegal as no warrants had been issued. With that decision on the books, the police saw that their case of The Queen versus Calf Robe was destined to suffer a similar fate, so the District Crown Prosecutor withdrew the charge.

The aftermath of the decisions rebounded through the offices of commissioners and bureaucrats in the nation's capital, with the Mounted Police demanding that the Bloods be forced to remain on their reserve and not be allowed to roam at will. But Agent Pocklington remained firmly on the side of his wards. "The Indians are not confined to their reserve by any law or regulation," he pointed out, "and the Indians know that they have the right to go and come as they please."[25]

But the Mounted Police had the reputation of always getting their man, and Sam Steele was not to be denied. Later in August the police caught Crazy Crow with liquor and threw him in jail for a month at hard labor; in November they caught Prairie Chicken Old Man and Young Pine in the same situation and gave them a month each at hard labor. With those symbolic acts of justice, the whole episode of the war party came to an end.

Prairie Chicken Old Man's foray had been the last of its kind. In the months and years that followed, a few other small raiding parties left the reserve in search of horses, but none ever reached the heights achieved by Prairie Chicken Old Man in his search for adventure and glory. His raid was the last to involve open conflict across the International Boundary and the last to take a human life. It was the end of an era, the passing into history of the scalping knife and the war trail.

The Snake Man

The Indian watched with amusement as the pale-skinned intruders recoiled in horror and fear. One moment they had been chattering gaily in their own strange tongue and now they were transfixed at the sight of the great Blood warrior who stood before them. A white woman was near fainting while a thin-faced young dude, presumably an Englishman from across the water, looked as though he was going to be sick.

For a mere twenty-five cents each, they had just witnessed the Blood Indian sharing one of the strangest secrets of the Canadian West. From his blanket coat he had taken a huge rattlesnake, petted it lovingly, then crammed its head eight inches (20 cm) down his throat. Now it was back in its nesting place in his robe, but the fear and apprehension of the onlookers remained.

The man was *Onista'sakaxsin*, or Calf Shirt; his secret was a strange power over rattlesnakes. He also was a paradox, for in his fifty-seven years of life he played with equal dexterity the diverse and often contrary roles of mystic and entrepreneur, war chief and politician, convicted criminal and police scout.

But his power over rattlesnakes was his strangest trait, a gift of his own religion. This power came to him when he was thirty-six years old, just before the Bloods and their Blackfoot allies began to experience the bitterness of life on a reserve and to hunger for the vanished buffalo.

Born in 1844, Calf Shirt was the son of The Shoulder and nephew of the great chief Calf Shirt who had been killed by whiskey traders in 1873. Shortly after the murder, Calf Shirt had taken his uncle's name. This was a common practice among the Blackfoot tribes, where a name was considered to be a family possession that was used during a person's lifetime and then passed on to a younger man after he performed some notable achievement such as capturing an enemy horse, taking part in a dangerous raid, or experiencing a vision.

As a young man, Calf Shirt joined several war parties, mostly against the Crows in Montana, and was so highly regarded that he became a leader of revenge parties. These were formed whenever the Bloods or their allies suffered a humiliating defeat at the hands of an enemy.

He took part in a great battle between the Crees and Blackfoot near the present city of Lethbridge in the fall of 1870. He had been out hunting, and upon his return, he was told by his aged father that the battle was in progress. The young warrior let his father daub bright paint on his face, and as a gesture of scorn, he promised that should he be struck by an enemy arrow, he would leave it in his body for his father to remove.

Grasping a double-bladed knife from his religious Bear Medicine bundle, Calf Shirt arrived while the battle was in progress and in time to see the Crees being trapped in a long shallow coulee. Among those making a stand were two warriors, one tall and the other wearing a calfskin robe. Other Blood warriors warned Calf Shirt to leave those Crees alone; they had killed several men who had attacked them and no one could harm them. But the war chief ignored their cautions. Armed only with his bear knife and singing his war song, he rushed the men but took an arrow in the wrist before he reached them. Heedless of the shaft, the Blood warrior grabbed the enemy's bow with his wounded hand and struck the tall Cree a mortal blow with his knife. The calf-skinned comrade, waiting for a clear shot, was stabbed to death in a similar manner.

After the fight, other warriors offered to pull out the enemy arrow, but Calf Shirt told them of his promise to his father and accompanied the victorious Bloods back to their camp. On the way, his wrist became so swollen that he could not travel unaided but he still refused to remove the arrow. Finally he was lashed onto a travois and dragged into the camp, where the arrow was finally removed. This was done by cutting the shaft close to the wrist and then using a pair of brass tweezers to pull out the remaining wood.

By this time, the Indian's whole arm was swollen, but Calf Shirt was able to doctor himself. He went through a ritual four times, and each time the swelling went down a little more. Finally, after the fourth doctoring, he peeled the old skin off his arm and he was cured.

According to Blood elders, Calf Shirt received his special rattle-snake powers through a vision a few years later in the 1870s. The event occurred shortly after Calf Shirt's parents died, first his father and a short time later, his mother. At that time the Bloods were camped in a rattlesnake-infested area east of the present city of Medicine Hat at a place called "Where We Drowned." Everyone knew that a man in mourning cared little for his own welfare, so his relatives kept an eye on Calf Shirt to see that he didn't become lost in a region that was so close to hostile tribes. But the area was so hilly that one day Calf Shirt wandered away without being noticed. He walked aimlessly in his sorrow until, at last, he lay down exhausted on a sand hill and fell asleep. While there, he had a dream in which a person appeared before him.

"I've heard you mourning the loss of your father and I've taken pity on you," the man said. "My father has sent me to you to say that you'll be his son and we'll be brothers. All of our people who live here are his children and now you're one of us. You'll become a leader of your people and we'll watch over you. Always carry some sagebrush with you so that we'll know you and so you can use it to treat those who are sick."[1]

In his vision, Calf Shirt saw the person but did not recognize him. Realizing this, the figure said, "I'm from the Big Snake tribe; our people are rattlesnakes. When you die, you'll become one of us."

Returning to his home village, Calf Shirt soon demonstrated his newly gained powers. Picking up a rattlesnake, he wrapped it around his waist, carried it before a startled group of Bloods, and played with it as though it were a child. At first his friends shunned him, for they feared the rattling serpents, but in time they learned that they had nothing to fear, for the snakes were his brothers and did his bidding. If he whistled, they slithered through the grass to his feet; if he made a sign, they quietly slipped away.

By the time the Bloods settled on their reserve in 1881, Calf Shirt had become a prominent member of the tribe. He was in the Many Tumors Band, which was under the leadership of the aged Medicine Calf and his younger brother, Strangling Wolf. The snake-loving Calf Shirt had been a warrior leader and was considered by many to be an unofficial chief, but government recognition had been denied him. He realized that when Medicine Calf died, Strangling Wolf would become the sole chief of the band unless he did something about it. Calf Shirt was quick to appreciate that the agent was the man who held the real power, so he set out to impress the government official.

His first move took place shortly after the Indian agent made it clear that he wanted the Bloods to turn to farming. With his chief's blessing, Calf Shirt joined with a number of other members of the band to plant turnips, potatoes, wheat, and other crops in a small clearing along the river bottom near the now-deserted whiskey fort of Slideout. While most other Indians ignored the demeaning work of scratching the earth, Calf Shirt eagerly joined the movement and came to the favorable notice of the government agent.

He also welcomed missionaries to the reserve. When John Maclean, a Methodist preacher, arrived at the Many Tumors camp in 1881, Calf Shirt was one of the first Indians to greet

Calf Shirt, a nephew of the great chief Calf Shirt who had been killed by whiskey traders in 1873, played the diverse and often contrary roles of mystic and entrepreneur, war chief and politician, convicted criminal and police scout. But it was his power over rattlesnakes that was his strangest trait. *Collection of the author*

him. Maclean considered him to be a wise and intelligent man.

"Sitting in his lodge," commented the missionary, "I have listened to his glowing recitals of brave deeds upon the battle field, and I have seen the strong man bowed down with grief at the loss of his friends."[2]

Like other visitors to Calf Shirt's tepee, the missionary could not help notice the man's affinity for snakes. "By some peculiar method," said Maclean, "he was able to go alone upon the prairie and secure very large rattlesnakes, one of which he would carry inside of his blanket coat. The Indians are afraid of snakes and the power possessed by Calf Shirt increased their regard for him. They were not alone in this, for we all respect the man who can do one or more things that are beyond our ken."[3]

Blood Indians and missionaries, ca. 1880s. *(Back row, left to right)* Reverend George McKay, Calf Shirt, remainder unknown; *(front row, left to right)* Robert Whitney, Tom Lauder, Dave Mills (interpreter), Reverend Sam Trivett, remainder unknown. *Courtesy Glenbow-Alberta Institute/NA-691-40*

Calf Shirt dug a hole in the ground near his bed and there a large rattlesnake usually lay coiled. Calf Shirt placed his tobacco board over the hole to keep the snake from wandering. When visitors arrived, the Indian would remove the board and proudly show off the reptilian side of his family.

Calf Shirt's relationship with Maclean remained warm and friendly during Maclean's entire stay with the Bloods. He taught the missionary to speak Blackfoot, and although the Indian never became a convert, he encouraged Maclean to open a school and teach the children.

Calf Shirt's most impressive action to gain the attention of the Indian agent occurred at the autumn treaty payments in 1884; it called upon the snake-wielding leader to take a moral stand against many of his tribe. As the agent later explained to his superiors, "Calf Shirt sat at the pay table with me and through his honesty I was in a position to refuse paying a number of South Peigans representing themselves to be Bloods. Through services rendered, this Indian has got the ill will of all the Blood tribe . . . I may state that of his own free will he reduced his family three souls."[4]

At this time, government officials were concerned that the Indians were padding their ration lists and claiming to have more persons in their families than was the fact. This, they said, often was accomplished by borrowing friends' children and dressing them so they would not be recognized when they came back for a second time during treaty and ration payments. In this way, a starving family could receive larger rations of beef and flour.

The government was concerned because it was going through the process of surveying the Blood Reserve, and under the terms of the treaty it had to provide land on the basis of five persons per square mile. By the time Calf Shirt was finished, the population on the ration lists had been reduced by over a thousand persons, and this new census became the basis for measuring the reserve.

Shortly after the death of Medicine Calf in October 1884, Calf Shirt reported to the agent that white men were selling alcohol to the Bloods in the form of Jamaica ginger, essence, and Pain Killer. Then, during the 1885 Riel Rebellion, he assumed the vital role of peace-maker and conciliator.

"I told Red Crow to have nothing to do with the Crees at all," said Calf Shirt, "that the Bloods got along all right, and if the Crees were in trouble with the Government to have nothing to do with them. The whites treat us good. Let the Crees fight if they like; we will not."[5]

Calf Shirt kept the agent informed of all activities, rumors, and gossip among the Bloods during the rebellion, as well as intelligence of any couriers or visitors from other tribes. He also intercepted war parties returning to the reserve and turned their stolen horses over to the police. Throughout the unsettled period, he was a steadying influence for peace and reason. Not surprisingly, two months after the rebellion, Calf Shirt was appointed a minor chief of the tribe to replace the deceased Medicine Calf.

Some indication of Calf Shirt's leadership ability was demon-strated early in 1886 during a lengthy interview with George H. Ham, a reporter from a Toronto newspaper. At that time, the rumor reached eastern Canada that when spring arrived, the Indians of the western prairies would explode in a new rebellion of bloodshed and destruction that would make the Riel Rebellion look like a tea party. It was not true, of course, but the reporter found this out only after traveling to a number of reserves.

When Ham reached the Blood Reserve, he spoke to the leading chiefs of the tribe. At this time the Bloods were split into two groups for rationing purposes. Red Crow lived on the upper waters of the Belly River, while Calf Shirt with the Many Tumors, Scabbies, Black Elks, and All Short People bands, lived near the Lower Agency. "Calf Shirt, although a minor chief," observed the reporter, "is the most influential individual amongst the Indians of the lower camp."[6]

Ham was extremely impressed with the chief, both for his astute political diplomacy and his power over rattlesnakes. He noted that Calf Shirt was the only leader who did not use the opportunity of the interview to complain about food nor to ask for an increase in rations. Realizing the gravity of the enquiry, he kept the discussions on a high plane as he tried to convince the reporter that the Bloods had no plans to rebel.

"All the Indians now are pretty quiet, and there is no trouble going on," he assured the reporter. "I'll let the whites know if there is any bad news. All know Calf Shirt to be honest, and when any trouble comes I will try to stop it and talk to my own people. I have a good heart. My band always behave themselves. When there are any stolen horses or bad news, I tell the whites and don't lie. I tell the truth."[7]

Now that Calf Shirt was a chief, he had no further need to impress government officials. Yet his natural inclinations were those of cooperation and peace. Usually, his efforts were directed towards a progressive and law-abiding reserve. In 1886, Agent William Pocklington referred to him as "probably the most reliable Indian on this Reserve."[8]

However, if the pride or reputation of the tribe was at stake, Calf Shirt had no hesitation in ignoring the white man's laws. One such occurrence happened late in 1886, when the Bloods learned that six of their men had been killed and scalped by Assiniboine Indians in Montana. This tragedy affected Calf Shirt in a personal way, as three of those slain were close relatives. As a ripple of excitement swept through the camps, the usually peaceful Calf Shirt stirred the young people into action. He organized a revenge party of some two hundred warriors, just as he had done in the buffalo days, and was prepared to lead them out against their enemy when an autumn snowstorm cut short his plan. Continued cold weather made the raid impractical, and before the snows had melted in the spring, Red Crow and other chiefs had made a peace treaty with their old enemies.

In the following winter of 1887–88, Calf Shirt displayed his further disregard for the white man's law when he smuggled a supply of whiskey onto the reserve. Then, sitting placidly in his tepee, he bragged that the Mounted Police were afraid to arrest him. This time he was wrong and was sentenced to a month in the Fort Macleod guardhouse.

During these years, Calf Shirt continued to live with his snakes and to turn his remarkable gift into a profitable enterprise. As early as 1881, he was a visitor to Fort Macleod, where he collected money for performing tricks with a large snake. On one such visit a local newspaper man wrote that "Calf Shirt is the snake charmer of the Blood branch of the great Blackfoot nation, and he handles the deadly rattlesnakes with the most consummate indifference to the awful absolute death that is contained in its [*sic*] slender fangs. He keeps it coiled round his body next to the skin, inside the shirt, where it lovingly nestles, and anyone who is willing to pay for his curiosity can see him put his hand in and drag the living, writhing death out."

"Calf Shirt claims," continued the writer, "to have some subtle power over snakes and to see him take his present specimen up, she measuring about three feet long, catch it by the neck and cram about eight inches of it, the deadliest reptile in America, head first down his throat, is calculated to make the marrow in any man's bones shiver. He also puts it out on the ground and playfully pats it on the back of the head with his fingers, till the snake rattles as if it was performing for the benefit of all the babies in Canada. It is not a pleasant sight for one with weak nerves and who understands what a rattlesnake is."[9]

During the years that Calf Shirt visited Fort Macleod, he became well known for his sense of humor. To put it plainly, he liked to scare the hell out of unwary white people.

Take a visiting Englishman, for example. Calf Shirt immediately recognized him as a greenhorn and decided to play a trick on him. First, he tried to communicate with the visitor by using Indian sign language, an eloquent expression of arm and hand movements that tell a story. The greenhorn, entranced, did not notice that Calf Shirt was drawing closer and closer to him. At last, when only a pace apart, the Indian suddenly pressed both arms tightly to his sides. The action disturbed a snake that was coiled around his body and hidden from view; angrily its triangular-shaped head and beady eyes darted from the protective folds of the blanket and almost into the face of the startled visitor. The forked tongue and hissing noise left no doubt as to the identity and anger of the ugly creature. By the time the amused Indian eased the pressure on his arms and returned the snake to its fold, the terrified greenhorn already was running for his life.

Calf Shirt also played a joke on one of the town's old-timers, a veteran freighter named Missouri Bill. The man was so badly crippled with rheumatism that on warm sunny days he would take a few drinks and find a seat in front of Kamoose Taylor's hotel. There he would spend the entire afternoon, lazing around and complaining of his infirmities.

Calf Shirt noticed this habit, so one day he crept around to the side of the hotel until he was within a few feet of the old freighter, but still out of sight. There he released a couple of his snakes and pointed them in the direction of the sleeping man. A few moments later, a cowboy walking down the street shouted a warning to the old-timer.

"Bill turned his head in the direction indicated," noted an eyewitness, "and saw the snakes approaching him at a rapid rate. With a startled screech he jumped to his feet, his cane forgotten in his haste, and hitting the high places was soon lost to view."[10]

Interestingly enough, the next time anyone saw Missouri Bill, he was completely cured of his rheumatism, and the problem never plagued him again.

But these were merely diversions. Like most Indians of that period, Calf Shirt had practically no source of income; the weekly rations and garden vegetables barely kept his family alive. So when he realized that his unusual gift could also be a source of revenue, he had no hesitation in accepting money in return for demonstrating his ability to handle snakes.

According to an early Mounted Police officer, there was one time when Calf Shirt played a trick that could have caused him serious trouble among some of the hardbitten frontiersmen who still felt that the only time an Indian was good was when he was dead. Calf Shirt slipped into an old sod-roofed saloon in Fort Macleod where several men were playing cards. From a sack he carried, the Indian surreptitiously released several snakes, which were soon slithering over the earthen floor. As there was no back door, the gamblers scrambled on tops of tables and chairs while the snakes vainly searched for a way to escape from the log structure.

At this point, Calf Shirt innocently ambled into the saloon and offered to remove the offending reptiles. A collection was taken up, and although they were suspicious of the Indian, the frontiersmen were more terrified of the snakes and opted for the lesser of the two evils. When he had enough coins, Calf Shirt scooped up his pets and left the angry white men to return to their cards and chips.

In 1888, Calf Shirt broke away from the Many Tumors Band—which was still nominally under the leadership of Strangling Wolf—and with about forty followers he settled at the northern tip of the reserve, just across the river from the town of Lethbridge. Here he formed a new band, which others soon dubbed the *Namopi'si*, or Crooked Backs. This name was given after members of the band had been seen at the town dump, bent over looking for scraps.

The new location had two good features for the snake-loving

chief: it was close to the only supply of rattlers on the reserve, and it was almost on the outskirts of the coal-mining town. Calf Shirt soon became friends with the shopkeepers and regularly earned money by performing with his venomous pets.

The location also created problems for the chief, for being so near the town, it became a convenient point for prostitution. To discourage this demoralizing practice, the government had forbidden the Indians to enter white settlements without passes. However, the location of Calf Shirt's camp made it easy for female members of the tribe to slip into town in the evening, or for whites to come out. The situation was criticized by the Indian agent, who said that "the authorities in Lethbridge will not allow Indians to stay in the town, consequently these Indians having good-looking squaws want to get as near Lethbridge as possible so that they can run back and forth . . . "[11]

To combat the problem, Calf Shirt was appointed a scout for the North-West Mounted Police. During the time he held this position, he fought to keep the undesirables out of his camp and succeeded to some extent in stamping out prostitution. As a scout he also mixed with white people more than any other Blood chief, and his facility for handling snakes was enough to grant him respectful attention from his non-Indian audiences.

One day, when a circus featuring a female snake charmer came to Lethbridge, a number of fun-loving citizens paid for Calf Shirt to see the show. The Indian watched the entertainer pick up her defanged reptiles, then twist them around her body and over her head. Calf Shirt was unimpressed. The townspeople, who crowded the tent to see the Indian's reaction, did not have long to wait. As soon as the show was over, Calf Shirt nonchalantly pulled a venomous rattler—one of his biggest—out of his shirt and offered it to the charmer. The woman took one look at the beady-eyed reptile, screamed, and fled. Calf Shirt snickered, returned his pet to its resting place, and commented in broken English, "I gave that pretty white woman something to wear around her neck, but she nearly jumped out of her nice dress to get away from it."[12]

On another occasion, a rancher brought a live rattler into Lethbridge to show the townspeople. The clerk at the Hudson's Bay Company store saw it as a unique attraction, so he bought the reptile and put it on display. But no sooner had the snake been put into its rudely constructed cage than it escaped and disappeared into a stock of dry goods.

Frightened, everyone fled the store and the clerk had no idea what to do next until someone suggested getting Calf Shirt. The scout was summoned, and agreeing on a price for his services, he went into the store, poked about the counters, and finally found the missing reptile curled up in some cotton goods. The Indian picked up the creature and played with it while carpenters hurriedly built a sturdier cage.

Calf Shirt's exploits became so well known that in 1889, two entrepreneurs from Maple Creek who organized western Canada's first wild west show, invited the Indian to join them as a performer. For the entire summer, amid Texas longhorns, bucking competitions, and fancy riding, Calf Shirt demonstrated his prowess with rattlesnakes. When the tour reached Winnipeg, he was advertised as "a Blood Indian snake charmer who picks up and handles rattle snakes."[13] From the prairie city, the show traveled east to Port Arthur and on to other Ontario centers.

In 1895, when plans were made to hold a large Territorial Exhibition in Regina, Calf Shirt again was an obvious choice for the program. Not only was he happy to make the journey with his pets, but he confided to his friends that the territorial capital was close to the Sand Hills, so he might have a chance to pick up some new friends.

The exhibition was the biggest ever held in the West. There were two circus tents, agricultural exhibits, rodeo events, and examples of Indian life, past and present. Calf Shirt was depicted as part of the "pagan" past and happily demonstrated his unique control over snakes. Some people did not believe the performance was genuine, however, and accused Calf Shirt of using defanged snakes. They were convinced of this when they saw the Blood chief put a snake's head into his mouth and down his throat.

"Calf Shirt told one white man that, if he would give him a dollar he would allow the snake to bite a dog that was standing near," commented a newspaper reporter. "The white man put up the dollar and the Indian immediately made one of the snakes bite the dog, which died in a few minutes."[14]

Another incident with his snakes occurred at Calf Shirt's home camp when his sister, Only Killed Him, had a fight with her husband, Coming Singer. He had collected their treaty money, but being an inveterate gambler, he had lost it and came home with nothing. In anger, his wife left him and moved in with Calf Shirt. When her husband asked for her to be sent back, Calf Shirt commented that the woman was not being forced to stay with him but added, "If you really want your wife back, you do as I say."[15]

Calf Shirt pointed to a coulee and told the man to ride in that direction until he found two rattlesnakes together, then to pick the biggest of them and bring it back. Coming Singer went as directed and soon found the two snakes coiled and ready to strike.

"Don't do that," he told them. "Calf Shirt has sent me to get you." The Indian then chewed some sagebrush, as he had been instructed, rubbed it on his hands and as he walked close to the biggest snake he spat some of the mixture on its head. The reptile immediately uncoiled, allowing Coming Singer to pick it up and put it inside his shirt. There the snake coiled tightly around the body of the frightened man. Riding back to the camp, Coming Singer tried to trot but the jogging made the snake tighten its grip, so he slowed to a walk. By the time he reached the camp, he was shaking with fear and the sweat was trickling down his brow.

The chief, gathered with others in front of his tepee, took the snake and praised his brother-in-law for proving that he truly wanted his wife back. "You gambled away your five dollars treaty money," he said, "but I'm a chief and get fifteen dollars. I'll give you five dollars for this deed and tell my sister to go back home with you."[16]

During the latter years of his life, Calf Shirt lived in a small log cabin with his wives Double Killer and Many Stars. Visitors observed, sometimes with anxiety, the numerous snake holes under the cabin's log walls and the dusty trails across the earthen floor. Sometimes, if he felt in a good mood, the chief might whistle to bring one of the reptiles slithering across the room to be with its human brother.

After his death in 1901, Calf Shirt was buried on a lonely hill near his camp, not far from Snake Coulee. Soon after, travelers swore that a huge rattler had joined the pack and liked to lie in the sun near Calf Shirt's grave, just as though it belonged there. And perhaps it did.

Man of Steel

S teel had lost his horses.

One morning in October 1891 he had gone outside his tepee at his camp on the west side of the Blood Reserve and noticed that his horses were not grazing where they should have been on a nearby hill. A quick check of the area determined that they hadn't been stolen; rather, they had wandered down to the banks of the Belly River and had disappeared. Likely they had followed the gravelly shores of the low water and had crossed somewhere to feed on the other side. That would have taken them off the reserve and out onto the grazing lease of the Cochrane Ranche Company.

Steel was a proud man. At twenty-eight years of age he had gained an enviable reputation for himself as a warrior before his people had been obliged to settle on their reserve.[1] Now he was content to raise horses and to take part in the religious activities of the tribe. In fact, his native religion was very important to him, occupying much of his time in the rituals and prayers that went along with owning medicine bundles and other holy objects.

But now his horses were gone: his wife's pack ponies and his spare riding horses. Luckily, he had always followed the precaution of tethering his best horse to his tepee, so he wasn't entirely afoot.

After explaining the situation to his wife, Medicine Pipe Woman, the warrior dressed in his finest clothes, then donned his white Hudson's Bay blanket-coat and a wide leather belt with a knife and scabbard attached. Steel was extremely conscious of his appearance, and whenever he left camp he always dressed well. Picking up his Winchester rifle, he waved goodbye to his wife and set out along the river.

He wasn't really worried about losing his horses, for they had drifted away before. There weren't many horse thieves around; in fact those kinds of problems had virtually ended five or six years earlier when the ill-fated Riel Rebellion up north had caused the country to fill up with soldiers from the East. They had stayed only a few weeks, but they were there long enough to discourage the kind of intertribal raiding that had been part of everyday life for many years. Each spring, the Bloods used to steal horses from the Crows, the Crees would raid the Blackfoot, the Peigans would go after the Assiniboines, and pretty soon the whole country was dotted with little war parties out searching for somebody else's horses. The Bloods had been the last to give up raiding, but after there had been a big blowup at the Sun Dance two years earlier—all because of horses—most of the Bloods had decided to call it quits.

Steel was one of the Bloods who had made a successful transition to reservation life on his own terms. He had not become a farmer, as the Indian agent wanted, nor had he become a dispirited ex-warrior who still dreamed of the past. Rather, he had accepted the new life and had learned how to survive comfortably within its confinements.

Perhaps his age had been a factor, for he had just turned twenty when he came to the reserve and had already seen his days of war parties and the spilling of enemy blood. In fact, he had spilled a little of his own and had a chest wound to prove it.

As Steel rode along the river, looking for telltale signs of hoofprints, he remembered the time when he was barely out of his teens and had gone to raid the Crows. At that time, too, he had kept a close watch, but that was for enemy scouts, not for missing horses.

On that occasion he had left the camp with three companions, Thin Wolf, Night Gun, and Rope Chief. They had gone south on foot so that they could bring back plenty of enemy horses. Ten days later, they had crossed the Yellowstone River, found a Crow camp, and successfully taken some animals from their herds. Once they were out of earshot of the camp they had galloped all night and had taken refuge in a grove of trees. Next morning, they had set out again but had gone only a short distance when Steel realized that he had left his scalping knife behind. He doubled back to his old camp, but he had no sooner approached the grove of trees when he saw that the hills were thick with angry Crows. Either they had followed the trail all night or another band had inadvertently stumbled across their track.

The other three Bloods had taken refuge in hastily dug trenches on a low ridge so Steel made a desperate effort to join them. Spurring his horse forward, he dashed through the enemy lines but caught a lead ball in the chest just before he leaped into an entrenchment.

In the confusion that followed, the well-armed Bloods were able to keep the Crows at bay. The ridge provided an excellent defence against attackers, for there was no way that an enemy could stay hidden if he tried to mount the slope. Of course, the stolen horses were recovered by the Crows almost immediately, but no one seemed prepared to make a suicidal attack up the hill. Yet the barrage of bullets, balls, and arrows had a telling effect on the Bloods, and before the day was over, Rope Chief had been killed.

Meanwhile, Steel had prayed to his spirit helpers, the owl and the thunder, to protect him and his companions from further harm. The bleeding in his chest had stopped so the young warrior joined in the fight until after the sun went down. The night proved to be dark and cloudy, and in spite of the fact that the Crows ringed the ridge with bonfires, the three surviving Bloods were able to slip through the enemy lines and make their way to freedom. Back in the lodge of his foster father, Ghost Chest, the young Indian was gently nursed back to health and made a full recovery.

Yes, mused Steel as he rode along, absently fingering the scar on his chest, those had been exciting days. Other raids had been more successful, but that one had given him his only wound. At least no one would ever point a gun at him again, now that they were at peace with their enemies.

At Heavy Shield's camp, Steel learned that someone had seen his horses a few miles west near the Waterton River. Good, he thought, I can round them up and be home before nightfall. Across the river valley and over the ridge, he saw his small herd grazing peacefully in the distance. A couple of them raised their heads as he approached, but the rest just kept on munching the hay that seemed so much better than the stuff they got at home.

Steel rounded up his little band of cayuses and was just topping a ridge when he heard someone call his name. Surprised, he reined in his horse and looked around. Below him, in a small secluded hollow, five Indians were busily engaged in skinning a beef. He recognized three of the boys as relatives—First Charger, Owns the Paint, and White Man Sleeps. Then there was Crooked Tail and a young lad he didn't know.

Steel realized right away what was happening. The boys had slipped away from the reserve, and within the hidden confines of the hills, had killed one of the cattle from the Cochrane Ranche. Hunger was a common complaint among the Bloods; numerous petitions had been sent to the government but to no avail. And young boys with voracious appetites were in the worst position of all; sometimes their weekly rations of beef and flour were consumed in a day, leaving them to starve until the next slaughter took place. These boys couldn't wait; they were doing their own butchering.

"Here," one of the rustlers called to Steel, holding aloft a piece of freshly cut meat, "take what you want."[2]

Steel shook his head. He had no qualms about accepting a gift of stolen meat, but he was too proud of his appearance to venture into the mess of butchering. "Give me what you want," he said, "and take it home for me. I don't want to soil my clothes or saddle."

The boys finished their butchering and loaded the meat on their horses just as Steel decided it was about time for him to go home. The long shadows of evening were spreading over the prairie hills and the colors of day were fading into the grays and dusks of night. The sky was cloudy, adding a monotonous pall that shrouded the countryside. Trees resembled gray, uneven rocks; rocks looked like sleeping cattle; and an evening stillness hung in the air.

Unknown to the covey of Bloods, word had been passed to the North-West Mounted Police detachment at Standoff that some whiskey traders had crossed the line from Montana and were taking their load of booze northward along the foothills. On that afternoon of October 19, Staff Sergeant Chris Hilliard had divided his small force into two groups, the officer going to intercept the bootleggers about ten miles (16 km) south, while Constables William Alexander and Patrick Ryan were instructed to follow the Belly River to the place where it was crossed by the Cochrane Ranche trail. If they didn't see the smugglers they were to head towards the Waterton River and search for their trail in the rolling hills.

The two police officers rode along the route and arrived at the hills just as Steel and the cattle killers prepared to go their separate ways. In the haze of dusk, all the patrol could see in the distance were two fully loaded packhorses, several riders, and some loose horses. Believing they had found the elusive smugglers, they let out a whoop and went forward at full gallop. Ryan immediately drew his revolver but Constable Alexander didn't bother; he had neglected to load it before they started out on the patrol.

The first thing Steel heard was a shout from one of the cattle killers. Turning in the saddle, he saw two police officers riding towards him at top speed, one waving his revolver dangerously in the air. Because he had separated from the others, Steel was the closest to the oncoming redcoats, so he rode forward to explain his innocence. However, he had just raised his hand and called out a welcome in Blackfoot when two shots were fired and the bullets whistled past his ear.

Oh no! Not again! He had seen it all before; the last time it was a Crow Indian and he still had the scar to prove it. That time he had run for cover; now he would stay and fight. The fact that they were police officers and that there might be dozens more over the next hill was unimportant; they were trying to kill him and he was a Blood warrior.

Halting momentarily, Steel swung his Winchester into the crook of his arm and shot the first officer when he was only a few feet away. The bullet nipped off Constable Alexander's ear lobe, grazed his neck, and tore the collar off his jacket. As the constable reeled from shock, Steel fired at the other man but missed. By this time he was almost surrounded by the two redcoats so he spun his horse around and headed for cover; he had gone only a few paces when a bullet from Ryan's gun caught him in the back.

Steel felt the searing pain rip through his body and he knew he had been shot. Determined to die fighting, he turned back to his attackers and fired again at Ryan, but already the warrior's eyes were cloudy and his mind confused. The bullet went wide and moments later the Indian slipped from his horse and fell to the ground.

No one knows when Ryan and Alexander realized they were chasing Indians instead of whiskey smugglers. In the semi-darkness of evening, the figures had been unclear from a distance, but as they drew near they must have discovered their mistake. By that time, Ryan's revolver was already barking and the fight was on. Of course, had they realized from the beginning that the men were Indians, there still would have been arrests. But both police officers had had long experience with Indians and knew that all they had to fear was the loss of prisoners escaping in the darkness. It was unlikely they would put up a fight, not like the hardened smugglers from Montana who had a lot more to lose.

But now it was too late. The five young Indians, the two packhorses, and the loose animals had all disappeared into the night. All that was left was an Indian lying on the ground, his horse standing patiently nearby. As the two police officers approached the dormant figure, Steel rolled painfully onto his side.

"You've already nearly killed me," he groaned. "Don't shoot any more."[3]

The two men were appalled at what had happened. Indian agent

Pocklington described Alexander as "a particularly nice, quiet young fellow, as is also Ryan," and that the former had been at the Standoff detachment for years.[4] Now they saw the Indian's blanket-coat streaked with blood and realized he was probably dying. They tried to get him on his horse but he was too weak; instead, he tried to walk along beside them, but after a short distance he collapsed again. The officers didn't know what to do, so they left him there and galloped off to the detachment for help.

As soon as the shooting had started, the five boys had dashed for safety, then made their way to Steel's camp. After they told his wife what had happened, they packed a few belongings and lit out for relatives in Montana. They would stay there for a year or so until the police had forgotten about them.

When she heard about the fight, Medicine Pipe Woman took one of the horses that the boys brought back to camp, hitched up her travois, and went to search for her husband. Everyone else in the camp was frightened so she had to go out into the darkness alone. She knew the shooting had taken place not far from the Big Rock, but when she looked, there was no sign of her missing man. She was on her way back home, just passing a small lake, when she heard a faint cry for help. Upon investigation, she found her husband. He had walked, stumbled, and crawled halfway back to his camp. He was pale and the upper part of his blanket-coat was matted with blood.

When she got him back to the reserve, Medicine Pipe Woman took her husband to the nearest cabin, one belonging to Running Wolf, and gently laid him on a buffalo robe. There Steel calmly smoked his pipe and sang his medicine songs as he waited to die.

One of the first men to see him was his brother, Thunder Chief, leader of the All Black Faces Band and a head chief of the tribe. He was angry about the shooting and set out immediately to see his fellow leaders. As soon as head chief Red Crow heard the tragic news, he personally arranged to give ten horses for the services of the three most powerful healers on the reserve—Low Horn, Black Eagle, and a medicine woman, *Kitsin'iki*. There was little hope that the Indian could survive the gunshot wound, but they would try to cure him.

As soon as the police learned of Steel's whereabouts—on October 20—an officer was sent to get his statement while the police surgeon, Dr. P. Aylen, went to inspect the wound. He found that the bullet had penetrated the man's back, punctured the right lung, and come out his chest. He was too weak to be moved and everyone agreed with Indian agent Pocklington that there was "very little hope for the

Indian,"[5] and no one argued with the newspaper account that said "he has only one chance in a thousand of living, and it will be admitted that this is pretty slim."[6]

Meanwhile, the Bloods reacted angrily to the shooting. Ermine Horse, a prominent chief, visited the wounded man and commented, "The Police will make us lose a brave man. If this happens we will take revenge against them."[7] Red Crow, always the diplomat, wanted the police to pay compensation to prevent further trouble, but they refused. The chief was following an age-old tradition of the tribe, one that often avoided long-term vendettas between families. On the reserve, word of the shooting spread like wildfire. Indians who had been working for ranchers south of the reserve promptly quit and hurried back home, ready for trouble. Others spoke of retaliation if Steel should die.

Fearful of the way events were escalating, Red Crow went to an American trader on the Belly River who had the reputation of selling the Indians unlimited supplies of ammunition, regardless of government regulations. He told the trader that the Indians might have a war on their hands and that he must close up shop for a few months. Wisely, the trader went to Montana and stayed away for the better part of a year.

Red Crow then led a delegation of chiefs to see the Indian agent, William Pocklington, and from there they went to the Mounted Police superintendent, Sam Steele. Thunder Chief, Steel's brother, related the events as he knew them, but it was obvious that neither official accepted his account.

"I do not believe a word of the Indian's story," said Pocklington flatly. "I am pretty sure that he had been helping to kill the beef & being caught tried to scare the Police away by shooting at them & when shot decided to tell this yarn with a view to fooling us all. He is a bad character."[8]

The police claimed that Steel had opened fire first, and for a while they insisted he had been shot in the chest. Only after seeing the irrefutable medical evidence did they admit he had been shot in the back.

As the holy men gathered in Running Wolf's small cabin, all offers of help from white doctors were refused. First there was Dr. Aylen, followed by Indian Department doctor F.X. Girard; both came to the camp but were not permitted to treat the wounded man. Instead, Steel placed his trust in the Indian medicine men and women. Of these, Low Horn was the leader. A great healer, believed to possess supernatural powers, he was said to have been the reincarnation of a famous Blackfoot warrior. With powers given him by the white-headed eagle, he devoted all his attention to the curing of his people.[9]

The family also showed its support when Steel's sister, Under Wolverine, vowed to sponsor a Sun Dance should her brother's life be spared. And they offered most of their horse herd to the medicine men in addition to the gift given by Red Crow.

When the incantations started within the cabin, a Mounted Police scout, Cecil Denny, was permitted to watch. Like others, he had given up on the poor Indian and felt his death was only a matter of time.

Pushing through the crowd of onlookers, Denny made his way into the cabin, which was stifling hot and reverberated with the deafening sounds of drumming and singing. The pungent odors of sweetgrass incense and tobacco smoke permeated the air. Stretched out on blankets on the floor was Steel, entirely naked, his body covered with a thick coat of white clay. The only place free of the mixture was a small area where the bullet had burst from his chest and left an ugly wound. As Denny noted, Steel "looked as if he was already dead and no one would think he could possibly survive."[10]

As Denny watched in fascination, he saw the medicine man pray over Steel; then the Indian announced that the wounded warrior was still controlled by an evil spirit that had entered his body with the police officer's bullet. Once this evil had been removed, Low Horn said, Steel would recover.

The holy man began to dance to the accompaniment of the drums, sometimes praying aloud and at other times sweeping his hands over the prone body of the victim. As the tempo increased, he took a bone whistle, cutting the air with its sharp and penetrating sounds. Finally, he bent down close to the man's body and blew into his wound. He placed his hands over the area, paused, then threw himself back with a flourish.

There was a gasp from the crowd. The drums were silenced. Not a sound was heard. The medicine man had obviously drawn the evil spirit from Steel's body and now he held it in his fist. Then, carefully and dramatically, he opened his hand and held up the object for everyone to see.

It was a live white mouse.

Denny was as amazed as the rest. "Where the mouse came from I cannot tell," he said, "but I never before or since saw a white mouse in an Indian camp."[11]

The medicine man announced that the evil had been removed;

Steel, shown here with his wife, was almost given up for dead after being shot by a Mounted Police officer. He survived, however, under the careful ministrations of three powerful Indians healers, including Low Horn, said to be the reincarnation of a famous Blackfoot warrior. *Collection of the author*

now Steel would recover. And sure enough, when the Indian agent visited him eight days after the shooting, he couldn't believe what he saw. "If he had not shown me his wound," said a surprised Pocklington, "I could not have believed he was sick."[12] And on October 31— twelve days after he was shot and left for dead—Steel was strong enough to ride horseback to Red Crow's camp in order to be closer to Low Horn and the others and to continue their treatments.

During those days of miracles, Steel had slipped in and out of consciousness. Although he had faith in the medicine men, he thought his wound was too serious even for them to cure. He was at peace with himself and believed that if he was going to die, he would go as a warrior, a proud fighter who had wounded his enemy in battle. But after the incident with the white mouse, he felt the strength returning to his body and he knew that he would live.

With the miraculous recovery of Steel, the threat of bloodshed ended. But the Mounted Police, aware of the unsettled conditions created by the shooting, chose not to arrest the Indian as long as he stayed on his reserve. In spite of the charge of shooting with intent to kill, the police knew they would have a confrontation on their hands if they tried to take Steel at his home. After a while, however, they became impatient to get their man. Steel, now completely cured, kept away from the Mounted Police town of Fort Macleod; instead he moved to the north end of the reserve, a mere four miles (6 km) from the bustling town of Lethbridge. From there, he could do his shopping, laugh at the police, and be back on the reserve before anyone knew he had been away.

Finally, the Mounted Police determined that the only way they could capture Steel was to trap him. They engaged the services of a scout named Gambler and told him to find a way to get the Indian into town. The solution was easy; Gambler simply killed a bunch of rabbits and asked Steel to help take them to Lethbridge, where he had a sale for them. Obligingly, Steel agreed, and only after they reached the village did he learn that the "buyer" was the Mounted Police cook. Still taking his companion at his word, Steel accompanied Gambler to the barracks, where the cook took the rabbits and offered to give the Indians a free meal. But no sooner had they set their weapons aside to eat than the police grabbed Steel and placed him under arrest.

When he appeared in court on February 16, 1892, the two head chiefs, Red Crow and Thunder Chief, were there to protest. When they learned the trial was going ahead anyway, they stayed to watch. The chiefs were worried because the likeable Indian agent, William Pocklington, had been transferred; he had been replaced by A.G. Irvine, a former Mounted Police commissioner. Where Pocklington had carried on running battles with the Mounted Police in defence of his wards, Irvine was obviously part of the police fraternity.

And that's the way it was at the trial. Steel had no defence attorney, while the Crown had the able services of G.E.P. Conybeare from Lethbridge. There were only four witnesses—Constable Alexander, Constable Ryan, and Dr. Aylen for the prosecution, and one of the cattle killers, Crooked Tail, for the defence. Both police officers testified that Steel had been warned to stop, that he had shot first, and that Ryan had fired only after his companion was wounded and called for help. Crooked Tail, on the other hand, proved to be useless as a defence witness and more concerned with denying his involvement with cattle killing than helping Steel. He refused to admit the Indians had any stolen meat in their possession, denied that they had packhorses, and claimed that he had been searching for horses when he saw the police and had heard three shots being fired.

Faced with that kind of evidence, the magistrate found Steel guilty of shooting with intent to kill and sentenced him to two months at hard labor in the Fort Macleod guardhouse. The Indians were convinced if Red Crow had not been present, Steel would have been sent to Stony Mountain Penitentiary in Manitoba, where many Indians died of tuberculosis before finishing their sentences.

Steel served his time and came back home to pick up his old life. He did not, as some officials predicted, die a young man because of weakened lungs. Rather, he had a long and productive career. He should have been appointed head chief of the tribe when his brother died in 1907, but in the minds of Indian Department officials, the stigma of the police battle still hung over his head and the position was denied him. So more and more he turned to religious matters. Eight times he was a member of the sacred Horn Society; four times he owned medicine pipes; and twice he was the owner of the beaver bundle, the most ancient holy object on the reserve. He also joined several religious societies, including the doves, brave dogs, braves, Black Catchers, and dogs.

When he died in the spring of 1940, he had become recognized as a leading holy man and warrior. He had been a member of the Horn Society that year and his tepee had been pitched to hold their meetings. Around it he had placed a circle of stones in addition to the usual pegs and had marked two stone fireplaces inside. He told his son Bob that after his death, the lodge was to be moved and four lines of stones placed on the ground, each extending from the circle to the cardinal points, thus creating a medicine wheel.

"The lines signify that he was a brave man," said his son-in-law, "a leader who had been to war. It was Steel's wish to have this done in tribute to him as a warrior chief."[13]

The medicine wheel is still there today, an ancient tradition that stands as a reminder of a brave man who should have died in 1891, but didn't.

Deerfoot and Friends

*O*n the 1880s, just as southern Alberta was being opened for settlement, long distance running had become a fad throughout much of the world. Pedestrianism, as it was called, was man's answer to horse racing. Just as the thoroughbreds could draw crowds to witness their strength and endurance, so could foot racers exhibit man's superior condition and ability. As it happened, this philosophy fitted perfectly with the lifestyle of many young Indians who considered physical prowess to be essential for survival. An Indian who could excel through demonstrations of physical superiority was admired by all his people, particularly the young ladies.

Pedestrianism reached the community of Calgary in 1883, the same year that the railway transformed the sleepy village into a booming tent town of merchants, speculators, and ranchers. It was a wild town, and even though prohibition was in force the laws were being violated openly at sports events, parties, and other gatherings. Even members of the town council were being arrested for drunkenness or other liquor-related offences.

In this rough frontier society, gambling was almost as prevalent as drinking, and sporting events became an ideal outlet for wagering. So pedestrianism, together with horse racing, became prime targets for the gambler. Within months of Calgary's formation, a group known ominously as "the syndicate" was organized and gained the reputation of making an easy dollar by sponsoring and then manipulating sports events, either through bribery or fraud.

During this period, the outstanding abilities of a young Blackfoot Indian came to the attention of the syndicate. His name was *E'nuksapop*, or Little Plume, described as "small, snug, built like a sprinter but with the heart and lungs of a hunting hound."[1] He was the son of a leading Blackfoot chief named Big Plume and had the reputation for being a quiet and responsible young man. An ex-Mounted Police officer named Edmund Allen had witnessed the Indian's participation in a race at the Indian camps and immediately enlisted him to run in Calgary. Allen, one of the syndicate members, had been a sub-inspector in the Mounted Police, where he picked up the sobriquet of "Lying Allen." After some questionable activities as Indian agent at Fort Walsh and Qu'Appelle, he was finally dismissed from the government service in 1881 and showed up in Calgary a short time later.

Allen's opportunity to use Little Plume's talents came in October of 1883, barely a month after the railway had reached Calgary. Capitalizing on the thirst for entertainment, a professional long distance runner from Ottawa named George Irvine began to travel the new line between Winnipeg and Calgary, racing against anyone that the communities could sponsor.

Recalling the performance of Little Plume, Allen and other members of the syndicate sought out the Indian and offered him twenty-five dollars if he would race the eastern professional on a five-mile (8-km) outdoor track. When the young man accepted the offer, he was quickly taught the techniques of the white man's system of racing. Delightedly, the gamblers observed that not only did the Indian learn rapidly, but his speed far surpassed their fondest hopes. Little Plume, they discovered, loved to run.

A track was laid out on the east side of the Elbow River and there, on October 11, the unknown Little Plume was pitted against the eastern professional. Betting was heavy, with odds favoring Irvine, and by the time the race was underway, more than four thousand dollars was at stake.

At the signal, Irvine took an early lead, with Little Plume following confidently at his heels. In a strategy that had probably been laid down by his handlers, the young Indian re-

Sketch of "Lying Allen" made while he was a Mounted Police officer in the 1870s. Allen later became a member of the Calgary "syndicate," who were suspected of fixing a number of athletic competitions for their own financial benefit. *Courtesy Glenbow-Alberta Institute/Nevitt Collection*

mained in second place until the runners were within a few hundred feet of the finish line. Then, with an easy burst of speed, he dashed past the surprised Irvine and won the race by a scant three feet (.9 m).

The result caused a mixture of jubilation and dismay. The gamblers gleefully raked in their winnings, but some of the men who had bet on Irvine were convinced that the race had been fixed. No Indian could run that fast. A loser identified only as Smith became so irate that he attacked a winner named Grant—probably one of the syndicate. The Mounted Police were forced to intercede and ended up frog-marching Smith back to the barracks, where he spent the night in jail. Next morning, both men appeared before the magistrate, charged with being drunk and creating a disturbance.

Irvine had won just about every other race during his tour, so his loss to the unknown Indian was sporting news. As far away as Winnipeg, a newspaper observed that Irvine had "met with a foeman worthy of his steel, in a dusky Blackfoot Indian named Little Plume, son of a chieftain."[2]

The financial advantages of scheduling a rematch in the more populous city of Winnipeg were immediately evident to the syndicate—who already were the real winners—as well as to Irvine and members of the Manitoba sporting fraternity. Grudge matches always brought out the crowds and the bettors. Before he left Calgary, Irvine issued a challenge to meet Little Plume in a ten-mile (16-km) race, preferably in Winnipeg or St. Paul, Minnesota. Each side was to put up five hundred dollars.

The syndicate acted while enthusiasm was still high. Within two weeks, a half-breed interpreter named Tony Cobell had been engaged, and with three leaders of the syndicate—Lying Allen, his father, and J. McLaughlin—they set out with Little Plume for the Manitoba capital.

It was an interesting quirk of fate that Little Plume was probably the first Indian from the Alberta prairies to travel east on the new railway. Even the great Blackfoot chief Crowfoot did not make the trip until almost a year later. Little Plume's love for running, and the avariciousness of his backers, gave this signal honor to a sports figure rather than to a political leader.

Little Plume had never been out of Blackfoot country before. Winnipeg, with its rows and rows of stone and brick buildings, milling crowds, and strange new sights, both frightened and fascinated him. Shortly after his arrival, he was taken to the fire hall, where more surprises awaited him. A reporter commented:

While he was gazing in wonder at a large steamer, one of the boys touched the whistle valve, which sent forth a screech that sounded all through the hall, much to the amusement of the little brave, but when the gong was sprung, doors thrown open, and the splendid horses came bounding to their places, he actually jumped with delight.[3]

But if Little Plume was captivated by Winnipeg, the people of that city were enchanted by the youthful runner. He was the center of attention as he wandered the streets, his hair in long braids and tied with red ribbons, his ears ornamented with shell earrings, and his face covered with yellow ceremonial paint. "Citizens must have observed during the past few days," commented a newspaper reporter, "a pleasant-faced Indian, dressed in gay leggings and wearing a gaily-colored blanket about his shoulders, walking about the city. It was Little Plume. By his unostentatious demeanor he made many friends and when he stepped into the ring he got many a friendly nod and approving look from those who had become attached to him."[4]

Little Plume and his backers had come to a city that was at the height of its enthusiasm for foot racing. Unlike Calgary, the sport had been well controlled and had remained relatively honest, in spite of the fact that the wagering was heavy in all events. Earlier in the year, several professional runners had competed in events that had drawn large crowds. Two visiting sprinters, Sadler and Fraser, individually had wiped out most of the local runners and had finally met in a match at Dufferin Park. There, amid heavy betting, Sadler won the 100-yard dash with a time of ten seconds flat. Later, Fraser took on another professional, T.H. Tait, and beat him in the 220-yard dash. There also were several long distance runners competing during the season, including Thomas Headley, A.G. Ross, W. Bennett, and H. Cameron. When George Irvine had arrived from Ottawa, he had beaten most of the local and professional competition, including the highly rated Headley.

The Irvine–Little Plume race, occurring late in the year, was supposed to be the last of the season. In order to allay any fears about the honesty of the Calgary delegation, Lying Allen assured the press that there was no way Little Plume could be bribed.

"There is a certain sense of honor among Indians," he said glibly, "which no amount of money can overcome. Little Plume's reputation is so much at stake among his own people that if he does not outstrip his opponent it will not be from failing to try to the utmost of his ability."⁵

Shortly after the arrival of the Calgary group, a formal agreement was prepared between George Irvine and Lying Allen on behalf of Little Plume. The site for the ten-mile (16-km) race was to be an old skating rink, where there would be fifteen laps to the mile. Each side deposited two hundred and fifty dollars when the agreement was made and another like amount would be forthcoming on the night before the race, winner take all. Gate receipts at the indoor rink were to go first for advertising and rink rental, then to cover the travel expenses of Little Plume and his party. Any balance was to be evenly divided between the two runners.

As expected, the advance publicity drew a large crowd to the event on the evening of October 26, so that the Calgary syndicate would have had very little trouble wagering the "several thousands" of dollars they had brought with them.

The odds favored Irvine at two to one. However, at the last minute the Calgary gamblers lost their nerve and laid out only about one thousand dollars of their cache, as though they were not sure if Little Plume could win in the strange city.

When the signal was given, the Indian, bare-footed and dressed only in a breechcloth, dashed to the lead and remained there for the first four miles (6.4 km). Irvine then spurted past him and held the spot for two miles (3.2 km), when Little Plume pulled ahead again. From that point until the end of the event, the lead position seesawed back and forth between the two runners.

The race was a clean one until the beginning of the last mile. At that point, Irvine tried to spurt far ahead of his Indian opponent but Little Plume overtook him. Then, just as the Indian was passing him, Irvine pushed Little Plume into a wall and knocked him to the ground. The crowd yelled "foul" but the Blackfoot runner jumped quickly to his feet and soon caught up to the leader. As he surged ahead, Little Plume either stumbled or was tripped and when he fell to the floor, Irvine trampled on his left hand with his spiked shoes. Again the plucky Blackfoot arose and with blood streaming from his hand, the crowd encouragingly shouting "Go to it, Nitchie," he raced forward, passed Irvine, and won the race with six feet (1.8 m) to spare. The recorded time was fifty-three minutes.

Exhausted and sore, Little Plume collapsed on the floor but was quickly hoisted on the shoulders of his backers and carried through the crowd to the Grand Union Hotel, where a doctor dressed his wounds. Irvine also felt the effects of the race, fainting as soon as he crossed the finish line. Later he was reported to be bleeding at the lungs.

"The universal opinion seemed to be that the best man won," commented a reporter, "and that the race was 'square,' though considerable dissatisfaction was expressed at the condition of the track, and particularly at the corners, where the Indian had to make a big sweep, otherwise he fell down, as he wore no shoes and the sawdust slipped from under him."[6]

Irvine's backers immediately demanded a return race, and accordingly, arrangements were made for a five-mile (8 km) duel on November 1, with each side putting up two hundred dollars.

Apparently the Calgary gamblers were angry with themselves for not betting more money on their man while they could still get good odds. Now that Little Plume had beaten Irvine twice in a row, the odds began to favor the popular Indian runner. At this point, evidence is lacking, but it is likely that Lying Allen and his crowd tried to talk Little Plume into losing the next race. In any case, a bitter argument ensued, with the matter not being settled by the end of the day. Next morning, before sunrise, Little Plume crept from his hotel room and began to walk the nine hundred miles (1,448 km) back to Calgary. By the time the syndicate had discovered he was missing and had traced his route, he was already several miles west of Winnipeg, and only after the gamblers promised to let him run a fair race would he agree to return for the match on the following day.

But the skullduggery was not over. On the night before the race someone—likely from the Calgary syndicate—mixed broken glass with the sawdust on the track. One of the sharp-eyed judges spotted it prior to the race but Lying Allen said it would cause no trouble and that the race should proceed. Little Plume, however, decided to pull his moccasins over two or three pairs of socks before going on the track. Betting by this time was two to one in favor of the Indian. "A great deal of money was staked on the results," commented *The Sun*, and one might speculate where the Calgary cash had been placed.[7]

At the signal, Little Plume and Irvine set out on the five mile (8-km) run, using the same skating rink where they had met previously. This time, in an attempt to prevent any fouling or interference, judges were stationed at each of the turns. From the beginning, there was no doubt that Little Plume planned to run a fair race. Irvine pulled into an early lead and held it for the first four miles (6.4 km), but the Indian was constantly at his heels, showing frequent bursts of speed, causing his adversary to press harder than he intended in order to maintain his lead. The Indian's strategy was to tire the front runner, and as soon as Irvine showed signs of fatigue, Little Plume dashed ahead of him and maintained a lead that he increased to twelve yards (10.9 m) at the finish line. His time was twenty-seven minutes, twenty-two seconds.

At the end, Irvine was so weak that he stumbled off the edge of the track and into a wall before collapsing. Little Plume, on the other hand, was exuberant over his win, and while he was being carried out on the shoulders of his admiring fans he claimed he could have run another ten miles (16 km).

Little Plume had so captured the hearts of the sporting fraternity in Winnipeg that before the race a number of pools had been formed to bet on the popular young runner. For that reason, the broken glass incident was the source of considerable indignation. Either with justified evidence or through suspicion, the Calgary crowd became suspect and Lying Allen felt obliged to defend himself in the press. After claiming that the glass was from a broken window, he went on to state that his people had seen it but "the glass was not raked out of the building before the sawdust was put on the course, as we supposed a thick coating of sawdust would render the track safe."[8] He further claimed that Little Plume had run in his bare feet during the race and had suffered no ill effects.

The *Free Press* called Lying Allen a liar.

"The assertion that the Indian ran in his bare feet is false," it began, "as our reporter was particular to notice that the Indian's feet were covered with moccasins."[9] It said Allen's story about the glass was "incredible," that the fragments were curved bottle glass, and that the whole story was "a very thin attempt to cover up a dirty piece of business."[10]

Little Plume was also angry about the broken glass incident and announced that he would not run any more races in Winnipeg. He planned, he told the press, to return immediately to his own reserve.

But during the next couple of days, the young Indian was persuaded to change his mind and agreed to run a three-mile (4.8-km) farewell race on the evening of November 8. Later, it was learned that he would not run for less than one hundred dollars, and he had to have the money in advance before he would agree to this last competition. Clearly he was disillusioned with the syndicate and so suspicious that he demanded far more than the twenty-five dollars promised to him in previous races.

The syndicate confidently put up their guarantee of one hundred dollars, and with the odds favoring Little Plume by two to one, they bet their entire bankroll on Irvine.

When the race was run, the Indian's lackluster performance was a surprise to everyone. It was suspected that he had been drugged just before the race. He ran like a novice and was never able to catch up with Irvine after the Ottawa runner had taken an early lead. When it was over, the befuddled Indian had lost by a full fifty yards (45.7 m). The press was so disgusted by the obvious crookedness of the event that they didn't even bother to write it up. It was, in the eyes of Winnipegers, "a put up job."[11]

After the race, Little Plume would have nothing to do with his backers. When he left, he refused to travel on the same train with them and, instead, went back to his reserve alone and humiliated. As a Calgary reporter observed, Little Plume had for a short time been "the source of prosperity for a group of Calgarians. The Indian ran for glory and white men reaped the harvest."[12]

Little Plume completely disassociated himself from the syndicate, but he continued to run for the fun of it. In the spring of 1884 he was invited to join in Calgary's celebration of Queen Victoria's birthday on May 24. The committee in charge of activities was made up of respectable merchants, and hundreds of Sarcee and Blackfoot Indians were witnesses to the event. Cheered on by his own people, Little Plume took the one-mile (1.6-km) race, beating out a fellow tribesman named Big Hawk and winning a meerschaum pipe and cigar holder. He also tried his first 200-yard (182.8-m) hurdle race but lost out to a local police officer. However, he placed second and won three dollars.

But Lying Allen and the syndicate weren't finished yet. They may have lost a prime profit-maker in Little Plume, but all they needed in order to make a comeback was a new runner. In the spring of 1884, Allen went to Winnipeg to assure sportsmen that he would bring Little Plume back for the July 1 races, even though he knew this would be impossible. Then, cagily, he hinted that if the Indian wasn't available, he had another Blackfoot "who can run a mile in 4 minutes and 17 seconds."[13] However, the race never came off.

The new man was *A'pikaiees*, Scabby Dried Meat, son of Medicine Fire and nephew of the great chief Crowfoot. He was described as standing "one or two inches over six feet in his deerskin moccasins, and he weighed perhaps a hundred and sixty-five pounds."[14] A Mounted Police officer said he was "a lean lanky built man, and as thin as a crane."[15]

Scabby Dried Meat was not an innocent nice guy like Little Plume. Rather, he was a wild, arrogant, hard-drinking, tough warrior who had already gained a questionable reputation among the young men for his daring and bravado. He was said to have eluded the police in Montana, and when he won his first Calgary race, *The Macleod Gazette* recalled that his running ability had been useful "when he escaped from the police guard room here some years ago."[16]

Scabby Dried Meat had no hesitation in allowing himself to be backed by the crooked syndicate, even though he probably had been warned by Little Plume. He entered into an arrangement with full knowledge of the kind of men he was dealing with. Yet the action was in keeping with Scabby Dried Meat's reckless nature. Not only was he supremely confident in his own ability as a runner but he was arrogantly sure that he could deal with any situation. He despised the white man, and with this attitude, he was neither cowed by them nor indebted to them.

He also shared a feeling common among some Indians of that era. Only four years earlier they had seen the last of the buffalo destroyed, and now they were dependent upon government rations for survival. So they blamed the white men for killing the buffalo and resented the life-and-death control they now possessed over the once-independent Blackfoot. As a result, some Indians felt they owed the white man nothing; he had stolen everything from them—their buffalo, their land, and their freedom. Therefore, young men in particular did not consider it a crime to steal back from the white man, whether cattle, horses, or goods.

Scabby Dried Meat shared this resentment and if he was involved with white men who stole from other white men, the matter was of no concern to him. What counted was that the syndicate was willing to pay him for what he enjoyed doing most—running.

No records exist to show if Allen was able to line up any races for the Indian in 1884. It is known that in September there was a match in Winnipeg in which a professional runner named Taylor defeated an Indian runner in a three-mile (4.8-km) race. However, the Native was not identified.

Little Plume and Scabby Dried Meat weren't the only Indian runners on the Canadian prairies, although they were among the best. In fact, Indians were such good runners that in some races they were barred from competing. In Regina in 1883, for example, there was a one-mile (1.6-km) race for the championship of the District of Assiniboia "open to all residents of the District, pure

Indians excepted."[17] A Dominion Day sports meet in Pincher Creek included a 100-yard dash that was "open to whites" only.[18]

Any plans the Calgary syndicate may have had for Scabby Dried Meat's career were interrupted by the onset of the Riel Rebellion. All spring and summer in 1885, Calgary was filled with troops from the East who had come to fight Indians, not to race them. As a result, most Indians stayed out of the town that summer and if races were held, they were limited to engagements among the militia, Mounted Police, and local townsmen.

By the spring of 1886, Calgary had changed from a frontier settlement to a substantial town of wood, brick, and sandstone buildings. The population had grown from about three hundred persons to more than one thousand, and had seen the establishment of many social amenities, including five churches, a school, theater, turf club, and race track. During these months of growth, the syndicate had been active in Calgary, turning its attention to horse racing in the absence of foot-racing competitions. But the gamblers were as crooked as ever.

"Put up jobs are the order of the day in every class of competition," complained the *Calgary Herald*. "One striking feature about these transactions is their extreme transparency. If a horse is to be pulled, he finishes with his head somewhere in the neighborhood of his rider's knee; and the same palpable trickery is observable in almost every class or event to which the attention of the sporting public here is directed."[19]

Calgary lacked indoor sports facilities until early 1886, when F.J. Claxton constructed the Star Rink for skating, running, and other events. To celebrate its opening, he announced a "go-as-you-please" race to take place from June 2 to June 5, four hours a night for four nights. The person covering the greatest number of laps during that time would be declared the winner.

The only competitor from Calgary was James Green, a member of the North-West Mounted Police who had been a professional runner in Montreal. Little Plume had been out of circulation for more than a year, but when Claxton prevailed upon him to enter, he reluctantly agreed. The syndicate also brought out their runner, Scabby Dried Meat, whose name was sometimes mistranslated as Bad Dried Meat.

On the first night, Little Plume and Scabby Dried Meat slipped into an easy lead over Green, and like a pair of tireless trotting horses, they remained together lap after lap. By the end of the first night, the

Indians were two miles (3.2 km) ahead of their only competitor. Around them all evening the crowds had milled and urged them on, while a band played, and refreshments ranged from mild to strongly alcoholic. Little Plume was, by far, the most famous of the three and something of a local hero; Scabby Dried Meat was, as yet, a relative unknown.

On Thursday, the second night, Green apparently found his pace, and while he did not make up his lost mileage, neither did he fall farther behind the pacing pair. The next evening, however, proved to be a bad one for Little Plume, for somewhere along the course he apparently fell or was pushed to the ground. After three hours of running, he was obviously in pain and finally had to come off the track to be treated by a doctor. His knee was badly swollen, and although the doctor recommended that he withdraw from the race, he insisted on returning to the track and finishing out the evening.

Meanwhile, Scabby Dried Meat was having a different kind of problem. The night before, well wishers had supplied him liberally with whiskey and when he appeared for the third evening, he had a terrible hangover and at first refused to run. However, as soon as Little Plume and Green were on the track he could not resist the challenge and, according to a reporter, "for a man who didn't feel well he put in some fine work."[20] Although Green was in top shape that evening and was easily able to pass the injured Little Plume, he succeeded in gaining less than a mile (1.6 km) on the intemperate Scabby Dried Meat. By the time the night was over, Scabby Dried Meat had run eighty-four miles (135 km) and six laps, compared to Green's eighty-three miles (133.5 km) and one lap, and Little Plume's seventy-six miles (122 km) and six laps.

According to a reporter, Scabby Dried Meat bragged "he could beat that Nape-o-guoin [white man]; he could run him all tomorrow night and all next day, and not drink anything either."[21]

Bragging or not, Scabby Dried Meat made good his promise. Not only did he stay sober but he scored an easy victory over Green and took the championship. Little Plume, although gamely staying in the race, had been so badly injured that he virtually hobbled to a third-place finish.

Now that the gamblers had another sure winner on their hands with Scabby Dried Meat, they faced a unique problem. Little Plume's real name had a certain charm that seemed appropriate for the modest runner. But Scabby Dried Meat was an impossible name if the syndicate expected to put him into the professional circuit and to build up the romantic image of an Indian runner. After some discussion, they finally settled upon a new name.

Scabby Dried Meat became Deerfoot. It was a name that created the image of a fleet-footed warrior nimbly coursing the open prairie. It had a James Fenimore Cooperish ring to it that would appeal to the press and the public alike. However, the name was not Blackfoot; rather, it had belonged to a Seneca Indian who had gone to England in the 1860s and defeated some of the top runners in the world. The syndicate hoped the Blackfoot might bring them similar results.

A detailed account of the four-day race at Star Rink, together with photographs, appeared in the July issue of the *New York Sporting World*. In addition, the newly christened Deerfoot posed for pictures at a local photographic parlor and prints were widely distributed among the sporting fraternity.

Amid this publicity, the syndicate sent telegrams to promoters in Winnipeg and other eastern points, seeking competition for their new man. In the meantime, another opportunity for Deerfoot to race occurred in July 1886, during the

Deerfoot, shown here in 1886, was renowned for his prowess as a runner in the 1880s. Indians proved to be such good runners that in some races they were barred from competing. *Courtesy Glenbow-Alberta Institute/NA-3985-24*

Dominion Day celebrations in Calgary. Little Plume, Constable Green, and the new competitor were the three entries for a one-mile (1.6-km) outdoor race that Deerfoot won with ease. He also competed in a quarter-mile (.4-km) race and defeated the only other competitor, G.C. Ross of High River.

Over the summer of 1886, Deerfoot was involved in a number of local races while the syndicate was trying to line up a professional match. In one of these runs, according to the press, the Indian "came within a second of beating the record of a mile, and that notwithstanding the fact that he had amused himself by cutting up some antics on the way round the track."[22]

Another tournament, if true, went unrecorded in the newspapers but was recalled by an old Mounted Police veteran. He claimed that Deerfoot easily won the one- and three-mile (1.6 and 4.8-km) races, but had a desperate run against a police officer for the five-mile (8-km) event. Although starting strong, Deerfoot was matched by his opponent at the two-and-a-half-mile (4-km) mark and when only two hundred yards (182.8 m) from the finish line, the white runner took the lead by a few feet.

According to the story, Deerfoot was dressed only in a breechcloth and moccasins, and when he strained to pass his competitor, a cord snapped and the breechcloth fell to the ground.

> The Indian finished the race clad only in his bronze birthday suit, to the consternation of the fair ones directly in his path. Restoratives were administered to several ladies who promptly fainted, losing all further interest in the outcome of the race.[23]

Apparently Deerfoot lost this race by a full thirty yards (27.4 m) "much to the joy of the whites and the disappointment and chagrin of the Indians who were present in large numbers."[24]

By autumn, the Calgary syndicate had exceeded its wildest hopes in bringing a professional runner to Calgary. Not only did the gamblers succeed in persuading a well-known British pedestrianist, J.W. Stokes of Birmingham, to race against Deerfoot, but George Irvine agreed to return to the prairies later in the season to take on Little Plume's successor.

Stokes arrived early in September, but when the syndicate sent for Deerfoot they were told that the Indian agent refused to give him a pass to leave the reserve. No reason was given for the action, but it may have been caused by a concern that Deerfoot's frequent association with the gamblers had increased his drinking problem and made him all the more recalcitrant in his dealings with the agency staff.

While the matter was being appealed, the syndicate put on a fifty-hour "go-as-you-please" walking race at the Star Rink, with Stokes easily beating the local competition. However, the match revealed either that the gamblers were still crooked or Calgarians were ill-prepared to offer matches in a professional manner. Problems of crowd control, confusion over the procedure of recording the laps, and general mismanagement of the event resulted in local newspapers refusing to report it.

Hoping that the problem of Deerfoot's pass would be resolved, the syndicate scheduled a fifty-hour running race for September 15. But the Indian was still restricted to his home reserve, so Stokes took on a local man and easily beat him.

Early in October, George Irvine arrived from Winnipeg, and when word came that the Indian agent had finally agreed to give passes to any Indians who wanted to compete, a ten-mile (16-km) race was scheduled for October 21. As far as the syndicate was concerned, they could not resist confusing the bettors, particularly if it would improve their odds. Accordingly, when another Indian applied to enter the race, the syndicate took him in hand and registered him under the name of Bad Dried Meat. Realizing that Deerfoot had been running professionally for two years under a name that was often translated in that way, the syndicate hoped that a number of bettors would mistakenly support that man. Bad Dried Meat's real name was Runs Backwards and Forwards; he was a Peigan Indian who was married to a Blackfoot girl and lived on her reserve.

The only competitors to sign up for the Calgary race were Stokes, Irvine, Deerfoot, and Bad Dried Meat. It was a gala event with the Mounted Police band in attendance and a large crowd of spectators jamming the Star Rink. Betting was heavy, and in spite of the international reputation of Stokes and Irvine, the odds were in favor of Deerfoot. The race was considered important enough to be covered by a local correspondent for the *New York Sporting World*.

Surprisingly, as soon as the race started, Irvine dropped far to the rear of the pack while Bad Dried Meat was only slightly behind Deerfoot and Stokes. As they circled the track lap after lap, no one passed Deerfoot, and the Indian runner led the race all the way. When a jubilant Deerfoot finally crossed the finish line, he was greeted by a rousing cheer from his supporters. Their joy was short-lived, however, as the men who were keeping the official records made the astounding assertion that there had been an error and that Stokes had actually won the race by a full lap. The crowd was incredulous, but in the heated arguments that followed, the organizers stood firm. In the end, nothing could be proven, so the judges invalidated the whole race and all bets were off.

When he heard the news, Deerfoot sat down and cried.

Most of the spectators supported the Indian and they raised twenty-five dollars amongst themselves to give to him as a gift in lieu of his rightful prize. Deerfoot, however, indignantly refused the money, claiming that he had won the match fair and square. Angrily he stomped out of the arena and immediately returned to his reserve.

A local journalist observed that the decision was "an instance of the most consummate meanness, and the men who would lend themselves to the perpetration of such a fraud deserve to be made an example of."[25]

The pattern of events seemed to follow the syndicate's strategy of building up the odds on their own man, then fixing the race and betting on the opposition. In this case, they thought they could get the Indian drunk and in no condition to compete, but he fooled them. Facing potential ruin, the syndicate managed to invalidate the race and cancel all bets. The *Calgary Herald* had no doubt that the syndicate had manipulated the race. The next day, in an editorial, the newspaper commented: "A Calgary audience is one of the most good humored crowds in the world, or else some of these 'smart' gentlemen would have been pretty badly hurt before now. In most places somebody would have gone home on a shutter last night."[26]

After further discussion, Claxton agreed to pay first prize money of twenty dollars to both Deerfoot and Stokes, and to award the third-place purse of ten dollars to Bad Dried Meat. The medal designed for the championship was not awarded.

Stokes responded to the criticisms by issuing a challenge to the syndicate. "Seeing that so many people believe Deerfoot to be better than myself for a long distance," he said, "I am prepared to test the pluck of his backers and run him ten miles [16 km] in a fortnight's time."[27] Failing this, he was ready to run twenty miles (32 km) and give the Indian a quarter-mile (402-m) head start. Deerfoot's backers agreed to the challenge for ten miles on the condition that the unclaimed medal be awarded to the winner.

Deerfoot was reluctant to return to Calgary, and when he did so on November 7, he was both suspicious and truculent. Like Little

Plume, he had learned that the running game was often more of a contest of behind-the-scenes intrigue than of endurance or skill. He had thought he could cope with white men who cheated each other, but not until the ten-mile (16-km) race did he discover that he could become the victim.

Before the race, arrangements had been made for the two contestants to split the gate receipts. Because of the bad publicity from the previous meet and the suspicions of bettors, however, the crowd was not as large as expected. Before the race began, Deerfoot wanted to know how much he would get. When the receipts were tallied, his share came to a meager $12.50. At first he wanted the money placed in the hands of someone he could trust, but then, on reflection, he complained it wasn't enough and refused to run.

At this point, a collection was taken up and the ante raised to twenty-five dollars, but Deerfoot demanded fifty dollars and was hostile to everyone around him, particularly his backers from the syndicate. First he claimed the rink was too cold for running and then, remembering Little Plume's experience, he suspiciously asked to have the sawdust checked to see if it contained broken glass.

Meanwhile, Stokes demanded that the race begin, and if Deerfoot failed to participate, he would lose by default. When the judges agreed, the English runner set out alone along the track, while Deerfoot retreated to a dark corner of the rink where he morosely watched the proceedings. Then, after Stokes had covered several laps, Deerfoot suddenly jumped to his feet, threw off his blanket-coat and leather shirt, and dashed into the race.

At this point, the Indian was six laps behind, but within the next two miles (3.2 km) he had gained a lap, picked up two more before the fourth mile, and stood even with Stokes on the fifth. Deerfoot seemed to be traveling like the wind while his competitor, thrown off stride by the sudden change in his opponent, had trouble finding his pace. At the six-mile (9.6-km) mark, Deerfoot was a full lap ahead and had gained an incredible three laps over the Englishman by the seventh. This lead was maintained until the end of the race, with Deerfoot having covered the ten miles (16 km) in fifty-four minutes and thirty seconds.

Stokes immediately protested that Deerfoot had automatically disqualified himself by not entering the race at the outset, but this time the judges decided unanimously that the Indian had won the race and awarded him the championship medal. Instead of being elated, Deerfoot remained hostile and announced that he was finished with the syndicate and that there would be no more races for him that season, and perhaps forever. Now that winter had come to the prairies, he would stay on his reserve until spring.

That left the syndicate with the Peigan Indian, Bad Dried Meat, who had made a good showing in the race and had easily beaten the more favored Irvine. According to one observer, "Only Deerfoot was better than this sturdy brave on the long-distance contests."[28]

Still wanting to capitalize on Stokes's visit to Calgary, the promoters organized a four day "go-as-you-please" race, beginning on November 25. Deerfoot refused to attend, so the contestants were limited to Bad Dried Meat, Stokes, a police officer named Mellon, and two local Indians, Rapid Runner and White Cap. It soon proved to be a contest between Bad Dried Meat and Stokes, each running about thirty-two miles (51.4 km) an evening. However, the crowds were poor and as the rink was needed for ice skating, the match was shortened to three days and Bad Dried Meat declared the winner.

When the racing season started again in 1887, Deerfoot was back, drawn like a moth to a burning flame that might ultimately destroy him. This time, however, he came without the backing of the syndicate, and like his friend Little Plume, he was now a free agent. The gala event in Calgary that year was the Dominion Day holiday on July 1, which marked the fiftieth anniversary of Queen Victoria's reign. There was a parade down the flag-and-bunting decorated Stephen Avenue, followed by horse racing, track-and-field events, foot racing, and bicycle racing. The latter were relatively new to Calgary but had quickly gained enthusiastic popularity. Ultimately, they were to replace pedestrianism as a racing event.

The only Indian competitors in the foot racing were Deerfoot, Little Plume, and someone called The Nut. In the quarter-mile (402-m) race, the contest was between Deerfoot and George Irvine, the Indian easily beating out his opponent. In the half-mile (804-m) event, only the Indians finished in the money. Little Plume, taking part in the last recorded race of his career, was in first place, with The Nut second, and Deerfoot third.

A few weeks after this event, the circumstances of Deerfoot's life suddenly changed. During the latter part of August, he had been to Calgary with a number of friends to compete in local races, and they were on their way back to their reserve when they passed the cabin of George Madge, near Langdon station. One of the Indians noticed that the door was ajar and when they looked inside they saw that no one was home. Taking advantage of the situation, one of the

Blackfoot stole a revolver, while Deerfoot took a pair of blankets.

It was a simple case of theft but their timing couldn't have been worse. Since the beginning of spring, 1887, Indian "incidents" had been occurring at several points on the prairies and newspapers were predicting a major Indian outbreak.

Seven Blood Indians had been killed the previous fall but as their bodies were not discovered until winter, the Indians had waited until the spring of 1887 before launching several retaliatory raids into Montana. When a white settler was killed in Montana, Canadian Indians were immediately blamed, and even though the culprit later proved to be an American Indian, the sensational publicity only added to the tense situation. Then, in April, a pair of Bloods raided a ranch on the outskirts of Medicine Hat and traded shots with the Mounted Police. Later, these two Indians were apprehended but escaped from custody while on their way to jail.[29]

In addition, a number of break-ins had occurred at various ranches and farms throughout southern Alberta, and people were demanding action from the police.

Madge discovered the theft of his gun and blankets shortly after it had occurred and immediately notified the Mounted Police. A patrol of five officers and an interpreter set out for the reserve and had gone only a short distance past Langdon when they caught up with Deerfoot and arrested him for stealing the blankets. When asked who had the revolver, he said it was one of the Indians who had gone ahead, so the corporal left the prisoner with three constables and took the rest of his men in pursuit of the other thief.

Because Deerfoot was so well known, the constable in charge did not feel it necessary to handcuff him. Instead, they all rode over to a railway section-house where a few Indians were camped. Upon arrival, Deerfoot suddenly broke loose from his captors and tried to grab a rifle from one of the Indians. When he failed, he grappled momentarily with an officer, then broke free again and picked up an ax lying near the door of the section-house.

Brandishing this weapon, he kept the police at bay and then ran down the railway track. One man in his way tried to stop him, but the determined Indian swung his ax threateningly until the officer moved aside. Then, stripped to his breechcloth and moccasins, the Indian dashed down the tracks in one of the most important races of his life.

Realizing that they could never catch him afoot, two of the officers began to pursue him on horseback, while the corporal and his men, returning empty-handed after searching for the other

Indian, joined the chase. They succeeded in surrounding Deerfoot, but the fugitive swung the ax back and forth, saying he would never be taken alive and threatening to brain anyone who tried to stop him. Even when one of the police fired a shot at the ground in front of him, he refused to surrender.

"You had better shoot straight the next time," he said in a menacing tone.[30]

Not knowing if they had the right to shoot the wanted man, particularly when the original charge was simple housebreaking, the officers kept a respectful distance. The corporal begged him to surrender, but Deerfoot shook his head and began trotting down the trail towards the Blackfoot Reserve. The police followed him for about four miles (6.4 km), but when it was evident that he did not intend to surrender and that an attack would almost surely result in someone's death, the pursuit was called off.

Defiance of the police would have been a serious offence under any circumstances, but the matter was made worse because it occurred only a day after another incident in which a Blackfoot Indian had been killed and a white man wounded in a shooting incident. In that affair, which had happened only a few miles south of Deerfoot's confrontation, two settlers named William Thompson and Tucker Peach had found their cabin looted, and when they went to a nearby Blackfoot camp, they saw some of their missing goods. In the argument that followed, a Blackfoot named The Meat shot Peach in the fleshy part of the arm; at almost the same instant, Thompson shot an Indian in the chest. The latter person, Trembling Man, later died from his wounds.

Thus, in a matter of two days the usually peaceful Blackfoot had been involved in two serious incidents, one ending in death and the other in defiance of the police.

Upon their return to the barracks, all members of the patrol that had allowed Deerfoot to escape were placed under arrest. The commanding officer was so angry that after he had heard the evidence, he sentenced the corporal, his men, and the interpreter, to six months' confinement. Later, when cooler heads prevailed, the charge was reduced to time in custody.

Meanwhile, Deerfoot arrived back at the reserve and immediately went to the lodge of his uncle, Crowfoot, to explain what had happened. By this time, news of the killing of Trembling Man had spread rapidly through the reserve. Later, when The Meat was arrested for his part in the affray, the excitement turned to anger as the Blackfoot learned that the white man who had fatally wounded Trembling Man was still at large.

Reacting quickly to the situation, the Honorable Edgar Dewdney, who had the dual titles of Indian commissioner and lieutenant governor of the North-West Territories, traveled from Regina to the Blackfoot Reserve. There he spoke with Crowfoot and learned first-hand of the anger and uneasiness that existed among the Blackfoot over the Trembling Man and Deerfoot troubles.

"The Indians have all along been taught," said one observer, "that the Police were their friends, and that the Government would always treat them well. There has been a lot of talk among them over this affair, and their manner towards the whites has changed to suspicion and distrust."[31]

Dewdney and Crowfoot were old friends, and so after lengthy discussions, the chief agreed to have Deerfoot speak directly to the Indian commissioner. When the two men met, the Blackfoot runner agreed to give himself up in Calgary, but he failed to appear. Assistant Commissioner W.M. Herchmer notified the Macleod detachment to send fifty men from the south, Herchmer led another fifty from Calgary, and added to the ten men already on the reserve, he had more than a hundred police ready to seek out the fugitive.

Concern was expressed that the invasion of the reserve by a large body of police might trigger a fight with some of the more hot-headed young warriors. Actually, the opposite proved to be true. With the Macleod detachment searching the southern part of the reserve and the Calgary group the north, the Indians were conspicuous by their absence. Finally, after days of futile hunting, the police withdrew without their man.

There were many rumors as to the whereabouts of Deerfoot in the months that followed. Some said he had gone to Montana, or to his wife's relatives in Strangling Wolf's village on the Blood Reserve, while others placed him with the Peigans. In fact, he had never left his own reserve, moving quite openly in the camps where he received the admiring support of the young men. Even the chiefs, angered by the search of their reserve, made no attempt to have him apprehended, and the fifty-dollar reward offered by the police went uncollected.

Deerfoot remained at large through the rest of 1887. From time to time, newspapers clamored for action, the *Calgary Herald* in one instance stating that the "successful way in which Deerfoot has set the authorities at defiance will have the effect of opening many eyes as to the manner in which the law is administered in regard to the Indians."[32]

Then, early in January 1888, Mounted Police scout Robert Giveen was visiting a small stopping-house just north of Fort Macleod when the owner told him that an Indian runner was camped nearby. According to the proprietor, the man had a pair of running shoes, a photograph of himself, and a certificate that said he had competed in the Calgary races. When Giveen was given a description of the Indian, he concluded that it must be the elusive Deerfoot. Just then, the Indian came out of the stopping-house, so without warning, the scout grabbed him. The Indian panicked and pulled away, running towards his tepee. Afraid that the man was going for his rifle, Giveen opened fire, the bullet striking the Indian in the fleshy part of the thigh. The wounded man was able to flee to a nearby ranch house, and there he was surrendered to the police scout.

When the Indian was delivered to the Mounted Police barracks, the authorities learned they had the wrong man. He was identified as Bad Dried Meat, the Peigan Indian who had raced with Deerfoot and Little Plume in Calgary. He had been on his way to the Peigan Reserve for horses and had just come out of the stopping-house when he was suddenly set upon by a white man. Concluding that he was being attacked by a drunken cowboy, the Indian had broken free and was running away when he was shot.

At first, the Mounted Police tried to say they had the right man, but the truth could not be denied, and in the end an embarrassed government took steps to compensate him, giving him one hundred dollars and enough canvas for a new tepee. When Deerfoot heard about the shooting, he also felt partly to blame and presented the Peigan Indian with a horse and a gun.

Deerfoot remained at large throughout the whole of 1888. Then, in the spring of the following year, Crowfoot made overtures to the Indian agent about the surrender of his nephew. By this time, Edgar Dewdney had become minister of the interior, and with his help, assurances were given that Deerfoot would receive a fair trial. Dewdney even arranged for the influential Calgary lawyer, James A. Lougheed, to defend the Indian. By this time, the sensationalism of Deerfoot's escape was almost forgotten, and early in April, when the Indian delivered himself to the Mounted Police, the incident received only passing attention in the press.

"Deerfoot is at last a prisoner at the Mounted Police Barracks," observed the *Calgary Herald*. "Everybody who lived in Calgary two years ago knew Deerfoot, the noted Indian runner, the man who could outrun any white man in the country.[33]

When Deerfoot was charged with housebreaking and with "resisting the police," it was obvious that he expected to get off lightly, and at first he even pleaded not guilty. When the defence counsel, through the interpreter, explained the procedure, he obligingly changed his plea to guilty. The judge stated that "he had been spoken to by several on behalf of the prisoner" and he determined to be as lenient as possible under the circumstances. He then sentenced Deerfoot to thirty days on the first charge and fourteen days on the second, both at hard labor.[34]

Six weeks after the trial, Deerfoot was a free man. Even before he was released, a number of tepees had been pitched across the Bow River as admiring friends prepared to greet him as a hero upon his release. "His wife," commented a reporter, "who is a Blood and used to show her horsemanship on the streets of Calgary, is coming to join her husband after their long separation."[35]

At the beginning of June, the news flashed through the camp that Deerfoot had been released. "The Indians began to stream over Langevin bridge in large numbers," said a reporter, "to pay their respects to the 'free man,' who held levee all afternoon, receiving the congratulations of his red brethren."[36]

Now that Deerfoot was free he looked into the possibility of resuming his running career, but it was not to be. He found that bicycling had replaced foot racing and even the old syndicate had disappeared as Calgary became a sedate sandstone metropolis. Lying Allen was now a customs officer in Fort Macleod, and at the time of Deerfoot's release, he was trying to find his wife, who had run off with a lacrosse player.

Deerfoot, the onetime great runner and local hero, returned to his own reserve where he became a fractious troublemaker. He beat up his friends in needless quarrels, mistreated his wife and family, and was constantly involved in petty theft, gambling, and fighting. As his grandson recalled, "He was a mean man who used to treat his wife badly. She was afraid of him."[37]

During his running career, Deerfoot believed that he had special powers which he had received from the deer spirit. Now he attempted to use these powers to his own advantage, helping him to become one of the most successful gamblers on his reserve. All he had to do was make a certain kind of whistling noise to call up his spirit helper to guide him to victory.

Shortly after he had started running, Deerfoot had married Crow Howling Woman, and she bore him his first daughter in 1887 while he was a fugitive. He also had two other daughters by her, one in 1890 and another who died shortly after birth in 1892. In the meantime, he took a second wife after his release from jail and they had a son a year later. During the 1890s he took a third wife, Small Face, and had a daughter by her in 1896.

Deerfoot's first brush with the law after his release occurred in 1891 when, in company with a Blackfoot named Crow Chief, he broke into a settler's house near the Dunbow Indian Industrial School. Interestingly, the owner's name was Allen, but he was no relation to the Indian's old gambling nemesis Lying Allen. The owner discovered the two Indians while they were still in the house. Deerfoot reacted by drawing a knife, but before he could attack, the settler had both men in the sights of his Winchester. The thieves fled immediately, but when the matter was reported to the police, Constable Todd found their camp a short time later.

To indicate how the mighty had fallen, Deerfoot began to run away as soon as the police officer approached his lodge. However, Todd pursued him on foot and succeeded in capturing him after a run of eight miles (12.9 km). The officer simply overtook the onetime champion and handcuffed him after a severe struggle.

The two Indians languished in jail for three months, and when they finally appeared, the charge was laid by Constable Todd, with Allen declining to take action. After hearing the case, the judge concluded that there was not enough evidence to justify the charge of "assault with intent to commit an indictable offence," and the case was dismissed.[38] According to evidence given at the trial, Deerfoot had also "assaulted another man in the same neighborhood but a few days before his latest escapade but the man laid no information against him."[39]

Deerfoot was arrested for simple assault in June of 1894, and this time he was sentenced to two months at hard labor. By now, he had become a familiar sight in Calgary and spent a considerable amount of time in the camps across the river by Nose Creek. This nomadic village was a constant source of trouble for the police as it was a convenient haven for Indians who came to town for reasons of prostitution or petty theft.

Though Deerfoot was a leader within the camp, his personal problems continued to plague him. As humorist Bob Edwards commented, "His abortive efforts to bull the whiskey market had the usual result."[40] In 1896, Deerfoot again came to the attention of the authorities on his reserve after his daughter became ill and fears were expressed that she might die. Angrily, the Indian blamed his wife for the problem and threatened to kill her. He then stalked out of his lodge and when he met a man carrying a rifle, he snatched it from him and fled into the bushes.

By the time Sergeant J.J. Marshall arrived at the camp, everyone was excited and rumors were spread that "it was his intention to kill a White Man, the reason being that Deerfoot's daughter was expected to die during the night, and he wanted to kill some white people to get even."[41] If true, this would be remarkably similar to an incident that had occurred a year earlier when a Blackfoot Indian, Scraping High, had killed the ration issuer after his son died.[42]

With the help of a school teacher, Marshall was able to contact Deerfoot and to determine that his wife, not a white man, was his intended victim. The Indian soon calmed down and finally promised not to cause any further trouble. As it happened, his daughter's illness proved to be minor and she recovered a short time later.

But Deerfoot did not stay out of trouble for very long; a month later he was arrested by two scouts, Cut Bank and Red Old Man, and charged with assault and drunkenness. When he appeared in a Calgary court, he was given six months on the first charge and one month on the second. This time he was sent hundreds of miles away to the Regina jail to serve his sentence. Perhaps it was there that he contacted scrofula, a virulent form of tuberculosis. Such a disease often turned a simple jail term into a death sentence for an Indian prisoner.

By now, the reputation of Deerfoot as a runner was all but forgotten. Instead, he was simply a jailbird and a troublemaker. No sooner had he returned to the reserve than he was arrested again in January of 1897 by scout Red Old Man and charged with assault. He was sent to the Calgary guard room but was so sick that the doctor was immediately summoned. As the inspector explained: "The Indian had been suffering for some time from scrofulous enlargement of the glands of the neck. Acting Assistant Surgeon Sanson was in attendance upon him the whole time of his confinement here, the man being too ill to work."[43]

However, the Indian was too far gone for the doctor to help, and on February 24, 1897, Scabby Dried Meat, known to the world as Deerfoot, died. The verdict of the coroner's inquest was that the deceased "died by the visitation of God in a natural way, to wit, of tuberculosis."[44]

The orders were that Deerfoot was to be buried in the pauper's plot at the Calgary cemetery, with Archdeacon Cooper of the Anglican church conducting the service. According to a Native elder, however, some citizens complained about the Indian being buried in a "white" cemetery, and in the end he was interred in an unmarked plot on the grounds of the Mounted Police barracks. The site was just east of a Safeway store that once stood on Eighth Avenue at Fourth Street East.

Tradition also states that Deerfoot's spirit was angry at this ultimate rejection by the people of Calgary. His name, according to the tale, would forever be associated with Deerfoot's power to take revenge upon the white man.

In 1974, Calgary city council decided that a new freeway cutting through the city's industrial area should be named the Deerfoot Trail "in honor of a Blackfoot Indian who was a renowned foot-racer in the final decades of the last century."[45] Since then, this road, carrying thousands of motorists a day and passing just east of Deerfoot's last resting place, has been the scene of man's mechanized carnage. Each year, people are killed or injured on the Deerfoot Trail, a road that commemorates both a great runner and an Indian who, according to the old tales, has left his name as a memorial for revenge against the white man who brought so much grief into his life.

Scraping High and Mr. Tims

$\mathcal{A}$t last, after a cold and bitter winter, spring had come to the prairies. The crocuses poked their lavender heads between the drifts of snow, and the pussy willows unfurled their fuzzy heads to greet the warm rays of the sun. The brown hills along the Bow River were tinged with green, and a few daring gophers stood like sentinels beside their burrows.

But there was no joy in the Blackfoot camps to greet the new season, for the people were sick and starving. Not only had last year's crops been a failure, but by 1895 all of Canada was in the third year of a depression. To save money, a budget-conscious government had cut back on rations until it seemed as though the only cattle that made their bawling way to the slaughterhouse were little more than masses of sinew and bone.

The results had been disastrous. Eighty-eight members of the Blackfoot tribe had died that year, some of tuberculosis, some of influenza, and others from just plain starvation. It was a tragic situation that seemed to cry for action. According to the Anglican missionary: "Many of their people died in the spring & this they accounted to their small ration. This made them desperate & they wanted to fight & die, if they must die, fighting."[1]

One of those deeply affected by the sickness around him was a Blackfoot named *Atsa'oan*, or Scraping High, a man in his late thirties. He lived about a mile (1.6 km) from the South Camp agency in the camp of the Bad Guns Band, which was under the leadership of his brother, Medicine Shield. By the spring of 1895, Scraping High's once-happy family had been reduced to just three people: Scraping High, his wife, and their nine-year-old boy. During the previous four years, Scraping High's second wife had died in childbirth, a boy had passed away, and his eldest son, Dried Limb, had married and moved away. To add to the misery, a nephew who had been living in Scraping High's lodge had gone back to his own family.

During these days of hardship and loss, Scraping High had been approached by the Anglican missionaries and persuaded to send his last remaining son to the new boarding school that had been opened in White Eagle's village. Here, Scraping High was told, his son would receive plenty of food, good clothing, and a warm bed.

Scraping High was not a Christian, but he loved his son so much that he was willing to sacrifice his own happiness for the sake of the child. Perhaps he did not understand that once the child was in residence he could not go home again until he reached the age of sixteen—unless he received a special dispensation from the Indian agent, or was going to die.

During the previous year, Jim Crow Chief, aged eleven, had died of tuberculosis at the Anglican boarding school in Old Sun's camp, while six-year-old Rosie Running Marten had been sent home to die. The school in White Eagle's camp had opened only in the fall of 1894, but the potential for disease there was very real.

If Scraping High knew about the danger, he did nothing about it. He was not a dynamic leader like Big Plume, who, hearing that his son was unhappy in school, had forced his way into the building and taken little Tommy away. In fact, Scraping High's concern was centered on providing food for his family. Under government regulations, a little more than a pound (.45 kg) of meat and a third of a pound (.15 kg) of flour was rationed daily to each man, woman, and child.

When Scraping High went to the ration house after his boy was admitted to school, he was surprised to discover that his family's ration had been reduced by one third. The ration issuer, Frank Skynner, had the reputation of being harsh and dictatorial when dealing with the Indians, but he also had to abide by the rules. He told Scraping High, perhaps not too diplomatically, that the boy's share of the ration was now going to the Anglican school. When the Indian protested, Skynner threw him out.[2]

Skynner was a former corporal in the North-West Mounted Police and had been the ration issuer on the reserve for three years. Born in Toronto, he was the son of a militia colonel at Port Hope and was known to the Indians as *Sepistowapspix*, or Owl Eyes. He was thoroughly despised by the Blackfoot for his overbearing and autocratic manner. When Scraping High complained at the next ration day about his food, Skynner again ejected him from the building.

Meanwhile, Scraping High visited the school every Sunday and was allowed to see his boy after church services. The child had been baptized and given the Christian name of Ellis, had his braids cut off, and was dressed in a drab gray uniform. But in spite of the apparent regimental approach to education, the missionary and his staff seemed to have a sincere love and affection for all the children. There could be no question that they were dedicated to their work.

John W. Tims had been the missionary on the reserve for twelve years. He had opened a day school in Old Sun's village shortly after his arrival, and he had been tireless in seeking food and clothing for the Blackfoot tribe. Bales of old clothes came from Anglican parishes in Ontario to be doled out to the aged and needy. Government officials were petitioned to increase rations of beef and flour, and constant efforts were made to convert the Indians to Christianity.

Like many other missionaries, Tims's ultimate goal was conversion. He decried the pagan influences on the reserve, tried to keep his adherents away from Native rituals, and was virtually close-minded about any aspects of Indian culture that he considered to be undesirable. On one occasion he complained that an ex-student had joined a warrior society and "has since married a camp girl of no education."[3] In another instance, he objected when parents asked for the release of their sick daughter. "As a Christian child," he said, "I did not wish her to be obliged to undergo the noise and manipulations of heathen medicine men."[4] He had also tried, unsuccessfully, to suppress the entire Sun Dance but had to settle for the elimination of the self-torture ritual from the event.

Tims's intransigence gained the ill will of some of the Indian leaders who found it necessary to question his actions. In 1892 and again during the winter of 1894–95, the chiefs became so frustrated by the missionary's unyielding and rigid attitude that they demanded he be removed from the reserve. "They said that the Revd. Mr. Tims was no friend to the Indians," reported Agent Magnus Begg.[5] The Indian Agency employees and North-West Mounted Police also had problems with Tims, as his narrow dogmatism made life difficult for them and could prove dangerous in the warlike camps of the Blackfoot. Perhaps the Indians were starving and dispirited, but they were still only a few years removed from the violence of their nomadic past.

By the time Scraping High brought his boy into the new school, Tims had become a major influence on the reserve. He personally supervised the boarding school at Old Sun's village, arranged for the opening of the new one under Reverend W.R. Haynes at White

Eagle's camp, and had a day school in operation at Eagle Ribs's village. The Roman Catholics, represented only by a mission house and day school at the South Camp, offered no real competition. Tims was firmly committed to the principle that successful conversions would come only through segregating the young pupils from influences of camp life and providing them with heavy doses of Christianity in their educational program.

Reverend J.W. Tims *(left)* and Reverend W.R. Haynes with five young Blackfoot boarding pupils who had just been issued with uniforms, ca. 1890. Tims came to be so despised by the Blackfoot tribe that they demanded and finally succeeded in having him removed. But his departure came only after a series of tragedies among the people. *Courtesy Glenbow-Alberta Institute/NA-1020-3-3*

Accordingly, he was pleased in 1894 when the Indian Act was changed to make school attendance compulsory and to give preference to boarding schools over day schools. Heeding the pleas of the churches, the House of Commons decreed that students would remain in school on a full-time basis and not be permitted out for holidays. The move was implemented because too many children left for a few days with their parents and never returned. The boarding schools were preferred over day schools because the missionaries could keep the pupils away from non-Christian influences, and with the government paying the expenses, they could hire staff to proselytize at little cost to their churches.

When the matter came to the House of Commons for approval,

some of the Liberal members expressed concern with the dictatorial powers of the government. The new act provided for "the arrest and conveyance to school, and detention there, of truant children and of children who are prevented by their parents or guardians from attending,"[6] and to fine or imprison the parents. It also gave the government the right to physically apprehend and force into a boarding school any Indian child under the age of sixteen.

One of the Liberal opposition members was worried about the clauses allowing "a power to restrict the liberty, not only of the parents, but of the students themselves."[7] However, the amendment passed with no significant changes. Presumably, people believed the deputy superintendent general of Indian Affairs when he stated that "it is very gratifying to observe that a marked change is in fact becoming apparent in the attitude of the parents generally towards the subject of the education of their children, and that they are beginning to realize its advantages, and to covet them for their offspring. It is the growth of this better sentiment that justified the introduction, without fear of exciting undue hostility, of measures for securing compulsory attendance at schools."[8] In fact, among the Blackfoot nothing could have been further from the truth.

Not only did they love their children, but the extended family was very important to them. In times of celebration or grief, everyone gathered together for mutual support. If a person assumed new religious duties, the extended family cooperated in sponsoring a giveaway; if someone died, the whole family shared the voluble outpourings of grief; and if starvation was a threat, everyone shared.

For that reason, parents automatically expected that their children would be sent home from school for a few days to support the family in religious rituals, share an unexpected workload, or to demonstrate family unity. The new regulations, however, completely ignored this aspect of Native culture.

The Blackfoot Indian agent, Magnus Begg, had no problems with the new regulations as long as they were tempered with reason and compassion. There were times when temporary illness, homesickness, or the cooperation of the chiefs, could best be served by permitting brief holidays. Tims, on the other hand, bitterly opposed letting students out for any reason.

At White Eagle's boarding school, the stringent edict was enforced. The deadly killer, tuberculosis, which might have been contained if the sick children had been allowed out into the camp atmosphere of sunshine and fresh air, was kept within the confines of

Anglican mission school at White Eagle's village on the Blackfoot Reserve, where Ellis Scraping High remained until near death. *Courtesy Glenbow-Alberta Institute/NA-4928-25*

the school and soon the disease was running rampant. By the spring of 1895, of the seventeen pupils registered, seven of them—more than 40 percent—had active tuberculosis in the form of scrofula.[9]

That was when Scraping High learned that his son was ill. Perhaps the boy already had the disease when he was admitted; no one will ever know for sure. But as soon as Scraping High saw the red open sores on little Ellis's neck, he was gripped by a cold fear. The symptoms of scrofula were all too familiar in the Blackfoot camps. From that time on, the boy weakened rapidly until that fateful day when the missionary told Scraping High he could take his son away. The boy wasn't sixteen; the father had sought no special permission from the Indian agent; so that left just one option: he was being sent home to die.

Ellis was too weak to stand by himself when Scraping High came for him. That night, as he was being nursed in his father's lodge, the boy looked up at Scraping High and said, in a fearful and plaintive voice, "Father, when I die, I'll be waiting for you at the Big Sand Hills."[10] This was the land of the dead, far to the east, where the Blackfoot spirits went after death. Sometimes, if the person was young and frightened, he might seek a loved one to accompany him. Little Ellis wanted his father to go with him to the Sand Hills.

Without hesitation, the grief-stricken father agreed, and added, "I am going to kill a white man."[11]

This was more than just a passing expression of anger at missionaries like John Tims and all the government employees who had caused him so much misery. Rather, Scraping High had committed himself to the practice of *iskohtoi-im'ohk'si-ow*, or "throwing his life away." This was an ancient custom followed by men who knew they were going to die—usually from a disease. Rather than passively accept their fate, such men went on the warpath and deliberately and openly attacked an enemy camp. They believed that all enemies they killed before they died would become their messengers to the spirit world. The more important the messengers, the greater would be their prestige in the land of the dead.

When they settled on reserves, knowledge of this practice continued but now there were no more enemy camps. Instead, the focus turned inward to the most important people on their own reserves. At the top of the list was the white man, with the tribal chiefs following a close second, and any member of the camp a poor third.

When a man made the commitment to throw his life away, he became a threat to everyone, even his own family. At such a time, no one was safe. And Scraping High had made this promise.

The next day, March 10, 1895, Ellis Scraping High died.

His father grieved and wailed as the boy's body was laid in a wooden coffin near the monument to the great chief Crowfoot. Scraping High cast off his clothing and dressed in rags, cut off his hair, and mourned the loss of his beloved son. As he wandered through the camps, dejected and sad, he told his brothers Medicine Shield and Poor Eagle and some of his friends of his awesome promise, and even to strangers he hinted darkly that he was about to "do something bad."[12]

In Scraping High's mind, his boy was waiting for him at the edge of the Sand Hills, afraid to make the final journey alone, yet the Indian hesitated to take the fatal step to join him. Finally, in the evening of April 3, a little more than three weeks after his son's death, Scraping High was playing cards with Duck Chief, Iron Shirt, Spring Chief, and Poor Eagle, when Duck Chief foolishly dared him to follow through with his vow—or had he just been bragging?

"Friend," said Duck Chief, "everyone is making fun of your name for saying that you were going to kill a white man, and now you are not doing anything."

"Do you mean that?"

"Yes, they're taking your name for fun."[13]

Perhaps Duck Chief meant it as a joke, but among the Plains Indians, he was offering a dare and this was a serious matter. As one Indian stated: "That age-old practice of daring one another has . . . caused us a lot of grief. It was very seldom that a man ever backed out of a dare."[14] Faced with this direct challenge, Scraping High returned to his lodge that night, took his rifle and set out along the river. He was ready to fulfill his promise.

The South Camp had only a sub-office of the Indian Agency. The main headquarters were located five miles (8 km) upstream, where the Indian agent, Magnus Begg, had his office. But to Scraping High, the South Camp was his home and the leading government man there was Harry Wheatley, the farm instructor. Quietly, the Indian made his way into the man's yard but found the house to be in darkness. The Indian concluded that the instructor was away. He was right; Wheatley was in the nearby town of Gleichen with the Reverend W.R. Haynes, attending a meeting of the Independent Order of Foresters.

Undaunted, Scraping High continued his deadly quest, passing a few more agency buildings until he saw a house where a lamp was casting its rosy glow into the night air. It was the residence of Frank Skynner, the fractious ex-police officer who had twice humiliated Scraping High at the ration house.

The Indian cautiously mounted the porch, being careful that no noise betrayed his presence. Peering through the window, he saw that the issuer was alone, his shotgun resting on the wall beside his fishing rod. The room was spartan; there was a table and sideboard that came with the building, while the only furniture brought by the issuer were a trunk, two chairs, and a cowhide mat. In the other room, Skynner had his bedroom suite and a metal bathtub.

Cocking his rifle, Scraping High rapped on the wooden door.

The unsuspecting Skynner arose from his chair and opened it to see who was calling so late in the evening. Without hesitation, the Indian shot Skynner in the head, the blood spattering on the door as the man crumpled to the floor of the porch in a gory heap. He was killed instantly.

Chanting his war song, Scraping High was jubilant. He had slain a white man! He had his messenger! Now he would look for others to kill before the police would come to take his life. He knew, and expected, that the Mounted Police would be his executioners. In this way he would die in battle and could lead his son into the Sand Hills with the pride of a warrior leader. Already, the white man, Owl Eyes, would be on his way as his messenger to prepare the spirit world for his arrival.

Scraping High went to Skynner's stable and took the dead man's riding horse, a large white mare. Mounted on this prize, he rode into the villages of the South Camp, singing and calling aloud, "Haiee!

Listen everyone. I have killed Owl Eyes!"[15] As he entered the village of head chief Running Rabbit, one of the Indians, Spotted Calf, ran outside his lodge to see who was shouting.

"I saw someone riding in the distance," he later explained. "When Scraping High got close to me, he raised his gun and I was afraid he would shoot me. I think he would have shot an Indian as soon as a white man."[16]

But Scraping High did not shoot. He was looking for someone more important than an ordinary Indian. He wanted to kill a chief. When he saw too many people milling around Running Rabbit's camp, he galloped over to Rabbit Carrier's village and went directly to the minor chief's cabin.

"I heard the dogs barking up the river," said the chief. "Then Crow Eagle came in and said Scraping High was coming. Scraping High came to my door and called me to put out my head. I said to my younger brother, 'Pity me,' as I thought he was going to kill me."[17] But Rabbit Carrier did not venture from the safety of his cabin and Scraping High was reluctant to force his way in. "I believe if I had put out my head," said the chief, "Scraping High would have killed me."[18]

As Scraping High left the villages, he shouted defiantly that he was going to his son's grave, and he would wait there for the police. "I have plenty of ammunition," he told them, "and I'll shoot white men and Indians alike of all who attempt to take me. I'll not be taken as long as I'm able to shoot."[19]

The news of Skynner's murder traveled through the villages like a prairie wind. Now everyone knew that Scraping High was dangerous as long as he was alive and that he was capable of killing again, regardless of whether the victim was Indian or white.

When Running Rabbit learned of the murder, he immediately despatched two messengers, Many Bears and Good Young Man, to warn Wheatley and the missionary to stay off the reserve. He advised them not to even consider returning until daylight. After he had told all his own people to stay indoors for the rest of the night, Running Rabbit went to town himself, and together with the farm instructor and Haynes, he broke the bad news to Indian agent Begg. By this time it was three o'clock in the morning, and at daylight their report was taken to the Mounted Police barracks.

Meanwhile, Scraping High had abandoned the white horse and walked up the hill to the graveyard. He passed by Crowfoot's coffin and the impressive monument that the government had built for him, and stopped near his son's grave. He had no fear of the spirits known to wander through the cemetery, for he soon would be one of them. He checked his rifle, counted his bullets, prayed to his spirit protectors, and settled down for the night. He wasn't afraid; rather, he had a sense of satisfaction that he had accomplished his mission and soon would be joining his son. In his grief, he felt that there was no reason for him to stay among the sadness and misery of his reserve. Perhaps in the Sand Hills he might find peace.

As soon as Mounted Police sergeant John Marshall received news of the murder, he telegraphed Calgary and then set out for the reserve with two constables, Magnus Rogers and "Scotty" Macnair, together with Wheatley, Haynes, and Running Rabbit. When they reached Skynner's house shortly after daybreak, they saw first-hand the grisly evidence of murder. Marshall reported: "He had been shot in the head; his brains were blown out and were spattered all over the floor of the porch and the ground outside. One eye was out and laid down over his cheek. He was lying on his back and from the position had evidently been standing on the door step when fired at."[20]

The officer observed that many of the Blackfoot families in the South Camp had struck their tepees or pulled their camping gear from their cabins and were moving upstream. By mid-morning, most of them would be squatting at Eagle Ribs's village seven miles (11 km) away. Scraping High's name was on every lip and fear was in the eyes of the women and old men as they looked for shelter from a warrior who had become a danger to everyone.

When Marshall enquired about the killer's whereabouts, the Indians pointed to a hill about a mile-and-a-half (2.4 km) away that jutted out into the valley. Although he had chosen it because of his son's grave, Scraping High could not have found a better defensive position. There were steep slopes to the south and west, a sweeping coulee to the north, and an open level ridge to the east, which offered no shelter for an attacker.

A number of Indians and civilians had been drawn to the scene by the excitement, and from them the sergeant tried to form skirmishing parties. However, most of the Blackfoot refused to participate, and even a reward of fifty dollars for the capture of the fugitive found no takers. Only after urging on the part of their agent did ten Indians reluctantly agree to guard the perimeter. They were placed at the bottom of the hill and along the coulees on the south side. The attacking party consisted of the sergeant, two constables, Agent Begg, and a local trader, R.G. "Cluny" MacDonnell.

They circled the site from the valley floor until they reached the rolling plains to the north. From there they moved forward, taking advantage of the low hills until they were within three hundred yards (274 m) of the defensive position. While this was going on, they could see Scraping High at the point of the hill. Periodically he waved his rifle or performed a few steps of a war dance. But when he saw the attackers moving in, the fugitive fired a few shots in their direction and disappeared among the graves.

Marshall still held out some hope that the Indian could be taken alive, so he had his men hold their fire and called for help from Medicine Shield, the wanted man's brother. The minor chief tried to explain that he could not approach the graveyard because even though they were brothers, Scraping High would not hesitate to shoot him. Finally, he agreed to call out to his brother, asking him to surrender. The reply was that Scraping High would shoot anyone who came near him, Indian or white.

The sergeant then gave orders to shoot to kill, and for the next few minutes there was rapid gunfire back and forth across the coulee. When no more shots came from the graveyard, Marshall rushed the site and discovered that Scraping High had fled down the south hill towards Hind Bull's village and into a densely wooded area. The Blackfoot guards had wisely galloped away when they saw their onetime friend running down the hill.

By this time, a few more curious onlookers had arrived on the scene, and Marshall succeeded in adding a rancher, Dave Brereton, and a cowboy, George Lee, to the posse. Another police officer, Constable David C. Baldwin, also came to help. It was now mid-afternoon and the sergeant was concerned that the manhunt might not be finished before sunset. The Indian had taken refuge in a grove of bushes about half a mile (.8 km) wide, which extended for about a mile (1.6 km) along the banks of the Bow River at Blackfoot Crossing. The officer was afraid that Scraping High might slip away and disappear across the river to the south, perhaps making his way to the safety of Montana.

In fact, escape would have been easy but the fugitive had no intention of running away. Rather, he was merely playing out his role of a warrior, waiting for a chance to kill another white man. But now his luck had changed. In the last exchange of gunfire on the hill, his rifle had jammed, and although he still carried the weapon, it was useless. Now he could rely only on his large double-bladed knife to finish his work. Looking up from the haven in the trees, he could see the posse spread out to guard the main escape routes, which led to the maze of coulees that funnelled back into the hills. His pursuers were too far away for him to attack with a knife.

Although a few Indians had sympathy for Scraping High, the only one brave enough to go in search of him was his nephew, White Headed Chief. Heedless of the warnings from his friends, he entered the woods and after a short search he found his uncle, the useless gun still held firmly in his hands. White Headed Chief tried to convince him to run away but he would not listen. Finally, just before he left, he offered his uncle a blanket to protect him from the cold, but the fugitive refused. "I guess he had already lost his soul," said the nephew sadly.[21] In Scraping High's mind, his spirit was already preparing to meet his little boy for the journey to the Sand Hills. The real world was no longer important.

Meanwhile, Marshall realized that his party was too small to effectively surround the bush, so he sent a messenger scurrying off to telegraph Calgary for reinforcements. He hoped that his superior officer, Superintendent Joseph Howe, could commandeer a railroad engine and reach the site before dark. At the barracks, Howe immediately readied twenty men for the trip, but there was neither a yard engine nor a freight train to be found in Calgary. The best that the Canadian Pacific Railway could do was to send out its express train when it arrived from the west at 8 P.M. However, this would be far too late to be of any help. Instead, Inspector D.H. McPherson and a dozen men set out on horseback for the seventy-mile (113-km) journey.

Marshall, in the meantime, decided he couldn't wait. He sent constables Rogers, Brereton, and Lee to guard the northeastern edge of the woods, while two search parties consisting of Constable Baldwin, Agent Begg, and R.G. MacDonnell in one group, and Sergeant Marshall and Constable Macnair in another, took on the dangerous task of trying to flush the fugitive out of hiding.

Scraping High heard the footsteps of the men as they made their way through the heavy brush, but he could not see them. Then suddenly, when he stepped into the open, there was a shout and several shots were fired by Baldwin's party. The Indian darted back into the bushes and headed north. Deprived of the use of his gun, he spent the next couple of hours playing a deadly game of cat and mouse with his pursuers.

Meanwhile, Rogers and Lee settled into a good defensive position in an old shack near the northern edge of the trees. They were both relaxing from the strain of the hunt when Scraping High unexpectedly appeared near a cutbank a short distance away. Rogers snapped off a quick shot, followed by a second bullet from Lee's gun, but the Indian disappeared into the trees.

Scraping High had been surprised. He thought all the white men were out beating the bushes for him. But now there was a man trapped inside the shack where he couldn't hide. Carefully the Indian circled the crude structure, keeping out of sight as he passed the open window and the door. He knew this was his last chance. Just as his ancestors who had chosen to throw their lives away had boldly attacked an enemy camp, so did Scraping High prepare to rush the cabin and hopefully kill the white man before being gunned down himself. Gripping his knife, he burst around the corner and dashed for the door.

He didn't know there were two of them. Lee, who was guarding the window, yelled a warning to the police officer, and when Scraping High reached the doorway, Rogers opened fire and killed the Indian on the spot.

It was all over. As far as the police were concerned, they had gunned down a crazy Indian who was running amok. They had no understanding of the Indian concepts of throwing your life away or killing spirit messengers, so they could only conclude that Scraping High had had a grievance against the ration issuer and had settled it in blood. The Indians knew better, but they said nothing. When McPherson's party finally arrived from Calgary, an inquest was held and the case was closed.

The Indians reacted with mixed feelings to the manhunt. Most were openly relieved that the threat had been removed from their midst, but others could not ignore the terrible conditions that had caused Scraping High to choose his fatal course. The next day, the Indian's coffin was placed in the cemetery next to his son. And in the minds of many Indians, his spirit would eventually depart for the east to meet his little boy, and to guide him into the hereafter.

Scraping High's relatives and many young warriors were angry about the killing. Perhaps Rogers had acted in self-defence, but he was still one of those white men who were keeping the Blackfoot caged and starving. He was one of the police who would go to Indian homes to pick up a student and take him back to a possible slow death in a boarding school. The police, the Indian Department officials, and the missionaries, were all part of the group that made daily life oppressive and the future bleak.

Realizing that Rogers might become the focus of the family's revenge, the commanding officer transferred the constable to Calgary. And to cool the situation, White Pup, a leading chief from the North Camp, presented the dead man's family with gifts of tea and tobacco. This was a traditional means of ending a possible feud and was considered appropriate compensation for the loss of a relative.

Later, the members of the Bad Guns Band gathered at the shack where Scraping High had been killed. There they outlined the shape of the dead man's body in white stones as their own small monument to their relative.

The officials at the Indian Department headquarters in Ottawa found the whole incident unsettling and may have wondered about the wisdom of cutting rations and allowing missionaries to hold sick children in their boarding schools. However, they rationalized that Scraping High's apparent insanity had precipitated the serious situation. As Deputy Superintendent General Hayter Reed expressed it: "The only thing connected with the most lamentable occurrence that tends to, in any way, relieve its aspect, is the consideration that the wretched perpetrator of the crime was not in sound mind, otherwise it would suggest the existence of a state of feeling between the wards and employees of the Department which would be most deplorable and point to something radically wrong about their mutual relations."[22] The bureaucrats almost got the message, but not quite.

Within a few days, the Blackfoot were back to their daily routines. Some were out planting vegetables and barley, hoping that this year the harvest might fill the bellies for a few weeks. Women went for firewood and water. Children played among the cabins and tepees. And the hungry dogs prowled through the camps, looking for a stray bit of food to steal from an unwary home.

Yet there was a difference. A pall of tragedy hung over the camps. It wasn't just the dramatic actions of Scraping High and his violent death. Rather, it was the accumulation of all the deaths that had taken place in the previous months, with many of the victims being young children; it was the sickness that did not seem to go away; and it was the boarding schools where Tims and the other missionaries held the children as virtual prisoners. The elders gathered earlier than usual to plan for the Sun Dance, for, as the Indian agent explained, "There have been so many deaths lately that the Indians wish to make Medicine for better health; during the month [of May] there were 12 deaths. There is also considerable sickness amongst them, and also amongst the school children."[23]

The children. It always came back to the children. The Blackfoot loved their young ones and would do anything for them. Now they watched helplessly as disease and hunger swept them away. Meanwhile, Tims fought his own bureaucratic wars. He protested bitterly every time the Indian agent permitted a student to leave his school, and complained further when the per capita grant for the child was withheld for the period the student was away. He seemed to be unaware of the growing sense of hostility on the reserve but continued to press for more students and less absenteeism. Even when, as he stated, "An Indian told me a short time ago that many young men were ambitious to follow in the steps of Scraping High and shoot a white man,"[24] he was unimpressed.

Blackfoot students at the North Camp mission school, August 1892. Teacher Hugh Baker is standing, left rear, with Reverend J.W. Tims on the extreme right. *Courtesy Glenbow-Alberta Institute/NA-1934-1*

Less than a month after the killing of Skynner, Tims learned that one of his students in the Old Sun boarding school was dying of "inflammation of the lungs"—a euphemism for tuberculosis—but he neither panicked nor tried to improve the conditions at the school. Rather, he followed his usual practice and sent six-year-old Roy Peacemaker home so he wouldn't die in school.

About this time, a thirteen-year-old girl named Mabel Cree also became ill, and when Doctor Neville Lindsay came from Calgary to examine her, he was unable to determine whether she had diphtheria or inflammation of the lungs, or both. Her family was terrified that her illness might prove fatal and rushed to the mission to see her. The first to arrive was the girl's stepfather, The Wood. When he dashed up to the matron's private entrance, he was immediately stopped by Tims. In a letter to the Mounted Police commissioner, Inspector Howe commented, "I understand that the Rev. Mr. Tims closed the door in his face and ordered him away, telling him that he should go by another door. I understand that the Indian resented this, as I think most White parents would do if placed in a similar position."[25]

In fact, The Wood was furious at this curt treatment and as he stalked away from the school, he turned to the missionary and hissed, "Beware! Beware! Beware Mr. Tims, if my child dies!"[26]

Tims apparently was unmoved.

Later, the girl's father, Greasy Forehead, and her uncle, The Cutter, came to the school and demanded that Mabel be released so they could take her to a medicine man. The Indian agent wanted to compromise by putting her in a tent on the school grounds where the medicine man could treat her, but Tims argued with him, saying that the girl had been baptized and should not come under non-Christian influences. He insisted that she would get better treatment at the school, where she would be tended by the matron and the doctor.

After earnest discussions among Tims, the doctor, and the Indian agent, the family reluctantly agreed to leave the girl in the school for two more days. If she had not improved by that time, they would take her to a medicine man. Like other Indians, they were aware of previous instances where "the child is kept at the school until given up by the white doctor and then, when too late, turned over to them."[27] Ellis Scraping High had suffered such a fate.

However, with assurances from Doctor Lindsay that the girl was in stable condition, Tims sent the family home and left for a meeting in Calgary. Only a few hours later, in the early morning of May 2, 1895, Mabel Cree died.

In the bedlam that followed the release of the shocking news, it is quite possible that Tims would have been killed had he been at the school. The resentment and hatred that had been building up over attendance regulations during the past several months now had a clear focus: John W. Tims. The death of Ellis Scraping High had occurred in a school under Tims's general supervision, but the missionary was not directly implicated. Now, however, Tims was the man who had ejected the girl's stepfather and was accused of keeping her family from taking the child to their own doctor.

It was as though the spirit of Scraping High was standing in the shadows, reminding everyone that his boy had died because of the Indian Department and the missionaries. Scraping High had revenged himself upon the government men, but there was still a score to settle with the Christian church.

On one side of the conflict were the Blackfoot Indians, who were suffering through hunger and disease; Scraping High had become their symbol of revolt. On the other side were the missionaries, who were devoting their lives to Christianizing the Indians but who were now perceived to be the wardens and destroyers of Blackfoot children; John Tims had become their symbol. In fact, ultimate control over the release of children from boarding schools was in the hands of the Indian Department, but to the Blackfoot, Tims was the culprit. This was due both to his insistence on keeping Indians in school and his overbearing manner; even his assistant indicated that he "lacked tact in dealing with them."[28]

Indians from all parts of the North Camp congregated at the boarding school when news of the girl's death become known. The women wailed the shrill death cry of the tribe as they sobbed in anguish, while the men expressed their anger and spoke of revenge. One of the ex-pupils, Thomas Calf Child, grabbed his rifle and set out for Calgary, threatening to kill the missionary if he met him on the trail. Only through the persuasive efforts of W.M. Baker, the farm instructor, was he convinced to return to the crowd.

In order to quiet the mob, the school staff hauled out their supply of tea and food, feeding the hungry and speaking earnestly to the parents of their flock. When Agent Begg arrived, he also ordered extra rations of beef and flour. He then held talks with the excited chiefs. As he noted, they "did not like Mr. Tims, and Mr. Baker informs me that they said there may be bloodshed if Mr. Tims is not removed."[29]

The crowd was eventually persuaded to go home, and that night four chiefs stood guard to prevent any young hotheads from causing trouble at the mission. The next day, while the schoolteachers made a wooden coffin, the family took the body to Calf Child's house, where they carried out the ritualistic mourning for the dead. When this was over, the school staff expected to give the girl a Christian burial, so a grave was dug and everything was made ready. Then the pupils of the school were lined up in pairs, in marching order, and together with the staff, they solemnly paraded towards the Calf Child house. However, they were only part-way there when a number of angry Indians burst out of a nearby house and ordered them to go back to the mission. Frightened, the school staff and students retreated in disarray while Mabel Cree's body was taken away for a non-Christian burial. This appeared to be the ultimate rejection of the missionary enterprise.

An hour later, the dead girl's mother, distraught with grief and perhaps believing that Tims had returned, dashed to the mission brandishing a knife and threatening to stab the first white person she met. She was forcibly restrained by two Blackfoot chiefs and was taken sobbing from the scene. Some time later, The Wood also showed up for a confrontation but was turned away.

"The Chief came along and told us to bar the doors," said the assistant principal. "The Chiefs were very much afraid we would be attacked by Mabel's people."[30]

Tims returned from Calgary that evening, and rather than being contrite, he responded to the situation with righteous indignation, believing that he had been victimized by Doctor Lindsay, who had assured him that the girl was in stable condition and in no danger of dying.

The next day, May 3, while rations were being issued to the Indians, a council was held among the missionary, government officials, bereaved family, and chiefs. Now that the missionary was back, the Indians vented their anger and demanded that something be done to rectify the situation. Agent Begg expected Tims to follow the Native custom of making a gift to the family, but when this didn't occur, he suggested that the missionary buy a horse from the government herd and present it to Greasy Forehead, the girl's father. At the same time, Big Road, a leading chief from the North Camp, offered a pony to the girl's stepfather, The Wood.

Tims disclaimed all responsibility for the girl's death, but finally he reluctantly agreed to make a gift of the horse. But he was obviously more worried about the cost of the animal than in calming the excited Indians. "As I could not see that any blame attached to myself," he said indignantly, "I felt that it was unfair to expect me to do this, and I did not feel I could afford to do so."[31]

Tims was convinced that all the problems of 1895 should be blamed on everyone but himself. He said the fault lay with the doctor ("I have been placed in an unenviable position through the unwarranted conduct of Dr. Lindsay"),[32] with the Indian agent ("Had the Agent always given me the assistance he might have done in the school work, there would have been no trouble over children to-day"),[33] with the Catholic Church ("This was . . . an attempt on the part of the R.C. Church to get my removal"),[34] and even with the devil himself ("The devil's kingdom was being assailed and he was using every effort to stay the flow of heathen into the Church of God").[35]

Four days after the meeting, little Roy Peacemaker died at home. This was the boy who had been released from the boarding school in the last stages of tuberculosis less than two weeks earlier. His passing only added to the anger and the pall of death that clung to the Blackfoot camps.

The next day, families began trooping to the mission and the Indian Agency, clamoring for the release of their children. Little Axe, one of the best farmers on the reserve, was concerned about his son "as he is very thin [and he] would like to have him at home for a while."[36] Pretty Gun, widow of Mounted Police scout Dog Child, wanted her daughter to help out at home. The Cutter, Mabel Cree's grieving uncle, demanded his four children be released, while farmers Raw Eater, Boss Medicine Ribs, and Dog, and police scout Red Old Man also sought holidays or discharges for their children.

Tims objected to anyone being let out, but Agent Begg, who seems to have been more sensitive to the dangerous conditions on the reserve, overruled him on a number of occasions. John Boss Medicine Ribs was let out for three weeks to be treated by a medicine man; Dog's daughter was permitted to attend the sacred tobacco-planting ceremony; and David Red Old Man was given time to help his father, who had an injured hand. Besides these students, as Agent Begg commented, "I have a great many Applications for leave for children at Old Sun's boarding school."[37]

One of the most disturbing cases, which indicates how closely the boarding school resembled a prison, was related by Agent Begg. He said that Raw Eater had signed an agreement with Tims for his boy to attend school for three years. During that time, the student had left school for one day without permission, returned voluntarily, but was given an extra *year's* sentence "for running away."[38]

If Scraping High had spoken to Raw Eater before he turned little Ellis over to the missionaries, perhaps some of the tragedies might never have occurred. It is possible that he might have changed his mind about the mission being a safe haven for his boy had he heard about the mandatory extra year in school Raw Eater's son had received. But it hadn't happened; Ellis Scraping High had died, Frank Skynner had been murdered, and Scraping High had been shot to death. Now, the little pebble dislodged by the death of Ellis was becoming a thundering avalanche that threatened everything in its path. If it was a contest between the actions of Scraping High and those of Tims to influence the future destiny of the reserve, the Indian was winning. If the dead man's spirit was still hovering about the reserve, it must have smiled with grim satisfaction.

The tensions and the problems at the Anglican mission did not go unnoticed by the bureaucrats, and in late May, Inspector Alex McGibbon arrived from Regina to conduct a personal investigation.

One of his first acts was to call a council of the chiefs and head men to hear their complaints. And they had plenty. At the top of their list was the expulsion of the Reverend Mr. Tims from the reserve and "a kinder man put in his place."[39] White Pup, the leading chief and a strong supporter of the Anglican church, had become an outspoken opponent of the missionary. He stated ominously: "Of the two grievances that my people and I had prayed to be removed, God in his wisdom and kindness of heart for his children had saw [*sic*] fit to remove one of them [referring to Frank Skynner]. The other still remains [referring to Reverend Mr. Tims]. I hope that God will not see fit to remove this man in the same manner."[40] And if Tims thought the devil was at work on the reserve, another chief agreed with him. "There was God and the Devil," he said. "God was good and Mr. Tims was the Devil."[41] The Mounted Police officer in attendance interpreted these comments to mean that if Tims wasn't removed, the Indians would do it themselves.

The anger over the deaths at the school and the virtual imprisonment of the students were hot topics of debate. The Cutter, still angry about the death of his niece, demanded that all students be given holidays for the Sun Dance in July. He said if his four boys weren't released, he would remove them by force.

The problem always came back to Tims and the school. McGibbon interviewed many people involved in the affair and could find no defence for the missionary's actions. He believed that barring The Wood from entering the mission was inexcusable, that his treatment of Indians was harsh and arbitrary, and that the missionary "was fully acquainted with the feelings of the Indians towards him, their dislike to him personally."[42]

Yet Tims remained unmoved by the comments and retaliated angrily, claiming that the whole report was "a clearly designed scheme to protect in every possible way the Department and its officers from any blame, and to throw the whole blame upon my shoulders."[43] In some instances, he responded to specific charges not by denying them but by challenging the inspector to prove them. For example, when discussing the claim that he knew the Indians disliked him, Tims responded, "I never stated so. I do not acknowledge this statement. The Inspector has no proof for what he affirms."[44]

Tims made no move to leave the reserve during the month of June, so the Indians' anger continued to seethe just below the surface. The Sun Dance was only weeks away, and already the excitement of planning for the ritual was beginning to grow. The Sun Dance was not simply a time for fasting and prayers; it gave the Indians an opportunity to recapture some of their old freedom. War experiences were recounted in the holy lodge; warrior societies conducted sham battles; and people from all parts of the reserve were drawn together in one huge village.

During the gathering, young men would ride through the camp, singing their war songs in the day and lullaby songs at night. A feeling of excitement prevailed as the Blackfoot forgot about their dismal life on the reserve and remembered the buffalo days. During the Sun Dance, any small incident could set off a dangerous confrontation. Under those conditions, Tims and the school question seemed like a veritable powder keg.

There were plenty of signs of unrest on the reserve. During June, an Indian refused to carry out instructions given to him by the Indian agent. When he was threatened with arrest, he fled to the woods where he painted his face and, armed with his rifle, dared the police to come and get him. He was ready to repeat the tragedy of Scraping High, but Agent Begg would not be goaded into a confrontation. He simply ignored the Blackfoot until the man gave up in disgust and went home.

About this time, some of the Indians began close-herding their horses so they would be ready in case of an emergency. They also returned to their old practice of carrying guns, just as they had when they first settled on the reserve. In recent years, a few guns had been seen, but most of the Indians had turned from hunting to gardening and had little use for the old rifles in their village life. But now the guns were back, and quantities of new arrows were being made. In addition, messengers were sent to the Blood Reserve, telling their allies about their terrible conditions and the danger of bloodshed.

These were all clear signs of the traditional actions taken by Indians preparing for war, and although Tims saw what was happening, the missionary chose to ignore the cold glances and threatening demeanor of parents whose children were in his school. He would not be coerced into leaving. When Agent Begg tactfully suggested that all the students be given holidays to attend the Sun Dance, Tims remained steadfast and opposed.

Matters took a further threatening turn in mid-June when The Cutter, still fretting over the refusal of the school to release his children, picked up his weapons and went in search of Tims. His announced intention was to kill the missionary. According to a report in *The Globe,* The Cutter "began chanting a death song and dancing the war dance in front of Mr. Tims' house. He was armed with rifle, bow and arrow and a knife."[45] However, the farm instructor disarmed him before he could do any harm.

A few days later, Indians attending the ration payments were in an ugly mood. As the meat and flour were being issued to the women, young men in war paint galloped around the ration house, waving their rifles and singing war songs. Finally, when the fever pitch reached a crescendo, a warrior rode down upon one of the many Indian dogs skulking around the building and, as he shot the creature, he shouted Tims's name in Blackfoot:

"Omuxistowan! Omuxistowan! Big Knife! Big Knife!"[46]

He was immediately followed by another Indian who killed a second stray dog, at the same time shouting the missionary's name. The message was clear.

When the Reverend Frank Swainson, who was married to Tims's sister, heard rumors about the ugly situation on the Blackfoot Reserve, he immediately realized that Mrs. Tims and her two children, as well as the obstinate missionary, might be in serious danger. Swainson was the missionary on the Blood Reserve, one hundred miles (161 km) south, but there the situation was calm and peaceful. Swainson had succeeded in bringing children into the Anglican boarding school and neither tuberculosis nor absenteeism seemed to be pressing problems. The difference was that he respected the Indians and they liked him. To investigate the truth of the rumors, Swainson made the long journey to the Blackfoot Reserve, arriving there on June 26. Brief discussions with some of the Indians convinced him that either during the Sun Dance or immediately afterwards, Tims would be killed. Some of the Indians begged Swainson to take the man away, for they knew that the missionary's death could result in violent retribution and a blood bath on the reserve.

With the Sun Dance only a short time away, Swainson rode to the Anglican mission and confronted his brother-in-law. To this point, Tims might have been deluding himself that nothing would happen, or perhaps he was simply being stubborn, but Swainson convinced him that his family and possibly the whole mission staff were in danger because of his actions. Forced by his fellow missionary to face the truth, Tims finally agreed to leave.

If the spirit of Scraping High was still hovering near the camps, it would have seen that the circle was almost complete. His boy had died because of the Indian Department and the missionaries. Frank Skynner's death had served as revenge against the government, and now Tims was fleeing amid humiliation and defeat. In the buffalo days, both of these events would have been considered victories for the Blackfoot.

Next morning, Tims was forced to add to the bitterness of defeat by asking for permission from Agent Begg for all the children to take a holiday. While he was away, he feared that the unrest might continue, so to avoid problems for the staff, he decided to close the mission temporarily and let the students out—just in time for the Sun Dance. Then, in a final gesture of professed innocence, he wrote to the Indian commissioner, blaming all the problems on the government administration and recommending that a force of two hundred Mounted Police be stationed on the reserve.

At last, he loaded his personal possessions into a wagon and, with his family, retreated from the mission to the safety of the Blood Reserve. Not until a week later did he officially ask his bishop for permission to leave his mission station.

When word of the flight reached the press, general sympathy was with the Blackfoot. A few newspapers made sarcastic comments, such as, "Blackfeet Indians at Gleichen recently chased out an obnoxious white missionary, and wished to celebrate that feat by holding a sun dance."[47] and "The Rev. Mr. Tims evidently believes in the Scriptural injunction:—'When they persecute you in one city, flee ye to another.'"[48] But most took a serious look at the relationship between the missionary and the Indians, and they didn't like what they saw. One correspondent noted:

> The Anglican mission has been for twelve years established there. Thousands and thousands of dollars have been spent for the purpose of converting them to Christianity. And, after all these years and all this expense, we find the Missionary deserting his post without a single convert. Nay more, he has exasperated the people against Christianity by acts of folly, and they are, perhaps, farther to-day from the Church's fold than they were before ever they had the Gospel preached to them.[49]

Even those who recognized Tims's devotion could not be completely complimentary about the missionary. Mounted Police superintendent Joseph Howe remarked: "In my opinion this man has attempted I believe honestly to carry out the instructions of his Dept. and educate the Indian children but he has undoubtedly a pugnacious and I might say an offensive manner which undoubtedly jars on the Indians' feelings."[50]

Within days of Tims's departure, calm returned to the Blackfoot Reserve. All talk of violence and bloodshed disappeared, and with the students back home, there was happiness in the camps. In the end, in spite of the missionary's comments to the contrary, it had been Tims and only Tims who had triggered the anger and hatred. A few weeks later, when rations were reduced to 1.15 pounds (.52 kg) of beef per day, there was not a murmur of protest from the reserve.

While the Blackfoot and the press belabored Tims, the missionary was welcomed back into the diocesan fold with open arms. Rather than chastise him for the debacle on the reserve, the Anglican Church shocked the entire region a few weeks later when it elevated Tims to the position of archdeacon and placed him in charge of all Indian missions in southern Alberta!

The Macleod Gazette summed up the matter very well when it commented: "The joke, for it rather partakes of the nature of a joke, is . . . the appointment to this archdeaconry of a man who is admittedly hated by the Indians of one of the largest reserves, and was intimidated by threats into abandoning his work there."[51] Yet the appointment remained, and Archdeacon Tims went on to take personal charge of the Calgary missions. In spite of his failure with the Blackfoot, Tims continued to be involved with Indian missions for the rest of his career. In later years, he was considered to be one of the grand old pioneers of southern Alberta, and was greatly respected for his work among the Indians.

As for Scraping High, the boulder effigy marking his death place remains to this day on the Blackfoot Reserve as a bitter reminder of the early residential schools and their role in destroying the lives of a child, his father, and a government worker. The catalyst in this disaster, the Reverend Mr. Tims, suffered only a temporary setback in his role of converting the Indians to Christianity. Scraping High's act had been brave and dramatic, but in the end it proved to be nothing more than a futile gesture. He had spoken with his gun but no one had listened.

The Transformation of Small Eyes

<hr/>

$\mathcal{O}$ n 1867, *Pokopi'ni*, or Small Eyes, was born into the Many Children Band, one of the most fractious, quarrelsome, and cantankerous groups of Indians in the whole Blackfoot nation. The date of his birth is remembered because that was the year when Buffalo Child, a great Blackfoot leader, was killed by the Crow Indians.

In some ways, Small Eyes must have been born lucky. He was lucky to have a rich father who was a chief. He was lucky to be healthy. And he was lucky to have survived that first year when so many babies died. But it wasn't all luck. On the day he was born, his grandmother prayed for the boy to have a long life. Then she blackened the end of his finger with charcoal, tightened a sinew thread around it, and severed the finger at the first joint. Carefully taking the tiny tip, she carried it to a nearby hill where she gave it as an offering to the Sun spirit. His grandmother, noticing that the other women were upset by the operation, said softly, "Do not cry for this boy. He is going to grow up because we gave his finger to the sun."[1]

After the ceremony was over, Small Eyes was wrapped in an otter skin, placed on his father's bed, and covered with the skin of a mountain lion.

Small Eyes wasn't his real name—not unless you consider that a mother's nickname qualifies. When he was born, he was called *Kai'sui-tsinamaka*, or Not Afraid of the Gros Ventres, but Small Eyes seemed to be so appropriate that pretty soon everybody was calling him that.

Small Eyes was a *mini'poka*, a favored child (or in the modern parlance, a spoiled brat). His father was Bull Back Fat,[2] a leader of a sub-group of the Many Fat Horses Band, and one of the richest men in the tribe. In fact, the band had been named because of its wealth in horses. Bull Back Fat and his wife, Little Walker, were active in the religious life of their people; when Small Eyes was three years old, his mother sponsored the Sun Dance. This was not only the most important religious event of the year, but it was a time for the sponsor's family to flaunt its riches by giving away many presents of horses, blankets, and other goods.

Because of the wealth of Bull Back Fat, people tried to please him by bringing gifts for his little son. As soon as the baby was old enough to sit up, an old woman gave Small Eyes a necklace consisting of a leather-covered *iniskim*, or buffalo stone. This was a good-luck amulet that was used in the buffalo-calling ceremonies. In the acceptance ceremony, the child's entire body was painted and a horse was presented to the old woman. Later, she also gave a brass button for Small Eyes to wear on a cord around his neck; for this the old woman was given blankets.

When the boy was five, his father joined the Horn Society, the most holy warrior organization in the tribe. When the leader saw how Small Eyes followed his father right into the sacred lodge, he said to Bull Back Fat, "You should have your son painted by the Horns because he likes to be with you and likes to be around our tepee."[3] So the boy was painted and was permitted to be present for the rituals, even though he was only five. This was a rare privilege.

That same year, a Peigan Indian came to Bull Back Fat's tepee with another gift for Small Eyes: the scalp of a Crow warrior. The man refused the gift of a horse. All he wanted was a keg of whiskey.

By this time, the Blackfoot country was in a state of chaos. American ranchers were accusing the Indians of theft and were threatening war, the United States military wanted control of the Indian Bureau, and Crees were pushing down from the north. But the biggest problem was whiskey. Since the end of the Civil War in 1864, freebooters had come west and made huge profits by selling whiskey to the Indians.

The Many Fat Horses Band was torn apart by the strife. Many Spotted Horses was the leading chief of the band, but Bull Back Fat was at the head of the sub-group named the Many Children. To the white traders, the family was known as the Mule Band, perhaps because of the obstinacy of its members.

The Bloods remember the Many Children as a wild, troublesome family who were decimated by whiskey. "They were a wild bunch," recalled Harry Mills, "and gradually they all got killed off, mostly by the Bloods themselves."[4]

"They were bad and mean," added John Cotton, another Blood

leader. "They kept fighting among our own people. When they were drinking they wanted to kill anybody."[5]

About 1871, when Small Eyes was still a child, the Many Children became involved in a feud with the All Tall People, another Blood band. Both groups had been visiting a whiskey fort when a brawl erupted between them. The Many Children were getting the worst of it, and as they fled from the camp, they killed a harmless old man from the other band.

This set off a blood feud that lasted for months. Whenever members of the All Tall People could kill a Many Children warrior, they did so. By the spring of 1872, a traveler noted: "At one time they numbered twenty-eight lodges—approximately between fifty and sixty fighting men. A feud broke out between them and another branch of the same tribe and at the time I speak of [1872] the Mule family had been reduced to two lodges and the survivors had taken refuge in the South Piegan camp in order to avoid complete extinction."[6]

During this period of dissension and brawling, Small Eyes's father was murdered. Like other chaotic events in the Many Children camp, the killing was directly related to alcohol.

During the passing months, Many Spotted Horses had become fed up with the proclivities of the Many Children. So the chief had moved a short distance away and taken his closest followers and friends with him. Among them was a man named No Chief, who was married into the Many Children clan. Some of Bull Back Fat's relatives were jealous about the move; they believed that Many Spotted Horses was favoring No Chief over his own family.

A short time later, a member of the Many Children Band arrived in the camp with a supply of whiskey, including a gallon (4 l) keg ordered by No Chief. When the Indian went to pick it up, he found the Many Children in a fighting mood. They immediately accused him of acting superior, and Hairy Face, a brother of Bull Back Fat, attacked him. As a crowd of angry men began to gather around him, No Chief panicked and shot his attacker in the back, killing him instantly.

Bull Back Fat, who was in his lodge with his family, heard the shooting and dashed outside. An elder explained what happened next:

> When he approached the killer, No Chief was trying to reload his gun. While he was doing this, [Bull Back Fat] grabbed him by the shoulders. No Chief dropped his gun and grabbed his war knife. As the crowd closed in, No Chief sliced open the

belly of [Bull Back Fat] from hip to hip so that his intestines fell out. The leader stumbled and fell to the ground mortally wounded.[7]

The other warriors angrily closed in on No Chief and after a short battle, he was killed.

Sadly, the Many Children carried the body of their chief into his tepee. Bull Back Fat's older brother, Porcupine Bull, centered his attention on the frightened little boy who had witnessed the killing. "Cut off some of that boy's hair," he instructed the others.[8] This was done, partly in mourning, but also so that the hair could be placed on the dead man's chest in the belief that in future the boy would not be lonesome.

Porcupine Bull took a necklace from Small Eyes's neck and exchanged it for the one worn by his father. Then an old woman told the boy to step over the body of his father four times and to kiss him goodbye. Amid the wails of grief, the sobbing Small Eyes was led outside and the body of his father prepared for burial in the branches of a nearby tree.

Small Eyes, the rich, spoiled six-year-old boy, son of a chief, center of attention, was now a poor, fatherless child. He was too young to have his own horses, so the herd was split up among his uncles. His mother could not maintain the tepee, so the covering and its contents were taken by other members of the Many Children Band. The family was left with virtually nothing.

These people were Bloods, but Small Eyes's mother was from the Blackfoot tribe, who hunted far to the north on the Bow River. Now that she was a widow, she had no wish to stay with the wild, drinking Many Children. Instead, she packed her few personal possessions and headed north to the lodge of her younger brother *O'toka-poksi*, or Yellow Turned Robe. There were four of them in the party—Small Eyes, his mother Little Walker, and his four-year-old brother, Takes a Handsome Gun, and an older sister.

When they reached the protected valley of the Bow, just east of the ford at Blackfoot Crossing, the contrasts were dramatic. Rather than cope with a wild bunch of Many Children who were constantly in trouble and were in the middle of a blood feud, Little Walker and her children entered the quiet camp of the Liars Band, where the use of liquor was not a major problem. Yellow Turned Robe was a good provider, and Little Walker was warmly accepted back into her extended family. When she made it clear that she did not wish to marry again even though she was still young, her wishes were respected. A few years later, when Yellow Turned Robe died, she took her family to the lodge of another brother.

One day, when Small Eyes was eight, his family moved their camp to the Sun Dance, a few miles upstream from Blackfoot Crossing. Ever since his father's death, the boy had stayed away from all ceremonies; he had loved his father and the reminder of happier days was too painful. Sometimes he looked inside a doorway where a ritual was taking place, but usually he just walked away.

This time he decided to watch the ceremonies of the Horn Society, just as he had done among the Bloods. During the singing and rituals, he was overcome with a great sense of awe, as though rediscovering the holiness he had shared with his father.

Later, when his mother announced she wanted him to take part in the Sun Dance ceremony, Small Eyes eagerly agreed. She got him to dress in his best buckskins and gave him the necklace and wristlet she had worn when she had sponsored the Sun Dance ceremony five years earlier. When he was ready, she handed him a pipe and a sacred offering—a yellow-painted calfskin mounted on a willow frame surmounted by a willow hoop to which seven eagle feathers were attached. It was one of the most holy objects a person could bring to the Sun Dance and would be mounted atop the main lodge as an offering to the Sun spirit.

While his mother handed out the dried buffalo tongues for the sacrament, Small Eyes was sent to the main lodge to sit with his uncle, Longtime Crow. When his turn came, he presented the offering to the Holy Woman for prayers and gave the pipe to the leading ceremonialist. The man lit the pipe, smoked it, and prayed for Small Eyes and his uncle.

In later years the boy saw many ceremonies—medicine pipe dances, warrior society rituals, women's society dances—but the Sun Dance and the Horn Society were at the center of his beliefs. They became an important part of his life.

Whether through resentment over losing his father or simply because of the way he had been raised—as a spoiled child—Small Eyes became aggressive and independent as he grew older. Even as a child he was described as "a tough guy."[9] With no father, he had to learn to fend for himself. In 1877, for example, when he was just ten years old and traveling with his family on their way to the Blackfoot Treaty, he found a dead eagle. Taking this prize, he traded it for a two-year-old mare and started to raise his own colts. Later, when one of the colts was a yearling, he broke it himself, using a saddle his mother had made for him.

During the treaty negotiations, Small Eyes met one of his father's brothers from the Many Children Band and rediscovered the other side of his family. In many ways, the surviving members of the clan were much like the boy: arrogant and tough. Once the contact was made, Small Eyes maintained it over the years, visiting his relatives whenever the Blackfoot met their southern allies.

After the treaty, the buffalo herds seemed to disappear from the Blackfoot's tribal hunting grounds. The area north of the Bow River was devoid of the shaggy beasts, and even to the south the hunters had to travel for miles before they could find enough animals to feed the camp. The Blackfoot had two choices: they could stay at Blackfoot Crossing and hope that the government would fulfill its treaty promises to look after them, or they could follow the buffalo herds into Montana. In the autumn of 1879, Little Walker, with Small Eyes and other members of the family, decided to go to the United States.

On the banks of the Missouri River they came upon a camp of Gros Ventre Indians and were invited to join them. At one time, the Blackfoot and Gros Ventres had been allies, but eighteen years earlier an argument over stolen horses had turned them into bitter enemies. Now, however, with the people facing starvation and threats coming from the Sioux, old animosities were put aside.

Small Eyes stayed with the Gros Ventres until the autumn of 1880, learning their language, and joining in their buffalo hunts. By now he was thirteen years old and responsible for the family's horse herd.

One morning, the boy went to round up the horses, when suddenly he was attacked by three Gros Ventres. They threw him from his horse and two held him while the third said, "Let's kill this boy."[10] When the man took out his knife and tried to stab him, Small Eyes swung one of his captors around to ward off the blow, then kicked his attacker savagely in the stomach. When the man fell down, the boy kicked him in the face.

"Did he hit you hard?"

"Yes," groaned the man, obviously in great pain.

"I'm going to kill him." As the Gros Ventre raised his knife, Small Eyes struck him with his whip and knocked the weapon out of his hand.

"Now I'm going to kill you with this knife," shouted Small Eyes as he picked up the weapon, "not you kill me."

Two of the men fled while the third, still injured and lying on the ground, begged the others to help him. Giving up any idea of revenge, Small Eyes rounded up his horses and took them back to camp. When he told his uncle what had happened, they quickly moved to a Blood village across the Missouri River. His father's relatives, the Many Children, were camped there. Later, Small Eyes learned that the man he had kicked had died of internal injuries.

The Many Children liked a good fight and congratulated the boy. But his uncle, just to be safe, bought a revolver for the boy and told him to be on his guard. There was always a danger that the Gros Ventres might try to avenge the killing, even though it had been an act of self-defense.

That autumn, when the first snowfall of the season blanketed the countryside, a Sioux war party raided the Blood camps. These were remnants of Sitting Bull's warriors who had fled to Canada after the defeat of Custer. Now, with buffalo almost nonexistent north of the border, they were forced to venture across the line, constantly hiding from army patrols sent out to arrest them. But the Sioux were a fierce and proud people, so they continued to follow their old ways, including taking horses from their enemies.

During the night, shortly after Small Eyes's uncle had returned from a successful deer hunt, the Sioux crept into the camp, and amid the blowing snow, stole all the best horses. These animals had been tethered in front of their owners' tepees, but even so, the Sioux had quietly cut them loose and escaped. At daybreak, a war party was organized to pursue the raiders, and like others in the group, Small Eyes was forced to ride one of the old pack ponies that had not been worth stealing.

A short distance from the camp they picked up the trail and followed it eastward for about fourteen miles (22.5 km). There, at a little backwater of a creek, they caught up with the Sioux resting with their loot. Small Eyes could see his own favorite horse among the herd. The Bloods and Blackfoot opened fire, but they were too far away to cause any damage. The Sioux returned the fire, then safely made their escape through a snow-choked coulee. It was too dangerous for the Blackfoot to pursue them, for every bend in the coulee would have been an ideal place for an ambush.

When they got back to their camp, Small Eyes's mother gave him her entire herd of ponies, five in all. They weren't racehorses or buffalo runners, but neither were the other horses that were left in the camp. He loved his mother and appreciated her generosity. In spite of his independence, he listened to her; she was the only one who could control him.

In the spring of 1881, the mixed camp of Bloods and Blackfoot moved to the Marias River, north of the Missouri. The Indians had accepted the fact that the buffalo were gone, and they had no recourse but to return to the reserves that had been set aside for them. They hunted deer in the valleys and ate whatever they could find. When they finally made their way to Fort Macleod, they were in pitiful condition. "They come in very destitute," reported Indian agent Norman Macleod. "They were nearly all on foot."[11] When they reached Blackfoot Crossing, they began to accept the daily handouts of beef and flour from the nearby ration house.

Small Eyes, now fourteen, was considered to be a man. Over the next few years, he was involved in breeding his horse herd, thereby adding to its numbers, and working for his uncles. He was strong-willed and tended to be a bully, but his mother kept him under control. She taught him good manners, how to keep himself neat and tidy, and above all, how to retain his pride and self-esteem. The latter was not problem; sometimes he seemed to have too much.

Then, during the winter of 1883–84, Small Eyes's mother became ill. She called her sixteen-year-old son to her side and told him to leave the reserve for a couple of weeks. She was going through a crisis, she said, and she didn't want her boy to see her pain. Always respectful of his mother's wishes, Small Eyes went to the nearby Stoney Reserve, and when he returned ten days later, the first person he met was his younger brother. As soon as he saw him, with his hair hacked short and the tears running down his face, Small Eyes knew that his mother was dead. A friend described his reaction:

> [Small Eyes] just went out of the house. He went up to the graveyard on top of the hill by the river. There he stayed all night crying. He started cutting holes in his arms and legs. He cut his hair short. He wore no shoes, no pants, just shorts and blanket. He had given up all desire to live. Towards morning the blood was all over him and he fell fast asleep.[12]

When the family found him, they led the distraught youth back to the house, where they cleaned and dressed his wounds. For the next few days, they watched him closely so that he wouldn't wander away to perish in the bitter cold. Sometimes when people like Small Eyes lost someone they loved, they tried to kill themselves so that they could go with their loved one to the spirit world.

After a few days, the young man asked his family to make him two pairs of fur-lined moccasins. He could not bear to stay on the Blackfoot Reserve so he had decided to visit his relatives among the Bloods. "Just go straight there," he was told. "Do not spoil your body again."[13]

A few days later Small Eyes set out on foot for the Blood Reserve, 120 miles (193 km) away. There was nothing between the reserves except open prairies, a few ranches, and a scattering of missions and Mounted Police outposts. He followed the Bow River down to the Catholic mission at Dunbow and spent the night in a haystack. The priest at the mission invited him to stay until the weather warmed up, but after four days he set out again. After a day of travel in the bitter cold, he dug a hole in a snowdrift, wrapped himself in his blanket, and went to sleep. Next morning, he shook the frost off his clothing, boiled some tea, and ate some of the dried meat he had brought with him. Later that day, while walking across the open prairie, he met a Blackfoot named White Louse who took him to his tent. It was lucky he did, for that night a blizzard swept down upon them and kept them inside for the next five days.

Setting out again, Small Eyes had just reached Mosquito Creek when he was struck by another blizzard. He made a small shelter out of willows and blankets and huddled there until midnight, when the skies cleared. Taking advantage of the calm, he walked for the rest of the night and all next day, often breaking through large snowdrifts. At last he came to a stopping-house run by an old German who had a Blood Indian wife. The man refused to let Small Eyes stay there in spite of the severe weather, and told him to sleep in the snow. Small Eyes didn't care; he was in such deep mourning for his mother that he seemed to be unaffected by the vicious cold. However, he was invited into another house nearby, where the owner provided him with food and shelter. Next morning, as Small Eyes was leaving, the man also gave him extra socks and some underwear.

After that, the journey was easy. For the next three days he walked south until he reached the Mounted Police headquarters at Fort Macleod. There Small Eyes was delighted to meet one of his father's relatives, Iron Shield, who took him to the Blood Reserve. Soon he was back among the Many Children Band at their tepees and cabins along Bullhorn Coulee.

Reservation life hadn't changed them much. Fewer in number after their interminable feuds, they were still wild and unpredictable. The Indian agent described them as "a very saucy lot [who] do not care about consequences" and claimed that "most of the scamps are in this band."[14] They drank when they got the chance, fought with their neighbors, and were active in the various warrior societies. They also were firmly committed to the religious rituals of the reserve—a fact that pleased Small Eyes. Tough-minded like them, he also felt strongly about the importance of the Sun Dance and the secret societies. Small Eyes stayed with the Many Children for the next three years, enjoying their lifestyle and joining in their escapades.

In the spring of 1887, he learned that two of his cousins, Big Rib and The Dog, were organizing a war party to raid the Gros Ventre Indians in Montana. Intertribal warfare was forbidden, even by the chiefs, and the practice had already died out on the Blackfoot Reserve. But the Many Children never followed anyone's rules but their own. Small Eyes, feeling reckless about his own life since the death of his mother, asked to go along.

Setting out from the Blood Reserve in April, the war party ran off a herd of horses from an unidentified enemy camp, but later they were attacked by a war party of Crees. While they were surrounded, Small Eyes vowed to go through the self-torture ritual at the Sun Dance if their lives were spared. Later, Big Rib returned from a reconnaissance to say that he had found a way to escape. The war party slipped away, but their horses were gone. They proceeded on to a ranch near Medicine Hat, where they exchanged shots with a white man and later fired several shots at a Mounted Police patrol that was hunting for them. Finally, they reached the outskirts of Medicine Hat, raided another white rancher, and tried unsuccessfully to kill a Cree they met along the trail. (These adventures are recounted in detail in the chapter "The Wild Ones.")

A few days after their return to the Blood Reserve, the Mounted Police swooped down on the villages and captured The Dog and his companion Big Rib. But Small Eyes successfully made his escape and headed back to the Blackfoot Reserve. On arrival, he went to the home of his uncle, Longtime Crow, and learned that the Mounted Police were searching for him. For the next couple of days he kept out of sight, but one afternoon while he was eating at his uncle's house, his aunt shouted that two police officers were coming down the road. Small Eyes immediately fled into the bush, and from his vantage point he saw a corporal and an Indian scout searching the area.

"If he had met a policeman then," said an informant, "he would have shot him."[15]

Small Eyes stayed hidden in a coulee all next day, cleaning his rifle and watching the trail. But the scout, Dog Child, had learned where the fugitive was hiding and silently crept up on him. As soon as Small Eyes saw him, he grabbed his coat and started to leave.

"You'd better stop," said the scout. "There's nothing wrong."

"Don't touch me! Don't bother me! I'll shoot you."

When the scout continued to advance, Small Eyes raised his gun in a threatening manner. "I'll shoot if you come farther."

"Don't shoot. There's nothing wrong between us."

"You're a scout."[16]

The two men stared at each other for a few seconds, then Small Eyes backed away and ran into the bushes. Dog Child made no effort to follow him.

Everyone heard about the standoff and feared a major manhunt would follow. Longtime Crow was worried about his nephew so he convinced the young man to seek the help of their great chief, Crowfoot.

Next day, armed with gifts of a Hudson's Bay blanket, tobacco, and a horse, Longtime Crow took the fugitive to the chief's house.

"Go in the house to see Crowfoot and give him the things," the uncle said. "Go up and kiss him. Tell him, 'Please, father, help me. Here is tobacco and a blanket and out there is a horse.'" Small Eyes did as he was instructed, and Crowfoot promised to help. The two of them went to the Indian Agency, and while Small Eyes stayed outside, the chief appealed to Agent Magnus Begg for clemency for the young man. At last, Small Eyes was beckoned inside.

"Well, my friend," said Crowfoot to the agent, "I brought [Small Eyes] to you to do what you want with him."

"You were crazy to go to the Bloods," the agent said to Small Eyes. "Why did you go to the Bloods? You were foolish."

"I don't like you to go hard on my people," continued Crowfoot, "so let him go."

Reluctantly the agent agreed. "You are very lucky that Crowfoot brought you up here," he said. He then sent a message to the Mounted Police, indicating that no charges would be laid against the young horse raider.

The incident made Small Eyes a hero on the Blackfoot Reserve. Not only had he taken part in a raid but he had eluded the Mounted Police and stood off a police scout. All the wildness and arrogance that had been a part of his upbringing now came to the surface. The years of being a spoiled child, the influence of his relatives among the Many Children, and his own personality, turned him into a ruffian and a bully. As one of his relatives observed:

[Small Eyes] was a tough guy. He wanted to run everything. He acted tough and mean. He would not talk mean with anyone but just try to beat him up. He also was a gambler; no one on the reserve could beat him at this. He would not stay home much but would go off and gamble. He always had good luck and came home with lots of horses. He was also foolish with girls.[17]

With his mother gone, there was no one to control him. He soon gained the reputation of being a wild, reckless womanizer. A handsome man, he had several affairs with married women. He drank whenever the opportunity arose, gambled far into the night, and neglected his work at his uncle's place.

Yet Small Eyes maintained his respect for his religion. He was a member of the Prairie Chicken Society and became the proud owner of weasel-tail leggings, a weasel-tail blanket, and other holy objects.

A year after his horse raid, when the time for the Sun Dance was approaching, the young man, now twenty-one years old, announced that he would fulfill a vow by going through the self-torture ritual. During the horse raid, when his life was in danger, he had promised to give himself to the Sun spirit if he managed to escape. His family tried to dissuade him because so many who had been through the ordeal did not live very long. But the young man was adamant; he had made a vow and he would honor it.

But he almost missed the ceremony. Shortly after the families had gathered for the Sun Dance, Small Eyes went out one night to listen to the men who were parading through the camp, singing serenade songs. As he walked across the encampment, someone grabbed Small Eyes in the darkness and tried to throw him to the ground. The young man thought that a friend was teasing him, but when he saw the glint of a knife blade, he realized the attacker was trying to kill him. The two men wrestled furiously for a few moments until the knife was knocked aside. As quickly as he had come, the stranger disappeared into the night; Small Eyes never discovered his identity.

"Don't try to chase other people's wives," he was lectured by Big Plume, a leading chief. "The man will always be after you. Stop going out and fooling around in the camps or you'll get hurt."[18] But Small Eyes didn't listen, and continued to pursue his favorite pastimes of women, gambling, and liquor.

At the society dances in the Sun Dance lodge, Small Eyes joined with others of the Prairie Chicken Society. He painted his face yellow, put eagle plumes in his hair, and wore his finest war shirt. During the dance, he gave away blankets and horses, and in exchange he received a ceremonial rattle. On the following day, he joined his uncle, Longtime Crow, in the sacred lodge, and gave away more horses and blankets to have his face painted, and to receive a headdress and a yellow-painted hide.

On the third day, Small Eyes took his pipe to Bull Head, one of the elders of the tribe, and asked him to guide him through the self-torture ritual. When the old man agreed, he invited another old man to help, and together they smoked the pipe and prayed.

Small Eyes was instructed to make a willow sweat lodge, and when it was ready, he purified himself. Then the old men prepared him for the ordeal. His body was painted yellow, with red dots below the eyes and lips, and down both arms and legs. A red half-moon was painted on his chest and a full moon on his back. Wreaths of sagebrush were tied around his wrists and ankles, and another wreath was made into a crown.

The young man then lay on his back, and while one elder held him down, the other pinched a piece of his breast between his fingers and prepared to cut two vertical slits in it.

"What do you want me to do?" asked the ceremonialist. "Cut the breast thick or pinch a little thin?"

"Suit yourself," Small Eyes replied.[19] He knew that the holy men usually did just the opposite of what was requested. If a man was frightened and asked for a narrow piece of skin to be cut, the ceremonialist would probably cut deep and thick. But Small Eyes, the tough guy, remained indifferent.

The cuts were made in both sides of the chest and wooden skewers run through the holes. The same was done with his back. When the cutting was finished, a hoop made of willows and eagle feathers was hung on the back skewers, while the ones in front were fastened to ropes that hung from the center pole in the Sun Dance lodge.

Small Eyes arose, hugged the center pole and prayed. "I started to cry," he recalled, "but not with much tears."[20] Then, under the guidance of Bull Head, he waved his arms in the air four times, shouted aloud, and tore the hoop off his back. As the drums began to beat, he danced a shuffling step away from the center pole, until the ropes were tight and tugging at the skewers in his chest. Pulling himself backward, he managed to rip the skewer free from his right side but the other one was in too deep. At last, one of the old men hacked at the flesh and the skewer popped free.

Weak and bloody from the ordeal, Small Eyes lay down while Bull

Small Eyes went through the self-torture ritual in fulfillment of a vow he had made to give himself to the Sun spirit. Above, a Blood Indian, Owns the Paint, is seen performing the ritual shortly before it was banned in the early 1890s. *Courtesy Glenbow-Alberta Institute/NA-451-2*

Head trimmed the wound so it would not be too ragged. The loose flesh was buried at the base of the center pole. The young man then hugged the center pole and was given a handful of ashes. This he held aloft to the Sun spirit and cried, "My promise has come true and I give you my body and flesh to eat."[21]

From the lodge, he was taken to the river to wash his wounds. They were treated with medicines and for the next four days the young man lived in agony. After the fourth day he was fine. "People thought more of him after that," said an informant, "for being brave and tough and that he kept his promise."[22]

Yet not everyone admired him. On the fifth day, Small Eyes dressed in his finest clothes, painted his buckskin horse on its joints and shoulders, and joined members of the Braves Society to recount his war deeds. As he waited with the other riders, a man suddenly emerged from the crowd and began striking his horse with a stick. The buckskin reared and plunged, almost unseating the rider, and not until the man had been dragged away was Small Eyes able to control his terrified horse. The attacker was another husband who suspected the young warrior of seducing his wife.

The next summer, Small Eyes returned to the Sun Dance. He was invited to be a servant of the holy man, burning the sweetgrass on the altar, and providing the pipe and tobacco for the ceremonialists to smoke. He also gave food and tea for the ritual and a shirt to the leader. When this had been done, Small Eyes offered a prayer and the holy man followed.

"My father, the Sun," said the leader, "I'm going to pray for this boy because he is helping us and I want you to show something that you hear his prayer." Then, turning to Small Eyes, he said, "Look towards the Sun and see if you see anything." It was a clear and cloudless day. Peering skyward, the young man saw a bluish-red light on one side of the sun.

"Do you see anything?"

"Yes."

"You will have your prayer answered."[23]

After the Sun Dance, Small Eyes went to work for Wolf Collar, herding his horses near North Camp Flats. One day, while searching for part of the herd, he found an old holy man, Small Medicine Pipe, seated inside a sweat lodge. He had been fasting for seven days and was near death. Small Eyes went to his uncle's place and got some meat, tea, and tobacco for the old man. He also gave him a black blanket for the cold nights.

In gratitude, the old man unwrapped a short staff that was lying on top of the sweat lodge. It was painted and covered with the feathers of many birds. A cluster of hawk feathers hung from its end. The old man prayed three times, then told Small Eyes to look in the sky. The young man saw two bars on each side of the sun, both coming down to the ground. This was a sign that the prayers would be answered.

After touching Small Eyes four times with the staff, Small Medicine Pipe said, "This is my body and life. I give this staff to you because you gave me things to keep me warm and food to eat. I have only this summer and the winter. Next summer I am going to leave."[24] As a Blackfoot elder explains:

> Whoever has power through the Sun will always be able to be heard by the Sun. Prayers are always heard. A man on a clear day may call for a rain and it will rain. If it is raining for days, he will call the rain to stop, and it will.[25]

In 1891, Small Eyes married for the first time. His young wife was a member of the Red Gun family. Small Eyes gave one horse to her father and another to her older brother as part of the marriage arrangements. His wife bore a son two years later, but she died in childbirth.

Shortly after his wedding, Small Eyes found a blind man alone on the prairie. He brought him to his tepee and had his wife cook a meal for him. While they were there, they could hear the sounds of distant thunder.

"What's this?" asked the blind man. "Is it going to rain?"

"There are a few clouds but the one towards the mountains is pretty heavy."

"Have you any arrows?"

"No."

At the blind man's bidding, Small Eyes got an arrow from a neighbor and the visitor painted it yellow. He then told the young man to tie it to the wooden pins outside his doorway. A short time later, a strong wind came up and a violent thunderstorm shook the area. After it had passed, a rider came galloping up to the tepee, telling them that the storm had killed ten horses and a little girl.

The blind man was not surprised. Handing him the yellow-painted arrow, he said to Small Eyes, "I am going to give you this so that in summer when there are hard storms, you may use it."[26] He taught the young man two songs that went with the arrow and instructed him in the ritual he should follow when he wished to ward off thunderstorms. He also told him to make an otter-skin bag for the arrow and to keep it as a holy object.

A year after the death of his wife, Small Eyes married two sisters, the daughters of Boy Chief. But he did not give up his old ways, particularly where married women were involved. This resulted in much anguish and resentment for his wives, but Small Eyes was a good provider and they stayed with him. However, after about two years, he became fed up with their constant fighting, so he sent the younger one away. Six years later his other wife died of a hemorrhage so he married *Anato'ksisi*, or Pretty Nose, the daughter of Bear Chief.

As he approached his late twenties, Small Eyes began working for the government stockman. He was a good, hard-working, reliable man and found steady employment whenever he wanted it. He lived on North Camp Flats, had a good-sized horse herd, and was among the first to raise cattle. He was, by Blackfoot standards, a rich and successful man.

He was still arrogant and bossy, but he had shown many qualities of leadership and had given up drinking on the advice of his blind friend. Gambling and women were still his main vices, and jealous husbands remained a problem. One day, for example, when riding across a bridge, he was attacked by two men, Bull Stone and Bad Young Man, who tried to throw him into the river. When they grabbed at his reins he struck one man with his whip and tried to run the other down with his horse. Breaking free, Small Eyes then drew his rifle and opened fire, but both men escaped.

Among Small Eyes's most prized possessions was a tepee bearing the painted bullrush design. But even more important was the marten-skin flag that went with the lodge. Many years earlier, a Peigan Indian had had a vision in which he was given the design for the tepee and was told to get a marten hide and decorate it with feathers and bells. "If this hide of the flag moves," he was told, "this design is true and you can paint it. If it stays still, don't bother."[27] When he made the flag, he tapped it four times and it came to life, running up the pole of the tepee and back down. But when he touched it again, it was just a decorated skin.

As an indication of the value of the tepee design and marten flag, Small Eyes had paid ten horses, a pile of blankets, a saddle, and a rifle for the right to have it. Each day he followed a ritual that included prayers and the burning of incense.

Much of Small Eyes's influence and prestige in the community came from his participation in the Native religion. He was an active supporter of the Sun Dance and the Horn Society. He owned many sacred objects and had the right to perform sacred rituals. He was prominent in four secret societies, and because of the powers that had been given to him, he was sought out to give prayers on behalf of the sick or injured.

Then his whole world was turned upside down.

In the summer of 1898, he had been out on the prairie mowing hay; the weather was so hot that he stripped down to his breech cloth. His wife came to see him in the fields, bringing him some water, and suggested that he get out of the sun. He followed her to their tepee and then went for a swim in the nearby Bow River. He had no appetite, so rather than eat, he sat in the shade until evening. The hot sun had made him very tired. He finally told his wife that he would sleep alone that night, alone with his sacred objects.

Just before sunset, he removed the marten-skin flag from its lofty perch above the tepee and took it inside. At night he always kept it in a special place above his bed. As usual, he made a smudge of juniper leaves and prayed.

Among Small Eyes's friends were a couple of ex-pupils from the Anglican mission school and a hard-working farmer named Little Axe. They went to the mission each Sunday, and Small Eyes began to hear their stories about Christianity. At first he wasn't interested, for there was no place in the white man's beliefs for the Sun Dance religion or the prayers and rituals of the Horns. But just last week he had gone to church with them for the first time, more out of curiosity than anything else. What he saw disturbed him, but he didn't know why. If he prayed to the marten skin, he hoped he might have a vision that would put his mind at ease.

He sang the songs that went with the tepee design, then lit his pipe and blew the smoke four times upon the marten skin. "I have respected you and have adored you as you wanted," he told the flag, "but I have heard the whites say there is a God up in heaven that made the people. So I would like to know who to worship. Tonight, the first person I see in my dreams, you are the God and I will stick with you."[28] Retiring for the night, he soon had a dream, or a vision. Small Eyes explained what happened:

> In my dream, I saw the whole camp of tepees, and among them was my tepee. I saw myself coming out of the tepee and went to the north side and looked away. Then I saw a church by the camps, about 500 yards from the camp. This took place on a Saturday night.
>
> I saw the church door open and a minister was there with a prayer book in his arm. The minister waved to me to come. The minister took me in. There I saw the flowers all nice. I kept walking around the church and walking up and up. I finally came out from the church above, just as if I were above it.

In his vision, Small Eyes saw a pillar the color of varnished oak. On it was a platform facing south, about as big as a tepee. He stood on the west side of the platform facing south, while the minister stood on the east side. In looking down, Small Eyes saw that the earth was shiny, just like a floor. Where he stood, it was as soft as a cushion and everything was green. When he looked up, he could see heaven.

> I put my hand behind to feel the pillar whether it was iron or hard wood. The platform did not seem to be supported and

I got nervous. I looked again at the earth and got more frightened, wondering how I would get down. The second time I looked down and then looked at the white man, he said, "Don't get scared. You can go back down by yourself. Don't you know why we are standing here?"

I didn't answer but thought to myself, "No." The minister said, "Our Father above sent me down for you. I pitied you." The man knew what I was thinking and I never had to answer the questions. The man said, "God sent me to take you here. He wants you to work for him." I thought, "I never turned down any work. I am a working man." The minister said, "It is not to work like you do but to give you a certain thing to do. The Father wants you to work for him." I did not know who the Father was, and I wondered.

Small Eyes then saw that the figure had changed into someone else. This man had long blond shining hair, and eyes that seemed to shine. He wore a white garment that hung down to his feet. Small Eyes could see the body and a sort of breech cloth through the robe. This figure held the same kind of prayer book as the other man.

He said to me, "This is the kind of job God wants you to do." I got scared of the man. He said, "There is no need of your being scared. You will be saved." I thought, "I'll take the job." The man said, "All right." Then he took my hand and said not to be afraid, that he would take me back. "God will give you a lift. Let's start down there."

Then everything was changed, and I saw another place like two walls at right angles. The man said, "Don't look down but look up. Just follow me. It is like walking down a packed snowbank." As he started down, the man was changed to the first man with a black suit and clerical collar. We went quite a ways down and the man started out from the church by the door used for coming in.[29]

The figure that Small Eyes had seen in the clerical garb was the Reverend Harry Gibbon Stocken, the local Anglican missionary. It was all so real that when he awoke he went outside and looked towards the mission. In the stillness of the night, he saw everything just as it had appeared at the beginning of his vision. The next morning, which was a Sunday, Small Eyes went to church and after services he announced to the Reverend Mr. Stocken that he wanted to become a Christian.

It was hard to believe that the transformation could be so sudden and so complete. One day, Small Eyes had been a wild, woman-chasing gambler who was utterly devoted to the religion of his people, and the next day he had cast it all aside to join the Christian church. He began taking instructions from the missionary and a short time later he was baptized. He was given the name of Paul Little Walker—Paul after the apostle, and Little Walker in honor of his beloved mother. His brother, Takes a Handsome Gun, decided to be baptized at the same time, taking the name of Timothy Little Walker.

Paul Little Walker was baptized and confirmed as a member of the Anglican church in 1898. Native religion had been a very important part of his life and he was respected among his people as a religious leader. But a dream convinced him to become a Christian. *Courtesy Glenbow-Alberta Institute/NA-346-2*

And just as Small Eyes—Paul Little Walker—had turned away from his old religion, so did he now reject the objects that went with it. He quit the Horns and the warrior societies, gave the marten flag to Bishop Pinkham, and turned the thunder arrow, painted staff, and the other holy objects over to his wife.

Pretty Nose was aghast at the actions of her husband. She had joined the Horn Society with him and had taken part in many of the ceremonies. She became angry when he started to give things away but no amount of arguing would change his mind. She reminded him of the power of holy objects and the misfortune that had come to others who had desecrated them. But he remained steadfast in his devotion to the new religion.

About four months after Paul's conversion, his wife became ill with tuberculosis and was moved into the mission house. There, just before she died, she decided to join her husband in the Christian church; she was baptized and given the name of Sarah. If, as some people gossiped, her death was Small Eyes's punishment for leaving his Native religion, her husband was unswayed. Not even when his painted tepee was struck by lightning during the summer of 1898 did he falter. He simply took the damaged covering to the cemetery and placed it over the grave of his wife.

A year later, when his brother Timothy died, many believed that the signs were too strong to be ignored. But Paul became more earnest than ever as a messenger for Christ. He was confirmed by the bishop and became a catechist and lay reader for the Anglican Church. He had never been to school, but he could read Blackfoot syllabics and spent all of his spare time studying the Bible.

While he was in mourning for his brother, Paul decided to visit his relatives on the Blood Reserve. In the months since he had last seen them, he may have changed, but his wild relatives had not. As soon as Paul arrived, he was taken to a medicine pipe dance that was being sponsored by Big Rib, his cousin who had been with him on the horse raid. There, rather than take part in the ceremonies, Little Walker called for silence and began preaching Christianity. The longer he talked, the angrier the Bloods became, until at last Big Rib was forced to lead him outside before the others attacked him.

The next day Paul went to the Catholic mission and engaged in a religious argument with the priest regarding the purpose of the crucifix and the role of the Virgin Mary.

Back home on the Blackfoot Reserve, Little Walker's zeal was soon felt by others in the tribe. He interfered in marital disputes, cautioned young men to be faithful to their marriage vows, and carried the word of God to anyone who would listen. Christian or not, Little Walker was still a domineering and quick-tempered man. "When he joined the church," said a Blackfoot elder, "some people did not like him, and hated him. But he just pitied them and helped them out."[30]

One day, while Paul was practicing his syllabic writing, the figure of a young woman appeared at his door. She wore a long, loose-fitting yellow garment and had on a yellow robe clasped at the neck by a brooch that shone like a star. Paul looked at her without knowing who she was.

"Paul," she said, "don't you know your wife? God has sent me to tell you He is pleased with you and wishes you to persevere."[31]

When he told the missionary about his experience, Stocken was skeptical.

> At first I thought he had fallen asleep and had had a beautiful dream, but no, Paul was quite certain he was wide awake and had hurried across at once to my study to pour out to me this wonderful experience. After much questioning, I was as satisfied as he was, that the vision and its message were real.[32]

A couple of years later, Paul took a new wife, a widow named Naomi who had been married to a Christian Blackfoot named Black Horse. When he died in 1895, he had left her with horses and cattle, and through her own initiative, she had become the wealthiest woman on the Blackfoot Reserve. She was one of the few Indians to keep her money in the bank in a nearby town.

Shortly after the turn of the century, Naomi selected Paul Little Walker to be her new husband. She believed he was a good man and a good Christian who would be kind to her and her daughter Ruth. So she went to him, proposed, and he accepted. After the wedding, Naomi became a housekeeper for the Reverend Mr. Stocken, who at that time was a bachelor.

Paul and Naomi were two of the most self-sufficient people on the Blackfoot Reserve, and two of the strongest Christians. Each Christmas, Paul would have a huge feast, and in the summer he ran his own store at the treaty payments. He often helped the poor and was generous to his friends and relatives.

But he remained so inflexible and tenacious where Christianity was concerned that he made many enemies. He refused to attend the Sun Dance and supported the clergy in attempting to suppress Native religion. Anyone he found gambling or drinking he reported to the police, and he was vocal in condemning immorality and sexual permissiveness on the reserve.

Yet his wealth and generosity won him many supporters, particularly among Christian converts, and even his worst enemies admitted that he had many qualities of leadership. Accordingly, when one of the two head chiefs of the tribe died, Paul Little Walker was elected as his replacement. From a warrior, to active participant in Native religion, to Christian zealot, to political leader of the Blackfoot tribe—Little Walker had run the gamut of Indian life. His pride,

Small Eyes (Paul Little Walker) after he became a chief. *Courtesy Glenbow-Alberta Institute/NA-667-88*

single-mindedness, and self-assurance may have been detriments, but they also contributed to his personal success.

The existence of two head chiefs for one reserve had come about because of the Blackfoot Treaty in 1877. At that time, one group of Blackfoot hunted in the north and another in the south. Accordingly, each was given its own head chief. When the Indians came to their reserve, the North Blackfoot settled at the west end where they came under the influence of the Anglicans, while the South Blackfoot camped at the east end where the Catholics established their mission.

By the 1920s, jealousies and arguments between the east and west ends were often based on religious differences. The missionaries added to the problems by their constant competition for pupils for their residential schools. At last, the government was able to get the Blackfoot to agree to have only one head chief for the entire tribe.

A new election was held, the candidates being Paul Little Walker, the Anglican proselytizer, and Water Chief, a traditional Blackfoot whose wife was a perennial sponsor of the Sun Dance. Little Walker was confident that the majority of Indians were nominally Christians and would automatically confer the leadership of the entire reserve upon him. However, the very arrogance that made him think that way also affected the voters, and to his amazement, he lost the election to his non-Christian opponent.

Little Walker became angry, disappointed, and ill. He was an invalid for almost three years. There was little solace in the fact that he was appointed a minor chief, nor that Water Chief failed to live up to everyone's expectations and was deposed. But in the end, this rejection by his tribe proved to be the best thing that could have happened. He finally started to show more humility and understanding in his dealings with his people. He began to attend the Sun Dance as an observer and became respectful of Native religion. Although he still had strong feelings about Christianity and was sincerely dedicated to gaining converts, he became less strident and dogmatic.

In 1925, for example, when he spoke in Blackfoot to an Anglican synod in Victoria, B.C., he was diplomatic and reserved. He commented:

> Please tell the people that I am glad to shake hands with them all, and to see that the women are doing such a noble work in trying to make the world better. When good women take the lead in any community that community must grow to the glory of God.
>
> Please remember that the greatest thing you can do for my people is to help them to be free from the liquor traffic. Please pray that the Blackfeet may be delivered from the curse of the drink.[33]

The path had been a long one, but when Paul Little Walker finally resumed his role of political leader and religious proselytizer after his long illness, he did so with more judgment and tact than he had ever displayed before. In the years before he died in 1952, he became one of the most respected Indian leaders in southern Alberta. He joined in the events of the Calgary Stampede each summer, wearing the full buckskin costumes of his tribe. He attended meetings of the Anglican synod, dressed in a modern business suit, and he assisted with services each Sunday in the white surplice of the Anglican Church. His chest still bore the scars of the self-torture ritual, and the joint of his finger was missing because of his Native religion, but ever since that night in 1898 when his vision had taken him to God, Little Walker had pursued only two goals in life—to be a Christian, and to bring others to his church.

Notes

The Wise Old Ones (pages 4–16)

1. Bobtail Chief, interview with author, Summer 1958.
2. Charles Pantherbone, interview with author, August 2, 1960.
3. John Cotton, interview with author, December 26, 1953.
4. Shot Both Sides, interview with author, September 3, 1955.
5. John Cotton, interview with author, June 3, 1956.
6. In 1855, the United States government concluded a treaty with tribes from the Upper Missouri River and Rocky Mountain regions. These included Peigan, Blood, Blackfoot, Gros Ventre, Flathead, Nez Perce, Pend d'Oreille, and Kootenay. It was variously known as the Blackfoot Treaty, Judith River Treaty, Yellow River Treaty, or simply the 1855 Treaty. It was signed by six Blood chiefs: Medicine Calf, Seen From Afar, Father of Many Children (or Bad Head), Bull Back Fat, Many Spotted Horses, and Calf Shirt.
7. John Cotton, interview with author. See note 3.
8. Ibid.
9. *Benton Record*, September 1, 1881.
10. Bobtail Chief, interview with author. See note 1.
11. Big Sorrel Horse, interview with author, December 26, 1954.
12. Mrs. Bruised Head, interview with author, August 12, 1955.
13. James Gladstone, interview with author, August 11, 1968.
14. Iron, interview with author, December 24, 1951.

A Friend of the Beavers (pages 17–27)

1. Stewart Culin, *Games of the North American Indians* (New York: Dover Publications, 1975), 704.
2. John C. Ewers, "A Blood Indian's Conception of Tribal Life in the Dog Days," *The Blue Jay* 18:1 (March 1960): 47.
3. Actually, the full name was White Clay on His Head. In another version, he was called Night Gun (James Willard Schultz, *Sun God's*

Children [New York: Houghton Mifflin Co., 1930], 108.

4. Richard Glover, ed., *David Thompson's Narrative, 1784-1812* (Toronto: The Champlain Society, 1962), 256.

5. Account by Holy Iron Woman, wife of Tom Scott, Peigan Indian, as told to Father J.L. Levern, October 1925. Levern microfilm, "Notes et souvenirs concernant les piednoirs," pp. 1-13. Glenbow Archives, Calgary. Unless otherwise cited, any conversations in this story are quoted from this source. My thanks go to Maurice Guibord for translating this account from the French.

6. In other versions, the comrade was named Wolf Tail (George Bird Grinnell, *Blackfoot Lodge Tales* [New York: Charles Scribner's Sons, 1892], 120); and Fox Eyes (Schultz, *Sun God's Children*, 108.)

7. About sixty miles (97 km) east of Calgary, just south of the village of Cluny.

8. Clark Wissler, "Ceremonial Bundles of the Blackfoot Indians," *Anthropological Papers of the American Museum of Natural History* 7:2 (1912): 193.

9. C.C. Uhlenbeck, *A New Series of Blackfoot Texts* (Amsterdam: Johannes Muller, 1912), 83.

The Reincarnation of Low Horn (pages 28-46)

1. The inference is that the sparrow hawk would give the boy supernatural powers and that when he grew up he would become a chief. Direct quotations of conversations are from an interview with Jack Low Horn, son of the Blood holy man, July 18, 1954, with James Gladstone interpreting. Other sources are: George Bird Grinnell, *Blackfoot Lodge Tales* (New York: Charles Scribner's Sons, 1892); and Henry John Moberly, *When Fur Was King* (Toronto: J.M. Dent & Sons, 1929).

2. *Kominakoos* was translated by Amelia M. Paget as "Looks Like a Pine Tree" (Paget, *People of the Plains* [Toronto: Ryerson Press, 1909], 145) while George Bird Grinnell translated it as "Round" (Grinnell, *Blackfoot Lodge Tales*, 88).

3. Moberly, *When Fur Was King*, 195.

4. This figure was given by Paul Kane, who was told the story in 1846, only a few months after it had occurred. (J. Russell Harper, *Paul Kane's Country* [Toronto: University of Toronto Press, 1971], 147). Kane refers to Low Horn as Big Horn and includes nothing of the spiritual elements of his story.

5. What ultimately became of *Kominakoos*? His name appears from time to time in Fort Edmonton records, and according to Moberly, he continued to live an exciting life. "He had been twice tossed by buffalo bulls and badly injured, twice pitched headlong from his horse with results disastrous to his bones. Deep scars furrowed his side where Blackfoot bullets had plowed round his ribs. He was a famous conjuror and his own

people believed he could not be killed, an illusion shared to some extent by his enemies. Before they ultimately took his own scalp, it was the boast of *Kominakoos* that he had slain fourteen Blackfeet" (Moberly, *When Fur Was King*, 195).

6. Grinnell's account lacks the supernatural implications of Indian narratives. He was told by Peigans that after the killing of Low Horn, the Crees were returning to their own country when six of their warriors were attacked by a grizzly bear. It killed five and the sixth returned to the others with the news. They were convinced that the bear had been the spirit of Low Horn. (Grinnell, *Blackfoot Lodge Tales*, 90).

7. Referred to hereafter as Different Gun, for simplicity.

8. For a detailed account of this cure, see the chapter "Man of Steel."

9. Letter, Dr. F.X. Girard to Indian commissioner, May 23, 1899. Blood Reserve letter-book, National Archives of Canada. As most of these letter-books were consulted at the Blood Indian Agency before they were turned over to the National Archives of Canada, that institution's full citations are not given.

10. Ibid.

The Amazing Death of Calf Shirt *(pages 47–58)*

1. James Willard Schultz, "Old Fort Benton," *Forest and Stream*, Oct. 6, 1900.

2. Joe Beebe, interview with Esther S. Goldfrank, in "Field Notes of Esther S. Goldfrank, 1939." Microfilm in Glenbow Archives.

3. Although not unknown, the killing of a wife for religious reasons or because of a vision was a rare occurrence.

4. *Benton Record*, Feb. 27, 1880.

5. S.H. Middleton, *Indian Chiefs Ancient and Modern* (Lethbridge: Lethbridge Herald, 1952), 159.

6. Middleton, *Indian Chiefs*, 162.

7. Middleton, *Indian Chiefs* 163.

8. Ibid.

9. Ibid.

10. Clark Wissler, *The Social Life of the Blackfoot Indians* (New York: American Museum of Natural History, 1911), 49. Winter counts formed a system of recording each year by selecting one important event from the year's significant occurrences. In this way, it was possible for people to indicate their age or some other event by comparing it with the winter count for that year; i.e., "I was born the year the stars fell," or 1833. See Hugh A. Dempsey, *A Blackfoot Winter Count* (Calgary: Glenbow Museum, 1965).

11. *Forest and Stream*, July 18, 1903.

12. Frank Red Crow, interview with John C. Ewers, Aug. 22, 1951, kindly provided by the interviewer.

13. *Benton Record*, Jan. 31, 1879.

14. The dead were identified as Franklin Friend, George W. Friend, Abraham Lotts, John Alley, John Andrews, N.W. Burris, Frank Angevine, Henry Martin, Henry Lyons, and James Berry.
15. Cited in John C. Ewers, *The Blackfeet, Raiders on the Northwestern Plains* (Norman: University of Oklahoma Press, 1958), 239.
16. *Montana Post*, Dec. 9, 1865.
17. Schultz, *Forest and Stream*.
18. Ibid.
19. The group included Kipp's partner, Charlie Thomas, as well as Diamond R. Brown, Dick Berry, Sol Abbott, Henry Powell, George Scott, and Jeff Devereux.
20. Schultz, *Forest and Stream*.
21. Ibid.

Peace with the Kootenays (pages 59–66)

1. Waterton was the European name for the stream. The Bloods called it "Where We Killed the Kootenays River," and for many years it was known officially as the Kootenai River.
2. Ambrose Gravelle (Kootenay Indian), interview with author, August 7, 1969.
3. Undated manuscript by Jim White Bull, in author's possession. White Bull, who died in 1973, was my wife's uncle.
4. Ibid.
5. John Cotton, interview with author, July 1954.
6. Ibid.
7. Undated manuscript by Jim White Bull. See note 3.

A Messenger for Peace (pages 67–79)

1. Edmonton House Journals, 1864–65, entry for Sept. 19, 1864, Hudson's Bay Company Archives, file B.60/a/34, Provincial Archives of Manitoba.
2. Edmonton House Journals, entry for October 5, 1863, file B.60/a/33.
3. Edmonton House Correspondence, 1857, 1864–68, letter, William Christie to the governor, March 24, 1866, file B.60/b/2.
4. Sometimes translated as Old Swan, Big Swan, or simply The Swan.
5. William Francis Butler, *The Great Lone Land; A Narrative of Travel and Adventure in the North-West of America* (London: Sampson Low, Marston, Low & Searle, 1874), 313.
6. Crooked Meat Strings, interview with Lucien Hanks, July 28, 1939, Lucien and Jane Hanks Papers, hereinafter cited as Hanks Papers, Canadian Museum of Civilization. The valuable interviews in this collection have been an important source of information on the Blackfoot tribe.
7. Ibid.

8. Ibid.
9. John McDougall, *George Millward McDougall, The Pioneer, Patriot and Missionary* (Toronto: William Briggs, 1902), 137.
10. Edmonton House Journals, 1869–70, entry for April 23, 1869, Hudson's Bay Company Archives, file B.60/a/37, Provincial Archives of Manitoba.
11. McDougall, *George Millward McDougall*, 139.
12. Alex Johnston, *The Battle at Belly River* (Lethbridge: Historical Society of Alberta, 1966), 3.
13. Crooked Meat Strings, interview with Jane and Lucien Hanks. See note 6.
14. One Gun, interview with author, March 5, 1957.
15. While Sweetgrass is not mentioned by name in accounts of this treaty, evidence would seem to indicate that he was the leader of the Battle River camp and the most likely person to have led the Cree delegation.
16. Crooked Meat Strings, interview with Jane and Lucien Hanks. See note 6.
17. Ibid.
18. Ibid.
19. Ibid.
20. Ibid.
21. Ibid.

The Orphan *(pages 80–92)*

1. The use of "Blackfoot" or "Blackfeet" has long been a subject of discussion and dispute. Neither legal nor linguistic evidence has proven one term to be right and the other wrong. However, the American government's official designation is the Blackfeet Indian Reservation, while the Canadian government uses Blackfoot Indian Reserve.
2. A number of dates were given for the boy's birth. The 1914 Blood paysheets show his birthdate as 1858; his church confirmation record in 1918 gives 1862; in a 1935 interview he places his birth between 1856 and 1858; and his obituary in 1936 gives 1854. However, John J. Healy's daughter, who was present at the affray, said he was eight years old when the incident occurred, which is close to his church confirmation date. Also, Iron, a patriarch of the Blood tribe, said he was a "small boy" when it happened.
3. Regina Mettler (daughter of John Healy), "Sketch of the Life of John Healy," Mettler Papers, Montana Historical Society, Helena.
4. Ibid.
5. John J. Healy, "They Had Always Been Friendly," in *We Seized Our Rifles* ed. Lee Silliman (Missoula: Mountain Press, 1982), 106.
6. Noel Stewart, "My Visit to the Home of Joe Healy," undated clipping from the *Lethbridge Herald*.
7. Ibid.
8. *Lethbridge Herald*, July 11, 1935, 51.

9. Ibid.

10. Ibid.

11. Stewart "My Visit to the Home of Joe Healy." See note 6.

12. *The Billings Times*, October 14, 1937.

13. Diary of Samuel Trivett, December 27, 1883. Church Missionary Society Papers, Reel A112, Glenbow Archives.

14. One of Joe Healy's daughters, Janie, married James Gladstone, Canada's first Indian senator. My wife, Pauline, is their daughter, and she recalls her grandpa Joe with fond memories. In 1967, I was honored by the Blood tribe by being made an honorary chief and given the name of Flying Chief, a family name that had gone unused since the death of Joe Healy in 1936.

15. *Lethbridge Herald*, October 6, 1937.

16. *Lethbridge Herald*, December 24, 1936.

17. Letter, Indian agent William Pocklington to Indian commissioner, June 26, 1888. Blood Reserve letter-book. As an aside, when Hughes came to in the hospital, he immediately asked for his overalls. When he was told they had been tattered by the lightning bolt and had been thrown away, he became very concerned and begged an Indian to get them. The man agreed, even though the overalls were covered with old patches and charred from the lightning. When they were handed to Hughes, he tore open one of the patches, and a handful of dollar bills fell out. "Figured this was a good way to carry my dough," he commented. (Iron, interview with author, December 24, 1951).

18. *Lethbridge Herald*, June 7, 1913.

19. Stewart, "My Visit to the Home of Joe Healy." See note 6.

Black White Man *(pages 93–103)*

1. James K. Hosmer, *History of the Expedition of Captains Lewis and Clark,* 1804–5–6, vol. 1 (Chicago: A.C. McClurg & Co, 1902), 108.

2. Sir George Simpson, *Narrative of a Journey Round the World,* vol. 1 (London, 1847), 80.

3. Hugh A. Dempsey, ed., "Donald Graham's Narrative of 1872–73," *Alberta Historical Review* (Winter 1956): 16.

4. Harry Mills, interview with author, December 26, 1953.

5. Letter, Indian agent Pocklington to Indian commissioner, November 9, 1885. Blood Reserve letter-book.

6. Ibid., September 30, 1884.

7. Harry Mills, interview with author. See note 4.

8. Letter, Indian agent Pocklington to Indian commissioner, April 4, 1891. Blood Reserve letter-book.

9. Letter, Indian agent Wilson to Indian commissioner, February 16, 1895. Blood Reserve letter-book.

10. Ibid., January 17, 1895.
11. Ibid.
12. Note from Percy Creighton in "Information collected by Marjorie Lismer, part of team working on the Blood Reservation, Summer 1939." Photocopy of Esther Goldfrank Papers in Glenbow Archives.
13. Tom Clarke, *Lethbridge Herald*, May 2, 1944.
14. Ibid.
15. Ibid.
16. *Toronto Mail*, January 28, 1886.
17. Ibid.
18. Letter, Indian agent R.N. Wilson to Indian commissioner, March 20, 1905. Blood Reserve letter-book.

The Wild Ones *(pages 104–18)*

1. Letter, Indian agent William Pocklington to Indian comissioner, August 4, 1891. Blood Reserve letter-book.
2. Letter, Indian agent Pocklington to Indian commissioner, May 18, 1887. Blood Reserve letter-book.
3. Observation by Mounted Police superintendent R. Burton Deane in *Report of the Commissioner of the North-West Mounted Police Force, 1889* (Ottawa: Queen's Printer, 1890), 42.
4. Rainy Chief was also known as Swan Shout, and Real Man's Shirt as Mike Snake Eater; Small Eyes was later baptized Paul Little Walker, and Coming Singer was also known as Dead Before.
5. Letter, Indian agent Pocklington to Indian commissioner, January 31, 1890. Blood Reserve letter-book.
6. *Macleod Gazette*, May 21, 1891.
7. Fort Macleod Judicial Notebooks, Fort Macleod Town Hall Records, Book 6, 48. Microfilm in Glenbow Archives.
8. Letter, Indian agent Wilson to Indian commissioner, August 4, 1894. Blood Reserve letter-book.
9. Ibid.
10. Those receiving two years were Never Ties his Shoe Laces, Wolf Child, Tough Bread, Nibs, Short Man, and Longtime Squirrel; six months went to Slap Face and Many Different Axes; and one month to Melting Tallow and Carries Something.
11. Letter, Indian agent Wilson to NWMP Supt. Deane, July 5, 1898. Blood Reserve letter-book.

The Last War Party *(pages 119–37)*

1. American soldiers.
2. The International Boundary between Canada and the United States was

called a "Medicine Line" because it seemed to have the power to stop U.S. soldiers from pursuing the Blackfoot north or the Mounted Police from chasing them south.

3. Wolf Sitting also was known as The Scout, while in later years, Hind Gun was given the name of James White Calf.

4. Richard Lancaster, *Piegan* (Garden City, N.Y.: Doubleday and Co., 1966), 302. Many of the details of the expedition were told to Lancaster by Hind Gun.

5. Letter, Indian agent William Pocklington to Indian commissioner, May 22, 1889. Blood Reserve letter-book.

6. Ibid., February 16, 1887.

7. Ibid., March 23, 1887.

8. Ibid., April 3, 1887.

9. "Peace Council held between the Bloods, Gros Ventres & Assiniboines at Balknap Agency the 9th June 1887." Blood Reserve letter-book.

10. Ibid.

11. Ibid.

12. Ibid.

13. This was the description given by a rancher whose horse was taken by the Blood raiders. *Billings Gazette*, May 9, 1889.

14. Lancaster, *Piegan*, 312.

15. Ibid., 316.

16. Ibid., 323.

17. Annual report of Supt. R.B. Deane, December 1, 1889, in *Report of the Commissioner of the North-West Mounted Police Force, 1889* (Ottawa: Queen's Printer, 1890), 37.

18. Telegram confirmed in letter, Indian agent Pocklington to Indian commissioner, May 17, 1889. Blood Reserve letter-book.

19. Ibid. He was referring, of course, to the incident that had occurred two years earlier.

20. Lancaster, *Piegan*, 329.

21. Toronto *Globe*, June 29, 1889.

22. Letter, Indian agent Pocklington to Indian commissioner, July 9, 1889. Blood Reserve letter-book.

23. Annual report of Supt. S.B. Steele, November 30, 1889, in *Report of the Commissioner of the North-West Mounted Police Force, 1889* (Ottawa: Queen's Printer, 1890), 65.

24. Letter, Indian agent Pocklington to Indian commissioner. See note 22.

25. Ibid., December 11, 1889.

The Snake Man (pages 138–49)

1. Jim White Bull, interview with author, December 29, 1955.

2. *Home and School*, December 27, 1890.

3. Ibid.

4. Letter, Indian agent William Pocklington to Indian commissioner, September 30, 1884. Blood Reserve letter-book.
5. *Toronto Mail,* January 28, 1886.
6. Ibid.
7. Ibid.
8. Letter, Indian agent Pocklington to Indian commissioner, February 19, 1886. Blood Reserve letter-book.
9. *Macleod Gazette,* November 2, 1894.
10. Tom Clark in *Lethbridge Herald,* July 19, 1931.
11. Monthly report for March, Indian agent Pocklington to Indian commissioner, April 8, 1888. Blood Reserve letter-book.
12. Joe Beebe, "Bygone Days of the Blackfeet Nation." Manuscript in author's possession.
13. *Manitoba Free Press,* Winnipeg, August 15, 1889.
14. *Regina Progress* as cited in the *Macleod Gazette,* August 23, 1895.
15. Jim White Bull, interview with author. See note 1.
16. Ibid.

Man of Steel *(pages 150–60)*

1. His name, *Ski'matsis,* was variously translated as Steel, Fire Steel, and Whetstone. The word refers to a metal tool originally used by women to start a fire by striking it with a piece of flint. After the introduction of matches, the tool was used for sharpening knives. His age, too, is in question. A letter in 1894 gives his age as thirty-two (born 1862), the band paysheets listed him as forty-four in 1907 (born 1863), a police report in 1932 showed him as sixty-eight (born 1864), while another police report in 1941 said he was "about eighty" (born 1861).
2. Laurie Plume (son-in-law of Steel), interview with author, August 5, 1955.
3. Indian agent William Pocklington to Indian commissioner, October 21, 1891. Blood Reserve letter-book.
4. Ibid.
5. Ibid.
6. *Macleod Gazette,* October 22, 1891.
7. Laurie Plume, interview with author. See note 2.
8. Letter, Indian agent Pocklington to Indian commissioner. See note 3.
9. See "The Reincarnation of Low Horn" for details of this medicine man's career.
10. Cecil Denny, "The Birth of Western Canada," manuscript in the Provincial Library of Alberta, 95.
11. Ibid.
12. Letter, Indian agent Pocklington to Indian commissioner, October 28, 1891. Blood Reserve letter-book.
13. Laurie Plume, interview with author. See note 2.

Deerfoot and Friends *(pages 161–85)*

1. L.V. Kelly in *Calgary Herald*, October 30, 1954.
2. *Manitoba Free Press*, October 24, 1883.
3. Ibid.
4. *The Winnipeg Daily Sun*, October 27, 1883.
5. *Manitoba Free Press*, October 25, 1883.
6. Ibid., October 27, 1883.
7. *The Winnipeg Daily Sun*, November 2, 1883.
8. *Winnipeg Times*, November 3, 1883.
9. *Manitoba Free Press*, November 3, 1883.
10. Ibid.
11. *The Winnipeg Daily Sun*, November 9, 1883.
12. L.V. Kelly, *Calgary Herald*. See note 1.
13. *Manitoba Free Press*, June 19, 1884.
14. L.V. Kelly, *Calgary Herald*. See note 1.
15. Thomas Clarke in *Calgary Herald*, August 20, 1938.
16. *The Macleod Gazette*, June 15, 1886.
17. *Regina Leader*, July 5, 1883.
18. *The Macleod Gazette*, July 6, 1886.
19. *Calgary Herald*, October 30, 1886.
20. Ibid., June 12, 1886.
21. Ibid.
22. Ibid., April 10, 1889.
23. Thomas Clarke, *Calgary Herald*. See note 15.
24. Ibid.
25. *Calgary Tribune*, October 22, 1886.
26. *Calgary Herald*, October 22, 1886.
27. *Calgary Tribune*. See note 25.
28. L.V. Kelly, *Calgary Herald*. See note 1.
29. For an account of this incident, see the chapter "The Wild Ones."
30. *Calgary Tribune*, August 26, 1887.
31. *Calgary Weekly Herald*, September 9, 1887.
32. *Calgary Herald*, September 14, 1887.
33. Ibid., April 10, 1889.
34. *Calgary Tribune*, April 17, 1889.
35. *Calgary Herald*, May 29, 1889.
36. Ibid., June 5, 1889.
37. Ed Yellow Old Woman, interview with author, January 10, 1981.
38. *Annual Report of the North-West Mounted Police for the Year 1891* (Ottawa: Queen's Printer, 1892), 159.
39. *Calgary Herald*, July 16, 1891.
40. *Calgary Eye Opener*, November 23, 1903.

41. Letter, Sgt. J.J. Marshall to officer commanding, Calgary, April 11, 1896. RCMP Papers, RG–18, vol. 114, file 24–96, National Archives of Canada.

42. For an account of this incident see the chapter "Scraping High and Mr. Tims."

43. Letter, Inspector Wood to commissioner, March 12, 1897. RCMP Papers, RG–18, vol. 126, file 4, National Archives of Canada.

44. *Calgary Weekly Herald*, March 4, 1897.

45. *Calgary Herald*, January 8, 1974.

Scraping High and Mr. Tims *(pages 186–209)*

1. Letter, J.W. Tims to Rev. Baring Gould, August 26, 1895. Church Missionary Society Papers, microfilm in Glenbow Archives.

2. Letter, Insp. A.M. Jarvis to officer commanding, July 5, 1895. RCMP Papers, RG–18, vol. 110, National Archives of Canada. The information was given to the Mounted Police officer by Blood chief Red Crow, who had heard it from a messenger, Pinto White Buffalo, sent by the Blackfoot to explain their troubles.

3. Draft letter, Tims to Bishop Pinkham, July 2, 1895. Tims Papers, M1234, Glenbow Archives.

4. Ibid.

5. Letter, Begg to Indian commissioner, August 26, 1892. RG–10, vol. 1152, National Archives of Canada.

6. "An Act further to amend 'The Indian Act,'" in *Statutes of Canada*, 1894, 57–58 Victoria, chap. 32, 232.

7. David Mills (M.P. for Bothwell) in *Debates of the House of Commons*. 7th Parliament, 4th Session, 5553 (July 9, 1894).

8. Hayter Reed in *Annual Report of the Department of Indian Affairs for the Year Ended 30th June 1894* (Ottawa: Queen's Printer), xxi–xxii.

9. Certification by Dr. N.J. Lindsay, Feb. 13, 1895. Blackfoot Indian Agency Papers, M1785, file 1, Glenbow Archives.

10. "Blackfoot Indian–1896. Are-jaw-wan, Scraping Hide [*sic*]." (Story of Scraping High as told by Paul Many Shots.) Glenbow Archives, M2359.

11. Ibid.

12. Testimony of Hind Bull at coroner's enquiry, April 5, 1895. RG–18, vol. 1345, National Archives of Canada.

13. White Headed Chief (nephew of Scraping High), interview with Lucien Hanks, July 1938. Hanks Papers, Canadian Museum of Civilization.

14. Joseph F. Dion, *My Tribe the Crees* (Calgary: Glenbow Museum, 1978), 12.

15. Paraphrased from a letter, Magnus Begg to Indian commissioner, April 6, 1895. Indian Department Papers, RG–10, vol. 1158, National Archives of Canada.

16. Testimony of Spotted Calf at the coroner's inquest, April 3, 1895. RG–18, vol. 1345, National Archives of Canada.

17. Testimony of Rabbit Carrier at coroner's inquest, April 5, 1895. RG–18, vol. 1345, National Archives of Canada.
18. Ibid.
19. Paraphrased from a letter, John Marshall to officer commanding, Calgary, April 4, 1895. RG–18, vol. 1345, National Archives of Canada.
20. Ibid.
21. White Headed Chief, interview with Lucien Hanks. See note 13.
22. Letter, Reed to A.E. Forget, assistant Indian commissioner, April 6, 1895. Indian Department Papers, RG–10, file 111, 762, vol. 4767, file 147, National Archives of Canada.
23. Letter, Begg to Indian commissioner, June 8, 1895. RG–10, vol. 1158, National Archives of Canada.
24. Letter, Tims to Indian commissioner, June 27, 1895. RG–18, vol. 110, National Archives of Canada.
25. Letter, Howe to NWMP commissioner, July 3, 1895. RG–18, vol. 110, National Archives of Canada.
26. Statement, W.M. Baker to Inspector McGibbon, June 6, 1895. RG–10, vol. 3928, file 117, 004–1, National Archives of Canada.
27. Letter, Begg to Indian commissioner, May 2, 1895. RG–10, vol. 3928, file 117, 004–1, National Archives of Canada.
28. Statement, L.V. Hardyman to A. McGibbon, May 2, 1895. RG–10, vol. 3928, file 117, 004–1, National Archives of Canada.
29. Letter, Begg to Indian commissioner, June 4, 1895. RG–10, vol. 1158, National Archives of Canada.
30. Statement, L.V. Hardyman, undated. RG–10, vol. 3928, file 117, 004–1, National Archives of Canada.
31. Letter, Tims to Hayter Reed, May 3, 1895. RG–10, vol. 3928, file 117, 004–1, National Archives of Canada.
32. Ibid.
33. Draft letter, Tims to Bishop Pinkham. See note 3.
34. Ibid.
35. "Indian Work," by J.W. Tims, in *Calgary Diocesan Gazette* (Christmas 1929), 24.
36. Letter, Begg to Indian commissioner, May 8, 1895. RG–10, vol. 1158, National Archives of Canada.
37. Letter, Begg to Indian commissioner, May 29, 1895. RG–10, vol. 1158, National Archives of Canada.
38. Ibid.
39. Monthly report of Sgt. Marshall, June 8, 1895. RG–18, vol. 110, National Archives of Canada.
40. Paraphrased from monthly report, Sgt. Marshall. See note 39.
41. *Alberta Tribune*, Calgary, July 10, 1895.
42. Draft letter, Tims to Bishop Pinkham. See note 3.
43. Ibid.

44. Ibid.
45. *The Weekly Globe*, Toronto, July 10, 1895.
46. Letter, Tims to Indian commissioner. See note 24.
47. *Moose Jaw Times*, cited in *Alberta Tribune*, Calgary, July 10, 1895.
48. *Alberta Tribune*. See note 41.
49. Ibid.
50. Letter, Howe to commissioner. See note 25.
51. *The Macleod Gazette*, August 2, 1895.

The Transformation of Small Eyes *(pages 210–33)*

1. Paul Little Walker and Joe Turning Robe, interview with Lucien Hanks, June 21, 1939, Hanks Papers, Canadian Museum of Civilization.
2. Actually, the man had several names during his lifetime. Originally he was called Tailfeathers. Then he inherited the name Not Afraid of the Gros Ventres from his father. When Small Eyes was born, he gave the boy his name and became Bull Back Fat. Most informants, however, remembered him as Not Afraid of the Gros Ventres.
3. L. Night Chief, interview with Lucien Hanks, August 5, 1939, Hanks Papers.
4. Harry Mills, interview with author, 1953.
5. John Cotton, interview with author, 1953.
6. Hugh A. Dempsey, ed., "Donald Graham's Narrative of 1872–73," *Alberta Historical Review* (Winter 1956): 17.
7. Jim White Bull, interview with author, January 1, 1955.
8. Paul Little Walker and Joe Turning Robe, interview with Lucien Hanks. See note 1.
9. Little Light, interview with Lucien Hanks, July 11, 1941, Hanks Papers.
10. Paul Little Walker and Joe Turning Robe, interview with Lucien Hanks. See note 1. All direct quotes in this story are from the same interview.
11. Reports, Indian agent Norman Macleod, April 19 and August 4, 1881. Blood Reserve letter-book.
12. Tom McMaster, interview with Lucien Hanks, June 24, 1939, Hanks Papers.
13. Ibid.
14. Letters, Indian agent to commissioner, March 16 and May 3, 1885. Blood Reserve letter-book.
15. Paul Little Walker and Matthew Melting Tallow, interview with Lucien Hanks, June 25, 1939, Hanks Papers.
16. Ibid.
17. Little Light, interview with Lucien Hanks. See note 9.
18. Tom McMaster, interview with Lucien Hanks. See note 12.
19. Ibid.
20. Ibid.

21. Ibid.
22. Ibid.
23. L. Night Chief, interview with Lucien Hanks. See note 3.
24. Ibid.
25. Ibid.
26. Ibid.
27. Tom McMaster, interview with Lucien Hanks. See note 12.
28. Ibid.
29. Paul Little Walker and Tom McMaster, paraphrased from interviews with Lucien Hanks. See notes 1 and 12.
30. Tom McMaster, interview with Lucien Hanks. See note 12.
31. H.W. Gibbon Stocken, *Among the Blackfoot and Sarcee* (Calgary: Glenbow Museum, 1976), 55.
32. Ibid.
33. "Chief Little Walker," in *Scarlet and Gold*, 6th annual, 1925, 24.

Index

Index

Index